THE PRINCESS
of
PROPHECY
HEROES OF THE TROJAN WAR, VOL II

by

Aria Cunningham

MYTHMAKERS
PUBLISHING

LOS ANGELES

All rights reserved.

Copyright © 2015 Aria Cunningham

Cover Art by JR Burningham

ISBN: 0991420144
ISBN-13: 978-0-9914201-4-8

Mythmakers Publishing is a division of Mythmakers Entertainment.
www.mythmakersent.com

To JR, my love.
To Karma, my heart.
To Tristan, my soul.

Acknowledgments:

As always, this book could not have been produced without the input and influence of many people.

A big thank you to my Betas: to Claire T.H., a lady of class and spirit who inspires everyone to follow their hearts; to Autumn, whose keen insight into behavior kept me striving to dig deeper into my characters; to Chris, whose unparalleled sense of story is a talent I will also admire; to Claire D., whose passion for the material reinvoked my own - thank you all.

To everyone at Mythmakers Publishing, for all the handwork and resources poured into this series, and your faith that a historic retelling of mythology was a venture worth printing. To my editor, Kati Volker, a tireless and giving collaborator, thank you for pushing me to a higher ideal. And to Julieanne, who shared the journey to print, your example is one I cherish.

Table of Contents

Prologue 1: Chaos & Order

Part One: In Grecian Waters 1
Chapter 1 - Coming Home 3
Chapter 2 - The Black Flag 15
Chapter 3 - Giving Chase 27
Chapter 4 - Untested Waters 35
Chapter 5 - The Traitor's Price 45
Chapter 6 - Restoration 55
Chapter 7 - Safe Harbors 73
Chapter 8 - The Watcher of the Winds 91

Prologue 2: The Battle of Kadesh 94

Part Two: In the Two Lands 97
Chapter 9 - The Delta 99
Chapter 10 - The Chancellor 117
Chapter 11 - The High King Returns 127
Chapter 12 - The Cobra Lies in Wait 135
Chapter 13 - The Court of the Sun 143
Chapter 14 - The Foreign Aphrodite 163

Chapter 15 - The Wives of Pharaoh 175
Chapter 16 - The Royal Heir 189
Chapter 17 - A Boy and His Master 205
Chapter 18 - The High Priest of Amun-Re 219
Chapter 19 - A Den of Thieves 237
Chapter 20 - Entertaining Seti 245
Chapter 21 - Lessons of the Vanquished Foe 261
Chapter 22 - Honor and Oaths 273
Chapter 23 - In the Marshland 287
Chapter 24 - Royal Reports 297
Chapter 25 - The Heifer or the Lioness 311
Chapter 26 - Salutations of Re 323
Chapter 27 - Proof of Conflict 331
Chapter 28 - A Poisoned Offer 341
Chapter 29 - Sacrifices to the Gods 349
Chapter 30 - The Swamps of Creation 363
Chapter 31 - The Phoenix Takes Flight 371
Chapter 32 - Rising From the Ashes 377
Chapter 33 - The Envoy 387
Chapter 34 - A Prince's Fate 399
Chapter 35 - The Joining of Houses 413
Chapter 36 - The Claiming of a Crown 425
Chapter 37 - A Twist of Fate 431
Chapter 38 - Brothers of the Sword 445
Chapter 39 - Parting Ways 451

Epilogue 455

Author's Note 457

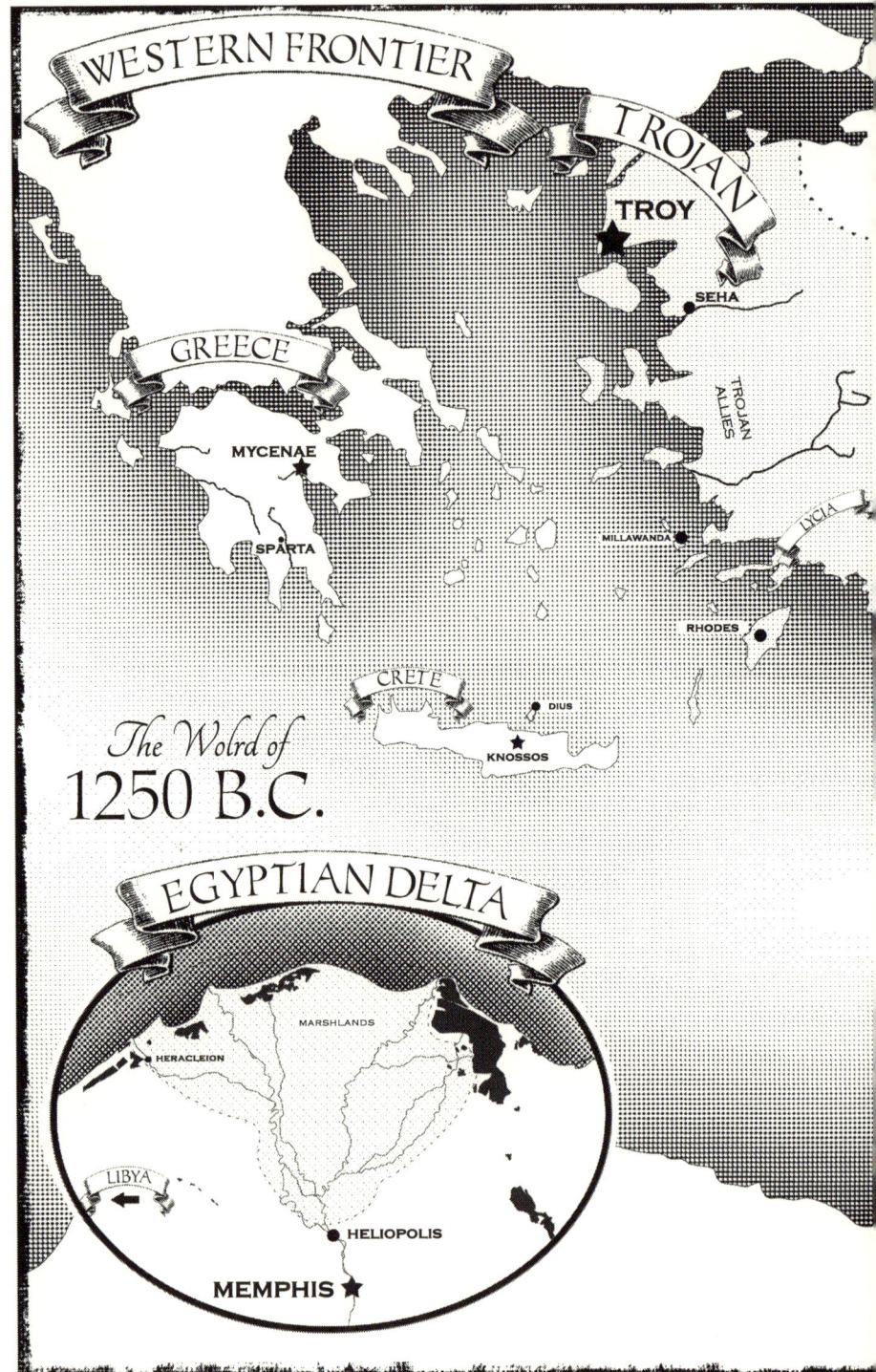

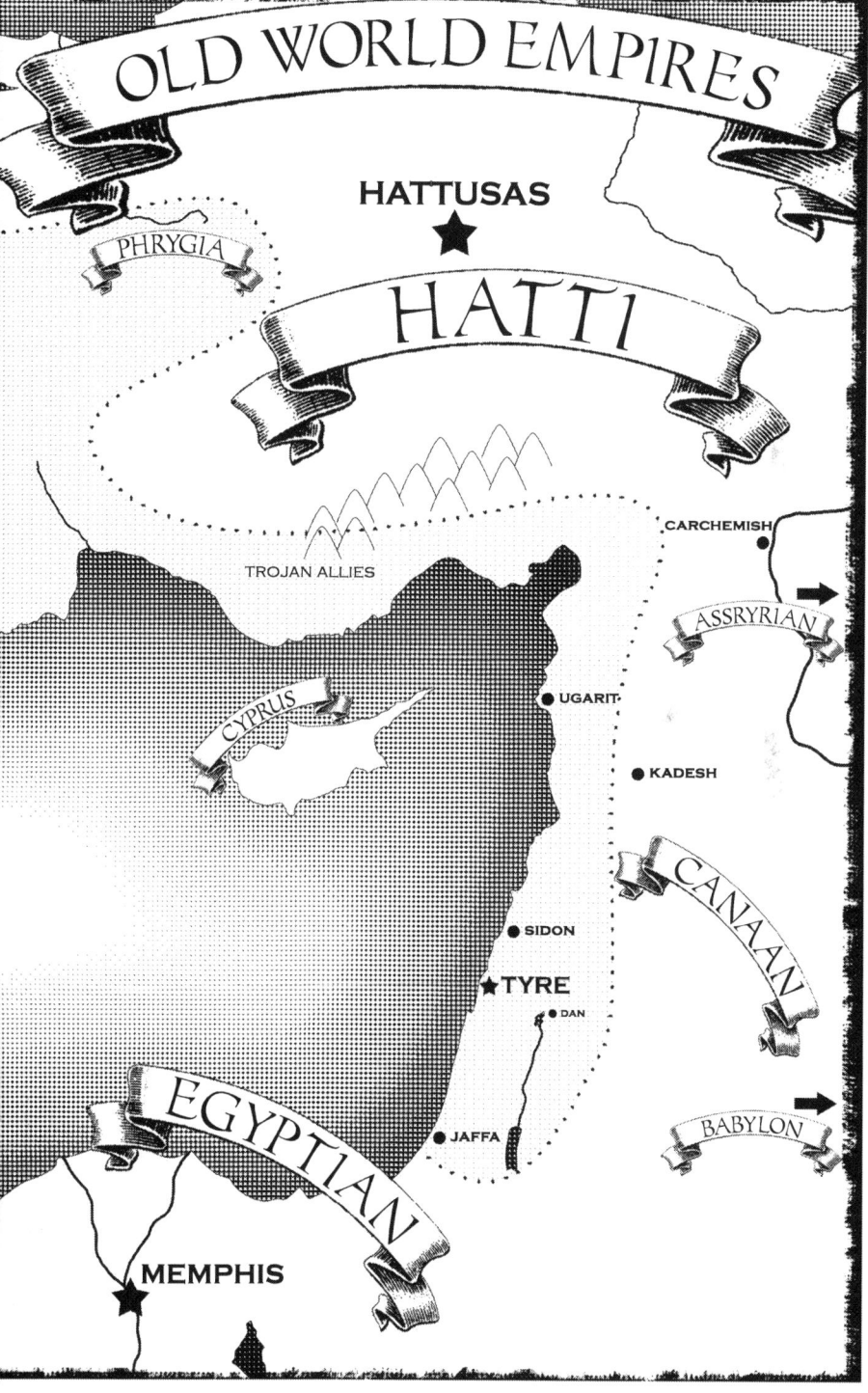

CHAOS & ORDER

OUT OF CHAOS, there came Order.

From the black void of nonexistence, the first God spoke and the Cosmos was borne. To the Greeks, the creator God was Gaia, the solid Earth which brought shape to the world of Man. To the Egyptians it was the Solar God Atum who ruled the sky. While each region envisioned the birth of the Cosmos differently, the underlying myth was universal: the Gods were Agents of Order keeping the dark forces of Chaos at bay.

For Ancient Man, this struggle of good versus evil, of civilization over barbarism, was maintained by the Empires. Mystic, priest, prophet and all-mighty king ruled with iron fists. The Rule of Law, skewed in favor of those in power, ensured that mankind would survive.

Inequality reigned supreme. Rulers abused their powers and enriched themselves at the expense of the greater good. With that abuse, the Old World Empires sowed the seeds of their demise.

In the years before the Trojan War, civilization unknowingly teetered on the edge of collapse. Palatial rule was failing, and the common man struggled to pay the oppressive taxes of their kings. Famine, plague, natural disaster and war had taken a mighty toll. The farmer who once worked the earth and the shepherd who watched over the flock, starved. With little to lose and their very survival on the line, these men became desperate...

And in that desperation they found their real power.

Shepherd and Farmer became Sell-sword and Pirate. Angry men marauded the open seas indiscriminately. The Scales of Cosmic Order became unbalanced, for these seafaring mercenaries fought without cause or country. They had no allegiance to good or ill. They were the Agents of Chaos.

Had the rulers of the time been wiser, they would have joined together to stamp out this nascent threat. But they were not. Shortsighted, these foolish kings bickered amongst themselves and even hired these Soldiers of Fortune to secure their borders and fight their battles.

For the mercenary, the gain was not only in gold, but also in status. For the first time in history, these once common men rose above the station of their birth. They procured a taste for power and began to question the right of any man to rule supreme, that perhaps the notion of monarchy and noble birth was a fabrication told to ensure the maltreated masses doubted their own strength.

Too late did both King and Pharaoh discover that their costly victories came at a price. The swords they had once hired in greed would soon become the swords they faced. Should that force ever unite, or find common purpose, it could break the world.

As the Age of Bronze drew to a close, revolution was in the air. The world needed but one war to begin an avalanche of deep-seated unrest, and with that clash, Chaos — the yawning abyss of darkness and disorder — patiently lay in wait to claim them all...

Part One:
In Grecian Waters

Chapter 1

Coming Home

HELEN STOOD AT the prow of the Trojan galley eagerly awaiting her first glimpse of Troy, the Golden City that was to be her new home. If the Gods were kind, they'd grant her this second chance. They'd let the horrors of her life in Greece be erased, so she could be Helen of Troy forevermore.

Fifty oars dipped into the aqua-marine waters outside the harbor, the steady swish of their passing the only sound in the early morning Mediterranean air. The night's sea fog clung to the ground obscuring the harbor city from view. It swirled around her like a steam of hot breath luring her ever onward.

Helen turned to her lover, the svelte and alluring diplomat beside her, entwining her hand in his. Paris Alexandros, the second son of King Priam and noble prince of Troy... the love of her live, the mate of her soul. He was almost too handsome to be real. She lost herself in studying his chiseled features. His curly, brown locks fell below his ears, and his almond shaped eyes never wavered their stoic gaze. For Paris she had fled the land of her birth and honor itself, for a fool's hope of happiness in his arms.

He watched the approaching dock, his back rigid with the stance of a man expecting danger. The circumstance of their flight from Greece lay on his shoulders with heavy burden. Helen shivered beneath her cloak, clinging to his arm. She was not the only one to shirk honor and duty to save her from her former life. Paris, too, surely faced the collective condemnation of the Trojan people for the troubles Helen drew in her wake.

She shook her head, trying to ward off those dark thoughts, but Paris' somber mood infected her. She began to imagine a wholly different homecoming, one where the citizens of Troy cursed her name and cast her from their shores. Silencing those imagined cries was difficult, and in that effort, she realized a silence of a different sort. One far more sinister.

Troy, the bustling market city, the hub of commerce between the Old World kingdoms to the east and those of the youthful territories to the west, was silent. Not a sound stirred in the abnormally thick air, the pall of the grave radiating around them. It was quiet. *Too quiet.*

Before she could query her lover, the sun crept over the horizon, its rays lifting the fog like a hand sweeping back a curtain.

And what it revealed was death.

All along the banks of the Hellespont lay the discarded bodies of Trojan citizenry. Blood trickled from their corpses into muddy pools, trailing off in rivulets to the Scamander river. Even at a distance the vast tributary was visibly tinged with the crimson matter.

Further inland, heat shimmered in translucent waves off the inner city of the acropolis. This was no ordinary heat. It radiated from the ground as though the Gods had opened the vents of the underworld and the flames of Tartaros had crept into the world of Men. As she watched, billowing clouds of black smoke rose into the air, and the city burned.

"*Helen,*" Paris' deep voice echoed in the silence. She spun, looking across the great plain of the lower city to where he pointed, to the beachhead of Troy...

Where sat the vast fleet of a Grecian army, an armada one

thousand ships strong.

Helen fell to her knees, a sharp pain penetrating her breast. They were too late. The wrath of her former lords had followed her to Troy. There was no escape for her, not in this life.

As though her fears summoned him, the silhouette of a single man emerged on the dock. Before his features drew into focus, she knew who it was. The barrel chest and warrior stature announced the presence of the Mycenaean king. Agamemnon waited for her as their ship glided into port.

Draped in his lion skin cloak, the king's eyes were as wild as the creature he once slew. The garment, like the man himself, was soaked in blood, as though the beast had just feasted on the flesh of his enemies. He lifted a finger to her, the force of his dark will stretching across the distance and making her pulse soar.

"*You are mine, Spartan. Mine. I have come to take my due.*"

Helen backed away from him, racing from the prow and nearly stumbling over her feet in her mad dash. But there was nowhere to flee. Agamemnon had come, as she knew he would. No place was safe. She fell to the deck and hands grabbed at her, pulling her around. In a desperate panic, she fought to remain free.

"Helen."

The female voice froze Helen's blood ice-cold. She looked up, her words of protest dying on her tongue as she stared at her twin sister.

"Helen," Clytemnestra's face was marked with horror. "*What have you done?!*"

Shame and fear flooded Helen as she backed away from her sister, incapable of response. A lifetime of suffering the abuses of king and husband had not prepared her to face this woman. She needed to get away. *Far away.*

She spun back to the prow just as Agamemnon raised his weapon: a fire-hardened short spear with a thick bronze tip that could penetrate any armor. He tossed the weapon into the sky, its dark shaft carving a path towards the ship and directly at Paris' back.

"*Paris!*" She desperately reached for him, but her prince, wholly unaware of the danger, was lost in shock as his beloved city burned. The spear found its mark.

And Helen's whole world was torn asunder.

"*Paris!*" Helen startled awake with a violent jolt. It took her a breathless moment to orient herself. In the pre-dawn darkness little was visible. Only the heavy scent of bitumen-sealed planks and the steady rocking of a ship at sea told her she was safe. Or as safe as a person fleeing for their life could be.

"Shhhh. It's okay." Paris stroked her back, continuing to whisper in her ear.

Precious air returned to her lungs. She clung to him, reassuring herself that he was real. Her hands roamed over his lean chest, up his chiseled jaw and into his hair. *Alive.* He was very much alive. The hammering of her heart began to slow as her brain finally accepted the information as truth.

"We're safe." She dropped her head to his shoulder and took a deep breath. *Safe... for now.*

Paris nearly cried out in relief. Since they left Mycenae a week prior, Helen's night tremors had only grown worse. Thick curtains separated the royal sleeping quarters from the remainder of the hold, providing what little privacy their circumstance afforded. Originally, he had given the space to Helen and her matron, trying for some semblance of honor in their questionable departure. Then the nightmares began, and try as Aethra might, the matron could not awaken Helen when the terrors took hold. Only Paris could, so each night he laid his bedroll within reach, ready to protect his love from her phantoms.

"Are you alright?"

"I'm fine." She spoke with a strength that belied her fragile psyche. "Don't worry about me."

He shared a worried glance with Aethra, the aged matron hovering near her charge. The woman's iron grey hair hung limp against a care-worn face, a face that bore more lines than when Paris had first met the woman. *She must know the source of these daemons.*

He held Aethra's gaze, that unanswered question lying heavy between them. The woman backed away, her tongue weighed down by some inner conflict. *Let her keep her secrets,* he grumbled silently to himself. *So long as she stays true to Helen.*

"Do you want to talk about it?"

She shook her head, a fierce resolve in her eyes. Her excuses varied whenever he asked. She didn't want to burden him, or, in this case, revisit her nightmares. Paris could only imagine what tormented her, what visions could cause her to thrash in her sleep and soak her bedsheets in sweat, a malady that only started when she set foot on his ship. He couldn't help but feel somewhat responsible. She would not be here if he had not convinced her to leave her homeland.

He ran a hand through his sweat-soaked hair. If Helen would not talk, then he had no choice but to find a way to help her forget. "Do you want to get some fresh air? It's almost first light."

Helen took a deep breath and nodded, grateful for Paris' patience. She quickly donned a fresh chiton, and he wrapped his cloak around her shoulders. Together, they quietly made their way above deck, careful not to disturb the score of sleeping sailors in the main hold.

A tremor of guilt pulled at her gut. Helen hated excluding Paris from her troubles, but the events on the night they left Mycenae, and those of her childhood, had left her scarred. Time and again her lauded beauty had subjected her to the sick attentions of powerful men. But this last abuse, by one whom she loved more than her own self, was beyond bearing. Helen felt saturated by a filth that penetrated far beneath the skin. Those type of hurts did not lessen when they were shared.

She grabbed hold of a rope ladder, climbing to the main deck, a task made difficult by the rolling swell of the Aegean. Fortunately, she had always been athletic and managed the task with grace. Once topside, the cool breeze off the pre-dawn waters instantly cleared her foggy mind.

A handful of Trojan sailors manned their stations, watchful for a change of winds or current. A young lad, no more than ten and seven years, tied off the main sail. He looked away nervously as she passed.

Helen flushed and hid her face in her golden tresses. Her interaction with the Trojan crew had been minimal at best. She found herself at a loss on how to relate with the hardworking men. They sailed for home, but under the dark auspices of having broken the bonds of *xenia*. Every shifted gaze or stiffened back made her wonder how many of them secretly wished to return her to Greece. How many wished to rid themselves of the wrath of the Gods that was sure to follow?

Paris told her not to worry, that his crew had faced death and more with him, but it was hard for her. What right did she have to ask that they risk so much for her freedom, especially when their kindness would earn them the undying hatred of the Mycenaean king? The fears that haunted her dreams were very real, and she would not suffer the fallout alone. Her presence on this ship placed the entire crew in danger. When they realized she was not worth the risk, not even Paris would be able to keep her safe.

Her prince took her by the hand and led her to the raised platform where Glaucus awaited them at the back of the ship. The stoic captain stood at the stern in the precise spot she had last seen him the night before. Did the man ever sleep?

"Paris. Princess," Glaucus grunted. It was as much of a greeting as Helen had come to expect from the quiet man. She had learned that Glaucus used his words sparingly because when he spoke, he wanted those words to matter.

"Any sign of pursuit?" Paris returned the greeting with similar gruffness.

"Not a sight of slip or sail." Glaucus kept his iron gaze locked over the grey-black waters. Scarcely a week from their flight from Mycenae, and they were still in Grecian waters. "Strange for these parts." The captain tightened his grip on the stern oar, making small adjustments in their course with the wide-bladed rudder. "Greeks are born mariners. If you prayed for secrecy, I'd say Poseidon favored your wish."

"Don't count your blessings yet," Paris scoffed. "We're not in safe harbors."

Helen shivered in agreement. An eastern zephyr had sent the Trojan galley off course, bringing them dangerously close to Crete, a kingdom almost as full of dangers to her as the one she left. The palace at Knossos was currently playing host to her husband Menelaus and his fearsome brother Agamemnon. At first, Helen thought the news of their grandsire's death, and their abrupt departure to observe the Cretan king's funerary rites, was a blessing. Their absence was akin to a cloak of darkness. With them gone, she was free to act unobserved, to escape with Paris. It was though Aphrodite removed all the obstacles binding her to Greece and illuminated the path to freedom and happiness.

But every gust of wind pulled them closer to discovery, back to the men who had made a prison of her life. If the Goddess was aiding her flight, then surely there were other gods who worked against them, vengeful gods who cared nothing for love and valued cold, dispassionate duty. It did not matter that her vows were sworn to a man who treated her wedding contract as thought it were a slaver's agreement.

"When will the port be in sight?" Paris tightened his arm around her waist.

"An hour. Maybe two." Glaucus offered the information with slight reluctance. "We could circumvent the island and try a port on the southern side—"

"No." Paris cut him off. "The sooner we get this done, the

better." Try as he might, Glaucus could not persuade his prince to listen to his reasoned advice. Having left in the dead of night, the Trojan galley was not prepared for a long voyage across open waters. They needed to procure supplies, preferably—Paris stressed—before news of her departure became public knowledge. But to dock at Crete?

"Dius is our best bet," Paris continued. "Any other port might not have enough stores to see us through to Troy."

The captain shifted his weight, a minimal indicator of his mounting disapproval. "There *are* other ports. Ones further away from Knossos..."

"*We are not stopping in Egypt.*" Paris shook with suppressed irritation as he repeated that command for the umpteenth time. "Get the men together. I want this stop to be as short as possible."

Glaucus grumbled something incoherent, then collected himself. "As you command, My Prince." With a curt nod to her and Paris, he turned to go. Glaucus bore the strain well, but the pressures of their questionable departure were beginning to bow his broad shoulders.

"Captain?" Helen rushed forward, untangling herself from Paris' arm. "I am sorry for the danger I have brought to you. And your ship." Stretching up on her toes, she planted a chaste kiss on the grizzled veteran's cheek. "Thank you... for your efforts."

Glaucus pretended indifference, but stood taller in the aftermath of her small token of affection. "Have no fear, Princess," he spoke with a fatherly frown. "I've spent most my life at sea. If the crown intends pursuit, they will never catch this ship." His certainty filled her with comfort, and then he left with no further comment.

Paris pulled Helen back to him and kissed the top of her head. "You will need to stay out of sight." He stroked the length of her hair.

She tightened her grip around his waist. "Do you have to go?"

"You don't have to worry." He lifted her chin and looked straight into her eyes. "The business of trade is straightforward. I've sailed into a thousand ports. This one is no different."

But the lie was in his eyes. *Everything* was different. "Please be careful."

"Of course I will." He placed a tender kiss on her lips. A chill ran through her body with his touch, a chill of longing and of foreboding.

She watched quietly as he left to manage preparations for the landing crew. The Trojan galley, nearly one hundred feet in length, was one of the longest ships she had ever seen, but it was hardly spacious. Almost all of their activities occurred above deck: cooking, eating, exercise, all while navigating the ship. Living in close proximity over the past week, she had seen first-hand how well loved Paris was by his crew, especially by his royal guard: the five elite fighters who joined him now.

She pulled a fringed shawl over her head and whispered a prayer, asking Hermes to send the message of her departure astray. It was a foolish hope—Agamemnon and his allies would eventually come for them—but when she had no options left, Helen always held to her faith.

Eventually, Aethra joined her at the aft-deck. Despite the early hour, her matron was a pinnacle of feminine propriety. Her thick woolen dress pressed tight to ample curves, and not a strand of hair was out of place on her proud head. Aethra would not have taken one step above deck otherwise. Her lips pressed into a firm line, the closest effort the woman ever made toward smiling.

For an hour they watched the men complete their work, not a word spoken between them. When the sun was fully above the horizon, the red-tinged glow making more than one sailor step cautiously, Helen could bear it no longer.

"Zeus strike me blind, you have never held your tongue this long," she snapped at her matron. "Do you have anything to say on the matter?"

Aethra raised an eyebrow at the hasty comment, an amused look on her face. "I speak when necessary. If you want idle chatter, you should have brought a chambermaid."

"I didn't bring you. You *insisted* on coming." Helen let that point simmer between them. The woman's claims of loyalty had been sorely tested with Helen's resurfacing memories. And though Aethra protected her as fierce as a she-bear defending her cub, Helen still had trouble trusting the woman. She had birthed a man so monstrous Helen shook at the barest memory of him. She had been only a child when Theseus abducted her, but the scars from his touch had yet to fade.

"You are a slave no longer." Helen banished the evil man from thought and focused back on what truly mattered. "You came of your own free will to advise me. *So advise.*"

"You wish to know my mind?" Aethra sounded surprised. "So be it. This flight from Greece is ill-conceived." She raised her head towards the bow of the ship, towards Paris. "He should have killed Menelaus when he had the chance."

Helen nearly choked. "You think Paris should have killed a member of his *host family*?" Did Aethra believe him completely bereft of honor? "*That is your sage advice?*"

Her matron shrugged. "It would have been cleaner."

"It would have been an act of war!"

But Aethra didn't flinch. She held firm under Helen's disapproving glare. "And how are his current actions any less?"

It wasn't. And Helen knew it, the words of her suitor's oath burning a hole in her mind. *To unite and defend against any wrong done to her husband in relation to their union...*

A cold chill settled over her, but before she could respond, the coastline of Crete came into focus on the horizon, and with it, the island port of Dius. She cast her matron one last frustrated glance and headed to the hold.

Events were moving too quickly for her to do more than

react. But the enormity of Paris' and her actions, and the repercussions sure to follow, were not lost on her. They had shirked the laws of Man to be together. Even though the Gods had given them signs, the world would take more convincing.

She caught one last glimpse of her prince before she kept her promise to stay out of sight. He had changed to a simple wool tunic favored by the common folk. Even dressed as a peasant, Paris was strikingly handsome.

Her heart ached with worry for his safety. If anything happened to him, her world would crumble. She whispered a prayer to Aphrodite that the price of their love would not be paid with swords, but the words died on her lips.

Perhaps this time, faith was not enough.

Chapter 2

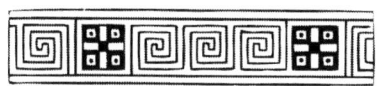

The Black Flag

"WHAT HOME PORT did you say?" the piebald harbor master asked.

Paris lounged behind Glaucus and Hyllos, trying to appear inconspicuous as they finished their exit interview at Dius' port entrance. The rat-faced official was the same unsavory sort Paris had run into a dozen times over in as many countries. Grease his palm and all manner of information would flow their way.

"Rhodes," Hyllos answered, sliding over a nugget of gold.

That part of their ruse had been Paris' suggestion. The best lies were always half-truths. As with the men of the Hellas, Troy shared a common ancestry and tongue with Rhodes. No one should suspect their true origin.

Rat-face tested the nugget between a pair of cracked teeth, pleased with the soft give in the metal that indicated purity. "And you've got nothing to declare?" His tone bespoke of how suspicious that circumstance was for merchants of the sea.

Hyllos grunted, playing his part perfectly. "We stopped in Mycenae and unloaded. I didn't restock, especially at Agamemnon's prices." He cast a nervous glance Paris' way.

Negotiations between Troy and Mycenae had been disastrous. There was no question that Paris' mission had failed. Agamemnon had delivered an ultimatum, one King Priam was sure to retaliate against in kind. In the end, Paris had gone a step further than his diplomatic authority permitted. By taking Helen, he had arguably "stolen" the greatest treasure of the Hellas, and he couldn't imagine Agamemnon would give her up without a fight. They were sailing home, but potentially with an army at their back.

"I prefer to deal with honest traders." Hyllos cleared his throat and continued on, "Thought it better to stop here."

"You thought right," Rat-face croaked. "Best you get down to The Chimera if you want to fill your larders before it's all gone. The trade master is a big fella by name of Xenocrates." He made a few notes in his ledger and waved them on.

Normally a comment like that needed explanation, but in the short time it took to disembark from the Trojan galley and walk to the harbor master's hut, seven wagons laden with sacks of grain, fruit and livestock rolled down the gangplank to awaiting galleys. Either a mass exodus was occurring on the island, or something bigger was afoot. Paris made to follow his men, but at the last moment his curiosity got the best of him.

"Messir, what's all the bustle about, keepin' us in the offing?" he asked, adopting the universal slang favored by sailors.

Rat-face gave him a funny eye, reading Paris' poor-posture and rough clothes as a marker of a grunt, hardly the sort that an important man like himself need answer. But the harbor master rolled his gold nugget around in his hand and decided it was worth the effort. "It's for the feast on the mainland." He pointed to the knoll behind them as though the answer was self-evident.

Atop a wooden flagpole, a black banner rippled in the gentle morning breeze. Stitched into its center were the white-winged forms of the baleful *keres*: the female death sprites who spirited away those who met a violent end.

Paris cursed under his breath. He had forgotten Crete was in the midst of mourning their king. The announcement in Agamemnon's court had happened too quickly for him to take notice. The Cretans would be on high alert, especially since their monarch was murdered by pirates.

"Seems the royal dead need enough food to feed a village." Rat-face grimaced. "Is a bloody waste if you ask me. But nobody does." His frustration was similar to what they encountered in the common folk at Mycenae. A poor harvest coupled with excessive taxes had made the commonwealth nearly mutinous.

Glaucus, at the crossroad into the city proper, was glaring at him to hurry up. "Best be on me way." Paris tossed the harbor master another nugget and rushed to join his captain.

"What are you doing?" Glaucus growled at him. "You are a Rhodian deckhand. Keep your purse out of sight. If anyone means to give us trouble, the first person they'll target is the man with the money."

Paris nodded, seeming for all the world a hired-hand getting reprimanded by his commanding officer. He dropped in line behind his tall captain. *Observe and keep quiet*, he chastised himself, remembering the promise he swore to Glaucus when planning this ruse.

It was a short walk to the tavern Rat-face indicated. The open markets where farmers and craftsmen displayed their wares were for women and old men. Real trade occurred in taverns, and the best prices always went to the man who bought the most rounds.

The Chimera was a fairly large establishment, two stories high and with its timber frame finished in stucco. Two voluptuous women of ill-repute dangled their legs out of the second story window, shouting out to potential marks.

"Soft-Cheeks!" a raven-haired trollop called down. "I've got something that'll make a man of you." It took a moment for Paris to realize she was talking to him, he being the only one in their retinue without facial hair. He almost laughed. It had been a long time since anyone had spoken to him so brazenly. As soon as he looked up, she let loose an intoxicated giggle and lifted her chiton, showcasing her wares.

Glaucus placed a none-too-gentle hand on his back and shoved him into the tavern. He stumbled ten feet before catching his balance and had to bite back an angry retort. His old friend was enjoying the reversal of roles far too much.

The common room was surprisingly full despite the early hour. A few men diced on a corner table, and others held conversations over their cups in groups of twos and threes. As soon as the Trojans entered, those lively conversations came to an abrupt halt.

"Shut the door," a lone man shouted from a darkened nook. He bounded to his feet and stalked over to where Glaucus entered. Though he stumbled on unstable legs, the irritated drunk was of equal stature with the captain.

Paris quickly made note of the man's thick leather garments and the sharpened sword at his hip. *A sell-sword.* And by his sloven appearance, one currently out of work. The practice of turning mercenary only happened in a region where the king commanded no loyalty, or when a man had no other way to feed his family. Apparently Greece was a mixture of both.

Glaucus stretched out a hand and shoved the heavy door, all-the-while glaring at the hostile Greek. As soon as the door slammed shut, the room, lit only by a handful of oil lamps, instantly dimmed. The air was thick with the stench of sour beer and fried bacon... and something unfamiliar. Paris grimaced. The place had the feel of an opium den.

"Sit down, Nikias." A middle-aged barkeep crossed the room to greet them. "I'll have you out on your arse if you harass customers." He wiped his hands on the filthy apron tied around his waist and turned to Glaucus. "What'll it be? Food? Drink? Or something else?" He nodded toward the back to the sounds of heavy grunts and rocking furniture.

"Drink. And the table of your trade master."

Paris blended into the crowd as Hyllos and Glaucus took a seat at a nearby table with a group of local merchants to haggle over wares. His other guards spread out across the room in an effort to glean more information. Brygos joined the dicers, Iamus and Ariston went to the bar, and Dexios stayed alert by the door. Ale was handed out liberally, and soon the atmosphere of the tavern returned to its steady hum.

He reclined in a shadowy corner, his back to the wall, and watched. The sell-sword was muttering to himself, a dangerous glint to his eyes. He had the look of a man wanting to pick a fight.

"What's your story, Sailor?"

Paris spun toward his addresser. A graybeard sat at the table beside him, the old man little more than a bag of bones with a weathered skin that would make a tanner envious.

"Nothing to say." Paris shrugged. "They drag me along when they need a back to haul their goods."

"Ah, but it's honest work, no? They pay you well?"

Paris gave the man a knowing smile. The graybeard was fishing for some liquid friendship. He signaled to the barkeep for two mugs and took the empty chair opposite him.

"Nikodaemos." The graybeard stretched his thin arm out as way of introduction.

"Piyama-rados," Paris offered in return. The name came spontaneously to his lips, a picture of the infamous renegade floating out of his distant memory. The wizened warrior had once taken refuge at his father's court. To a young prince, Piyama seemed all-powerful and ancient. Paris smiled at the old man across from him, knowing why the name had come to him now.

"Okay, old man. What's the story here? Why're the locals tensed like a cat in a boneyard?"

Nikodaemos buried his whiskers in the foam of his cup, a sad cast to his face. "There be talk of war."

Paris stiffened. Had news of their departure from Greece followed them already? A fierce defiance raged in his chest, and he gritted his teeth. He didn't care if he'd have to face an entire Greek armada, he was never giving Helen back. He had travelled the whole world over and never met a woman as thoughtful and compassionate as his princess. To have won her heart, that she was willing to fight for a life with him, defied reason. She was a slice of happiness he had no right to expect. He'd suffer the injustices of his life twice over if that path always led him to her.

"War? Is that so?" Paris took a long pull of ale, hoping the move masked the hammering of his pulse. "With whom?"

"To them bastards who killed King Catreus. Easterners, they say."

Paris sighed with relief and cast a nervous eye around the common room. The earlier hostility had vanished, replaced now with guarded whispers. The locals twitched at any loud sound, cagey as badgers guarding their dens. He had seen the look before, by men expecting to be pressed into service at any moment. This port was a tinderbox waiting for a spark to set it off.

"Your king was well loved?"

"No more than two shits and a fart," Nikodaemos grunted. "But he left no heir, which means some mainland prat will claim the throne."

A sour realization gripped Paris' stomach. He could guess which king would be eager to claim that honor.

"Mycenae? How long were ye in port?"

Paris' ears perked up to the conversation at the adjacent table. The crowd at Hyllos' table had grown. Trade Master Xenocrates, a burly merchant with shoulders set as wide as an ox, asked the question while his partner measured Glaucus' purse with a set of scales and balances.

"A few days. Just long enough to unload and avoid extended port taxes." Hyllos used the same cover story they planted at the port.

"Did ye get a gander at the Trojan prince?" Xenocrates' voice was amplified in his inebriated condition and it easily carried across the common room. "Rumor has it the perfumed lordling is a dead-man walking. Cursed by the Gods."

Hyllos tensed, his eyes darting unconsciously in Paris' direction. "The only Trojans I saw were in the market. I don't mingle with princes."

"Pity," the trade master cast him a sick grin. "That's a sight I'd pay a dram to see." He laughed loudly, a mocking sound picked up by his fellows.

Paris steadied his hand on the table, feeling the heat of embarrassment flush his cheeks. The dire warning of his birth omen hung over him like a storm cloud. In Troy, he was prepared to face the slander of Hecuba and her sycophants. But here in the West, at the edge of the civilized world? To have that humiliation be common knowledge everywhere he went?

He took a deep breath, pressing the anger and shame away, tucking it into a corner of his soul that he never let loose, just as he had when Clytemnestra exposed him to the Mycenaean court. He would not let that dark vision be the measure of his worth.

His companions, however, were not so good at containing themselves. Iamus marched from the bar and grabbed Xenocrates rough by his tunic. "Where did you hear that?" His face was devoid of color. The entire common room turned to watch the two men.

"Go back to your drinks, Sailor," Glaucus growled in a vain attempt to control the situation.

But the damage was done. The locals were looking at Paris and his men in a new light, the tension in the room as thick as the smoke. The sell-sword left his table again and struted over to Glaucus.

"You are no man of Rhodes," Nikias simmered. "You hide it well, but I've seen your like before... *Lycian*."

It seemed impossible, but the tension in the room

increased. The word "Lycian" rippled through the gathered men like a dirty epithet. Paris slipped out of his chair and cased out the danger. The sell-sword was the biggest threat, the only real warrior in the tavern. But the West bred hardy men, and the locals—merchants, farmers and fishermen—looked as dangerous as any battle-hardened solider.

Glaucus stood to face his accuser, not an ounce of emotion showing on his face. The stoic captain had been in Paris' guard for so long he had forgotten about the man's questionable past. In spirit, Glaucus was as Trojan as he was. "Say that again." Glaucus' voice rumbled with the threat.

"Lycian." Nikias spat. *"Pirate."*

Glaucus didn't have time to move; two Cretans grabbed him from behind. Paris' other guards were in a similar plight as the brawl broke out. Fists flew, crockery shattered, and shouts filled the air. But hot-blooded as the local merchants were, it was the sell-sword who was the ringleader. He pulled his sword free of his belt and advanced on Glaucus.

Paris was on him with lightning speed. He grabbed Nikias' outstretched arm and spun, launching the sell-sword over his back and slamming him down on the mud brick floor. The man gasped for breath as the air was knocked clear of his lungs. While he struggled to get up, Paris stomped a foot down on his neck.

"STOP!" he shouted to the room at large, using his most authoritative voice.

Slowly, the violence halted, every eye on him to see his next move. He twisted Nikias' arm, forcing the man to drop his sword, while keeping pressure on the man's neck, ready to snap it without a moment's hesitation.

"You brain-soft idiot," Paris hissed at the man. "If we were pirates, would we be here bartering for goods? Or would we wait on the high seas and pillage your ships as they left port?"

Nikias' hate-filled eyes narrowed with fear. He gagged as he stared up at Paris, a man who knew he looked death in the face.

THE PRINCESS OF PROPHECY

The Cretans had taken the quiet moment to regroup. A dozen armed merchants had joined ranks with Xenocrates forming a formidable barrier. They watched Paris warily. Even Nikodaemos looked at him as though he were a Titan in their midst. His moves were too acrobatic for a common deckhand. Paris had exposed himself as either a nobleman or assassin of the highest caliber. From the look on the faces of the honest tradesmen, they did not desire the company of either sort.

"It's time you go," Xenocrates told them darkly, a deep murmur of agreement coming from behind him as his numbers continued to swell. By Paris' quick count, they were outnumbered three to one.

"Go?" Glaucus growled in protest, pressing forward heedless of the danger. More than a few merchants took an unconscious step back from the irate man. "Our business is not finished!"

"Yes, it is." Xenocrates signaled his partner, and the merchant tossed back their sack of gold. It fell to the ground with a resounding thud. "Your metal is no good here, Lycian. Hoist anchor and set off. No one in Dius will trade with your kind."

For a moment, Paris wondered if Glaucus was going to call the man's bluff. Xenocrates was flushed with drink, as were the other merchants. Even if they were sober, he'd give his captain even odds at taking down this back-alley mob. There might have been a time when Glaucus would have invited such a fight in defense of his honor, but those days had passed. Paris needed to end this, and preferably without further risk to his crew.

"We're leaving," Paris ordered his men in a tone the bore no argument. "*Now.*"

The other Trojans, save Glaucus, sprung to action. Hyllos collected their gold as the other guards exited the tavern. Only after the last man was safely out of the melee, did Paris drop his hold on Nikias and grab Glaucus by the arm, towing the captain to the exit. The Cretans backing away from them as they passed by.

Once outside, Paris regrouped with his men, frustration heating his blood. Would he never be free of the omens of his birth? He shook his head. There would be time to deal with his personal troubles later. His first priority was the welfare of his men. Iamus' chest heaved as he recovered from a berserker fit and Brygos had a bloody nose, but no one else looked worse for the wear.

Glaucus, however, was an unhealthy shade of white, a picture of fury incarnate. "There's only one way the Mycenaean queen learned of that god-forsaken curse, and you all know it. Someone talked." He glowered at his troops, his six foot frame towering over them. "*I want the traitor found!*"

"Glaucus—" Paris tried to find words, but failed. There was no doubt someone on their crew had betrayed them by divulging that sensitive information to Helen's sister, but continuing the witch hunt, turning soldier against soldier, only served to destroy what loyalty remained.

"It's insubordination." Glaucus refused to back down, trembling with pent-up fury, a man hellbent on enacting justice. He took the presence of a traitor on his ship personally. "It will not stand!"

A bone-chilling silence invaded his men. As sworn swords of the Royal Guard, they made a sacred vow to defend Paris' life and honor. To have a traitor in their midst tarnished them all. To a man, they were in agreement with their captain.

It sickened Paris that the horrible circumstances of his birth would claim someone else's life. His curse was an infection that undermined every relationship he held dear. He backed off, giving Glaucus leave to handle this situation as he saw fit.

"We've already interviewed the entire crew," Dexios stated grimly, a firm cast to his sun-bronzed face.

"Then do it again," Glaucus ordered. "Each sailor is on double-duty until the culprit is found."

As they returned to the harbor, Paris' mood soured for the

worse. Dius had been a mistake. They had not procured the supplies needed to see them back to Troy. Still in enemy waters and with no other choice before him, he'd be forced to brave more perilous harbors.

But if Glaucus was right, if one of Paris' men had truly betrayed him, then the dangers of an enemy port were minuscule compared to what hid beneath his deck.

Chapter 3

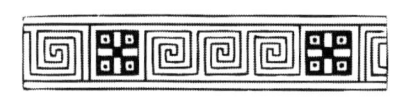

Giving Chase

HOW COULD SHE leave me?

Clytemnestra lamented silently to herself, the heartbroken thought becoming a mantra in her mind ever since she learned of Helen's disappearance the night prior.

The sun was at its zenith now, and the queen rode through the lower city of Mycenae in a raised palanquin. The lightweight carriage required only four slaves to hoist it, but today Clytemnestra had a dozen men in attendance. A show of strength was necessary, she reminded herself, especially after the insolent actions of that vile Trojan prince.

Her face flushed with heat. The barest thought of the foul man who seduced her sister was enough to send her into a fit. *We should have killed him the moment he stepped off his cursed ship.*

Ichor boiled in the queen's blood. This mess she'd been forced to handle was all Paris' fault. The Trojan had bewitched her sister, feeding her lies about love, while offering Helen nothing but a tarnished reputation and eternal damnation from more powerful men. That insipid prince was going to pay for his crimes if it was the last task Clytemnestra meted out on this earth. If not for him, she would not have had to treat her sister so roughly...

A pang of regret stirred in her bosom. Nestra *had no choice* but to shock her twin back to reason, to prove to her the feelings Paris evoked were not special. Anyone could stir them. Helen was too innocent to see through his empty promises, defenseless against his devilish charms. She trusted naively instead of holding the man suspect. As she should hold *all* men suspect.

Clytemnestra sighed. Perhaps she had pushed Helen too far. She was was not ready to accept the cruel truths of this world. Of course she had run away. If Nestra could only talk to her, she could explain that she would never hurt Helen without reason. Her punishment, while harsh, was nothing compared to what Agamemnon would do. Helen had to understand...

A painful sob constricted her chest, the loss of her twin more devastating than Clytemnestra could have ever imagined. Helen was her only ray of sunshine in this God-forsaken world, her sister's joyful spirit the only thing that made living at Agamemnon's side bearable.

And now she was gone...

A sharp pang seared through Clytemnestra's head and the confined space within her palanquin went out of focus. Her breaths came in shallow gasps. It was happening again. A foreign prince had abducted her twin, disappearing into the night to inflict his sick pleasures on her body. The girls had been only eight the first time it had happened, and the stain of that dark memory haunted Nestra thereafter.

The cry of alarm rang through their father's camp. Nestra burrowed beneath the furs in their tent just as the raiders threw open the flap. But Helen was too slow. She was caught in the open...

Nestra would never forget the sound of her sister's screams as that vile Athenian king took her away. Or the feeling of utter helplessness that paralyzed her body as she quivered beneath the blankets. Nestra had been too weak to save Helen from Theseus, and it disgusted her. In the horrible aftermath that followed, she made a solemn vow to herself: to banish all weakness from her heart and to protect her twin at all costs.

But how could she save Helen from herself?

A jolt in the litter stirred the queen from her dark thoughts. Nestra pulled back the gossamer curtains hiding her from view and surveyed her surroundings. The entourage had moved off the smooth limestone streets of the main city and onto the hard-packed avenues of the lower fields.

Mycenae had grown too quickly for any sort of rational plan. Pockets of occupation popped up as more peasants migrated to the great city. Unfortunately, that brought as many unsavory sorts as hard-working citizen.

Layabouts, thieves, and rapists, Nestra sneered, dabbing her nose with a perfumed cloth, a futile attempt to block the stench of sewage running down the street. The locals had dubbed this precinct "Vagabond Fields". Only the truly desperate came here. Or those looking for the desperate.

A pair of children ducked into an alley at the sight of her palanquin. Probably orphans by the state of their disheveled dress. They stared at her with dark, beady eyes, and there was a glint of hunger in their hate-filled glare that did not desire food.

The queen glared back. Her husband spent too much time pursuing enemies abroad. Only a fool ignored a threat in his own house. If Nestra had her way, she'd purge the entire district. It was better to strike than wait to see what damage your enemy could inflict.

The slaves halted fifty feet away from a dilapidated hut. The thatching on the roof was newly mended and the paint on the door fresh. The work masked the bones of a questionable structure, and it spoke of occupants who could not afford the copper or time to build something better.

"Are you sure this is the place?" She turned to Belos, the dark-skinned captain who commanded her guard.

"I knew him well, My Queen. He is the one you seek."

Nestra nodded and Belos gave the command for his men

to spread out and secure the perimeter. Her guardsmen feared Belos like they did the wrath of Zeus. The muscular warrior hailed from the southern continent and resembled the black jungle cat of his homelands in both ferocity and temperament. Nestra placed all her trust in the man, as she could not with Agamemnon's lackeys. Belos' fortunes were tied to her own, unlike the Mycenaean soldiers who owed her no such loyalty.

"Once it's clear, take only the men you trust inside. I don't want talk of this meeting spreading throughout the city," Clytemnestra instructed him.

"Of course, My Queen." He departed immediately to oversee the task.

Nestra wrung a kerchief in her hands, the small square of linen damp with tears. This plan had to work. Each day, *each minute*, she delayed put Helen's life further at risk.

Belos waved to her from the hut. Her men were ready. She gave him a quick nod to proceed and watched as Belos kicked in the door and stormed the interior with five equally muscular men.

There were sounds of struggle from within. Belos had promised to make short work of the man, but it continued for long, tense minutes. A baby wailed, crockery shattered, and a man screamed in pain.

Clytemnestra froze, the threat of danger urging her to run. Had she made a mistake? Desperation brought her to this dilapidated place, and for an angst-ridden moment, she doubted the wisdom of her plan.

The hut fell to silence, and Belos finally stepped out the front door. "We are ready for you, My Queen."

Clytemnestra closed off the pathetic yammering of her heart, slamming shut a stone door on any emotion. Now was the time for strength. She strut into the house like a true Spartan, her back stiff as a corpse and an arrogant sneer on her face. She wanted this man to have no mistake where he stood in her favor.

There had been quite a battle. The one-room hovel was

completely turned out. A wooden table, now missing a leg, was smashed against the wall. One of her guards gasped for breath while clutching his ribs, the white tip of bone protruding from his tunic. Feathers from slashed bedding filled the air, cascading around them like flakes of snow. Nestra kicked aside broken pottery as she entered, her eyes boring straight into the man she had come to see.

He was tall, over six feet, with sandy-brown hair that hung to his shoulders. His clothes were poor, the fabric thin, but beneath that wrapping lay the body of a well toned warrior. He brandished the missing table leg like a man familiar with combat. Behind him, an exotic, dark-haired beauty grasped his arm, an infant at her breast and another child, but one year older, clinging to her leg.

"What is the meaning of this? I've committed no crime!" he shouted, his petulant tone reminiscent of the toadies in her court. Was this really the man Belos had told her of? He seemed no more dangerous than the unsavory men who traded in dark alleys.

"You dare to speak that way before royalty?" Belos growled. "You should *kneel*, you *meshwesh* scum." One of her guards stepped forward, an arrow drawn taut in his bow.

"There is no need for formalities." Nestra crossed the room to stand before him. The man was far from the type to bend the knee. "I know who you are, *Scylax*."

He froze. That infamous name was poisoned with the spirits of the countless dead he had dispatched. His arm tensed, pushing his wife further behind him. "I am not that man."

Clytemnestra was taken aback by the heat in his voice. Not a flicker of emotion crossed his eyes, those crystal blue orbs as cold as ice. They were a strikingly pale blue, like the pallor of a two-day-dead corpse. They froze her heart and warned her of danger. Clytemnestra laughed at her own foolishness and cast the man a devilish smile, deciding it was his best feature.

"You're a *mercenary*." She let the word drip with the

revulsion she felt. Sell-swords had no honor, they stood for nothing and no one, save their own advancement. In the eyes of the Gods they ranked just above merchants as the lowest form of humanity.

"But you aren't just any mercenary," she continued. "You commanded a company of Greeks in the employ of Libyan rebels. You tried to unseat a sitting Pharaoh. Any man who thinks he can topple kings is one I pay close attention to." She moved in dangerously close as she spoke, delivering her next words with the seductive cadence of a lover. "It's important to know who your enemies are. Are you my enemy, Scylax?"

The man was completely at her mercy, and he knew it. He flinched, pulling away from her uncomfortable presence. "I'm not that man. Please, leave me and my family be—"

She gave Belos the pre-arranged signal. Her guard stepped forward and yanked Scylax' wife away by the hair, placing a naked blade at her throat.

The change happened quickly. With lightning fast reflexes, Scylax pounced forward clubbing the first guard who attempted to subdue him. He took hold of Belos' sword arm, wrenching the blade loose. It was an incredible display of strength. He was about to pick up the weapon for murderous effect when a cry cut through the din.

"Scylax, *no!*" his wife sobbed, her pitiful cries freezing the man in place.

A tense moment of silence followed while her royal guards stood motionless, fear of their opponent writ large on their faces. But Clytemnestra knew how to end this stalemate. Scylax' weakness was obvious: *his family.*

"Is this your daughter?" She plucked the toddler off the ground. The sell-sword had forgotten the child in his mad rush to save his wife. The babe wailed in Clytemnestra's arms, confused at the identity of this stranger who was clearly not her mother.

Scylax hesitated, stuck halfway between her and Belos. He could not save one loved one without endangering the other.

The desperation in his attack drained from his body. In its place grew something far more dangerous. He crouched low, the stance of a man prepared to unleash bloody revenge.

Clytemnestra laughed. She was wondering when the man would reveal himself. This was the true Scylax, the ruthless killer whom even the brave knew to fear.

"I'll ask you again. Are you my enemy, Scylax?" She added her own murderous heat to her words. "Or would you rather be my ally?"

That was not what the mercenary was expecting. His muscles relaxed as he reconsidered the possibility of escaping this encounter with the lives of his loved ones intact. "I have nothing of value for you. That life is behind me. On my honor."

She laughed again, a bitter sound meant to wound the pride. "Honor? Your honor is held by the highest bidder. Which is what I mean to be. I have a task for you, Soldier. But I'll have your oath now before another word is spoken. Will you continue your anarchy or would you rather have a queen in your debt?" She pinched the child's tender skin for good measure, making the babe cry out in pain.

"Yes, yes. I'll serve you. Zeus strike me blind if I prove untrue," he swore. "Just put her down."

Nestra practically dropped the brat. Nothing set her teeth on edge like the piercing cry of a baby. Of her three children, only Iphigenia had been blessedly quiet. The Gods favored her with that lovely child.

Belos regained his sword, and the family huddled together in the corner of the room. Scylax eventually coerced the child to hush and turned back to her.

"What is this task you'll have of me?"

Clytemnestra caught her breath, preparing herself for that first lie. Helen had placed her in a terrible predicament. If Agamemnon found out about her affair with the Trojan prince, of her willing abduction from the capital, he would invent a new method to reap pain and suffering from Nestra's twin.

Her life would be forfeit. There was only one way Helen could return to Mycenae and still live.

"My sister Helen, the Princess, was kidnapped."

Scylax shared a shocked look with his wife. Helen was well loved by the common folk. This news came as a horrible surprise to the man.

"The Trojan prince stole her from her rooms two nights past. You are to take a ship and sail after them. Find them and bring my sister back to me."

It was a simple search and rescue endeavor, a task Scylax was over-qualified to conduct. He turned to Belos, a look of distrust in his eyes. "But why me? Why not the royal armada?"

"Because they can't be trusted!" Nestra snapped, committed now to this lie. "Someone helped the Trojans escape. I cannot rely on anyone who had contact with their delegation. It has to be you."

It was a convincing argument. It had won over Belos and the few guards she dared tell of Helen's departure. Scylax glanced at her warily, slowly accepting this pretext, and he began to hammer out the finer details of the quest with her commander. She would equip him with whatever he needed so long as he set sail on the next tide.

"And what of the king?" the mercenary hesitated, a look of disgust on his sharp features as he mentioned her precious husband. "Should I stop in Knossos to inform him of these events."

"Tell no one of your mission," Clytemnestra forbade him. "Stop for nothing. Helen's safety is all that matters. You bring her back to me."

She did not need to see the concern on her commander's face to know she was losing her tenuous grasp on control. But it was too late for half-measures. "Kill the Trojan." She trembled with the heat of that need; it burnt out all reason.

"The more he suffers, the greater your reward."

Chapter 4

Untested Waters

BARELY A DAY had passed since the Trojan galley cast off from Dius' harbor. Glaucus unfurled the sails, taking advantage of the western zephyrs, but it was a short-lived burst of speed. The sun set, the wind died off, and then he put the oarsmen to work, forcing double-shifts until Dius was well behind them.

Paris joined his captain at the stern early the next morning, neither man having rested. The interrogations began as soon as Glaucus felt comfortable leaving the helm. The captain insisted on conducting the investigation for their traitor himself, claiming he knew his men better than anyone. If someone tried to lie, he swore he would be able to tell. Thus far, however, no suspects had emerged, and half the crew had been cleared beyond doubt.

"You should get some rest." Paris tried to relieve the man. It was difficult to tell when Glaucus was tired, he bore his aches without complaint.

"As should you." Glaucus cast him an equally appraising eye.

Paris yawned, knowing he must look like the aftermath of a stampede. He stretched out muscles cramped from long hours of standing in the cold night. Most ships travelled by line of sight, requiring a clear view of the coastline to navigate. Only the best mariners could pilot by the stars, and besides Glaucus, Paris was the only one on board who could read the Cosmos. He had taken Glaucus' place sometime past the witching hour.

"I'll rest when I'm dead." Paris grunted. "Or maybe not even then. It'll depend whether or not I have anyone still alive to haunt." He laughed at the thought. The way his life was shaping up, there would be a long list.

Glaucus laughed with him. It was good to see the man relax somewhat. He bore too much responsibility on his shoulders, and had taken the presence of a traitor in his crew personally. "There's only one person on this ship who is doing any haunting." Glaucus turned his attention down to the main deck.

Helen walked amongst the oarsmen, bringing a bladder of water to the thirsty soldiers. She tried to strike a conversation with those who drank, but most of the men were too shy to say more than a few words. She had a way of tying even the most confident man's tongue.

Paris savored this view of his princess from afar. Glaucus was right. Helen had a face that would haunt him for the remainder of his days. He never thought he could love another human being as much as he did Helen, nor fear her loss more than he did his own life. But the Spartan princess had turned his life upside down from the moment he first spied her in the mist. For her, he'd forsake Honor itself.

As he watched, Helen eventually gave up her attempts to mingle, a look of frustration on her face. He knew she was making efforts to know his crew better, a task made more difficult because of the ongoing interrogations. The entire crew was on edge, ready for all manner of dangers—both from within as without. Still, he hoped she did not get discouraged. Setting sail for a new life in the company of strangers took courage few could muster. He didn't know where she found the fortitude, but every day she tried just a little bit harder, a fact that made him admire her all the more.

After a quick stop at the cook station, she joined them at the aft-deck, carrying two wooden bowls filled with a gruel fashioned out of stale bread and a copious amount of their dwindling drinking water. "It isn't much, but it's hot."

"Thank you." Paris took the meal, trying to appear grateful for the repast although his appetite was nonexistent.

Glaucus couldn't make it past two mouthfuls. He let the gruel drip from his spoon with an unceremonious plop. "We're not going to make it another week without fresh supplies, let alone all the way to Troy."

"I know," Paris admitted ruefully. "We'll have to try a port along the southern coastline. Maybe word of our departure hasn't travelled that far."

But Glaucus wasn't content to let that matter lie, and he picked up the conversation that Paris had been hearing all night. "There are other ports, Paris. Ones not linked by kinship to Greece..."

"*No.*" His curt reply shook with more force than he intended. "That is not an option."

"Well, it very well might be." Glaucus glowered back, casting an embarrassed glance to Helen. The captain was always uncomfortable questioning Paris in front of company, but proper or not, Glaucus would not let this matter drop.

"We are *not* going to Egypt. Now put it out of your mind."

Helen tried to ignore their squabbles when they arose, but this last part intrigued her. She turned to Paris, puzzled. "What's wrong with Egypt?" Mycenae's interaction with their southern neighbors had always been friendly. They were a good trade partner. She couldn't imagine formal, sophisticated Egypt would be hostile to a traveling diplomatic ship.

"Trade in Egypt is controlled by the crown." Paris gave Glaucus a warning glance, making sure the man knew this discussion was not an invitation to alter their plans. "*All trade.* One does not simply drop anchor and barter for goods. There are strict formalities that must be observed. Local governors take part. It's complicated..."

But both Helen and Glaucus were staring at him as if he were paranoid. Paris ran a hand through his hair, trying to find words to describe his concerns. "Egypt was the first kingdom I visited as an ambassador. That was about ten years ago, right after Rameses, the second of his name, died."

Paris remembered that ill-fated trip as though it were yesterday. "Ozymandias sat his throne for sixty years, and the fallout of his death was like nothing I had ever experienced. It reached every level of society. Brother turned on brother as every man who envied Pharaoh rushed in to grab what influence they could."

He paused, worried he was letting emotion cloud his reason, but it was difficult to separate the two when discussing the Two Lands. "My trip was meant to be a short mission, a show of respect from one great king for the passing of another. I was scheduled to stay for a fortnight at best. I did not leave for *six months*."

Helen's eyes grew wide, some small understanding reflecting on her face. If such a delay happened to them now, their dreams of a future in Troy would be forfeit.

"Egypt is a dangerous place," Paris pressed on, "unlike any land I've visited. It is steeped in traditions that are mysterious and completely foreign to men of the North. One false move, one accidental insult to their Gods, and we'll find ourselves hopelessly mired into their world." Like quicksand, Egypt would bury them in their never-ending plots and squabbles. With the wrath of Agamemnon that was sure to follow them, he would not risk the uncertain harbors of Egypt, no matter what arguments Glaucus presented.

"That was ten years ago, Paris," Glaucus persisted. "I'm sure the kingdom has stabilized by now."

"They can't be trusted." Paris shook his head, unrelenting. There was no other way to interpret the series of mixed messages presented by the Egyptian Empire. "I won't risk taking Helen there, not if there is another option."

Helen blushed, turning her gaze to the floorboards. This complication was because of her. The crew suffered, Paris suffered, all to keep her safe. And she was impotent to help them. She hated this feeling of utter helplessness.

"Captain!" Hyllos hailed from the deck. The Trojan trade master approached the helm with a grim face.

Glaucus exhaled heavily, a dark pall overcoming the man with a swiftness that stunned Helen. "A confession?"

"Well, not exactly." Hyllos' face pinched tight as he struggled to find his tongue. In the end, words failed him.

"Then what?" Glaucus growled at the thin man, his lack of sleep making him quick to ire.

"We have... information. But you need to hear it from the source." Hyllos' gaze darted from the captain to Paris and dropped to the deck. Paris had never seen the man seem so unsure of himself. When he spoke again, his voice was so low Paris had to strain to hear it. "For what it's worth, he came to us."

"Hades Hounds," the captain cursed, rolling his eyes. "If you will excuse me, Your Grace, I have a traitor to catch." Glaucus dipped into a sharp bow, leaning in close to deliver his next message with a lowered voice. "I'm not done with this conversation."

"I am," Paris snapped with finality.

The captain snapped his heels together and joined Hyllos. They were both below deck in four powerful strides. Helen watched them disappear, her earlier frustrations finding a safe target. Someone on this ship had betrayed Paris to her sister. Someone had broken his oath, bringing ruin on the entire Trojan delegation. It sickened her to no end. No Spartan could live with that shame. Any one of her countrymen would have laid down on his sword on principle.

"You're worrying again."

She spun back to Paris, burrowing her troubles deep

inside. He had enough burdens without her adding to the list. "You mistake me, Trojan." She planted her arms across her chest, a show of mock offense. "I am merely being cautious. You promised me a new life, and I plan to hold you to your word."

"You'll have it," he promised, lifting her chin for a chaste kiss. Then his voice dropped, all hint of playfulness gone. "All that I have, all that I am, is yours, Helen. Trust me to see you home safely." His kiss led to another, this one deeper.

Helen's heart leapt in her chest. They were in public—anyone could see. Even now, leagues away from her homeland, she couldn't shake the feeling of disobedience, that the powerful people who ruled her life were watching and waiting to make her pay for this indiscretion.

But a rebellious fire burned inside her. She squelched the voice in her head that screamed at her lewd behavior—a voice that sounded eerily similar to the sister she left behind. Helen did not care if she acted no better than a bathhouse trollop. She loved this man, body and soul.

"I trust you, Paris," she whispered fiercely, pressing her lips to his ear.

Paris had to restrain himself. The power of the emotions she invoked was almost frightening. He didn't know if he believed in other lives or the immortality of the soul, but Helen's touch, the way she said his name, felt like a familiar caress. He had never felt more vulnerable, and yet *accepted,* in his entire life. With Helen by his side, he had finally found a place he belonged.

He tickled a sensitive spot on her neck with the day's growth of stubble on his chin, and she squirmed in his arms, giggling. It was a musical note, one that filled him with warmth. He loved the sound of her laughter. They had spent too much of their lives under the thumb of those who reaped sorrow instead of smiles. Gazing into her jewel-blue eyes, the orbs a deeper blue than the finest lapis-lazuli, he vowed silently to make up for those lost years.

THE PRINCESS OF PROPHECY

"Your face is made for the bards, My Love."

Helen closed her eyes and let his touch wash over her. "A pretty face? Is that all it takes to turn your head?" Goosebumps ran down her back. "Prince Paris the Lovelorn... struck dumb by beauty? I thought you Trojans were forged from stronger metal than that."

He laughed at her jest and tucked a loose strand of golden hair behind her ear. When he touched her temple, she winced and pulled back.

Paris cursed at his clumsy mistake. He hadn't meant to touch the wound. The bruise, once a deep and angry purple, had faded to a pale brown. He suspected the pain wasn't physical anymore, but a lingering sting, like a poison that couldn't be leeched free. The joy, which a moment before lit up her face, had vanished.

"Do you want to talk about it?"

She shook her head and retreated further back into her own space. Although it burned, he swallowed his next question. He had found her bruised and battered on the northern precipice at Mycenae just one step away from ending her life, and he still did not know the reason why. He wanted to respect her privacy — she would share when she was ready — but that unanswered question was a widening crevasse between them, keeping him at arm's length.

"It doesn't matter. None of that matters," she answered a bit too quickly for it to feel genuine. "It's in the past. I want to talk about the future — *our future*. Tell me again about Troy?" She forced a smile, a brave attempt to appear cheerful, although it did not touch her eyes.

Paris sighed, allowing her the deflection. He led her over to the port railing and pointed behind them towards the northeastern sky just shy of where the morning sun hung low on the horizon. "She's there. The Golden Gates of Troy."

Helen blinked. "Behind us? Then why are we sailing south?"

He grinned, amused by her sweet confusion. "This side of

the Great Sea is plagued with currents and foul winds. When the winds are wrong, our oarsmen can't match their power. We have to navigate around the perimeter, like water swirling in a bowl, to get back to where we came from. The journey home always takes longer than the ride out."

Helen stared out into the great expanse of turquoise-blue waters. *The journey home... my home.* Would it be? It had been so long since she felt she belonged anywhere. She could not help but voice her concerns. "Do you think they will like me?"

"They will *love* you."

He sounded so confident, but Helen wasn't reassured. "And if they don't?" Before the fabled halls of Troy, before the sophisticated aristocracy of the Old World, how would a wild and impulsive daughter of Sparta compare?

Paris followed her gaze to the tiny speck on the horizon where Troy lay. "Then we don't have to stay." It pained him to consider that option, but he was no fool. The likelihood that the Trojan nobility would reject them was far greater than the odds of a warm reception.

But he could not help but hope. Priam promised him he could stay this time, that he would denounce the omens that had haunted Paris from birth... a promise he had made not knowing Paris would return with another man's wife. The king had instructed him to quell the rebellious Greeks, not provoke them to greater fury.

Paris quickly played out the interactions he'd had with Agamemnon over his weeklong visit to Mycenae. He was sure he had no alternative but to leave. Agamemnon was searching for a war. No act of diplomacy, whether the silk glove or the fist, was going to stop that. Priam had to understand.

"They *will* love you," Paris repeated, knowing the true source of danger in their return. "It's me they might turn away."

Helen slipped her delicate fingers into his, giving him a reassuring squeeze. "They will love you, too. Once they know the omen is false, they'll see you for who you truly are. As I do."

He leaned in, pressing his forehead to hers. "It would take a miracle…"

"Then have faith." There was a firm cast to her face that matched her stubborn core. "The Gods brought us together — for what purpose, I don't know — but there *is* a purpose, Paris. Trust in that, if nothing else."

He wished he shared her faith, but he had seen too much of the world to believe blindly. If the Gods were real, they cared little about the havoc they sowed on mankind. In his opinion, the Immortals should be feared, but never trusted.

Helen's conviction, however, did not waver. He marveled again at the events that brought them together, that a woman of such fortitude and grace would give her heart to him. If miracles were a real phenomena, then Helen's love was certainly one.

He gripped her hands solidly in his own. "I trust in this. Whatever follows, follows." He wished he had a better plan, that he hadn't convinced her to abandon her old life for a fool's chance at happiness, but in these chaotic times perhaps a fool's chance was better than none. "So long as we are together, I don't care what anyone says."

"Together," she promised, gracing him with one of her rare smiles. "To the very ends of the earth."

Commotion broke out on the deck below. They both spun toward the noise just as the sailors on duty pulled in their oars, backing away from the remaining crew who poured out of the hold. Every hand was on deck, and they spread out into a circle, gathering around the mast.

"What is the meaning of this?" Paris shouted down.

Before anyone could answer, Glaucus emerged from the hold towing Iamus by the neck. He slammed the unsteady soldier against the mast and placed the edge of his blade to the royal guard's throat.

"MY PRINCE," Glaucus called to him. "I have found our traitor!"

Chapter 5

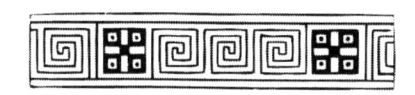

The Traitor's Price

A STUNNED SILENCE followed Glaucus' announcement. Paris dropped Helen's hands as a cold shock took hold of him. A pain he could not describe laced through his chest.

Iamus? The man had been part of Paris' royal guard for as long as he could remember. He was a grizzled veteran of many campaigns. *Iamus* had betrayed him to the queen?

Paris leapt down to the main deck, practically flying into the midst of the Trojan sailors. They instantly parted, and he closed the distance to the mast in three powerful strides, his shock lending him speed.

"Is it true?" he asked, his tone thick with disappointment.

The man before him hardly resembled the Iamus Paris knew. His pallor was a sickly off-green. His muscles sagged, and his silver-kissed black hair was plastered to his skull. But it was Iamus' eyes that gave Paris the biggest pause. They were liquid pools of sorrow.

Glaucus tightened his grip around the soldier's throat. "Your prince asked you a question. *Answer him!*"

"I... I don't remember fully, but it must have been me." Iamus croaked, his voice breaking as he spoke. "I am sorry, Your Grace. Forgive me."

Brygos stepped forward and spat on Iamus' face. "You bloody hypocrite, Iamus. You don't deserve his forgiveness."

The crowd pressed in, their shouts of outrage heating to a clamor. Paris grimaced, sharing in their disgust. The vows of the royal guard were explicit. Iamus had condemned himself. The long years of his valued service could not save him. Blood would be shed, but before the guard paid the traitor's price, Paris needed to hear it.

"How? *Why?*"

Perhaps it was the disappointment he laced into the word, but Iamus nearly broke with his confession. With guilt-laden eyes, he answered: "It was an accident, My Prince. A... a courtesan. That raven-haired vixen... she plied me with drink." He swallowed hard, the bulge in his neck dropping dangerously close to Glaucus' blade. "She wouldn't stop asking about you. I didn't mean to mention the curse. It slipped. And when I woke the next day, I thought I had dreamt it."

A deep shame colored his cheeks. The man had to know his words condemned him, but some deeper sense of honor forced Iamus to continue on. "I should have come to you sooner, but everything happened so quickly. I wanted to see you safely out of Greece. I... I am sorry."

As am I. Paris sighed and exchanged looks with Glaucus. There could be no weak link in their company, no question of loyalty in his guard. For a lowborn soldier like Iamus, there was no room for mistakes. Princes governed by the Old Code, and — when that code was broken — they extracted the blood price. Paris was powerless to change tradition.

His gut twisted. This felt wrong. Iamus had served him loyally for many years. He should not die for a simple mistake. The man deserved a chance to redeem himself, to pay for his error and regain his honor. But mercy was forbidden, a cruel fact of life which Paris knew best of all. His role as an outcast from the Trojan court had been a consequence of that rigid dogma. If he stayed his hand, he would lose the respect of every man on board.

Paris bent down and withdrew a hidden dagger strapped beneath Iamus' shin guard, a blade the man had used in his defense more times than he could count. With a heavy heart, he gave the knife to Glaucus.

The captain raised the weapon by its ivory hilt, prepared to enact the sentence.

"WAIT!"

A hundred sets of eyes turned to the aft of the ship, to Helen. The crowd parted for her as they had for Paris. Even now, her beauty affected them. Their angered muttering silenced to a hushed awe.

Helen swallowed nervously and stepped forward on unsteady feet. She had called out without thinking, only knowing the guard had more to account for before the mercy of a swift death. Yet, with every man on board staring at her, their gaze lingering in an uncomfortable way, her conviction wavered, and her body shook with the urge to run.

Shame filled her. Such fears were unworthy of a Spartan. She could not allow herself to be weak. With a shuddering breath, Helen mustered her courage to do what she knew she must. Marching down to the mast, she pushed Glaucus aside to stand toe-to-to with Iamus, glaring up imperiously on the condemned. She waited, unmoving and disturbingly close, until he met her unforgiving gaze.

"You betrayed your prince's confidence?"

Iamus nodded, dropping his head in shame. "I did, Princess."

"This information was used to humiliate him before the entire court at Mycenae. Knowing the power of that information, knowing it would jeopardize your mission and wound the man you swore to serve, and you let it 'slip'?"

Iamus winced, the power of her words cutting him as deeply as Glaucus' blade could. "It's a weakness, Your Grace," he confessed. "When my head is stuffed with spirits I cannot control what I say."

But his words did not soften her. "If spirits are your weakness, you should banish them from your life. It is an infection that leeches you of honor." She stepped back and looked him over, measuring the worth of the man. "The queen played you for a fool, Soldier. You have wronged your prince, making him appear weak when the weakness was your own." The memory of the ill-fated banquet returned with Clytemnestra's cruel words lingering like a pestilence. Her twin's vicious revelation was meant to wound both Paris and Helen alike. "You have wronged *me* as well." Helen grimaced as a righteous anger filled her. "That information was meant to turn my heart, to make me look upon Paris the way I am looking upon you now."

Shame overwhelmed the guard. Iamus fell to his knees and he gazed up at her, tears streaming down his face. To his credit, he no longer asked for forgiveness. From the look she cast at him, he would not receive it.

Through this exchange, Paris could scarcely breath. Helen was terrifying. *She was awe-inspiring.* She stood over Iamus, the silent judge, the arbiter of righteous indignation, commanding every man on deck to a higher ideal. Paris knew that honor was sacrosanct for the Spartan princess. But the way Helen defended it... If he had to describe her actions, *she was regal.*

"What do you know of this curse?" Helen shook, scarcely containing the emotions boiling inside of her. She wanted this man cowed, for him to pay for the suffering he caused Paris, for him to know just how deeply he wronged his prince. "Tell me all of it."

"Helen—" Paris moved to intercede, a specter of embarrassment on his face.

"No." She stood her ground. "If he is going to die for it, then the others need to know why." She saw the struggle play out on Paris' face, the desire to hide from the darkness in his past overwhelming him. To his credit, he did not give in to that urge, and a hard look creased his face as he nodded to her, allowing her to proceed. Difficult as facing these daemons

THE PRINCESS OF PROPHECY

might be, until they dealt with it, the omen of his birth would forever overshadow their future.

"*Speak,*" she demanded of Iamus.

The guard hesitated, the scrutiny of his fellow soldiers weighing down his tongue. "I know little..." he started to protest. Helen refused to relent. She raised her fist, daring the man to stay silent a moment longer. "There was an omen on the night of his birth," he added with great haste. "It was so terrifying the Temple demanded he be sacrificed to the Gods, and the queen tried to kill him as he slept. But Priam stopped her. The prince was raised outside the palace, and when he came of age, the king made him an ambassador to keep him out of sight of the Trojan court. That is all I know, I swear it."

Helen stepped away from the mast. She had heard the same from Paris' lips. It had made her heart bleed then as it did now.

How could she? What kind of a mother would harm her own flesh?

And what kind of a queen? Her thoughts strayed, unbidden, to Clytemnestra. Was the whole world ruled by cruelty and lies? She fought down her disgust, knowing very soon she would meet the Queen of Troy.

"That omen is false."

The crew broke out into a shocked murmur from her declaration. Their reaction surprised her. She could hardly be the first person to question the validity of the Temple priests. But if the world needed more convincing, so be it. She turned back to Iamus, drawing the Trojans' attention with her.

"In Greece we believe that the whole of mankind is a shimmering light holding the dark forces of Chaos at bay." She shivered, feeling that darkness surrounding her. "Prometheus gave Man the first fiery brand, a gift from the Gods. It was what I was named after."

Iamus stirred beside her, his dark eyes riveted to her face.

"When Chaos is at its strongest, our torch must burn stronger," she continued, speaking more to herself than those around her. "The brighter the flame, the greater the courage that fuels it. Every man I know dreams his flame will burn brighter than all those who came before him." Her father had such dreams. Dreams that for the past ten years she believed she had destroyed. A tear fell down her cheek.

"Hecuba dreamed she gave birth to a fiery torch whose flame burned her very soul. In the West, that omen would herald the birth of a great hero, a mighty defender of men. It was your *priests* who claimed it otherwise." The tear became a stream. She made no move to dampen its flow.

"Do you understand?" She stared out into the crowd, refusing to let any man turn from her gaze, her need for truth overcoming any fear she once had of these strange men. "The Temple knew her child—*your prince*—was special. They *feared* him. And in that fear, they manipulated your queen. Do not let them manipulate you as well."

She locked eyes with Paris. He was still as a rock, his thoughts unreadable. She hoped he was not terribly upset with her for forcing him to relive these dark memories. "With your leave, My Prince, I would like to sentence the traitor myself."

Paris flinched at her formal address. He was shocked to his core at her pronouncement. The devotion she showed, the faith in his character... it was completely foreign to him. He wanted to warn her that he was not the man that she claimed. But, by all the Gods, he wished he could be. "You have my leave."

Helen turned to the condemned. "Rise."

Iamus stood on wobbly legs, the shame he effused earlier tripling. "I am so sorry, Princess. I did not know."

It was too late for small gestures. Helen raised her hand, ready to sentence him to death. The words were on her lips. They beckoned her to speak...

But something stayed her hand. The trembling mass before her was not Clytemnestra, who mistook cruelty as a form of justice. Iamus was not Agamemnon, a man whose heart was filled with hate. Nor was he the detestable Hecuba, a queen who let her fears control her. Iamus was simply a man. A man who had made a mistake. Could she condemn him?

"*The worth of a man is not only determined by what he has done, but by what he WILL do.*" Her father's words echoed back to her across time. When Iamus blinked in response, she realized she had spoken out loud, albeit softly. Clearing her throat, she thought hard on what Tyndareus would do in her stead.

Then she knew.

"I hold your life in my hands, Soldier. You know the damage your careless words have caused. You know the pain. Now I would know what punishment *you think* your actions deserve."

The man could scarcely look at her. It was cruel to humiliate him before answering for his crime, but she had to make this point explicitly clear. No one was going to use this information to hurt Paris again. *No one.*

"I... I am deeply sorry for the pain that I've caused you, Princess. I will carry that shame for the remainder of my life." Iamus choked on his words. "But for breaking my oath to my prince... I deserve to die." A wave of relief washed over the man when he sentenced himself, as though in accepting his punishment he could now face his death with dignity.

"I'm glad that you feel that way," she said softly, then turned and raised her voice for all to hear. "For my part, I can forgive you."

The crowd broke out into harsh mutterings. Only then did she realize they expected her to be soft, to accept his apology and show mercy. The Trojan men were formidable, their training strict, but they had not grown up in Sparta. She would show them Spartan mercy.

"BUT," she continued, shouting above the din, "your crimes against Paris I cannot forgive. Forty lashes. Let the Gods decide if they claim your life. If not, then reclaim your honor."

Paris drew a sharp breath between his clenched teeth. *Forty lashes?* There were few men who could survive such a beating. He would have been content to let Iamus walk the plank, or a quick and clean death by Glaucus' blade. His past loyalty surely deserved that leniency. And yet, surprisingly, Iamus looked upon Helen not in horror, but with grim acceptance.

If the crew had been shocked by her actions before, they were beside themselves now. Glaucus looked to him for guidance and he could only nod.

The captain grabbed Iamus' tunic and pulled it over his head, shoving the man up against the mast. The guardsman never took his eyes off Helen, and she crossed to the opposite side of the post as Glaucus bound his hands.

"You might want to go below deck, Princess," Glaucus grunted.

But Helen refused to leave. "If he has the courage to bear it, then I have the courage to watch."

The captain cast her a steely eye, but when she did not budge, he repositioned her out of the strike zone of the lash. His bosun handed him the weapon, a vicious-looking length of braided leather with beads of bone woven into six dangling tails. The bone would act like claws, tearing into the flesh. The captain snapped a practice whip into the air, the tips rattling together sharply.

Iamus winced in anticipation of the blow. Sweat broke out on his brow. On impulse, Helen grabbed his hands. He looked up to her in surprise, and she tightened her grip, locking eyes with his just as the first lash struck its mark. The tremor of pain that ran through Iamus' body pulsed through to her. It was a strangely intimate feeling, like she shared in his punishment.

"ONE." The bosun shouted out the tally.

"This is all your fault." Nestra's voice whispered from inside her head. Some part of Helen believed that. If not for her, the queen would never have attacked Paris' character. If

not for Helen, Iamus' loyalty would not have been placed in question.

But it had been. And Iamus failed. He would pay for his failure. As would she.

Another lash fell, and another. By the fifth blow, Iamus was crying out loud. By the tenth, he was shrieking. He clung to her as though Helen was the only thing keeping him upright.

"TWENTY TWO. TWENTY THREE."

She saw the moment when his mind shut off from the pain. His eyes became lucid, the pupils dilated, unable to focus. He stopped breathing. He was on the verge of death, his spirit broken.

"I forgive you, Iamus," she told the Trojan as the next blow fell, somehow knowing he needed it. "I forgive you," she said again in rhythm to Glaucus' lashes. "I forgive you."

"THIRTY FOUR. THIRTY FIVE."

His eyes constricted, and Iamus drew a long and shuddering breath. "I'm sorry," he gasped, his words incoherent for all but Helen. "I'm sorry..."

"I know. I forgive you."

"FORTY."

When the last lash fell, Iamus was still breathing. He managed to survive the punishment, but he was hardly out of danger. Helen did not need to see his back to know it was a ruined landscape. The pool of blood on the deck was evidence enough.

No one spoke. A solemn pall had gripped the crowd the second she stepped forward as witness. She turned to them, knowing the second danger Iamus faced.

"He's paid the penalty. In the eyes of Zeus, the crime is wiped clean. Never speak of it." She turned back to the soldier and tucked his disheveled hair away from his face with a gentle hand. A fevered glow lit up his eyes as he stared back at her. She had expected anger, hatred, anything but the adoration he poured in her direction. She leaned in and spoke for his ears alone.

"Never hurt him again."

Chapter 6

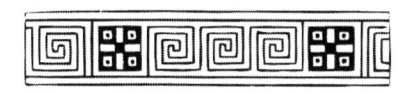

Restoration

AS THE DAY wore into evening, Helen avoided all company. After the events at the mast, she drew more odd looks than usual from the Trojan crew. If the hold had not been so cramped, she would have hidden herself below deck. She eventually retreated to the prow. The long stem, elegantly carved into a rearing horse head, did wonders for blocking the wind and gave Helen a comfortable vantage point to watch the waters ahead.

She was not alone. Paris had tried to offer her company, but she insisted she was fine. Now, more than ever, he needed to be with his men, which left Helen with Aethra, her elderly matron blessedly silent about the morning's activities. They sat for hours watching the empty horizon. For lack of anything else to occupy her hands, Aethra brushed Helen's hair, plaiting her golden tresses into intricate ropes. When the call rang out for supper, Aethra finally broke the silence.

"It would have been kinder to let the man die." She raised her head towards the back of the ship, towards the wounded Trojan.

Helen suppressed a wave of guilt. It would have been kinder, but hardly fair. There was no mistaking which alternative Aethra would have chosen, however. The matron was quick to dish out punishment for any transgression. "He made a mistake, Aethra. Does that become the sum of his worth? Can't he emerge from that shadow for some greater good?"

Aethra folded her arms beneath her ample bosom. "Are we talking about the Trojan or someone else?"

Helen avoided her steely gaze. She knew better than to play coy with the woman. It was Aethra, after all, who taught Helen her first lessons in introspection, but guilt was gnawing at her, like a swarm of beetles devouring the summer crop. It stripped her soul bare, exposing her traitorous heart. "I swore an oath to Menelaus, *an oath I broke.*" She shuddered against the cool breeze. "If I deserve a second chance, why not him?"

Aethra sighed, her dark eyes filled with pity. "Do you need to stand before the mast before you can forgive yourself, Child?" She laid a gentle hand on Helen's back. "You broke no oath that he had not already shattered by his own deeds. The sons of Atreus left you no option but to leave. Do not play the fool for crimes committed against you. You are stronger than that."

Helen gazed across the galley toward Paris. He sat with his men before a burning brazier. As though by instinct, he looked in her direction, his quiet affection piercing her heart.

She *had* played the fool. Her entire life had been one compromise after another until she met the Trojan prince. Through Paris, she discovered a part of herself she had long thought lost: a vein of strength and moral fortitude. He had proven to her there was still honor and goodness in the world. He was a rare, precious human being, and she was going to protect him at all cost.

"You've held yourself apart for too long." Aethra added, watching the gathering men like a commander surveying enemy troops. "You are a stranger to the crew. A foreigner. Men fear what they do not know. We should join them."

"Are you suggesting I *fraternize* with the lowborn?" Helen

faked a smile, adopting a light-hearted tone. In Mycenae, that sort of behavior had earned her more lectures from her stern chaperone than she cared recounting, precisely the sort of topic to distract the woman from the current line of conversation. "How uncharacteristic of you, Aethra."

"Are you avoiding them on purpose? How uncharacteristic of you, *Princess*," Aethra quipped back, not fooled for an instant by the deflection.

Helen tightened a shawl around her chest to help mask her discomfort. How could she explain the doubt she encountered every time she faced an unknown warrior? Or her fear of trusting her safety with a man, *any man*? With everything that had happened in Mycenae, from even her own sister... Helen doubted she would ever trust again.

"Not all men are like Greeks." Aethra continued to lecture her like a child. "Show these Trojans how you expect to be treated and they will see you as a queen. In that, you should trust me." She stood and offered a hand to Helen, beckoning toward the main hold.

Were it so simple.

But Aethra *did* have experience in the matter. Although technically a slave, one would be a fool to not recognize the woman came from royal blood, albeit a tainted line that Helen's father had all but wiped out. Her matron had reinvented herself more times than Helen could guess.

Helen softened. If this voyage was truly taking her to a new beginning, then perhaps she could leave her old self behind and become some one else. Maybe even the person she always dreamt she would be. Regardless if she felt like that person yet, she could at least try.

"By all means," Helen waved Aethra onward. "After you."

Paris took a seat beside Glaucus and ladled himself a portion of mutton stew. The meat was tough, salvaged from the leftovers of their meal three nights past, but still savory. And warm. It was the best the crew could expect under the circumstances.

"If we have to eat slop, it'd be nice to have something to wash it down, Captain," Brygos suggested, trying hard to make the request sound innocent—a difficult endeavor for the bulky man.

"You'll wash it down with salt water, you lazy dog." Glaucus simmered. "We need to keep our wits about us, not pilot this sea-bitch three sheets to the wind."

"Let them have it," Paris interrupted what he was sure would be an epic tongue-lashing.

"But, Paris—"

"A round in honor of our brother, Iamus." He hushed his captain.

A bawdy cheer ran through the crowd, loud enough—he hoped—for the recovering guardsman to appreciate. Over their boisterous cries, Paris leaned in and whispered into Glaucus' ear. "They have done all we have asked without complaint. Give them one night of rest."

Glaucus nodded, the stress-lines along his neck unclenching. "As you wish."

Joyful conversation broke out at the announcement, many in thanks to their disgraced companion, an unexpected side-effect that convinced Paris even more of the wisdom of his decision. From the men surrounding him, the elite fighters of his royal guard, the conversation was more intimate, for they knew Iamus best.

"Do you remember the time Iamus barged into the bathhouse in Rhodes claiming someone had stolen his purse?" Dexios recounted, waving Brygos over to top off his cup.

"Don't you mean the *ladies'* bathhouse?" Brygos added with a grin, replacing the stopper in the clay amphora.

"I don't think that was an accident." Paris joined their round of laughter, taking a sip of the tart Grecian wine. "But he *did* find the cutpurse hiding in the steam room. How many purses did he recover?"

A fair number of hands went into the air.

"Only after he made right by the bath madame," Dexios said with a sigh. "Lucky bastard. She was a lovely dame at that."

Paris couldn't help but grin. The infamous guard was almost as good at getting out of trouble as he was at getting into it. Despite his disappointment in the man, he was glad Iamus was not dead. Losing him would have left a gaping hole in the hearts of his crew.

How had Helen managed such a miracle? He replayed the events of the morning over and over again in his mind, shocked to his core by what he had witnessed. Helen's act of mercy should have been met with ridicule and outrage. Instead, she had won the loyalty of every man on board. Standing before the mast, she refused to buckle to tradition and challenged everyone to rethink their concept of justice. She showed a courage he had rarely seen in his lifetime, even from himself.

As though the thought summoned her, Helen appeared at his side. She carried a bowl of stew in her right hand, and with her left she stroked his cheek. Her touch, as usual, stirred his blood.

The conversation died off the moment she stepped into the light. Brygos in particular was coughing nervously. Paris wondered what crudity the man had last uttered.

"Join us." He shuffled aside on the rowing bench to make room for his beloved.

"Thank you." She smiled, but then crossed to the opposite side of the fire, taking a seat between his guardsmen. Ariston barely managed to make room, the youth was so mesmerized.

Paris grinned. It was entertaining to see his men struggle to find their words. Helen's presence cowed them faster than one of Glaucus' famous salt-baths. When she asked what they were drinking, Brygos hastily offered her his glass.

"That's dreadful!" Her face puckered from the bitter vintage. "I hope you didn't pay much for that. I've tasted better swill from the bottom of the jar."

Hyllos, who sat to her left, looked away sheepishly. "Not much..." the trade master muttered into his cup, which, of course, earned him a round of heckles from the crew. It was a conservative jest they had on Hyllos behalf, the men still unsure what behavior was expected of them before a princess.

"You are a merchant, no?" Helen asked. Hyllos nodded, too tongue-tied to answer. "I thought the gift of barter ran through a tradesman's blood." She leaned forward with a mischievous grin. "Or did you lose your wits to a woman, the same as your bloodied mate?"

It was too much for Brygos, and the hefty man—already deep in his cups—guffawed loudly. He was quickly joined by the others.

Paris watched Helen with a new appreciation. She deftly put the gruff soldiers at ease. She was clearly a woman raised by men.

Or perhaps, he mused, *Spartans hold to a different ideal of female conduct than their Argive cousins.*

"To be fair, Princess," he interrupted their laughter, "the women of the Hellas have proven to be more intoxicating than the spirits in a cup. If Hyllos was besotted, then perhaps the blame was not entirely his own?"

"A fair argument, but perhaps the prince should save that excuse for his own transgressions?"

Paris whipped around to find Aethra standing behind him. The rigid woman was watching their gathering with a bemused smile on her aged face.

Aethra, smiling? He had thought the woman was born with a frown.

"There is no excuse for botching a trade," she continued, taking a seat beside him. "Especially where wine is concerned."

His shock must have played out on his face, for Helen's merry laugh followed. "Indeed, My Lady!" She raised her cup with great fanfare. "Perhaps you can teach him how it is done since you are so good at knowing everyone else's business." Aethra was not amused by the jest. Paris wondered, once again, what was festering between the two women.

Once his men settled down, Helen turned to Ariston with a look of mock seriousness on her lovely face. "My matron is full of useful advice of late. She reminded me that I have been remiss in offering gratitude to the men who so bravely freed me from my palatial prison. Yet how am I to thank you if I don't know your names?"

Dexios prodded Ariston in the back as the youth squirmed under her prolonged attention. "Uh, Ariston, Your Grace." He knuckled his forehead.

"Ariston," she tried out the word, causing the poor guard to blush three shades red. "You seem young to be in the company of these veterans. How did you join their ranks?"

After several failed attempts to speak, Dexios finally spoke for the lad, "He's good with his sword." There was an awkward pause before Dexios realized his poor phrasing. "I meant—" But he was drowned out by the roar of laughter.

"I see." Helen looked aside, a blush of her own gracing her cheeks.

"I never—*I wouldn't...*" Ariston tried to protest, stammering like a spirit-soaked goat herder.

Paris looked around at his crew, at the many joyful faces. All beaming, and all *red*. He wondered just how many jars Glaucus had fetched. Farther down the galley, a few oarsmen had procured a pair of lyres and were playing a lively tune. Some of the sailors even danced a jig.

He stretched out, feeling a sense of ease he hadn't experienced since arriving on Argive soil. If Paris was truthful with himself, he hadn't felt this good... well, *ever*. He looked over to Helen—his beautiful, sweet Helen—and knew it was all because of her.

She held her own with his guardsmen, Brygos attempting to elicit one of her musical laughs with another tale of questionable behavior. She countered with one of her own, something about Spartan manhood rituals that sounded decidedly unpleasant.

"They really go naked?" Ariston asked, his eyes wide in disbelief. When Helen opened her mouth to elaborate Paris decided it was past time to rescue her.

"I'd say that's enough vulgarity for one night." He walked over to his beloved, offering her his hand. "I should have warned you, Princess. When you consort with sailors, your manners will be corrupted."

She took his hand, a spark of challenge in her eye. "And what happens when you consort with princes?"

"That depends on the prince." He winked at her.

The musicians switched songs, plucking out a sweet tune. He pulled Helen after him, dragging her away from the crowded deck to the more spacious and darkened corner at the bow. His guardsmen howled at their departure, but Paris wasn't about to give her back to those hooligans. He wrapped her arms around his neck, and led her into a slow dance.

"You truly are amazing. Do you know that?" Her sweet perfume of lilac and rose inundated his senses. He inhaled deeply, letting her intoxicating presence soak into him. He doubted ambrosia tasted as sweet as her ruby kisses.

Helen's heart pounded against her chest. The way he was looking at her, with complete adoration... she was powerless in that gaze. She could deny him nothing. And when he ran his hand down her back, every nerve in her body began to tingle, responding unconsciously to his touch. Perhaps it was the wine, but she was suddenly overwhelmed with desire for him. It had been too long since they had been together. Not since the night they left Mycenae, before... *other things*... had transpired.

A silent tremor ran through her body. After that night, could she physically love again? It seemed irrational, but a portion of her soul felt dirty, used up... broken. Paris hadn't pressed her to perform, despite the ample opportunities for him to have done so. His patience allowed her a safe haven in his arms. Safe, like she would never feel in the outside world again. Helen pulled in closer to his chest and met his loving gaze, astonished that he could care for her so deeply, especially when she came with nothing but troubles.

A new fear took hold of her. If she was truly damaged, as she feared her sister's punishment had left her, would Paris still want her by his side? Men had needs, and if she failed to meet them? That fear threatened to unmake her. In her mind's eye, she saw herself broken and bloodied in her royal apartments, the delicate little princess who was eternally the victim of a cruel and vicious world. That person *disgusted* her. She was weak, unworthy.

Helen couldn't let Nestra infect what she and Paris shared. She had to purge those fears. For this man she could at least try. Lacing her fingers through his hair, she pulled Paris' lips down to hers. His touch ignited her blood, the heat of his hot breath kindling a flame within. Nestra's lingering presence, that spike of icy fear, tried to battle the inferno inside her. If she loved Paris less, that ice storm might have won out. But not this day, not before the flame of this man.

"Can we go somewhere more private?" she asked in a voice she scarcely recognized as her own.

"Are you sure?"

Helen nodded. She had never been more certain of anything in her life.

Aethra watched her charge disappear below deck with a frown. The child was reckless. One moment Helen presented herself as a fearsome queen, demanding—*nay, deserving*—respect. And the next? A shameless minx at the mercies of her lusty nature. Aethra chewed her lower lip, trying to bite away her frustration. Her efforts to preserve the girl's virtue were a losing battle. Sparks flew when Paris and Helen were together. It would take more than a disapproving chaperone to pull them apart.

"Dare I ask who has offended you, and should I give them fair warning before you strike?"

She turned to the unwelcome disturbance. The Trojan captain climbed the final few steps of the aft-deck, two steaming cups in his hands. She sniffed in disapproval before finally accepting his offer. "You best not be trying to drug me."

"If I thought it would mellow your acerbic tongue, I just might." Glaucus grunted. "Peace woman. It's only tea." He settled himself against the sternpost beside her and added, "It is not yet summer. Nights on the Great Sea can be unforgiving."

She pulled her wrap around her against that cold. Perhaps the man wasn't completely without use. She sipped her tea and studied the rigid captain.

His hair had been black once, before it turned to grey—an unfortunate curse of aging that Aethra was all too familiar with. The lighter color suited the man, it lent him an aura of grizzled wisdom not found in the cocksure Trojans in his charge.

"You're not one of them, are you?" she exclaimed with sudden realization.

His pale-grey eyes hardened. "What makes you say that?"

"You have an accent." Aethra delighted in his surprised look. "You roll your r's. It's subtle, but noticeable. The Helladic dialect is not your native tongue."

That much was obvious, that and his broadly set shoulders, had set him apart. She wondered where he hailed from. One of the southern isles?

"Lukka." He offered without her asking. It wasn't the first time Glaucus had correctly read her thoughts.

"Lukka?" She frowned. She knew of no such place.

"Lycia to you Greeks. It's along the southern reaches of Anatolia, in the shadow of the Great Taurus mountains."

"Lycia!" The disapproval escaped her lips before she thought to censor herself. Lycia was home to notorious pirates and derelicts. Why would a Trojan prince sail with such a questionable character? "Should I be concerned?" She eyed him warily.

"So you've heard of it?" He seemed mildly amused.

"By reputation." She sniffed again. "And don't take that as a compliment." A small grin threatened to make his face pleasant, which meant he looked like a wolf playing with a meal.

"You are well versed in foreign cultures." Glaucus continued, ignoring her subtle hints for solitude. "Unusual for a—"

"A what?" She cut him off sharply. "A slave? For a man with large eyes you see little."

Her barb had no effect on the man. His face was like stone. "...For a *Westerner*. Careful of hasty judgements, My Lady. They blind you from truth."

She swallowed her quick reply. Glaucus came offering a kindness and did not deserve her barbed wit. Helen's rash behavior had put her in a mood. The girl no longer respected her as she once had, and now Aethra found herself fighting against any slight, perceived or real.

It still galled her to be considered a slave. Aethra had years to accustom herself to her lowly station, but for some reason Glaucus, more than any other man, made her feel the absence of her crown. She wanted him to see her as she once was: a queen of a mighty kingdom.

She looked away, banishing the tears that threatened her stoic composure. That life was a distant memory now. This was her new world, and Helen her salvation. The Winds of Change filled their sails. Clinging to a distant past was a mistake for the weak of heart, *not her*.

They sat in silence for a long while, each guardian enjoying a moment of peace. The steady slap of waves on the hull and the jangling of halyard rings above created a sense of solitude from the festivities on deck. As captain of this ship, Glaucus should have been with his men, enjoying a night of respite. Yet, he was here keeping her company. That, more than his refusal to leave, lulled Aethra into lowering her stalwart defenses.

"Do you miss it? Your homeland?" She offered the first olive branch.

"I had a wife once." His face creased at the memory, a dark shadow overtaking him. "She was taken from me. Lukka wasn't home afterwards." She thought he was finished, the brief dialogue more words than she'd heard from the man in one sitting. When he continued, it was like the confession was battling to come out. "I didn't care much where I went, or who I worked for, until Paris found me. Not many men would have bothered cleaning up a spice-addled soldier of fortune, let alone a prince. But he did. I have been Trojan ever since."

"How—" she bit her tongue. "Forgive me, it's none of my business."

"The Hatti." He delivered the word devoid of emotion. It gave her the chills all the more for it. Without realizing she had done it, she placed a sympathetic hand on his arm, knowing too well the toll of war.

"And what of you? You do not strike me as a spinster." His gruff manner softened. By that, he was slightly less rigid than carved stone. She took her arm back, folding it beneath her bosom.

"I had a son. He is dead now." The captain had been forthright with her, he deserved an honest answer in return, but the window of openness closed shut within her, as any mention of Theseus was apt to do.

"Condolences, My Lady. No mother should have to bury her son."

She waved off his concerns, feigning indifference. "He earned his grave." She hardened her heart. "Please, pay him no mind."

He was not deterred. "The world is not so cold that a mother cannot mourn her own flesh. No child is born deserving death. Whatever sins he committed, that child was blameless."

Aethra clenched her mouth shut. His words were surprisingly kind, but they could not change the horrors her son committed, nor the obligations Theseus had left behind him. With lust in his heart, he had kidnapped an eight-year-old girl. It was only a matter of time until the Spartan army arrived in Athens to take Helen back. Aethra had lost her only child that day. But Tyndareus had lost two, and in recompense, he claimed Aethra as slave. A queen turned slave… Not once in the many years that followed, did she disagree with his decision.

She straightened her back, banishing those old memories to the past, her thin frown firmly back in place. Glaucus' words sparked a lingering curiosity in her. *A child not deserving death...* Aethra often wondered why this unforgiving man had devoted himself to Paris. Surely he knew of the dark omen foreshadowing the prince. Knew and did not care.

"You love him, don't you? The prince, I mean."

He cast her a too-knowing glance. "As much as you love your charge."

That was hardly possible. There were oceans of duty tying Aethra to Helen.

"He is the son I will never have," Glaucus added, refusing to elaborate further.

Aethra sighed. She had spent the past week in constant anxiety, unsure how to help her princess. If Glaucus was in the same position, perhaps it was best to combine their resources? "Then you should be as concerned as I. This mad flight from Greece? The bards might romanticize these antics, but it will not sit well in Troy."

The captain stiffened. "The king will see the necessity of it."

"*I'm not talking about the king.*" Great Gaia! Were all men blind to the real power behind the throne? "Whatever life they hope to create, whatever happiness they seek to enjoy, will be poisoned the second they step off this boat. The nobility will never accept them."

The captain, however, was unmoved. "You are letting your fears get the best of you."

"Am I?" She rounded on the man. "What is Helen to Troy? An adulteress? Worse, a whore? They will not have the privilege of seeing her as the noble princess she is, or the horrible life she left behind. They will judge her."

A sliver of realization sparked in his eyes, but it wasn't enough.

"And Paris?" she continued on. "They will dub him a seducer and a thief. Forget his misaligned birth. For snatching another man's wife, they will shun him. This deed will confirm every bad thought they ever had of the prince."

"You will not dissuade him." Glaucus grimaced. "I know. I tried."

Aethra released a tense breath, relieved she was not alone in her concerns. "But he listens to you? He takes your counsel?" She was loath to admit that Helen would refuse her advice. There was a mountain of trust Aethra had to rebuild.

"What are you suggesting?"

"She cannot enter Troy as his lover."

Glaucus listened patiently as she explained the rest of her plan. With any hope, he could convince the prince it was the best course of action. If not... Aethra let her shawl slip, allowing the cool ocean air to caress her skin. If not, there were worse things than living out the remainder of her life at sea. The company was turning out to be better than expected, too.

The captain offered her his cape, refusing her protests for him to keep the garment. When he turned to drape the fabric over her shoulders, he froze, his gaze held fast by the waters behind them.

"It can't be..." His face drained of color.

"What is it?" She stared into the black abyss, but her aged eyes were unable to spot what gave him pause. His hand tightened on her shoulder, pushing her down behind the safety of the hull.

"We're not alone."

Paris led Helen to the hold, practically flying down the rope ladder into the darkened space below. The second Helen stepped down, he scooped her into his arms. A handful of ceramic oil lamps burned in carved-out nooks across the ribs of the ship, their shadows dancing in a flicking pattern. The dim light made it difficult to find a footing, but Paris didn't stumble. He stepped across the exposed beams in stride, trusting to his keen sense of balance, a trait he had been blessed with even as a child.

Not that Helen made it easy. She nuzzled his neck, her soft kisses driving him to distraction. Aside from a few sailors snoring in their hammocks, they were alone. It took all his willpower to continue on to the back of the ship and to the privacy of their royal quarters. Once inside, he laid her down on the blankets and secured the curtains behind them.

Paris was no stranger to what would follow next. But seeing Helen in his bed—languid and stretched out like a jungle cat—he felt like a virgin boy before a Goddess. His pulse raced. He had travelled the world over, and not once in his myriad of explorations had he seen her equal.

She rose to her feet, her chest, like his, rising and falling with heavy breaths. With an eager hand, he caressed her face, following the perfect line of her prominent cheekbones, tracing his fingers across her open lips. Those lips were a rich shade of pink, and full, like a spring rosebud. Lips that begged to be kissed. She was a vision. Any man would be lucky to simply worship at her feet.

Worship all they like, they cannot have her heart.

That heart was his. He could see it in her eyes as she stared deeply into his own. Trembling ever-so-slightly, she pulled the corners of her chiton off her shoulders, the woolen material dropping to the floor boards. Gathering his hand in hers, she pressed her lips to his open palm, then guided that hand down to her naked breast.

Paris could scarcely breathe. He wrapped his arms around her, feeling every voluptuous curve, every soft crevasse. Her skin was exquisitely soft. He could spend a lifetime discovering Helen's body, and it would be a life well spent.

He pulled her mouth to his, drinking of her lips, slowly at first, then with a thirst that could not be slackened. Infused through this influx of senses, was a deep and unequivocal knowledge that this love, this union, *was right*. He belonged with her. Every ounce of his being yearned for her. He always had, even before he knew she existed. Her body was bare, but he was the one standing naked before her.

She quickly rid him of those bothersome garments and they collapsed to the bedroll, bodies entwined. Instinct took over—he had no sense of conscious thought. He had only one purpose: to please this woman. And thus began the delectable game of yearning and fulfillment, of caressing, stroking and kissing. Each tantalizing contact hinting at something more.

Despite her best efforts to remain quiet, heavy moans escaped Helen's lips. Her cries were an inarticulate sound of longing. She pressed those luscious lips to his ear as he mounted her, her voice thick with passion as she moaned his name.

The bonding was the same as in Mycenae. With every thrust he felt himself melting into her, as though their bodies became one. He slowed his pace to a stop, savoring a moment of pure intimacy.

"I love you," he whispered into her ear, words he had never spoken to another soul. She trembled beneath him. He pulled back to gaze into her eyes—

THE PRINCESS OF PROPHECY

And that was when he noticed she was crying.

"Helen? Are you alright?"

She smiled through her tears, pressing her lips to his. "I... I love you, too." But still the tears flowed.

"We don't have to do this. I can wait until you're ready—"

"No, I want to." She shifted beneath him, encouraging him onwards. "I need to."

He was worried about her. She held her secrets close, but not as well as she thought. Not to him. He could feel when she was near. He was beginning to suspect he could feel when she was hurting as well. When she kissed him again, it wasn't pain she was expressing, but a tender, bittersweet love. She held his face in her hands.

"Please. Don't stop."

He started again, slow, and in even rhythms. Helen raised her hips to meet his, matching him. He let her set the pace. She was fighting, for what he couldn't say, but he knew he had to help her. So when she rose to meet him, he thrust deeper.

Helen's body spasmed as the first wave of the Goddess' touch rolled over her. She pressed a pillow over her mouth, trying to stifle her involuntary cries. Every muscle went taut as the quickening of her blood peaked. As quickly as it descended on her, it was gone, leaving her utterly spent. She fell back against their blankets unable to move. Unable and unwilling.

At first, when Paris touched her, she could not banish the image of Clytemnestra forcing herself on her. Her sister's face was replaced with that of Agamemnon, and Menelaus, ending finally with Theseus—the last more of a dim memory than vision of flesh and blood.

Then her fears of intimacy were lost in the torrent of love Paris evoked. With three heartfelt words, he burned away her shame and fear as surely as the blazing torch of his birth omen. He ignited her. She cursed herself for not giving herself to him sooner. The past week had felt so hollow without this embrace.

Paris lowered himself to her side, lifting the pillow just enough to see her face. There was a healthy flush to her cheeks, and on her lips was the dazzling smile that always left him speechless.

"Was I loud?" she asked.

"Not much," he lied.

She traced the lines of his face, the almond shaped curve of his eyes, those piercing dark orbs that saw right through to her soul. She kissed him tenderly and whispered a prayer of thanks. Aphrodite blessed their union. She was sure of it.

A deep grunt came from outside the curtains, the sound of a man clearing his throat - *loudly.*

"What is it?" Paris snapped, imagining a world of tortures for whoever decided to interrupt them.

"You're needed topside."

It was Glaucus. Paris had never wanted to throttle the man more than in that moment. "Can't it wait until morning?"

The captain cleared his throat again, answering with stoic cool. "There's a ship off our stern."

Both Helen and Paris instantly sat up.

"We're being followed."

Chapter 7

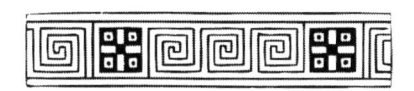

Safe Harbors

THE OARSMEN GLIDED the Trojan galley into a sheltered cove along the eastern coast of Crete. Paris stood at the prow surrounded by his advisors. A somber pall fell over the crew as they neared the small island. Glaucus had managed to slip their pursuer in the dark of night, but the sun was rising, and any ship out in the open would be easy to spot. They needed cover.

The oars dipped soundlessly into the turquoise waters, navigating their ship around towering pillars of limestone, stone megaliths that stretched from the ocean floor toward the heavens like the fingers of Poseidon. The porous rock was coated with white droppings from nesting falcons, the bird's mournful cries echoing down to the galley and reverberating off the tall cliffs of the nearing cove. To Paris, those cries were like trumpets warning anyone within earshot that strangers approached. He grit his teeth and tried to steady his nerves. His mind was playing tricks on him.

"How do we know the island is deserted?" He turned to Hyllos, the trade master deeply engrossed in studying the papyrus he acquired in the Mycenaean port.

"It's not." Hyllos rolled up the document, tucking the

papyrus into his belt. "There's a Temple of Dionysus on the far side facing the Cretan coast. Two priests and a full cult contingent live and forage on the topside."

Glaucus glanced back to the stern, to the helmsman manning the rudder. Timon kept one eye behind them and the other in front as he guided the ship into hiding. The natural caverns along the steep limestone cliffs were favorite anchorage for pirates and thieves, a constant danger in these parts of the Great Sea. Now they would serve to keep the Trojan galley out of sight. "We shouldn't dally here, Paris." The captain tensed beside him. "I can evade one ship easy enough, but where there is one, there are bound to be others."

It was a chilling thought that stole sleep from Paris' night. Who was on this mystery ship? Was it simply another trading vessel, or had Agamemnon's wrath followed them already? Whatever the answer, he was now a marked man and would forevermore be looking over his shoulder for Mycenaean spears.

Paris shook those dark thoughts away. He didn't have the luxury to indulge in fear. He had sworn to protect Helen, *to protect his crew*, and that meant making all haste back to Troy. "If we must wait out this ship, then let's use that time wisely. We can't afford to stop at another Cretan port, not when there are hounds in pursuit. Send a team topside to forage for supplies."

"There are safer harbors. Ones not surrounded by our enemies," Glaucus pressed.

Paris resisted the urge to shake the man. They had been over the matter countless times. He was not going to risk the uncertain shores of Egypt, not unless Poseidon Himself forced his hand. "Ready the foraging team."

Glaucus stifled his dissent, the aged captain too tempered to let his irritation show beyond a grimace. Paris turned to go, but Glaucus halted him, grabbing him by the elbow. "There is another matter."

"Something more important than the safety of our crew?"

Paris raised a brow, taken aback by his friend's strong grip.

"The Greeks are not the only danger we face." Glaucus shifted nervously, his reluctance to speak writ large on his broad face. "The vipers behind us are nothing compared to the those in Troy. You cannot lead us homeward with your eyes closed."

Paris flushed an angry red. Is that what Glaucus thought he did? Travel blindly and trust to hope? He opened his mouth to refute the claim just as his captain's next words chilled his blood.

"It's time to discuss what you plan to do about Helen..."

Helen gripped the railing of the ship as they dropped anchor in a cove, her knuckles blanched white as she clung tightly to the polished wood. Their ship was almost the full length of the depression in the coastline. With the rocky outcrops behind them, they would be invisible from any ships sailing the perimeter of the island. Yet still she felt exposed. No amount of land nor sea could keep her hidden from the powers that sought her.

The deck became a hive of activity. Helen, hoping to keep out of foot, crossed to the far side of the ship where Aethra stood at the aft-deck watching the brightening waters like a silent sentinel.

"I owe you an apology."

Aethra turned to her, a look of surprise stamped on her face. "You do?"

"I have been blaming you for something you did not do," Helen continued. "It's not fair to you. I've been angry and irrational, and you have been the one to suffer for it. I am sorry."

Her matron was completely taken back. Aethra covered her heart as though it might break. "I... I am sorry, as well. I should have come to you sooner, told you the truth. I honestly thought you chose not to speak of it, not that you had forgotten."

Helen waved her off. She had no desire to discuss the horrors Theseus inflicted on her. Not when a new danger literally loomed on the horizon. "I want you to know I harbor you no ill will. In case..." Her eyes drifted nervously back to the water, expecting to see a ship at any moment. "In case I never see you again." She tried to sound strong, but her voice cracked, betraying her true emotions lying beneath.

Aethra watched her with sorrow-filled eyes. "You know I've seen much of war."

Helen nodded, too wound up to answer verbally.

"Then I want you to trust me, and see these events through *my eyes*." She took Helen by the arms and spun her around toward the milling Trojan troops. "That is a full contingent of Trojan warriors. They are disciplined, fierce and well trained. Any one of them is a match for a man of the Hellas. Whatever is following us—*these men will turn back*. The captain is talented; the ship is sound. No one is going to take you away."

"I suppose you're right." Helen forced a smile, but she couldn't stop shaking. Aethra meant well, but she had no way of knowing the future.

Her matron pulled her around again, holding firm to Helen's arms. "I'm serious, child. Men spoke of the might of Troy in my halls at Athens, and always with deep respect. You could not ask for a greater protector." She pulled Helen into a tight embrace. "You do not need to fear the fools of your past. The danger is in what lies ahead. It is your future you must be concerned with."

Helen froze. What did Aethra mean by that? She spun back to the main deck, searching for Paris, and was surprised to see him rushing in her direction. Glaucus, as ever, was at his side. The two men were in the middle of a heated argument.

"ENOUGH," Paris shouted at his captain. "I've heard all you've had to say. I don't need to hear another word."

She waited for him to catch his breath. Paris so rarely lost his temper. "What's wrong?"

"We're sending a team topside to forage for supplies."

But he was still fidgeting, his agitation raising her alarm. "What else?"

"I need to get off this ship. Clear my mind." He ran a hand through his hair. "Helen, we need to talk."

Dexios tossed a grappling hook up the hundred foot cliff, a shower of pebbles trickling down to the deck as barbed tips found purchase in the soil above.

"We're climbing up there?" Helen's eyes were as wide as saucers. Dexios ascended the rope hand over fist, making the effort seem easy, but it was still a considerable climb.

Paris almost suggested she stay on the ship. Twenty-five men were going topside, leaving seventy-five to defend the galley if the Greek vessel returned. Helen would be well defended here, yet a nagging feeling told him to not let her out of his sight.

"We'll pull you up. You'll be safe," he assured her, then took his turn on the climb up the thick rope.

It felt good to stretch out his muscles. Barely a week on deck and Paris was already feeling the pinch of living in tight quarters. There was scarcely space to walk, let alone get any real exercise. Muscles needed to be set in motion, or, like a blade left to rust, they became fragile from lack of use. Nothing could sap the battle-readiness of a soldier like a long voyage at sea.

He pulled himself over the ridge, accepting a hand up from his guardsman, and immediately began scouting the perimeter. The landscape of the high plateau was mostly flat and consisted of tall grass and scrub brush like juniper. In the distance a grove of cypress trees blocked out the western vista.

"Three groups," Glaucus ordered the milling troops. "Dexios, take five men and go north, see if you can find any fresh water. Brygos, do the same but go west. See if there's any decent foraging in that grove." He grabbed the soldier's tunic roughly. "Favor fruit before roots, unless you fancy a bout of scurvy. Understood?"

Brygos nodded, the soldier smart enough to keep his grumbling under his breath.

"The rest of you are with me," Glaucus pulled a short spear holstered on his back. He gave the weapon a quick whirl, checking its balance. "String your bows. We're going hunting."

A pair of broad-shouldered soldiers finished hauling up the repel line with Helen securely tied into a loop on the bottom. Paris made to join her, but Glaucus grabbed his elbow.

"And what about you?" The captain pulled him aside.

"We'll head south along the perimeter. Not too far, half a league at most." Paris pulled a shadow clock from the travel pouch tied to his belt. The wooden rod was roughly the length of his hand with a t-shaped raised bar at one end. He held the object flat in his palm and positioned himself in the path of the sun. Its shadow landed halfway down the shaft at the second of four, irregularly-spaced grooves. "We have an early start, but let's return here by one mark past midday."

"Agreed." Glaucus nodded. He cast a nervous eye to a set of storm clouds gathering on the horizon and then back to the princess. "Don't get too distracted. There's a foul taste in the wind."

Paris bit back a bitter retort. Of late, his passions were overwhelming reason. Glaucus was more likely concerned with their welfare than in meddling in his personal affairs. And even if he did mean to meddle, as much as Paris was loath to admit it, his personal affairs concerned them all now.

"I won't. Safe hunting." He slapped Glaucus on the shoulder, then joined Helen on the bluff.

"I haven't gone climbing since I was a child." She grinned, a flush of exhilaration on her cheeks. "I'd forgotten what it felt like to stand on top of the world." She leaned far over the cliff for a better view, fearless like a she-bear.

He took her by the hand, leading her along a small game trail, wild goat by the look of the tracks. "Is Sparta a mountain country?"

"No, we live in the valley plateau, in the shadow of the mountain." Her smile grew with the memory. "I was outside as often as the elements allowed. I loved to explore the wild lands with my brothers." Her face tensed with that divulgence. She seemed strangely confused.

It was the first time Helen mentioned having brothers. Paris frowned, trying to remember their first meeting, certain he was missing something. When her smile returned, he shrugged it off.

"It was the same for me. Hector and I spent our boyhood on the slopes of Mount Ida." He paused, remembering those carefree days. Ida was freedom for a prince rejected by the court. In the privacy of its rocky cliffs, Paris was able to reinvent himself, to become the person he wanted to be, not the one the Temple claimed was inevitable.

Hector had been his constant companion then. Through a multitude of adventures, they challenged each other, influencing the men they would ultimately grow into being. Paris treasured those days.

"The shepherds will be grazing their herds in the high meadows by now." He turned back to Helen. "And when the summer temperatures thaw the ice caps, the most beautiful waterfalls will cascade down the hills. I'll show it to you, if you want."

"I'd love that," Helen said, surprised at how much she meant it. So far, the prospect of escaping to Troy had filled her with anxiety. Yet, when Paris spoke, a peaceful smile spread across his face, and she knew it must be a land of many wonders. Despite everything that happened to him, he deeply loved his homeland.

They continued down the trail, hand in hand, talking of pleasantries — of memories distant past and ones they'd soon form. The scrub brush gave way to grass and wildflowers, the island a canopy of color with brilliant red poppies, yellow-faced daffodils, camomile, iris, and hyacinth. There were even herbs. Helen knelt along the cliffside to collect some dittany, the round and fuzzy little leaves oozing a sweet juice onto her fingers.

"For Iamus," she explained, wrapping her bundle into a piece of cloth.

He eyed her suspiciously. "*Erondas*? Newly weds take that... to, um... increase their ardor."

Helen laughed. "That's one use for it." She licked her sticky fingers, curious to see if she would feel any amorous side-effects. "It's a powerful healing plant that also dulls pain. Iamus has endured enough for one offense, don't you think?"

He seemed amused. "Another act of mercy, Princess? One more display and I'll have to declare you a rebel."

The jest gave her pause. Mercy? Agamemnon thought mercy a weakness in his neighboring rulers. A kind heart was an invitation for other more powerful kings to crush. Her father believed that punishment should equal the crime—an eye for an eye, a tooth for a tooth. Justice was black and white. When Tyndareus dealt with men who compromised their honor, he showed no mercy in favor of person or circumstance.

But Helen didn't feel that way. Her years in Agamemnon's court had shown her the world was not as simple as her father's tutelage had led her to believe. When she answered Paris, it was without any trace of humor. "Mercy can be warranted." Her voice dropped darkly as she reconsidered that thought. "But only for those who deserve it."

The moment of gaiety had also slipped from Paris. He had the look of a man facing an insurmountable problem. "Helen, we need to talk... about what comes next."

She tensed, as she had when he first uttered those words on the ship, dreading what would follow. "We do."

He pulled her off the trail and they sat beneath a lone

cypress tree, its wind-sculpted trunk curved in a twisted spiral toward the sun. The thick needles provided decent shade, and they reclined in its shelter.

Paris took a deep breath, wondering how to start. He wished nothing more than to enjoy a peaceful afternoon with Helen and delight in her pleasant company. But he could not deny the dangers their actions had set into motion. Glaucus was right. There was too much at stake to simply trust to hope. He wanted to believe Priam would take his side and welcome Paris home as he promised, but that safe return depended vitally on what Helen said next.

"We... I broke the bonds of *xenia* when I took you from Mycenae. I will have to answer for it when we return to Troy. I will most likely lose my position as Ambassador and what little standing I have with the court." She moved to protest. "It's all right." He cut her off. "I would not have acted if I cared about those trifles. You are the only thing that matters to me now."

"And I, you. You must know that." She gripped his hands tightly, her deep blue eyes darkening with intensity.

No one had ever espoused such feelings for him before, such devotion. He couldn't shake the feeling, as he did when she denounced his birth omen before the crew, that he didn't deserve that esteem. He could only fail her. But hero or accursed, he had come too far to turn back now. They could not move forward with their eyes shut to the dangers ahead.

"We are riding the razor's edge of honor," he continued, regretting the next words he knew he must say. "There are many in Troy who believe I have none. They will use any misstep against me, and... unfortunately, that now includes you."

She bowed her head, a mix of guilt and anger playing out on her face. "What are you saying? Will we not be safe there?"

"I'm saying we have to be smart. Be prepared for anything, and *survive*." It bothered him that he had to play the courtiers' sick games. He wished the world rewarded honesty and the forthright, the sort of bravery Helen showed when she spared Iamus, but he had been an ambassador long enough to know that true power dealt in shadows. A man didn't live long if he couldn't see into the dark. "Aligning yourself with me might be a mistake. At least at first."

Helen pulled away from him, her pale face tense with shock. "What are you saying?"

"The Oath, Helen." Paris pressed on, hating the pain he saw etched on her face. This was precisely what he told Glaucus he didn't want to happen, but it was too late to worry about hurt feelings. "I know of it, and the soldiers do as well. We cannot keep it secret. I need to know the terms, the *exact words* they swore at your betrothal."

Helen took a deep breath, forcing herself to relax. Paris wasn't like the men of her homeland. He didn't crave her for the spoils or glory of her hand. She was no trophy that elevated his standing amongst his fellow brother-at-arms. He loved her without need for benefit, unlike the suitors who came to Sparta so many years ago.

The memory came vividly to her mind's eye. Her father had thought himself clever to have devised a way to keep the quarrelsome kings and princes from fighting over her hand. An oath to protect her. Little did he know it would forge the bars of her prison. The words they swore were burned into her mind and she repeated them now with little hesitation.

"Come all who would be my son. Come and swear this sacred oath. To defend and protect he who is chosen like a brother of your blood. Swear to defend him against any wrong done to him in regard to this union. Swear by the blood of this sacrifice and share in the protection of Artemis and Her Almighty Father."

Paris' mind whirled, trying to find a way out. *Any wrong done in regard to this union...* that was the linchpin securing Agamemnon's army. If the Greeks came in full force, Priam might reconsider the wisdom of subduing a quarrelsome neighbor. But if Mycenae was forced to stand alone? Troy would scatter Agamemnon's forces to the ends of the earth and teach the insolent king a lesson the West would not soon forget.

"How many swore?"

"Forty. Almost every realm in the Hellas." She had once been so proud of that number. Now it filled her with dread.

"And will they all unite? Can Agamemnon command their loyalty?"

She nodded. "Their loyalty or their fear. Some who made the vow are already dead by his hand. He would not hesitate to make an example of any others who tried to shirk their obligations."

"That means his leadership is tenuous at best." It was the barest sliver of hope, but Paris would take it. "We'll need to undermine it further. If you came to Troy seeking sanctuary, not because of me, then no harm was done to Menelaus in regard to your union. The oath will be useless."

Helen trusted Paris. She did not doubt he was unmatched in his ability to maneuver politics and diplomacy. But denying her love for him felt wrong. It played into the falsehoods about his birth, an injustice Paris seemed all-too-willing to accept. "Agamemnon will come regardless. He hungers for war," she protested. "My leaving is nothing but a convenient fiction of insult. He will find another reason. I don't see the point—"

"*We* know that," Paris interrupted her, "but the Trojan High Council will not be so easy to convince. I can't risk the chance they might call his bluff and try to return you to him." He shook his head, his mind made up. "You need to go before the king. Ask for sanctuary. Tell Priam the true nature of Agamemnon and how you have suffered under the fist of Mycenae's king and queen. They will rally to defend you, I know it."

That was the last thing Helen wanted to speak about, to anyone, let alone the entire Trojan court. "*No!*"

"Helen?" Paris reached for her, taken aback by her impassioned response.

She pulled away, her body shaking uncontrollably. "You

promised me we would have a new life. *Together.*" She was having trouble breathing, her agonizing breaths coming in painful hiccups. "But you want me to go before a court filled with strangers—*alone*—and tell them... tell them—" She couldn't finish the sentence, the idea was so reprehensible to her. She leapt to her feet, desperate for escape. Spinning on her heel, she fled into the meadow.

The tall grass cut into her bare legs as Helen ran. Blood trickled down from a dozen little cuts. It didn't take long for her feet to falter. The world went in and out of focus. The green blades of the meadow intermixed with a scattering of poppies, the vibrant flower creating an illusion of a sea of red, a sea of blood. It surrounded her. She had nowhere to go where bloodshed would not follow. Helen fell to her knees as a pervasive numbness enveloped her.

Paris froze, unsure if he should follow after. He finally made up his mind to give pursuit, rising to his feet just as Helen fell from hers. He took his time to reach her side, hoping to give his princess a moment of respite.

He felt horrible that he caused her such pain. He had a tendency to think clinically, to shut off emotion when considering a course of action. It was how he survived. But Helen was not built like him. Compassion ruled her heart. It was what he loved about her.

She was also strong. It was easy to forget that she had suffered through a number of atrocities that would have broken a lesser woman. And when he saw her, huddled on the ground and moaning softly as she rocked on her heels, his heart bled. What had those evil parasites done to her? He crouched beside her and pulled her into his arms.

"Why didn't you just let me die?" she moaned.

He tightened his arms around her as if to squeeze out those horrible thoughts. "*If you die, I die.*" He shook with that promise. "There is no world for me without you in it. Helen, please. You wouldn't have to say anything you didn't want—"

"Then don't ask this of me!" she fired back. "Don't make

me walk into your kingdom a beggar. Don't make me pretend there is shame in loving you. Do not make me their victim..."

Her voice broke. Her demons were ripping her apart, festering in her soul. She could not be the person Paris needed while in their shadow. She had to purge those memories and harden herself against this weakness.

Paris tried to still her trembling. He was not blind, something was deeply wrong with his beloved. Helen was no coward, but it was as though a dark veil had come over her that she could not bear to face. This was not a response to a simple beating. He gathered his courage, knowing he was treading into sensitive territory. "What happened with the queen, Helen? What happened the night we left Mycenae?"

"Nothing happened." She pushed away from him, hiding her face in her golden locks.

"But the nightmares—"

"It's... it's just bad dreams. I have no control over what visits me in my sleep."

She was lying, her falsetto tone, her posture, every part of her screamed of falsehood. "Just dreams? Does Aethra know of those dreams? Would she say the same thing if I asked?"

Helen's head snapped up. *He wouldn't dare...*

But there was a hard line creasing Paris' brow. She'd seen that stubborn streak in him before. If Paris planted his feet in the sand on this issue, she doubted she could deter him.

"Why do you press this?" she groaned, her plea sounding desperate even to her own ears. "How often do you turn your head, a shadow of your past haunting your eyes? Do I ask you to disclose its source?"

His face blanched as though she plunged a blade in his gut. "No, you don't. But if you asked, I would tell you."

And there it was. The challenge had been thrown down. If she evaded him again, the gulf between them would widen. She tried to speak, but her tongue would not move. She thought of Theseus, of Agamemnon... her own sister. The pain, the shame, *the guilt* of their actions invaded her. She felt unclean.

It was foolish not to confide in Paris. He probably suspected the truth—of Agamemnon if no one else—but she couldn't help but feel that speaking the words somehow gave the people who had wronged her power. She dropped her head, too ashamed to meet his discerning eyes.

A small sob escaped her lips. She'd sever her own arm before she'd let it do Paris harm, but here she was—keeping him at a distance. As everyone he'd ever known surely had done. She couldn't stop the tears now. She hiccuped violently, trying hard to stifle those traitorous tears.

Paris cradled her to his chest. He stroked her long hair, not saying a word as she spent herself crying. When her sobs were no more than soft gasps, he finally released her. "It's not your fault, Helen."

"But, I-"

"It's not your fault," he repeated firmly. "It happens... these horrible things happen. But it isn't your fault. The people who do them—the blame lies on their shoulders. Do not carry it for them."

Paris lifted her chin, his fingers tracing over the nearly faded bruise on her temple. "She abused you, didn't she? More than just this." His eyes were filled with somber understanding.

Helen hesitated. Leaning into his hand, she nodded, her eyes never leaving his.

Paris had to mask his own pang of guilt. He should have been there to protect her. He had known there was something amiss that night. He should have trusted his instincts. It was a mistake he would not make twice.

"And there were others? Agamemnon?"

She nodded again. He swallowed the ball of bile creeping up his throat and continued. "And the queen... had she ever... before?"

"Nnnno. She saw us together. I've never seen her so angry. I... I couldn't stop her."

The queen had seen them together? His blood instantly froze. "I am so sorry, My Love."

Slowly, her tears ceased, and Helen leaned on his shoulder, her body drained of energy. As her breathing returned to normal, he held her close, amazed at her courage in the face of such depravity.

"You don't have to worry about them any more." His arms tightened around her with that promise. "You will never fall back into their hands. That life is behind you, I promise."

"I... I know," came her shaken reply.

Paris grimaced, regretting the additional pain he knew he must inflict upon her. "We are very close to that new beginning. But, as much as I want to declare my love for you before my king," his voice cracked and he paused, swallowing his misgivings before continuing on. "It is too dangerous. I... am disgraced. To the Trojan court, everything I touch is tainted."

Helen moved to protest.

"No, hear me out." He waved her off. "It is madness to deny the truth. I am *cursed*, an ill-favored son of Troy. If you enter the realm as my lover... if the nobles suspect I persuaded you to abandon your husband... my shame will become yours." Paris shook involuntarily, horrified at that thought. "*I cannot do that to you.*"

Helen froze, her hand half-outstretched to Paris, his heartfelt sorrow infecting her. The guilt of their flight from Greece lay heavily on his soul. It conflicted with the duty he owed to Troy and his king. In that tangled web, where did love factor in? She lowered her head, the ball of hope that resided in her chest quietly snuffing out. She could not place a greater burden on his shoulders.

"What would you have me do?"

"I need you to trust me." He sighed heavily, his face marked with sadness. "Where we go now, our enemies are ahead of us, not behind. They fight with whisper and shadows, weapons that cannot be defeated by bravery alone. If we let anger or fear dictate our actions, what safety we could hope for in Troy will be lost. We must not play into Agamemnon's hand."

"I understand." Helen cursed her naivety. The childish hope she harbored for a future of love and acceptance in Troy was but a tale for the bards. In the real world, there was no song honoring a woman who forsook her vows. Helen would go to Troy a refugee and sing a tale of woe, and in doing so, curse herself to forever be Agamemnon's victim, a stigma she knew now she would never escape.

"I'm sorry it has to be this way," Paris added, hating that he must ask this of her. Helen deserved better than this—she deserved better than *him*. But if he was to protect her, he had to do it the only way he knew how. "This is for the best. For both of us."

Helen nodded, her hand shaking as she accepted his help up from the grass. If not for the cry in her heart, his words would seem like wisdom. Paris was so capable and brave. He risked the wrath of kings on her behalf.

She could not help but wonder, when would he do the same for himself?

They walked back to the ship some time later, neither Helen nor Paris electing to speak. For the first time since they met, Paris felt a wedge growing between them, a shadow of duty that threatened to keep them apart. When they reached the cliffside, Glaucus had already returned, a similar gloom hanging over his host of men.

"What is it?" Paris rushed to his captain's side, fearing the worst. But one glance down to the rocky cove below showed the galley still at anchor. Glaucus' ire came from another source.

"A small herd of goats and a few roots tough enough to break teeth." He nodded back to their meager haul. "With the winds blowing from the east, we'll starve before we make berth at a safe harbor in Canaan. Paris, I implore you. Be reasonable."

A peal of thunder broke out overhead as a dark cloud crossed over the sun. The hair rose on Paris' neck. *The Gods mock me...*

"We'll resupply at a military fort along the delta. No one will know you are there," Glaucus promised, using Paris' stunned silence as a chance to argue his case. "I will deal with the overseer. We'll resupply and wait until the trade winds turn and take us back to Troy."

What Glaucus promised was no simple feat. That voyage would entail a dangerous delay, and if they were discovered, every skill Paris possessed as a diplomat would be required to see them through. Even though he new there was no other option, he still hesitated.

"Where are we going?" Helen came to his side, slipping her hand into his. Looking into her careworn face, knowing the dangers she had survived and how bravely she had faced them, he knew he could do no less.

"To Egypt." The words stuck in his throat. A quick glance to Glaucus confirmed the relief that admission imparted to his captain.

Egypt, the land of the eternal sun. The one place Paris hoped to avoid at all costs.

Chapter 8

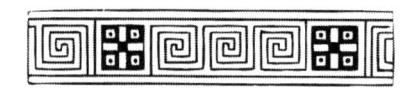

The Watcher of the Winds

SCYLAX STOOD AT the bow of his ship staring out over the empty waters of the Aegean. Some evil sprite lent his quarry speed. He had worked his crew near to death to catch up with the Trojan galley, and right when he caught sight of the wooden beast, it disappeared.

The Gods were punishing him, he decided. Scylax had chosen Mycenae to start his new life, believing the power of the Greek capital would render it immune to the many wars of conquest that frequently set the countryside in flames. But that bitch of a queen had dug him out of his den, forcing him back into the dark underworld he had helped to create.

Scylax glared at the pathetic crew the queen had provided him, his hand inching toward the whip at his belt. He longed to make those lazy dogs fear him more than sore muscles. They groaned like babies, taxed by the swift journey to Crete. When Scylax discovered they had missed their quarry in Dius by mere hours, he set an even harsher pace. Every day that the Spartan princess eluded his grasp was another day the queen held his family in ransom. He'd beat them all bloody if it brought him home quicker.

The pacemaker set a steady beat on his drum, and the

oarsmen threw their backs into their work, flinching away from Scylax' ice cold gaze. He unclenched his hand. He was a fool to expect anything of worth from this motley crew. They were no Brothers of the Sword, but desperate men taking whatever work they could attain. In the days to come, they would be as useless to him as the vermin that prowled the lower deck. No matter how much he longed to strike out, beating these men would bring him no closer to his quarry.

He took a deep and measured breath, remembering Dora's lessons on how to quell his temper. He was in control. Scylax. Not the violent titan of his past.

He saw the terror in his wife's eyes when he accepted this charge. Dora feared he would become the monster that he once was back when they first met. He shared her fear. A blinding rage beckoned to him. It was the familiar embrace of an old lover. That Scylax was an agent of death, a man who would think little of ripping a queen's spine from her throat. When Clytemnestra threatened his children, he briefly considered that action, but Scylax knew, in taking the bloody path, he'd lose Heliodora forever, and her gentle love was the only reason he still lived.

Yet, in doing the queen's bidding, he was nevertheless on the path for blood. This time, however, only one man need die. Scylax went over the queen's description of the Trojan prince again, each detail given equal weight. It was important to know your prey, how they thought. That advantage meant Scylax could anticipate the prince's moves, and given time, lie in wait.

Only a coward kidnaps a married woman while her husband is away. His thoughts turned again to Dora, alone in Mycenae. If anyone dared to touch her...

Scylax grit his teeth as a red haze clouded his sight. Dora would have to forgive him for this murder. The Trojan had earned his death.

A gust of wind stirred from the north, raising the hairs along Scylax' neck. With it came the heavy scent of earth that spoke of summer squalls. A lifetime at sea had taught him to read the winds, and these zephyrs were blowing them to the southern continent.

I can't go back there... Bile rose in his throat. He had agreed to run down the Trojan galley, to return the princess to Greece and no more. There had been no mention of Egypt. The queen could not ask him to return to that pit of deceit.

But she wasn't asking...

A return to Egypt meant facing his past. It meant inviting daemons long buried to take root. Could he face that temptation and return again?

Scylax swallowed his misgivings, the bile burning the tender flesh of his throat. For Dora he'd descend into Hades itself. If Egypt was where the Trojan prince thought to hide, so be it. The cloak of darkness would not avail him. No amount of tricks would turn Scylax off course.

"Baradas!" he shouted to his helmsman. "South by southeast. Everyone is on double-shifts until we see the southern continent." He ignored the pathetic groans from his oarsmen at the announcement, a grim determination taking root inside him. He'd hear no objection to the task that lay before him.

When the Trojans entered the Two Lands, Scylax would be waiting for them.

THE BATTLE OF KADESH

SINCE THE DAWN of civilization, the holy lands of Canaanite and Syria have been the source of constant warfare. In the twilight years of the Late Bronze Age, these fertile lands were contested property between the mighty empires of Egypt and Hatti. Satrapies were won and lost in their never ending tug-of-war of power.

A short time before the birth of Helen and Paris, an historic battle was fought on the plains of Kadesh. Rameses the Great, the second of his name, fought bravely against a Hittite host twice his army's size. In the end, neither king could claim victory, and both monarchs lost their appetite to rule a ruinous land destabilized by their bloody campaigns.

A truce was called. And with the ratification of the Treaty of Kadesh, Egypt and Hatti—the mortal enemy of Troy—formed the world's first peace treaty, a feat so momentous it was immortalized on the walls of Karnak and the annals of Hattusa. A princess of Hatti was wed to the Pharaoh, and thus the pact was sealed in blood as well as stone.

Rameses ruled in Egypt for another 50 years. While none

THE PRINCESS OF PROPHECY

would question the rule of their God-King while he still drew breath, many factions in Egypt detested calling their once great enemy, "friend". They whispered that this alliance of empires was in truth a desperate attempt to preserve the legacy of a failed king, of a Pharaoh so weak he let slip the slaves of Israel and conceded lands once held by their ancestors—lands won by the blood of Egypt.

By the time of Rameses' death, these factions had taken root in the royal household. Pharaoh had sired countless children with his numerous wives and concubines, many of whom he outlived. While tradition held that the crown prince would ascend the high seat, there were many contenders vying for power. In the aftermath of Rameses' death, brother turned on brother, and neighboring kingdoms pecked away at Egypt's borders. Danger was ever-mounting.

In those troubling times, it was not the sons of Pharaoh who posed the greatest threat to Egypt, but a princess of mixed Hittite and Egyptian heritage, a princess with ambitions to become Pharaoh herself. Twosret, Daughter of Re, Lady of Ta-merit, Twosret of Mut... a woman as devious as she was cunning.

A woman who would destroy her family's dynasty.

Part Two:

In the Two Lands

Chapter 9

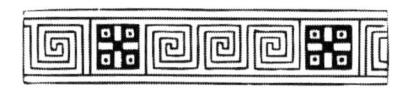

The Delta

THE NORTHERN ZEPHYRS blew relentlessly off the Great Sea the week following the Trojan's departure from Crete. Just when Paris thought they neared the Egyptian coast, the winds would shift, pushing their galley off-course and losing the distance they had gained the day prior. To the Trojan prince, it seemed the Gods were in flux, as undecided as he about their destination.

On the fifth day, just after sunrise, the lowlands of the Egyptian delta came into view. The marshland, dense and green, was surrounded by yellow desert sands on both sides. Any manner of danger could hide in the blind channels that flowed from the Nile into the sea. Danger or not, that was their destination.

"Trim the sail," Glaucus barked out to his bosun, and a team of sailors set to work on the rigging. As soon as land came in sight, the captain had taken point position at the helm. He navigated the ship around wooden beams jutting out of the water. Those timbers were not the branches of flooded trees but masts from a vast ship graveyard, the forsaken vessels run aground on the treacherous sandbars lining the coast. Only an experienced helmsman could read the correct path to the reach the delta. It was as much of a deterrent for a sea invasion as having an army stationed at Egypt's border.

Paris ran a hand through his salt-crusted hair. He hoped his paranoias were just that. But knowing the Two Lands as he did, it was best to approach the Egyptian shores with caution.

"Have you thought through what you are going to tell them?" Paris asked again.

"As little as possible." Glaucus unconsciously gripped the hilt of his sword. "Just enough to get to the trading post along the delta. If you stay below deck where no one can recognize you, I should be able to handle the rest."

They had agreed to continue the subterfuge they adopted in Crete. Complicated questions arose with the presence of a royal diplomat... questions and obligations they both wished to avoid. Glaucus insisted Paris stay out of sight. Due to the lengthy time he had spent in the Two Lands, there were good odds he would be recognized by a local governor or vizier. Trojan merchants restocking their larders, however, would pose no great interest.

"You've told the men to deny this is a royal ship?"

"Only fifty times." The captain grunted. "No one will betray your presence." He seemed almost eager to prove that fact.

Glaucus was strangely in favor of this detour. When Paris pressed, the gruff man simply stated that he was a soldier and soldiers preferred offense to pretense. When Glaucus refused to elaborate, Paris could only guess it had something to do with Helen. The captain watched over her as assiduously as he did his prince.

He looked across the ship to the bow where Helen was replacing Iamus' bandages. After their sojourn on the Cretan isle, she had taken responsibility for the soldier's care. Iamus was back on his feet within a day and insisted on taking his turn at watch, although anything more rigorous was still beyond him.

Helen raised her head and smiled at him. Over the past

week that smile had grown more brilliant, as though she meant to pack in a lifetime of affection before they reached Troy's golden shores. Each day was more precious than the last, a stolen moment of happiness they were both desperate to preserve. He wished it could last forever. She practically radiated with joy.

Her mood also infected the crew, many of whom seemed to think this visit to the Two Lands was simply another adventure to notch in their belts. That left only Paris to worry about what lay ahead, and his tongue had grown more acidic the closer they ranged to the southern continent.

He excused himself from the helm and joined her at the bow. Helen had just finished placing a salve on Iamus' welts, a mix of honey, dittany, date juice and goat brains. It smelled terrible. Paris was grateful when she placed fresh bandages over the mess.

"Don't touch it this time," she warned the soldier, tying the linen in pace. Iamus grunted under the tight knot, but made his promise with little complaint. When he caught sight of Paris, he hastily pulled his tunic back on, his eyes darting nervously.

"Your Grace." He looked like he wanted to say more, but clamped his mouth shut.

"Go on with it." Helen prodded the man, poking him none-too-gently in his tender back.

"I was wondering—" he looked to Helen for reassurance, "hoping... you would let me return to your royal guard."

Paris was unprepared for that question. He paused, considering the man before him. There was remorse in his eyes, but was it enough? When Helen told the crew that in the eyes of the Gods Iamus' crime was wiped away by his punishment, it seemed a viable prospect. But could he trust Iamus not to fail him again?

"We'll discuss that when we get back to Troy." He shook his head, still uncertain. "Rest up, Iamus. You'll need your strength."

"Yes, I will. Thank you, My Prince." He quickly rose to his feet and shuffled away, his walk one of a man who still assumed his guilt.

"Did you put him up to that?" Paris turned back to Helen. She was watching him intently, an unspoken question in her narrowed eyes.

"No. I merely encouraged him when he asked if it were possible. Every man deserves a chance to redeem himself." She crossed to his side and took his hand in hers. "Does that sound so unreasonable?"

The ship banked hard to starboard, turning into a channel of the delta. They were quickly surrounded by towering reeds that blocked out the horizon. The rumble of waves crashing against the hull, that steady sound Paris had become so familiar with over the past two weeks, faded away. A new hum took its place, this one of marshland insects and songs of frog and heron. With the cool ocean breeze gone, the humidity of the swamp soaked into his bones. The change came suddenly, as if they crossed an invisible barrier, and once on the the other side, there was no mistaking that the land was as ancient as it was unchangeable. This was the feel of the Egypt he remembered.

"Paris?" Helen tightened her grip on his hand, a crease of worry on her lovely face as she stared into the marshland. "Are you sure this is the right decision?"

"Absolutely." He squeezed her hand back, a surge of guilt flooding him. His pensive mood had not gone unnoticed, and while a foray into Egypt unnerved him, the last thing he wanted was to scare her. "I'm sorry if I've worried you. I like to be prepared when I go into a new land. Ideally, I'd send in scouts, assess the atmosphere of the capital before entering." He grimaced, knowing he was still saying too much. "Forgive me, Helen. Glaucus is right. I am paranoid. Egypt is not as bad as I make it out to be. In some ways, it truly is an advanced culture, one that far surpasses any other in the world."

She tucked a strand of hair out of his face and cast him a

gracious smile, one those rare smiles that she shared only with him. "Really?" She settled in against his chest, finding the nook in his arm that seemed to fit her shape perfectly. "Tell me more."

"Well," he started, pulling her closer, the warmth of her skin chasing away his earlier anxieties, "for example, women have many rights in the Two Lands and can even own property."

Helen laughed at that outlandish statement, a concept completely foreign to a Greek. A woman was *oikos*, the property of her *kyrios*, her guardian who was first her father and then the husband he chose for her. In Sparta there were some exceptions, where citizens believed that the women of Lacedaemonia were superior to other females in Greece. Though that belief came with greater privileges, any woman who claimed herself equal to a man was courting madness. The rule of the earth was granted to men, not to their female counterparts.

"And the Temples!" Paris continued. "No house of the Gods can compare with the Temples of Egypt. The priests of Re are mighty magicians and have rituals that can purify the soul, erasing the sins of a man's past as though they never were."

Erasing your past? "They can do that?" Helen sat up, suddenly very interested, her eyes wide with incredulity.

"Yes." He perked up at her interest. "And often. Egyptian priests are obsessed with purity."

Slowly, her amazement shifted to doubt. "Powerful women and temple zealots, these are the fearsome folk you wished to avoid?" Her banter was light, hiding how truly stunned she was by this revelation. What awaited them in this mysterious land they now travelled? "Don't fret, My Love." She batted her dark lashes at him playfully. "I won't let them hurt you."

Paris pulled her into his arms, reaching in to kiss her neck, delighting in her musical giggles. "Is that so?" He laughed with her. "Perhaps I've been focused on the wrong danger. Should I be more mindful of the lioness in my bed?" Her laughs turned to squeals as he tickled her, and she squirmed in his hold, as feisty as a minx. Doubling his efforts, Paris decided this was far better use of his time than obsessing over events he could not change. Just when he thought he had the best of their bout, Helen froze.

"That's strange." She tensed, her attention drawn to the obscured coastline. The channel had narrowed. The encroaching marshland was so close to the galley they could almost stretch out over the hull and touch it.

"What's that?" He reluctantly pulled away from her.

"That sound... I could swear it sounded like a summer thrush. But those birds are native to Thessaly."

The warble came again, louder now. Paris' throat constricted. That call came from no bird. "GLAUCUS!" he shouted behind him, pulling Helen down to the deck.

The attack came swiftly. The camouflage curtain, a thick netting of reeds and swamp undergrowth, dropped to the ground and revealed a band of bedouins behind it. The nomadic fighters, draped in linen robes and headscarves, charged the Trojan vessel with swords brandished high.

"PIRATES!" The cry rang out through the galley. Trojans spilled over the hull to meet their enemy head on. The ring of metal on metal filled the air.

"Stay on deck." Paris warned Helen, pushing her out of the line of danger. "Whatever you do, do not get off this ship."

"Paris!" She tried to hold on to him, but he was fast after his men.

Glaucus was in the thick of the battle. He wielded a short oar like a quarterstaff, swooping two men from their feet and spinning around to catch the blade of another. Two dozen bedouins had emerged from the reeds. If there were any more of them lying in wait, this would end badly. Paris scanned the remainder of the field, looking for the leader. He needed to finish this quickly.

THE PRINCESS OF PROPHECY

The bedouins were covered head to toe. It was difficult to determine if one was dressed more finely than the others. One man had cleared a space around him. Brandishing twin sickles, he mowed down Paris' soldiers like blades of grass. The Trojans were grudgingly giving him space, and by the nervous glances from the other pirates, it appeared the bedouins feared him as well. He had to be their leader.

Paris launched himself off the ship, somersaulting over a line of fighters. Dropping into a lunge, he sprinted across the spongy earth toward his mark. The pirate was prepared for him and caught Paris' sword between his two, twisting the weapon wide. They circled each other, both men hunched low, their blades flicking dangerously back and forth between them.

"ⲱⲣⲟ ⲱⲉⲛⲧ ⲏⲟⲩ?!" Paris shouted to the pirate leader in Egyptian. Strangely the man did not flinch. Paris tried again. "ⲇⲟ ⲏⲟⲩ ⲙⲓⲛⲇ ⲱⲣⲟ ⲓⲱⲣ ⲉⲍⲓⲱⲧ? ⲱⲧⲟⲡ ⲧⲣⲓⲱ ⲙⲇⲇⲛⲉⲱⲱ." Again, no response.

The pirate initiated a counter attack, his sickles spinning so fast they seemed a single blade. Paris barely managed to parry, the curved edge of his enemy's weapon coming dangerously close to his head. That lunge brought the pirate within striking range, too close for Paris' sword but just near enough for his fist. He whipped out his hand, palm-edge first, knocking the man hard in his throat. The pirate leader fell to the ground, choking from the blow.

Paris kicked the sickles out of his enemy's hands. Reaching down, he yanked the scarf from the pirate's head, exposing his face for the first time. As Paris suspected, his skin was not the taupe hues of the desert nomads, but a sun-darkened olive. The pirate leader was not Egyptian. Paris hauled the man up by by his short black hair, and brought his sword under the man's exposed neck, trying one last time to communicate.

"I am ⲧⲣⲟⲭⲁⲛ," he shouted in Babylonian, followed by "ⲧⲁⲩⲣⲓⲱⲁ," in Akkadian, and then finally in his common tongue: "*Troy!*"

That finally got the reaction he was waiting for. The pirate blinked back his confusion. He seemed less ready for violence than a moment before.

"Tell them to stop or I will slit your throat." Paris hissed in his ear. The pirate made a valiant effort to dislodge him, trying to ram his head at Paris' face, but Paris was too quick. He dodged the blow and slammed his knee between the pirate's legs, dispelling any more fight the man had left. "DO IT!"

"CEASE YOUR FIGHTING," the pirate shouted to his men in a commanding voice.

Slowly, the battle came to a halt. Glaucus quickly rounded up their enemies' weapons, the Trojan soldiers battle-ready for whatever order Paris next decreed.

"That is a diplomatic ship, River Scum. I'm sure you recognize the craft or you're less a pirate than you are an Egyptian."

"Piss off, Trojan." The leader growled, a dark spike of anger simmering behind his eyes. "Slice me, or admit you lack the stones."

Paris ignored the barb and balanced himself for another attack should the man prove foolhardy as well as blind. "That is no merchant vessel, and I know you know the difference, so don't play dumb." He pressed his blade dangerously close to the pirate's throat, the sharp edge shaving bristles off the man's day-old stubble. "I'll ask you one last time. *Who sent you?*"

"Paris!" Helen, having ignored his instructions, stood at the bow of the ship, her face blanched free of color. "Wait." She delicately leapt to shore and pressed her way through the throng, heedless of any danger. Stopping before the pirate leader, her eyes were as wide as saucers. "*I know you.*"

The pirate tensed. A similar discomfort ran through his brethren, many of whom glanced at the pile of weapons with an eager eye as though they meant to reengage.

Paris tightened his grip, cognitive of the mounting danger. "Helen—"

"This man is Greek." She continued to stare at the pirate leader, utterly confused. "He's a farmer. From Phthia."

"Myrmidon, Princess," the leader said with a sigh, finally accepting his captive status.

"I met your boys," Helen continued, her shock blending with disapproval. "On a state visit from Mycenae. They were nearly eight and six." She drew a sharp breath of realization. "Deukalion, what in Great Gaia's name are you doing in Egypt?"

The pirate tensed at the mention of his name and a dark cast came over his face. "Drought and famine took the boys. What little we had left on the farm went to the tribute collectors. Egypt was as good a place as any other, and better than most, Princess."

Paris yanked on the man's hair. "He is lying, Helen."

She pushed his blade aside, staring the man directly in the eye. "Are you here to harm me, Deuk? Is that the man you have become?"

Deukalion shifted, uncomfortable under the scrutiny of the petite woman. "I mean you no harm, Princess, but a man has to eat. Your king has squeezed the freemen too long."

Helen was disgusted by that news. She knew Agamemnon's greedy trade policies were beggaring the outer villages. He failed to take responsibility for the suffering his desire for glory and riches created. "*He is not my king,*" she said with considerable heat. "Paris, this man is not our enemy."

Deukalion's head jolted up in surprise. As did Paris'. Helen's intentions were noble, but he was not going to let an enemy walk away only to ambush them again. "His blades look plenty sharp to me."

"Promise me." She turned back to Deukalion. "Say it plain. You will not follow us or raise arms against us again. Say it, and I will believe you."

The pirates moved to protest but Deukalion waved them down. "I so swear. Zeus strike me blind if I forsake it." Helen seemed satisfied, and with her nod, the pirate leader shoved off Paris' hold. He waited expectantly for the Trojan soldiers to follow her lead and release his men.

But Paris signaled Glaucus not to lower his guard. "You're not walking out of here without answering some questions first."

A trumpet call blasted through the air, its clarion note joined by four others. The reeds surrounding them shifted from a force that was not wind.

"Royal army," Deukalion hissed, turning to run. He met Paris' extended blade and stopped short.

"*Paris,*" Helen pleaded.

Something about this encounter struck Paris as false, and it began with this man. His gut told him to keep this Deukalion close, to interrogate him, but the trumpets were nearing. Paris had no wish to be the center of a royal purge of local pirates, be that what the man truly was or not.

"Go!" He finally lowered his sword. He didn't need to turn to know Glaucus was glaring in his direction. Deukalion collected his blades while his crew slipped away into the marsh.

"I owe you a debt, Trojan." He tucked his headscarf back into place and saluted Paris with his sickle. The trumpets rang out again, and Deukalion rushed after his men, the whole host disappearing like a flock of water fowl gone to nest.

"That wasn't wise, Princess." Glaucus stalked over to them.

"Maybe not." She glared back. "But it was *right.*"

The captain did not have time to respond as a full squadron of Egyptian military entered the clearing by the channel. Their commander, atop a jet black stallion, galloped to their side, his dark eyes assessing the situation in mere seconds.

"*Foreigners?*" he shouted down to them in Egyptian. "*Who are you? In the name of Merneptah, Pharaoh of the Two Lands, explain yourselves."*

Paris exchanged a nervous glance with Glaucus. He had meant to stay below deck and let his captain handle their trade. But Egyptians were finicky about status, and dressed as he was, there was no mistaking Paris was noble. The commander watched him expectantly, waiting for an answer, and Paris struggled to provide one. Glaucus' ruse would not work.

Pressing Helen behind him, he responded in the man's native tongue. *"We are pilgrims,"* he lied. *"From Troy. We were in route to Heliopolis when we were stopped by pirates –"*

"Pirates!" The commander spun from him, shouting orders to his infantry men. They set forth immediately into the marshland, leaving only a small contingent with their commander and Paris' men. Once they were gone, the severe man studied Paris again, a distrustful look on his face. *"Pilgrims?"*

"Yes," Paris insisted.

The commander dismounted, the beads braided into his shoulder-length black wig clacking ominously as he strode over to Paris and Helen. *"The delta is a dangerous place for pilgrims. We have pirates and smugglers about. Even those who mean to do our great Pharaoh harm."* He eyed Paris suggestively, as though insinuating that was precisely what the Trojan galley intended.

"So I've noticed." Paris bit back his anger at the man's gall. *"But I am from a minor house in Troy come only to marvel at the Temple of Amun-Re. Our intentions are peaceful."*

The Egyptian peered over Paris' shoulder, his eyes widening with appreciation as he spied Helen. Paris shifted, cutting off his view.

"It pleases me to hear that," the commander added with a perturbed tsk, *"but you will have to get clearance from our administrator in Heracleion. Foreigners are not allowed in the Two Lands without his say."* He turned to bark more orders to his remaining soldiers, leaving Paris to explain to his crew.

"Where?" Glaucus growled, his grey eyes thunderstorm-dark as he studied the Egyptian commander.

"A military outpost, less than a league away." Paris grimaced, less than pleased by this predicament. "It's all right," he added off Helen's worried look. "I told them we were pilgrims. We'll file a report of our activities with the local magistrate, restock the galley, and be on our way back to Troy. Nothing has changed."

Helen seemed relieved. Paris wished he could share her ease. For better or for worse, they had entered Egypt. It was too late to turn back now.

※

As Scylax slid into the marsh, thick reeds fell back into place, obscuring the Trojan galley from sight. He yanked his blade free, taking his frustrations out on the unoffending stalks, each stroke abating the mounting need inside him to destroy something.

The Trojan and the princess had slipped through his fingers. Surrounded by a squadron of the Egyptian royal army, they might as well have been spirited to Mount Olympus, they were so hopelessly beyond his reach. He had this perfect moment to complete his mission, and now it was gone.

Scylax had made landfall on Egyptian soil shortly before the dawn. With his crew exhausted, and many of them little more than untested whelps, he was forced to make other arrangements in laying his trap.

At first, he thought hiring Deukalion to be a clever ruse. The queen had ordered this task done, but there was no reason Scylax himself must hold the blade. His old swords brother and fellow commander in the Libyan campaigns was more than capable of flushing out a few hares. By using Deukalion, Scylax was afforded the unique opportunity to case out his enemy, to see the prince in action and know how capable the man was.

THE PRINCESS OF PROPHECY

Then everything went horribly wrong, and Scylax knew he had made a terrible mistake.

You weak fool, he scoffed at himself. *If you are incapable of killing the Trojan yourself, the princess is as good as dead. And if she dies, so do your girls.*

He ran a hand over his face, trying to rub some sense back into his head. Why did he delegate this task? The old Scylax would never have let others do his work for him. He would not have hesitated to join the battle and bloody his hands. He would have pounced on this opportunity. The Trojan would be dead, and the princess back on a ship with him to Greece.

Scylax slashed at the reeds again, the tip of his blade hitting the stalks awkwardly, sending a jolt down his arm. He cursed his bad form, spitting his frustration onto the spongy soil. He was as rusty with a sword as those soft-cheeked boys on his ship.

But his waning skill was telling, and he could not lie to himself. He was not the man he once was. It had been five years since he'd last killed a man... five wonderful years with Heliodora and their girls. The old Scylax was lethal, a killer who had earned a reputation of swift and silent death. That man would not have thought twice about taking a life, *any life*. Was he even capable of violence now?

The military horn rang out again, scattering a flock of grouse into the sky. He had dallied on the field too long. Ducking back into the thick cover, Scylax carved a trail through the undergrowth as he retreated back to the rendezvous point. Tips of broken papyrus flew through the air, cutting into his face with the sharp sting of a swarm of gnats. He cursed, slashing harder, mowing down row after row of the plant stuff, willing his body to remember the feel of his sword carving through flesh. A man was not much more than a bundle of reeds. When the time came, he *must* be ready to act.

Some distance from the river, a bedouin camp came into view. Scylax crept around the perimeter, staying clear of their lookouts. He located Deukalion's yurt and slipped in the back, bypassing the piss-poor excuse of a guard stationed at the entrance.

The interior was dark and smelled of the untanned leathers covering its driftwood frame. That scent filled Scylax with familiarity. This was a hunter's den, a place of refuge and security where predators lowered their defenses. He had spent most of his life on the outskirts of society in places like this.

As he waited, a sliver of fear wormed its way into his heart. Over the past five years, something inside him had shifted. With Heliodora's guiding light, he'd found a new appreciation for life. He had changed. *She had changed him.*

In the Underworld, however, that morality was a weakness. Only the strong survived here. If Deukalion suspected he had turned clean, if Deuk did not fear him, this mission would be over before it began. Scylax scoured his mind, trying to remember his old mannerisms, to find the correct response for a sword brother who failed his mission.

He did not have long to consider. In a short amount of time, Deukalion threw open the tent flaps and strode into the room. The blinding light of the mid-day sun flooded the yurt, forcing Scylax to avert his eyes. Fortunately, he didn't need to see. Deukalion, on the other hand, needed time to adjust to the change.

Scylax slipped behind him, the man's heavy breathing as conspicuous as the royal army's trumpets for one trained to listen. He pressed the tip of his dagger into Deukalion's lower back, relieved when the soldier tensed in surprise.

"You're getting soft, Deuk. There was a time when no man could get the best of you."

The raven-haired man shoved him off, the pinch of his face showing more embarrassment than irritation. "Hades Hounds, Scylax. You always were a bastard."

Scylax feigned indifference, lounging against a support beam and using his blade to pick dirt from beneath his nails. *Dismissive and cocksure.* He grinned as the memories flooded back to him. "I'd rather be a bastard than craven. You let that lordling disarm you."

Deukalion's blade flew from his hand and embedded into the wood beside Scylax' head with a solid thunk. An inch to the left and that blade would have punctured his skull, but the old sell-sword didn't want him dead; he was trying to prove something else.

Scylax glanced at the blade and back to Deukalion with a smirk. "Did I say something to upset you?"

Deuk stalked over to him and retrieved his blade. A fire burned in his eyes to match his mighty temper. Scylax was vaguely reminded of their time together in the field. Deuk always let his emotions get the best of him. In the heat of battle, he could break an enemy line, but for delicate matters he had the sophistication of a child.

"That was a royal ship, Scy. What are you playing at?"

"What do you care?" he fired back. "I'm not paying you for counsel. I bought your sword arm. You were supposed to detain them."

Deuk backed away and began to pace. "It's so like you to come down here where no one has seen you in years and act like you own the place. We have rules, arrangements with the magistrate. *We don't attack royal envoys.*"

Scylax grimaced. He did not have to feign the sour wave of disgust clenching at his gut. He pushed off the wall and stalked over to Deukalion on silent feet. "Arrangements. *With them.* I was wrong; you haven't gone soft. You've become a puppet for the crown."

He didn't need to say anything more. Service to Pharaoh, to any king, was as vile as the flesh-eating virus to the brothers of the sword. If Scylax had been any other man, Deukalion would have cleft him in two for that comment.

Slowly, with a Herculean effort, the sell-sword suppressed his anger. "I have no quarrel with Trojans," Deuk added, albeit with less verve. "And you could have warned me. I would have brought more men."

"It would not have helped you. That prince had your number."

Deukalion ignored the barb and tucked his sickles into his belt—an uncharacteristic display of control. Perhaps the man *had* matured in his tenure in the desert. "I know what you want, you sick bastard, and I won't help you get it. *'I need to reclaim stolen property'*. Bullshit! You're after the princess. I won't help you start another war!"

A knot of dread took hold of Scylax, its dark shadow clouding his vision. Scylax had told no one Helen had been abducted, just as the queen instructed. *How had Deukalion known?* Was that Mycenaean bitch playing him for a fool? Was he being set up to start a war?

It was the man's screams that pulled Scylax back to reality. In his rage-fueled haze, he had pinned Deukalion to the floor, the tip of his dagger plunged through the tender flesh of his swords-brother's shoulder, impaling the man to the hard earth.

"Get off me!" Deuk howled in pain just as his guard rushed into the yurt.

Scylax pulled another dagger free from his belt and held the weapon outstretched, ready to throw. "Leave us!" he hissed at the man. Whatever the guard saw convinced him to flee, and the two mercenaries were left alone again.

Some part of Scylax was horrified by his actions, but he couldn't control himself; his body moved on instinct. The priests who ran the orphanage at the Temple of Ares often told Scylax that the balance between sanity and madness was finer than the edge of a blade. If pushed at just the precise moment, any man could lose his reason to the fearsome God. As Scylax knew all-too-well. *"What do you know about the princess?"*

"Nothing!" Deuk shouted through grit teeth. "Take it out!"

"Don't lie to me," Scylax lowered the tip of his dagger over Deukalion's eye, "or the next one won't be a flesh wound. Now tell me... *how do you know about the princess?"*

"I met her in Phthia!" the mercenary groaned. "She's a

good person, not like the other royals." Praise for any royal was a rarity from a brother of the sword, and when Deukalion's dark gaze narrowed and swelled with hate, Scylax took notice. "She doesn't deserve what I know you'll do to her. Just leave her in peace."

Leave her in peace? Scylax tensed with confusion. The princess Deukalion described hardly resembled the helpless prisoner he sought. His suspicions surged, more wary than ever that he was being manipulated by the crown. "Where are they going?"

Deukalion spat in his face. "Piss off, Scylax. Do your own dirty work. I won't help you take her."

Scylax twisted the blade in Deukalion's shoulder, watching the man writhe in pain beneath him. "I don't have time for your petty nonsense. If you are too craven to finish the job, I'll do it myself. *Where are they going?*"

"Heracleion, you bloody bastard," Deuk cried, sweat breaking out on his brow as desperation tensed his face. "But Chancellor Bay will detain them. With the right introductions, you can collect them."

Scylax stood up, his frustration mounting. "No, Deuk, he won't. They won't be staying in Heracleion."

A royal, foreign or not, would not remain at the mercy of a local magistrate for long. Egypt had them now, and once the prince was caught in its web, there was but one destination possible: Heliopolis, and the Court of the Sun—a vile den of corruption that would make his job infinitely harder. He planted a foot on Deukalion's chest and yanked his blade free.

"The Gods curse you and your black soul," Deuk spat, cradling his wound and lurching to his feet.

"They already have."

Scylax watched his once-friend with a touch of pity. Egypt had taken ahold of him, too. Under its blistering sun on the edge of society, Deukalion lived and fought for nothing. In the sad saga of his life, he wouldn't know what it felt like to love someone so dearly he'd risk his very soul to protect them.

"For your troubles." He tossed his old comrade a purse of gold and exited the yurt.

Scylax snuck outside the camp with relative ease, stealing a camel as he left. With the sun beating down on his headscarf and an open road ahead of him, he tried to prepare himself for what lay ahead. This unfortunate delay in the Delta had not been entirely useless. He had witnessed the Trojan in action, and the prince had proven himself extremely capable. He displayed an agility Scylax had rarely seen in battle. With his own skills uncertain, he wasn't ready to take the Trojan in direct combat, ambush or not.

No, this matter would not be resolved by the sword. It would take cunning to get the prince to lower his defenses, something, as a former commander of the rebel forces, Scylax excelled at.

He had time to make up if he was to reach the sacred city before the Trojan envoy. Kicking his camel into a gallop, he pressed the animal for more speed, a hard resolve taking hold of him as he began forming his plan.

Chapter 10

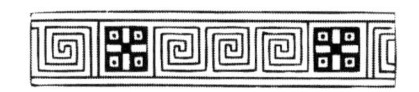

The Chancellor

PARIS AND HELEN entered the port city of Heracleion by chariot. The Egyptian commander insisted they accompany him personally, refusing to let the noble couple out of his sight.

Heracleion was a city under construction. A half-finished temple to Amun was covered with stoneworkers, its walls of dark-grey diorite sparkling under the noonday sun. The "roads" leading into the city were in fact a network of man-made canals, allowing the river trade to thrive in the Delta outpost. It took some persuasion, but Glaucus returned to the Trojan ship and brought the galley down the channel behind them.

The commander, who refused to give his name, steered their chariot down a dusty path to the most impressive building the city could boast: a military outpost with thick defensive walls. The fort's gypsum-coated exterior was brightly painted in hues of red and green and two sixteen foot statues flanked its massive door.

Thoth, Paris surmised, recognizing the ibis-headed Egyptian god of scribes. The dwelling was certainly the domicile of a magistrate.

Helen could scarcely keep her eyes inside her head. She

had travelled much of the Hellas. While no other Greek kingdom came close to the architectural wonders of Mycenae, Egypt was a level of magnificence all its own. Its buildings were exotic and constructed on a massive scale. The use of angles and decorative elements created a sense of perfection she had never seen in Grecian works. Even half-finished, Helen knew she was looking at the work of masters.

As she watched, an Egyptian overseer let fly his whip at half-naked men pulling a laden cart of stone. Their pitiful cries were unheeded, and the overseer brandished his weapon again. *"What are they doing?"* she whispered to Paris, alarmed.

"Slaves." A twinge of disapproval crossed his face. "Egyptians always use slave labor when constructing their monuments."

"But some of these people are old men. They couldn't possibly have been taken in battle."

Paris sighed. Helen had so much to learn of the world. Unfortunately, it was not all going to be pleasant. "Egyptians don't enslave just prisoners of war. They take whole families." Theoretically those families, in time, could become Egyptian and contribute to the crown levies, but Paris had yet to see that promise hold true. A king who gave up a favored toy was a rarity.

Helen bit her tongue. She had been warned to guard her feelings, to be careful to make no offense, but it was difficult. Her Spartan upbringing placed her at a disadvantage. She had been taught that a virtuous man had nothing to hide. He wore his opinions as plain as his face. One look to their stern captor, however, suppressed that thought. Helen doubted her Spartan virtues would be appreciated here.

Paris dismounted from the chariot and offered her his hand. They followed the commander into the fort, a path that took them down a long columned hall where pillars were covered in artful hieroglyphics. Guards fully-armed with spear and helm were stationed at each portal, their stature so rigid even a Spartan would envy it. The commander passed them by without comment, leading the pair ultimately to the back of the fort, to an inner chamber remarkable only for its lack of decoration or design. The room boasted four straight white walls, no windows, and a single desk at the far corner where a man poured over papyri reports stacked high before him.

"Can't you see I'm busy, Khamet," the magistrate spoke, never taking his eyes off his documents. "You're supposed to be in the channels safeguarding my next shipment, not escorting prisoners to the fort. I pray you don't need my advice on how to handle river scum."

The commander paused mid-step and cleared his throat. "This was a special case, Chancellor Bay. I thought it best if you cleared these travelers."

The chancellor looked up and Helen got her first full look of the man. Bay was past his prime, aged two-score at least. His head was bereft of hair save for the patch on his chin, and he twined those long strands of black in his fingers. His angular features were different from the Egyptians Helen had seen thus far, and his skin a lighter hue of brown. The contrast made Bay seem out of place. He was foreign in a way that sent shivers down her spine, and when he laid his eyes on her, she had a sudden flash of Agamemnon. She distrusted this chancellor instantly.

"Well, well... this is not the treasure I was expecting. What have you brought me, Khamet?"

Paris immediately stepped in front of Helen, cutting off Bay's view. "Chancellor? I am Alexandros, from a minor house in Troy. My friends and I are expected at the Temple of Amun-Re in Heliopolis."

Bay reclined on his stool. "Are you now?" He studied Paris, his eyes glinting with the knowledge of a man who knew far more than he let on.

"They travel on a warship, Chancellor," Khamet added. "With a full contingent of Trojan warriors."

Paris tried to interject, "I never travel with less—"

"So say the men we capture who raid our shores." Bay cut him short. "So say the men who try to bypass this port and cheat our Pharaoh of his well deserved duty. So which are you, Trojan? Mercenary or smuggler?"

Paris chewed back his ire. The chancellor wouldn't dare speak to him so disrespectfully if he claimed his full titles. He could feel Helen beside him, her body language speaking of her similar distrust. Bay was an ant blocking his path from bringing her to safety. He could swallow his pride if it brought him closer to that goal.

"Neither, Chancellor." He grit his teeth. "We were, in fact, beset by pirates before your commander found us. I was fortunate to have my guard. We barely fought them off."

Bay stood and left his desk, crossing the short distance to stand before them. He twisted his short beard in his fingers and stared at Paris with eyes so dark they seemed to swallow the light around them. Even Bay's sunken cheeks seemed cadaverous, as though something ate his flesh from within. "So, you're not a smuggler?" His tone indicated disbelief. "And my men will find nothing suspicious on your vessel when they search it?"

"Of course not." Paris rankled with indignation, wracking his mind to remember if there was anything incriminating on board. "I'll lead your commander through the inspection myself."

Bay turned to Khemet who nodded back. "No need. The inspection is already underway. You may wait here until my man reports."

Paris inhaled sharply. *The gall of this man...* But he made sure his concerns did not reflect on his face, adopting instead the bored airs of courtly indifference. "Good. The sooner it's done, the sooner you can send us on our way."

Bay, however, was finished with him, and he turned his attention now to Helen. "And what is this vision? I am surrounded morning, noon and night by all the beasts of the Nile and you have brought me a lily." He took Helen's hand, bringing it to his lips for a lingering kiss.

Helen stiffened, her skin crawling from where he touched her. "I prefer roses, Chancellor," she responded with a tart tongue. "Roses have thorns. You pay the price if you try to pick them."

"Indeed, My Lady." Bay laughed. He slapped his hands together with two sharp claps and a servant ran into the room. Dressed in a half-skirt of white linen and wearing twin golden bangles wrapped around his arms, the servant bowed low, pressing his forehead to the floor—a display of subservience Helen had rarely seen even for royalty.

"Bring us refreshments," Bay commanded, and more servants ran into the room carrying stools for the official and his guests. Helen took a seat, disturbed by how close Bay chose to sit by her.

"What is your name, My Lady?"

"...Helen." She responded with some hesitancy and could not help but glance nervously to Paris as she spoke. It felt strange to use her real name, but Paris assured her it was safe. Having treated with the Egyptians in the past, he was in greater danger of exposure than she. It was best to lie only when necessary.

"Helen," Bay caressed the word with a thick tongue.

The brazen behavior was too much for Paris to stomach. "You can address your concerns with me," he interjected. If Bay touched Helen again, he was going to crush the man's throat, and Paris didn't fancy his chances of fighting their way out of an armed fort.

"I'm sorry," Bay oozed with insincerity. "Did I say something to upset you? Is this your wife?"

The question stumped Paris and he answered before he gave it much thought. "Well, no—"

"Then you have no reason to deny me, a chancellor in the royal employ of Mighty Egypt, the pleasure of her company." His eyes gleamed with a sadistic joy. "Isn't that right, Alexandros? Forgive me, but which *minor house* did you claim?"

Paris had not the chance to respond as another commander stormed into the room. He was a similar age to Bay, but this Egyptian was built like an ox, robust where Bay was gaunt. The leather breastplate covering his tunic was dented from use, and he held the hilt of his sword with a familiar grip. "Are you conducting military operations in my jurisdiction again, Bay?"

"General Setnakhte." The chancellor took his time to rise from his seat. "How pleasant to see you again."

"None of your games, Bay. Why are your men raiding a galley docked at my city?"

"We found them in the company of pirates—" Khamet tried to interject.

Setnakhte rounded on the man. "Who was speaking to you, *Commander?*" Khamet flinched and shrunk back into his stool. "You overstep your bounds, Bay. Or need I remind you that your powerful friends hold no sway in Heracleion?"

"Is that so?" Bay was clearly not intimidated. If anything, his smile grew. "Then why was I sent here from the capital to clean up your mess? Had you done your duty and purged the raiders from the delta, I wouldn't be forced to spend my days in this rock pile of a city surrounded by imbeciles and base-born mongrels."

Setnakhte flinched at the insult. There was no question of whom Bay meant when he uttered those last words. "And who did you pay for that honor?"

"What does it matter? The tides of power are changing, and in this district, *you* answer to *me,* General. I would think a soldier would understand the concept of chain-of-command."

A fire lit up the general's dark brown eyes. "You play your role well, Chancellor, but never forget, I know from whence you came. You should think twice before you seek to place yourself above honest Egyptians, *you ill-bred cur."*

"Paris," Helen whispered into his ear, her urgent tone pulling him away from the drama unfolding before them. He took her hand and began to quietly inch away from the two irate men. If the Egyptians raided their ship, Glaucus would suspect Paris was in trouble. He would send reinforcements. With Bay and Setnakhte distracted by their heated argument, Paris weighed the wisdom of making a run for it.

"*You should crawl back under that rock in Ugarit where you came from,*" was followed by "*It's a pity a dog does not recognize when its days are done. You should lie down and accept this transition.*"

Paris pulled Helen closer to the door, the princess amazingly adept and silencing her step. As he reached for the latch, it was thrown open from the other side. Sheltering Helen under his arm, Paris pulled her out of the path of the guard who entered.

"Chancellor Bay!" the guard shouted as he rushed into the room. The Egyptian was nearly out of breath and carried a parcel wrapped in cloth.

Bay collected himself and pulled away from his rival. "You'll have to excuse me, General. As much as I enjoy our little talks, I have work to do. And it appears my search has born some fruit."

Paris froze, exchanging a nervous glance with Helen. There was nothing on board that would incriminate them. He was sure of it. His royal signet ring was hidden in the secret pocket of his cloak. If no one talked, Bay had no proof.

The Chancellor unwrapped the parcel and gasped, what he discovered taking his breath away. Paris had only to glimpse the colored reflection of the object's jeweled surface to know his lies had been undone.

You careless fool, he cursed himself. He had forgotten about the *kerykeion*, the scepter only the highest level of diplomat carried. The *kerykeion* insured immunity for the bearer, a person almost always of royal lineage. Setnakhte recognized it. The general immediately stalked over to Paris, violence leaping from his eyes.

"Who sent for you? Which prince?"

Paris pressed Helen behind him and rose to his full height. The time for pretenses was gone. "No one sent us. We are traveling to the Temple in Heliopolis. No farther."

Bay cradled the *kerykeion*, a fevered glow in his eyes. "They are pilgrims, from a minor house of Troy. Why would a minor lord have such a treasure?"

"Don't be stupid," Setnakhte snapped at the chancellor. "He is no minor lord." He turned back to Paris, more desperate than ever. "*Who sent for you?* What is your name?"

Paris opened his mouth, scrambling for the right answer to get him and Helen out of the room safely. But he took too long, and Bay answered for him.

"He said it was Alexandros. Why? Is he lying?" The chancellor tightened his grip on the scepter as though he meant to claim it for his own.

Paris could see the name settle into the general's mind. His eyes widened with shock and he dropped to one knee. "Forgive me, Your Grace. I did not recognize you."

Paris cursed under his breath. He cursed all the Gods and their capricious natures. They took his every fear and made them come to be.

Bay charged to the general's side. "What are you doing? Get up."

But Setnakhte grabbed Bay by his tunic and brought him down to his knees. "He is the second son of King Priam, you fool. He is a prince of Troy."

The sniveling official scowled at Paris with disbelief, the truth crawling over his face like news of the plague.

"That's enough." Paris sighed, waving them back to their feet. He held his hand out expectantly to Bay, and the chancellor reluctantly gave back the *kerykeion*. "I don't know what is going on between you two, and I don't care. I want nothing of it. I spoke the truth. We are traveling to Heliopolis and no farther."

"Of course, Your Grace." Setnakhte ducked his head with

respect. "I'll accompany you to the palace myself."

Paris shook his head. He had to salvage something out of this mess. "No. We are restocking our larder and going to the Temple. I will meet with the vizier afterwards."

Bay and Setnakhte shared a confused look, neither wanting to speak first. "But surely you must know—" Bay started first.

"What?" Paris snapped back.

"The royal family is there." Setnakhte shifted nervously. "Pharaoh and his sons hold court in Heliopolis."

Paris groaned. *The full court?* There would be no escaping notice now. No visiting royal could deny an audience with Pharaoh. Such disrespect would cause a deep rift between their nations. Priam would never condone it.

"Then we are fortunate," Paris lied to them both, feeling the bars of his royal cage locking into place. "Please, General. Lead on. And don't stop until we stand before the king."

He exchanged a quiet nod with Helen, a crease of concern tensing her lovely face. Yes, they would stand before the king, and once there, Paris would have to explain what they were doing in Egypt.

And if Pharaoh didn't like what he heard, there was very little Paris could do about it.

Chapter 11

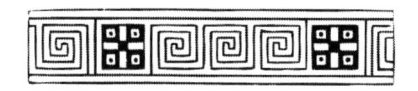

The High King Returns

"STRAIGHTEN YOUR BACK," Clytemnestra snapped at her youngest daughter while fanning herself on the balcony of her royal apartments. Electra scowled in her direction, the girl's tense eight-year-old face resembling her fearsome father more each day. With features so mannish, it would be feat to secure her a proper husband.

"A curtsey is a show of respect." Nestra slapped the wooden fan down in her palm, the sharp sound making the maids jump nervously. "You represent the honor of your house when you bow before a king."

"*I'm trying.*" The girl made another awkward attempt.

Nestra groaned. She was starting to believe the task hopeless. "Iphigenia, please. Show her how."

Her eldest stirred from the padded chair along the chamber wall where she had taken refuge. At nearly twelve, Iphigenia was considered a lady-in-training, having set aside the garments of childhood. Though she wore an ankle length chiton that flowed gracefully over her sun-kissed freckled skin, Iphigenia still lacked the curves that would ultimately declare her of child-bearing age. She remained Nestra's lovely girl.

"Yes, Mother," came her dutiful reply. The princess rose from her perch doing her best to hide the melancholy that invaded their household since news of Helen's abduction became common knowledge. She cast her royal mother the tender smile she had inherited from her aunt and dipped into a curtsey, proceeding to take over Electra's lessons.

Nestra allowed her attention to wander, gazing across the palace grounds towards the Khavos ravine and the turbulent sea beyond. Far off shore, dark storm clouds gathered on the horizon, and forks of purple lightning burned an afterglow into Nestra's eyes. She prayed it was a small squall. Summer heat bred the worst sort of storms, sending even the best mariners down to the depths of Poseidon's realm. With no word from Scylax, Nestra could only assume her twin was still out there, the dangers to her life mounting ever greater.

"That's it!" Iphigenia chimed, clapping at her sister's successful curtsey. "Head held high, and dip." The girls enacted the move in unison, giggling like a pair of maids.

Clytemnestra envied her children and these years of innocence. It was a shame it would be short-lived. Times of war scoured away traces of childhood as quickly as dry tinder took to spark. She remembered her own transition only too well. She had not been much older than Iphigenia when Agamemnon demanded a Spartan bride and forced her to his bed. Innocence was a luxury one could not afford when joining the house of Atreus. She would not have lived long in Mycenae without learning to put aside her childish ways.

"Again," she instructed her daughters, studying their form with her keen eyes, ensuring there was no flaw.

The doors to her chambers flew open and Astyanassa rushed to her side, the raven-haired chambermaid's eyes wide with fear. "The King has returned," she gasped as she knelt by Clytemnestra's side. "He is headed this way."

A vein of panic gripped Nestra's stomach as she steeled her nerves. "Go. And remember what I told you. If anyone asks, you tell them what we agreed and nothing more."

The sultry woman nodded. There was a hint of untamed spirit in the maid that made Nestra more than a little nervous. Everything relied on their interchangeable stories. That hot-blooded vixen had best not fail her now.

Astyanassa scurried back to the door, nearly running head-first into the mountainous chest of Clytemnestra's husband. He shoved the maid out of his way, his obsidian eyes held firmly on his queen.

"Is it true?" Violence simmered beneath his deceptively calm exterior. Nestra lost her voice as she rose on shaky legs.

Iphigenia instantly grabbed Electra by the arm, the two girls inching back towards the door, their eyes darting between their parents. This was far from the first episode they had witnessed between Clytemnestra and her husband. Her eldest had learned early to disappear or share in his wrath.

"Father." Electra strained against her sister's hold, her voice laced with an eagerness to please. "I've missed you, Papa."

Agamemnon ignored her, his body shaking with suppressed rage as his eyes bore into his queen. *"Is it true?!"*

Clytemnestra rushed to her daughters' side, pushing them out of Agamemnon's path with hasty hands. "Go back to your chambers."

Iphigenia began to protest, hesitant to leave her. "But Mother—"

"Now!" Nestra shouted at the girls. The older princess quickly collected her sister, a pained look of concern on her face as they exited the royal apartments.

"Answer me, Woman. Did that perfumed lordling... *take Helen?*" Agamemnon trembled with suppressed rage, and Nestra prayed to Hera he did not find a new outlet of release.

"Yes." The word escaped her clenched throat. "The night after you left. The Trojans escaped under the cloak of darkness, like thieves raiding a village. We did not know of the prince's depravity until well into the next day."

Agamemnon paced the antechamber, eyeing his queen with unveiled disgust. "That was almost a fortnight ago! Why didn't you send for me?"

"You were observing your grandsire's funeral rites, surely that took precedence—" She gasped as his hand whipped out, tightening around her throat.

"*Nothing takes precedence over this!*" He spat on the floor, his eyes wild with wrath. "Curse you, Woman. You sat here on your backside, in the luxury I provide for you, and did nothing!"

She struggled for air, his fingers constricting so tightly she feared her neck would break. "No," she choked out. "Not nothing... I sent...an...assassin," she wheezed, clawing at his hands, black specks dancing across her vision. "To kill the Trojan...and reclaim...what he took from you."

Agamemnon tossed her to the ground and she gulped in precious air. "You stupid woman! You play at politics, meddling in matters you cannot possibly understand." His pacing began anew.

Clytemnestra took a moment to clear her senses. She knew what she said next would determine her fate—hers and Helen's. Rising to her feet, she presented herself before her king, dipping into a humble curtsey Electra would have envied.

"You are right, My Lord. I acted foolishly, believing a swift and deadly response to be best." She flinched as his hand tightened into a fist. Agamemnon was always loath to admit when she spoke sense. It was best to say her piece quickly before his temper ran wild. "I thought such actions would go unnoticed by those who would tarnish your reputation. I am but a woman. I might be queen, but I could not presume to lead in your stead. *You* are the king. And one day soon, you will be High King. The formal response need must come from you."

Slowly, the muscles around his neck unclenched and he lowered his fist. Clytemnestra breathed a sigh of relief, careful not to make any sudden move that would agitate him.

"I *will* be High King," her husband growled with that promise. "And you would do well to remember your place *behind me*. You take too many liberties, Wife."

Clytemnestra lowered her eyes, hoping to mask the spike of rebellion flaring within her. Agamemnon would never be High King without her help. One day he would recognize the benefit of having a Spartan bride at his side. That or pay the consequences of underestimating her potential.

"As you say, My Lord. Your throne and the glory of Mycenae are all that matters."

༄

Agamemnon watched his wife humble herself before him, her moment of humility not enough to mollify his wounded pride. This rebellious behavior was unacceptable. How could he command the respect of the Grecian kings if he could not manage the affairs of his own house?

"Tell me what you know. All of it."

She recanted her tale, of how the prince raided his treasure room and Helen sought to stop him, of how she was taken captive and smuggled to the Trojan ship in the dead of night.

She lies... His fist tightened to strike her for the offense. The Trojans could neither have gotten past his guards at the treasury nor the traps he set within. Why would his wife fabricate these details? But, as his blood rose in temperature while Clytemnestra described the abduction, Agamemnon realized he didn't care.

That fool Trojan took the bait. He could scarcely believe it true. His idle threats and insults had proven enough to spur the insipid prince to this rash action. Helen's abduction was the inconceivable sin, the match that would ignite the flames of war. Tyndareus' ill-conceived Oath could be invoked, and his brother kings were honor-bound to answer his call. Years of planning would now bear fruit.

Agamemnon paced the anteroom of his bedchamber, his mind ablaze. Finally, his grand destiny would be realized. His war with the East was now justified. By the sword, he'd force the lords of the Old World to bend knee to *his rule*. They would tremble before the might of the West! Agamemnon would ascend his throne as Overlord of Greece, enshrined by the will of the Gods, just as Calchas prophesied. He should rejoice at these fortuitous chain of events.

But he did not.

Helen, delectable, sweet Helen, was gone. A white-hot rage burned inside him, threatening to obliterate all of his careful planning. Yes, Helen's abduction gave him a strategic advantage, but the thought of that pretty-boy prince having his way with his golden princess made him sick.

How dare he? I'll gut him like a suckling pig and toss his entrails to the dogs!

That madness bottled up within him. He needed a release. He swung his arm out, sending a decorative vase to the floor, the broken pieces of ceramic cutting into his fist. "A quick death is too good for that Trojan bastard." He turned to his wife and his fist flew free, knocking her across the temple. "*I will make him pay. I will make his whole bloody family pay. And anyone who dares stand in my way.*"

Clytemnestra raised her head, her lapis-blue eyes glaring at him with an unbroken spirit. Blood trickled down her face from a gash where her head had hit the stone. "His death *will not* be quick," his queen uttered with heat, picking herself off the ground. Her hate-filled gaze was flush with the same jealousy that raged within him, whether for the Trojan or Agamemnon himself, he could not tell. His wife was always prickly in matters regarding her twin. The first time she confronted him about his infidelity was also the last.

This display of Spartan courage deeply aroused him. It had been too long since he last showed her the rightful treatment of a king to his queen. Too long since he reminded her of the power he wielded over her body. He grabbed

THE PRINCESS OF PROPHECY

Clytemnestra by the throat again, pulling her to him for a bruising embrace. She did not resist. Only the spark of fury in her eyes gave hint of the spirit battling within.

He tore at her chiton, the embroidered fabric falling to the floor in rags. Pressing her down on their bed, he savaged her throat and breasts with a bestial hunger, his fingers crushing her tender flesh to him. With a few short moves, he rid himself of his kingly garments and mounted her, his frustrations fueling each powerful thrust until she cried out in a mix of pain and pleasure.

How different from her twin, his wife was. Clytemnestra hid nothing, defiant, daring him to do his worst. His queen seemed to welcome this exchange of wills, as though each tangle between the sheets somehow made her stronger, like a warrior who survived the battlefield.

Helen, in contrast, quietly accepted his attentions. Her soft yielding was intoxicating, some portion of her spirit hidden away, a tantalizing treat he could never reach. The promise of capturing that tender morsel kept him returning to her bed. She was a treasure his brother had no idea how to savor. One day he would possess her again.

With a shuddering cry, he climaxed, pumping his seed deep within his queen. He collapsed on top of her, feeling a peace he hadn't experienced in weeks.

"Clean yourself up," he commanded, pressing his lips to her ear as she squirmed beneath him. "You'll tell this tale to the *lawagetas* lords, and when the time comes, to the kings who assemble. You *will not* say one word that is not first cleared by me. Nod if you understand."

She nodded, a touch of fear-tinged respect finally constricting her face. He rose from the bed and donned his clothes. With strict instructions that he expected her in the megaron within the hour, he left the royal apartments.

He stormed down the long corridor, his confidence growing with each stride. He was but a child when Apollo's priest prophesied his grand destiny, but those words strummed through his veins with the same power.

Through a sea of blood and betrayal of kin, will the son of Atreus rise to power. All will bow to his majesty, and from the ashes of his victory, the world will be made anew.

Agamemnon would unite the Hellas. His destiny as High King was writ in the stars. It was time now to collect his crown.

And it all began with Troy.

Chapter 12

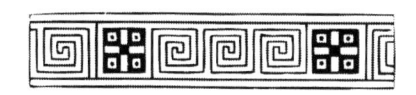

The Cobra Lies in Wait

THE ACRID SMOKE of torch fire stung Scylax' eyes as he travelled deeper into the dungeons of Heliopolis. Kenamon set a good pace. The Egyptian royal guard, though off-duty, wore the light armor of his office. Like many of his fellow guardsmen, Kenamon provided information to those who could pay, and if the purse was fat enough, he even provided favors.

Scylax kept a watchful eye on his Egyptian guide. Only a fool trusted someone who sold secrets. Too soon, one found himself paying for silence as well as information.

The prison corridor, although connected to the royal palace, angled downward and further away from the acropolis. The design was ingenious, following the septic lines back to the Nile, the refuse of society housed with the waste of the highborn. In Egypt, anyone who disrupted the established order of the realm was considered a loathsome creature, a traitor and miscreant.

A fire burned in Scylax' belly. It was not so long ago he walked these halls in chains, a prisoner of war. He knew intimately why the the Crown kept its prisoners stationed far out of sight where the sounds of their tortured cries could not reach refined ears. If not for a young healer of Isis, he would have died in the dank underbelly of Heliopolis' dungeons.

They neared a blind corner. Kenamon raised a hand to signal a stop, and Scylax immediately pressed back into the shadows, the cool touch of the stone walls tensing his muscles.

"*Wait here,*" Kenamon whispered, handing over the torch. "*The guards make rounds at top of hour. I will see, make sure they go, and collect you.*" He spoke in a pidgin language that was part Egyptian, part Greek, and part Akkadian, the universal language for the swordsmen who hailed from so many distant lands. Scylax made it a point to feign ignorance of the full Egyptian tongue. Men who could not be trusted often showed their hand when confident they could not be overheard.

Kenamon turned to go, but Scylax grabbed the man by the tunic. "*Be quick. Or I find you.*" He lifted the hilt of his sword so the guard did not mistake his meaning. Kenamon nodded nervously and slipped around the corner.

Slowly, the stillness of the place surrounded him. In the distance, a whistle of wind and steady drip of water echoed down the tunnels to Scylax' ears. With it came the muffled moans of human misery.

A chill that was not caused by the night breeze invaded Scylax. This deception was necessary. He needed access to the palace, and that required adopting a subterfuge that allowed him to maneuver openly. Foreigners weren't allowed this deep into Egypt without special permission. Only nobles and slaves were permitted, and since the prospect of impersonating a royal was beyond reprehensible to him, the dungeon was his only solution.

I am in control this time, he tried to reassure himself, but the months he spent in the black cells of this prison were enough to scar a rational man for life. It was fortunate for Scylax that during his time here, he had been far from rational.

Unwelcome memories flooded him. Of his time in the torture chambers and the wicked bronze tools designed for mummification his captors used instead on living informants. Of the initiate of Isis who was forced to heal him so he might last through the enhanced interrogations. If not for Dora, he would have lost himself to madness in this place. He would have ended his life on a suicidal mission to kill every petty king and royal bootlicker who betrayed him. But under her tender care, she showed him another way. Scylax discovered he was living to die and failing to embrace the possibility of something better.

A rat scurried down the corridor, its padded feet shying away from the circle of light thrown by his torch. It paused just outside the ring and rose on its hind legs, sniffing the space between them, curious. Scylax chuckled at its bold behavior. It was a good reminder of how ruthless scavengers thrived in the Two Lands. He would not survive unless he became just as ruthless.

The rat's ears twitched as footsteps rang out down the hall. Kenamon was returning. The rodent flattened itself to the floor and melted into the shadows. Scylax wished he could do the same. Having returned to Egypt, the land of whispers and double meaning, under the command of another royal, he was more confused than ever. He felt the mountain of stone pressing down on him, forcing him into the world he had long tried to escape.

The guard stepped around the corner and froze, staring at Scylax in disbelief. So lost in thought, it took Scylax several wasteful moments to realize this man was *not Kenamon*. When the guard's partner stepped beside him, Scylax finally sprang to action.

Scylax thrust his torch into the face of the first guard. The young man screamed in pain, backing up into the path of his partner. Scylax unsheathed his sword and crouched into a fighting stance.

You stupid fool. How could you be so careless? To mistake the footfalls of two guards for one? It was sloppy. Missing such details would get him killed.

The second guard untangled himself, leaping over his partner and into Scylax' reach. It was an arrogant move, one made by inexperience. Gauging by the smooth curve of his hairless cheeks, this guard was barely old enough to be called a man. Scylax envisioned the thrust that would put his enemy down, a single plunge through the heart, but when he shifted his weight to complete the move, he hesitated.

He's only a boy...

The Egyptian guard, however, did not hesitate, and his return stroke came dangerously close to Scylax' head. He blocked the blade by instinct, his counterstroke slicing cleanly through the man's throat. The guard fell to the floor, his mouth frothing with bloody saliva.

Scylax could not take his eyes off the dying soldier, the first man he had killed in five years. Some part of him registered that Kenamon had returned, his hireling snapping the other guard's neck as he groaned on the floor, but Scylax' sole focus was for the man at his feet. He knelt down beside him and watched the guard bleed out, a silent witness as the spark of life diminished in his fright-filled eyes.

A chill of remorse washed over Scylax. That boy was someone's son. Was there a wife who would never see her husband again, a child who would never know its father? He shook uncontrollably as a darkness began to take root inside of him.

You cannot think this way. He tried to collect himself. *If you are unmade at the death of some Egyptian lackey, how will you manage to kill a prince?*

Slowly, he rose to his feet. With a shuddering breath, he crushed those weak feelings into the void, letting the emptiness that remained fill him with quiet strength. But as his body drained of emotion, he could not help but feel it was wrong.

I don't want to be this person...

"*We must go.*" Kenamon urged him, panic leaking into the guard's voice. "*Before they find.*"

They mustn't find, not if Scylax expected his plan to work. He turned menacingly toward his uncertain ally, his voice laced with cool detachment. "Remove body first. Crocodile pit. Is near. You follow." He grabbed the arms of the man he killed and lifted him over his shoulder.

Kenamon moved to do the same, a suspicious look tensing his face. "How you know?"

Scylax didn't answer him. *He knew.* As all the prisoners of this dungeon knew. The masters insisted on feeding the royal crocs with live prey. Witnessing the deed was mandatory. The masters claimed it "good for morale".

After a few turns deeper into the darkness, the air became less oppressive. The stench of decay was mixed with bog water, and a small eddy of wind made the hall feel almost pleasant. Almost. An open window not much more than a rough break in the wall overlooked the interior of an adjacent tower. Some seventy-five feet below rested the muddy flat of the royal croc pen. Scylax lifted his kill over the edge, turning away before the body landed with a wet splash.

Kenamon mimicked his move, shuffling to keep ahead of Scylax as they returned to the main hall. The guard continued to glance over his shoulder at him, his nervous eyes asking what his cowardly tongue would not... *who are you?*

Scylax schooled his face to blankness, uncertain of that answer.

They passed several doors, some emitting soft groans and painful moans that indicated they were occupied, others as silent as the tomb. At one of the deeper levels, Kenamon finally stopped. Retrieving a ring of keys from his waistband, he set about unlocking a wooden door set into walls four feet thick.

The door groaned on rusty hinges as it swung open. Kenamon tried to wave Scylax through first, but after a severe shake of his head, the guardsman scrambled through the portal. Scylax followed, torch in hand.

It was a wide interior where the prisoners were kept. Each

man was shackled to the wall, afforded just enough chain to lie flat. Though they were dressed in fine linens, like the palace pets Scylax assumed they must be, the truth of their bondage was in their eyes: those empty pools of hopelessness. Some hardly stirred, their will to live barely present. Others sat up, fearful of what new torture this visitation would bring.

Scylax lifted his torch higher, surveying the company of men. Greek men. *His men*. Prisoners of an ill-fated war, these wretched souls were unfortunate to have survived the treachery of the craven Libyan king who hired them. They were strong enough to survive five years in captivity, but not enough to have escaped, as Scylax had. Some he recognized, others he did not, but—as a commander of great renown— they all recognized *him*.

Shocked whispers rippled throughout the slaves. Cries of *"He has come!"* to *"Free us, Commander!"*

Kenamon grimaced, his lip curling back in disgust at the prisoners as they continued to beg. When one strayed too close to the Egyptian, he kicked the man away, spitting on his head. *"Back off, you meshwesh filth."*

Scylax' heart turned to ice. He leaned in close to Kenamon, his voice dropping dangerously. *"Plan?"*

The guard pointed to the huddled masses. *"These belong to Crown Prince. You join. Take place. Overseer come each day. Collect you for work. I come back one week time."*

There was a brilliance to the plan, infiltrating the palace through those the Crown sought to conquer, but knowing Egyptian bureaucracy the way Scylax did, there was one major flaw. No overseer worthy of the title would overlook a miscount of heads.

"Join?"

Kenamon nodded, and without a second's hesitation, he lifted the nearest prisoner, a middle-aged pikeman with slanted eyes common from the Siculi islands, and thrust his sword into the man's chest.

Breath escaped Scylax. The hopeful cries of the other

prisoners silenced, and they quickly turned their heads, fearful of drawing attention. Kenamon hacked through the dead man's arms, freeing his shackles as though he were nothing more than a pig at the slaughter.

"*Join.*" He pointed to the space the man occupied. "*Take place.*"

Red clouded Scylax' vision. The hilt of his dagger had somehow found its way into his hand. It demanded to be feed. His pulse roaring in his ears, Scylax plunged the knife into Kenamon's neck.

The Egyptian made to scream, but Scylax twisted his blade, severing the man's tongue. As Kenamon spasmed in his hold, Scylax jammed his fist into the Egyptian's mouth, yanking free his foul tongue. When the guard kicked his last, he let the man fall to the floor with a thud.

Scylax took a deep, shuddering breath. His blood raced through his body, adrenaline coursing through his veins. Every nerve was taut, his senses hypersensitive. This was the feel of death he long remembered. His blood sang with it.

Beat by beat, his heart returned to a normal rate, and the world came back into focus. He looked down on the mangled corpse at his feet, surprised he did not feel the same remorse he had in the hall.

With a sharp laugh, he realized the difference. This was the sweet satisfaction of killing a man who deserved to die. The other slaves shirked away from him in fear, mistaking his amusement for something more maniacal. His mirth was aimed at himself, for ever doubting he was capable of completing this task.

Egypt would not claim him for a second time, and neither would the royals who sought to manipulate him. He would complete the queen's task, but on *his terms*.

He was ready now to meet the Trojan prince.

Chapter 13

The Court of the Sun

HELIOPOLIS, THE CITY of the sun. Helen's breath caught as she spied her first glimpse of the magnificent site. The Egyptian holy city was the origin of all life on Earth, or so the mystics claimed. Broad avenues lined with towering obelisks sparkled in the midday sun. The pyramid-tipped columns varied in color, and led in perfect symmetry to the distant acropolis above the flood plains of the Nile. Enormous buildings, of which Helen had never seen the like, populated the eastern bank, their plastered facades covered in dazzling reliefs like panels of history displayed for eternity.

She and Paris, along with a small retinue of Trojan guards, sailed up the river aboard Setnakhte's military barge. Her prince stood rigid, unable to relax for even a moment. He watched the still waters of the Nile like one expecting to be swallowed by them. The revelation of his royal status had afforded them a modicum of respect, but with it came obligations. Paris became distant, guarding his thoughts and feelings as was expected by a diplomat. For the first time since leaving Mycenae, she felt the layers of duty and propriety return, threatening to separate them.

She whispered a prayer to Aphrodite that this sojourn on

foreign soil would be short, that they could visit the Temple and be swiftly back in route to Troy. But viewing the city from afar, Helen could tell there was nothing swift about this place. A timeless beauty permeated every sculpted stone. The air teemed with magic. Helen found herself as captivated by this strange land as she was frightened of it.

Can the priests really absolve a person of their past sins, as Paris claims?

That nagging thought would not leave her be. For ten years, Helen clung to hope that the Goddess would fulfill the prophecy She had made to her so many years ago. Paris was her great destiny, she was sure of it. Even marrying Menelaus, and all the horrors that followed, was a necessary step down the path that led her to him. If the Gods truly planned for them to be together, could this purification ritual be their path forward? A way to legitimize their union before Gods and Men?

She scolded herself for indulging those frivolous thoughts, but ever since she agreed to Paris' plan to present herself to the Trojan court, she had been desperate to find another way. If only she could talk to Paris, to see if her hopes were even possible... but there was no time to get him alone.

Helen sighed heavily and pulled her shawl around her head, blocking out the intense rays of the sun. She turned back to gaze upon the city. Its brilliant colors were an oasis of life against a backdrop of yellow sand. Along the banks of the Nile, where green patches of reed and palm grew, fishermen hoisted nets into the water. On the flood plains, teams of workers collected the harvest: cabbage, onions, and a variety of other vegetables that sprouted from the nutrient-rich black soil. Other men, naked to the waist with sun-bronzed skin, used hoe and shovel to reconstruct the irrigation canals leading off the river.

Everywhere Helen looked, Egyptians went about their daily lives, the industrious people a thriving hub of activity and purpose. A few workers looked up from their toils as the barge passed, but seeing the royal standard flying from the mast, they quickly averted their eyes. It was an odd experience for Helen who was often received warmly by her common folk.

"It is truly a marvelous city." Bay slid beside her quietly. "*If* you have the right connections." His narrow eyes alluded to where she might find some.

Helen shivered. The chancellor insisted on accompanying their delegation, apparently as eager as the general for an audience with the royal court. He had barely left her side for the duration of their short voyage from Heracleion. With the general watching over Paris like a hawk, she was forced to deal with the unpleasant man on her own, and she was tiring of finding excuses to avoid him.

"It is beautiful," she offered pleasantly through clenched teeth, knowing how unwise it would be to make an enemy of the man. Bay reminded her of Rhopalus, one of Agamemnon's toadies. The Mycenaean Master-of-Arms hoarded power and influence like a badger defending its den. Though his strength came from the company he kept, the man's head was swollen with self-importance. Any insult to his person was met triple-fold, and not in the manner his enemy expected. Rhopalus once had a man's wife stoned for adultery because the woman refused his advances. Any man who pulled himself from obscurity to advise the royal ears was either highly accomplished or uniquely ambitious. Bay did not strike her as the former.

"Beautiful." Bay's voice dripped with unspoken meaning. "How astute of you."

"My Lady?" Aethra stepped between them. Her dark eyes dropped to the deck, a seeming gesture of deference, though Helen didn't miss her flash of indignation. "I have your things prepared, if you'd like to see?" Bay instantly gave the woman space, his lip curling in disgust. He pulled his hands away as though proximity to a slave might contaminate him in some way.

"Yes, of course." Helen silently blessed her thoughtful matron. "Chancellor." She dipped her head as way of dismissal and followed Aethra to the bow as the ship pulled into port.

Once they disembarked at the city dock, Paris took the lead of their delegation with the general and chancellor. He had switched out his travel clothes for the fine spun tunic of ivory he wore when she first met him. Adding in his crimson cape, the fabric so vibrant it was easily the richest patch of color in their decorated surroundings, he was a regal sight.

Helen, in contrast, opted for something demure. Her chiton was ivory as well, but unadorned with no sign of embroidery or flourish. On her left shoulder, the fabric was pinned with a golden fibula in the shape of an eagle, a symbol of her homeland that filled her with pride. Aethra hoisted a standard over her head to provide shade and Helen immediately grabbed the woman's arm.

"You shouldn't."

"I should," her matron insisted. Aethra gestured to the packed avenues where the lowborn scurried out of foot from more elite passengers. Many of the nobles were carried in palanquins, and not a single upper class citizen lacked an entourage of servants. "It is what they deem proper."

Helen dropped her hand and nodded, letting Aethra do as she pleased. As they walked, she could not help but feel exposed. Pulling her shawl around her face, she blocked herself from view. She needn't have worried. Trailing behind a Trojan diplomat, she might as well have been invisible. A single woman was little more than an idle curiosity compared to a foreign prince. Paris was the source of many heated whispers and excited gestures.

They made quick time to the acropolis, the raised mound sharing only the barest resemblance to the towering hills of Greece. Setnakhte led them to the palace, a complex so large it dwarfed any construction in the whole of the Hellas. A garden of sculpted plants opened up to a processional walkway, the narrow avenue lined on both sides with statues of kneeling bulls. The stone animals' elegant horns pointed to the mid-day sun.

And the palace itself! Towering pylons framed enormous portal doors, from a distance resembling the U-shaped throne of the kings of the Old World. On either side, massive stone statues guarded the entrance, the seated figures carved from a single block of polished, black basalt.

"Are they Gods?" Helen gazed up at the colossi in amazement. They towered some sixty feet above them.

"They are pharaohs," Paris answered, both he and Glaucus dropping back from their Egyptian entourage to join her while Setnakhte arranged for the gates to be opened. "But in Egypt, their king is a God." He shook his head, leaving his criticism of the Egyptian theocracy unspoken. "He is the living embodiment of Horus and gains immortality with death. Pharaoh is a supreme being. Remember that if they ask you to speak to him."

Helen grimaced. Honoring oneself above, or equal, to the Gods was blasphemy in Greece. It was an invitation for the Immortals to remind their human counterparts of the fragile nature of living flesh. Yet, Helen could not help but stare in awe. Surely some divine force favored this land to bless them with such abundance. Even in the far reaches of Sparta, she'd heard tales of Heliopolis.

"Helen," Paris hesitated, unsure how to explain the viper's den they were walking into. "Trust no one. No matter how sweet their smiles nor innocent their questions. Promise me."

She was taken aback by his intensity. Before she could answer, the massive gates began to stir. The ominous grind of stone on stone rang jarringly in her ears. The doors slid out, locking into deep grooves in the ground with a resounding boom. From the interior courtyard, General Setnakhte marched toward them with a contingent of royal guards.

"The court is assembled in the main hall, but I cannot present you yet." The silver-haired commander's face was pinched with irritation.

"Why not?" Paris looked over the general's shoulder to Bay, searching for some inkling of what lay in wait.

"They have discovered a new Mnevis bull," the chancellor offered, also with a touch of irritation. "Pharaoh must anoint the beast in service to Amun-Re. When the ceremonies are completed, *I* will bring you before the throne."

It seemed Setnakhte was none-too-pleased about that division of duty. He gripped his sword tightly and adopted the air of command he had in Heracleion.

"Follow me."

❖

They entered the palace through a set of columned porticos, the first courtyard open to the air with thick pillars stretching almost as high as the mud brick walls behind them. Setnakhte led onward without comment, stopping before a set of royal guards holding body-length staves tipped with curved blades. The men recognized Setnakhte immediately and moved aside, giving him access to the palace interior.

Helen entered the palace after him, the thin soles of her sandals slapping against the flagstone floor of the entry hall. The space was enormous, its corbeled ceiling soaring a hundred feet above her. A dozen columns, thinner and more richly decorated than those outside, divided the room into a set of corridors. Each wing branched off into even more corridors half the height of the room they stood in now. It created the dizzying affect of a labyrinth where one descended into the depths of the palace.

Helen was instantly disorientated as the general wove through a series of intersections, the stoic man leading ever onwards. In a manner of seconds she was hopelessly lost. The sheer scale of the architecture dwarfed her. She had no doubt the palace could have fit three Mycenaean fortresses side by side. Before such grandeur, she could not help but feel insignificant.

A spike of stubborn defiance flared within her. She squared her shoulders and lifted her chin. Perhaps others walked these halls and quivered with inferiority, but not a daughter of Sparta.

Nor a prince of Troy. Paris marched ahead of her, his eyes locked forward and his step confident. She was determined to match him stride for stride.

Bay and Setnakhte walked alongside each other, setting a fast pace as though each man vied to outdistance the other. She could not tell which man she distrusted more. Bay was a loathsome creature. There were a sick desperation and lust behind his vacant eyes. He was clearly a man without scruples. But Setnakhte was dangerous too, if in a different way. When he cornered Paris at the Heracleion fort demanding information on the Trojan envoy, she was certain he would have killed them all had Paris given the wrong answer. Such strength of conviction could be honorable... *if* the soldier fought on the side of justice. A distinction yet to be determined.

Trust no one. Paris' wise words echoed back to her.

They turned down another corridor and the distant sound of music greeted them. The instruments were familiar to her — a mixture of flute, harp and lyre, but the melody was distinctly foreign. It was strangely seductive, as though the plucky chords tugged directly on some force inside her.

Setnakhte halted just outside the main audience hall and Helen and Paris peered past him into a crowded room beyond. The throne room of Pharaoh was a spacious hall. Its vaulted ceiling was supported by two rows of columns. Between those columns several hundred nobles and officials milled about. The center of the room was open from the entry doors all the way to the throne, creating a processional walkway to a raised dais where the royal family presided over the gathering.

A band of female musicians performed before the throne, the women attired in shimmering gowns of sheer silk. Across from them, a troupe of dancers wove around the room, contorting into bends and flips with acrobatic ease. The dancers were both male and female, and wore only a colorful wrap about their hips. Some held ribbons, the vibrant colors of red, yellow and blue spinning in the air with their elegant moves.

Beside each pillar stood a priest, a censor of burning incense dangling from a chain in his folded hands. Each man was shorn of hair, and his body was draped in the archaic white robes of his office. As the dancers spun past them, they stared forward, never blinking.

The dancers came together in the center of the room, bending over backwards like petals of a flower unfolding before the sun. Their steps were in perfect timing with the quickening tempo of music. Beside the throne, a gong was struck, the resonant note hanging in the air. Dancers and musicians scurried out of the way as the crowd broke into a quiet hum of anticipation.

Helen craned her neck, trying to get a better view. As the musicians tapped a steady beat on their drums, a young calf was led into the hall by a coterie of female attendants. The animal shook with fear, cooing softly. His forlorn cry echoed throughout the chamber and back to the Trojans waiting in the corridor. It was a pitiful sound that reminded Helen of many similar scenes from her childhood. A pang of sorrow flooded her, knowing the future did not bode well for the poor creature.

He was a magnificent animal, even for one so young. His coat was the sleek black of the finest obsidian. Someone had bathed him in milk, making his hair shine under the light of a dozen braziers burning throughout the throne room. The attendants pranced before him, sprinkling lotus petals before the calf's hooves, their sleek young bodies and perfumed wigs making the women almost identical in appearance. Once they were within ten feet of the throne, the women fell to the floor, prostrating themselves before their king.

But the man who descended from the high seat wore no crown. His head was covered in a short black wig, a simple band of gold circling his noble brow. His skin was bronzed, a noticeable shade lighter than the workers Helen had spied in the fields. About his waist he wore a *shendyt*, a pleated kilt that fell to his knees and gathered into an ornate pendant at his pelvis. Bands of electrum decorated his well sculpted triceps and on his chest was the most elaborate piece of jewelry Helen had ever seen. The pectoral, in a dazzling display of color, hung to his breast and was inlaid with ivory, lapis-lazuli, garnet, and faience. He was of a similar age to Paris, but where her prince frequently wore a studious frown, this man smiled and effused an air of leisure and indulgence. Was this truly a God-king?

Paris drew a sharp breath and turned to their guides. "Where is Pharaoh?"

Setnakhte instantly shushed him. Chancellor Bay, ignoring his companion's dark glares, leaned in close to Helen and whispered in her ear. "The Crown Prince Seti II. A marvelous specimen of Egyptian nobility, wouldn't you agree?"

Helen stiffened and shifted away from the chancellor. "I couldn't rightfully say."

Inside the hall, Seti lifted an ornate headdress from a pillow offered by a priest. Two tusks of ivory framed a thin plate of hammered gold, the centerpiece shaped into a perfect circle. As Seti raised the sun-disk high, the musicians lifted their voices in a light hymn.

"Re, I call upon Him, in all His names, to provide protection for His chosen. To preserve the Mnevis' flesh in health, strengthen his muscles, maintain all his members in good condition and plenitude for all eternity, just as certain as Re rises in His solar barque across the sky." The prince placed the headdress on the calf's head, tying it into place. The poor creature could scarcely keep its head up.

Seti clapped his hands and servants spilled out of hidden alcoves carrying heavily ladened trays of food. They placed the trays in a fan around the calf. The steamy fragrance of stewed meat blended with the perfumed incense of the room to make a sickly-sweet aroma.

"Accept this banquet, Mnevis of Re, from your venerable father Horus, the Great God of the Sky. He praises you, He loves you, He preserves you, He strikes down all your foes!" The prince's voice rang out with authority.

The calf was too frightened to eat, so the female attendants took plates from the trays and tried to entice the beast, offering up the morsels like prayers before an altar. When it was clear the animal would not cooperate, Seti clapped again, signaling that the ceremony was over. The dancers and musicians started back up, and the hall broke out into light conversation.

"What of the calf?" Helen broke their company's silence, her curiosity getting the best of her.

"He is Mnevis of Re." Bay smiled at her ignorance. "He will retire to the temple where a whole priesthood and harem of heifers awaits him. You are fortunate to see this. A new Mnevis bull is only selected once every fifteen years."

"They don't eat him?"

"Of course not!" Setnakhte gagged at her innocent question.

Bay moved to intercede, but Paris stepped between them, his hulking presence a warning for the chancellor to keep his distance. "The Mnevis is a sacred animal endowed with the gift of prophecy, or so the priests claim. They will honor him as a god so long as he lives."

Helen turned back to the room, watching the attendants fawn over the innocent calf with a new understanding. They beseeched the animal for favor, cooing like vestal virgins before Aphrodite's altar.

Over an animal? She shook her head in disbelief. The practice seemed barbaric to her, like those of the pagan tribal men who dwelt in the northern ice lands. This place was truly as mysterious as it was strange.

"Are you ready now?" came Setnakhte's terse response.

THE PRINCESS OF PROPHECY

The general was oddly tense, like a man expecting a knife to be pulled on him.

"Whenever you are." Paris motioned Glaucus and his royal guard forward.

The Trojan and Egyptian guards preceded them into the hall, marching directly to the royal dais. With the jubilant atmosphere of the room, they stirred little notice. The crown prince lounged on a gilded chair, one leg strewn over its arm, as two servants cooled him with colorful fans of ostrich feathers. He was surrounded by various officials and a handful of elegant nobles. An expression of idle curiosity lit up his smooth face as he watched them approach. Bay immediately stepped before the prince and dipped into low bow.

"Your Grace," the chancellor simpered.

But Seti looked past the bald official to his military commander. "I thought you were stationed in the Delta, Setnakhte. What brings you to court?"

Chancellor Bay, reluctantly, quickly made room for his rival. Setnakhte stepped forward and fell to one knee. "An unexpected guest who needed a chaperone, My Prince." He waved Paris forward. "May I present Prince Paris of Troy, second son of King Priam." Ignoring the ugly sneer from Bay, the general stationed himself between the royal household and the Trojan host, his eyes darting between Seti and the other members on the dais, searching for the-Gods-only-knew-what.

"Your Highness." Paris bowed before Seti, holding the *kerykeion* out before him.

On sight of him, Seti leaned forward, his forehead furrowed in thought. "Do I know you?"

"It was a long time ago, Your Highness, but yes." Paris settled into a relaxed stance, allowing his role as diplomat to take control of his facilities. This opening of courtesies was a familiar role for him, and he knew to adopt the manner of his host or risk countless offense. Seti, it appeared, preferred a casual atmosphere. "I came to Memphis for the coronation of your father Merneptah."

"That's right." Seti pushed back into his cushioned seat. "Troy has long been friend and ally of the realm. May Amun-Re's light shine on you, Prince Paris." The prince sounded certain, but he gave a quick glance over his shoulder to a heavily robed advisor for confirmation. When the vizier nodded, a flash of color drew Paris' attention to the shadowed eaves of the platform.

He froze. *It was impossible.* The woman standing behind the throne was certainly a princess of Egypt, her dress and jewelry distinctly identified her from the Two Lands. *But that face...* sharp and angular with a yellow-tinged pallor, was not Egyptian. She had the blood of the Hatti in her veins, he would swear to it.

There was no doubt the princess was a great beauty. Her thick jet-black hair was natural, unusual for an Egyptian court that standardized the use of wigs. Her full bosom and lush curves were accented by a tight fitting dress, the gossamer fabric as light as spun gold. Her narrow hazel-green eyes, eyes that would have stuck an average man dumb, stared directly at him. He shivered despite the humid warmth.

A sharp grunt pulled Paris back to himself. The disgruntled sound came from the general beside him. Paris stepped back from the dais, trying to mask the revulsion he felt for his ancient enemy, a hatred that was instilled in his bones.

She is Egyptian, you fool. Not Hatti. He tore his eyes away from the royal woman just as Seti addressed him again.

"What brings our northern allies to the City of the Sun?"

"A spontaneous sojourn, Your Highness." Paris collected himself. "I am returning home from a voyage to Mycenae. I wished to show my companion the splendors of the Temple. Fortune graced us that the royal family was at court."

"Fortune, indeed." Seti nodded. "We are always pleased to host our Trojan friends. Welcome and well met, Prince Paris. I pray your company provides a much desired diversion to the crown before the river inundates again." He waved his guard forward, this final sign of acceptance apparently what Setnakhte was waiting for.

"We found the Trojans in the channels beset by pirates, My Prince." The general addressed the throne, the set of his shoulders indicating some minor attempt to relax. "The reavers are becoming more brazen in their attempts."

A stir of upset rippled amongst the gathered nobles. Bay stepped forward, his face flushed an angry red, discontent to be ignored any longer. "You should clear out the rabble, Great Prince. Take a phalanx of your best charioteers and chase them back to deserts and beyond. If you rode at the vanguard, like your noble father once did, victory would be assured!"

"*You dare?*" Seti snapped, a flash of anger directed at his chancellor. Every noble on the dais took an involuntary step back. "You open your mouth and I hear my brother's words parroted out to me. Do you serve the crown, Bay? Or Amenmesse?"

Bay immediately dropped to his knees, kissing the floor before the throne. "The crown, Your Highness! I serve Egypt and all Her glory. *You.*"

"Good. You'd do well to remember that." Seti settled back into his throne, his eyes ablaze. "My place is here, Bay. Not in the field, and not chasing rebels. I should strap your ears for spouting such foolishness while Pharaoh is ill."

Paris tensed. Seti's lightning fast switch to full fury was shocking. It was dangerous to deal with rulers who ran so hot and cold. The crown prince's moment of ire, however, was quickly masked with a false smile, and he turned back to Paris, a shade of embarrassment lingering on his face. "I am distressed you encountered troubles. These Sea-Peoples are becoming a greater nuisance. Some five years prior, Father dealt them a hefty blow, but still they continue to grow in numbers."

"Pirates trouble the northern seas as well," Paris agreed delicately, his eyes alert for any sign that would set the crown prince into a rage. "My father has formed an armada to keep them from Troy's golden shores. But Your Highness, did I hear you correctly? Is Pharaoh ill?"

A shadow of grief fell over Seti, and he slumped into his chair. "Pharaoh's light wanes on the western horizon. Soon he will join the Gods in the eternal twilight, and my time will rise as king of the Two Lands. The physicians say he will not see the river swell."

Paris swallowed a nervous lump. "My condolences, Noble Prince. We should not disturb you in your hour of grief. If it pleases you, I can retire to Temple and be about my business. My father is expecting a swift return at any rate."

"Nonsense." Seti waved off his protests. "As I said before, your company will be a much desired distraction from the events at hand. Stay, enjoy the endless summer." His invitation was resoundingly final and had the feel of command.

Of all the ill-fated luck... Paris cursed silently. He had witnessed the transference of power in Egypt before. It was not an experience he wished to repeat.

"I am honored by your hospitality." Paris began with slight hesitation, unsure how to continue without offending his host. "A respite in the Eternal Lands will be most welcome. Truthfully, though, I cannot dally long. My father *is* expecting our return."

"And your companion?" Seti asked, one eyebrow raised as he looked past Paris to the princess.

Helen had tried to stay inconspicuous throughout the royal exchange. They conversed in Egyptian, so she could not follow their conversation at any rate. She did her best to absorb what she could with her eyes.

To Helen, Seti's pampered manner seemed out of place for a ruling monarch, and the nobles behind him had neither the decency nor grace to mask their ill-mood. Their stiff posture and dark glares spoke of a haughty nature that oozed insult. Only the woman standing directly behind the throne, a princess of such exquisite beauty Helen had rarely seen her equal, held her composure. Her hazel eyes glinted with curiosity as she studied Helen from afar.

As Paris continued to converse with the regent, Helen found her attention wavering, and her eyes strayed over to the Mnevis. The calf cowered away from his attendants. He now wore several wreaths of flowers along with the enormous headdress.

Poor thing, she thought to herself, locking eyes with the terrified animal. She was so enraptured with the creature that when Paris took hold of her hand to pull her forward, she was taken completely off-guard.

"ⲁⲛⲁ ⲱⲟ ⲙⲓⲅⲧ ⲧⲣⲓⲱ ⲃⲉ?" Seti leaned toward her, an amused twinkle in his eyes.

"Introduce yourself," Paris interpreted into her ear.

Gracefully removing the shawl from her head, she dipped into an elegant curtsy. "I am Helen, Your Grace. From the—"

"She's an Islander," the robed vizier cut her off, hissing viciously and speaking in perfect Greek. "*From the North!*"

Helen was unprepared for such a negative reception. Every noble within hearing distance broke out into shocked whispers, pointing at her with angry fingers. She turned to Paris for direction, but he was at as much a loss as she.

"*Nemhet!*" Seti rebuked his official. "ⲙⲓⲛⲁ ϩⲟⲩⲣ ⲧⲟⲛⲅⲉ."

But the vizier was not content to follow commands. "You should heed my words, Highness. An unannounced foreigner lands on our soil caught in the company of pirates, and in his midsts he brings one of *them*? Pharaoh rots in his bed. You should not treat with those who tried to unseat him!"

How dare he? Helen bristled with deep offense. Even Menelaus at his most paranoid would not speak so brazenly of a guest before the court. "*Them?*" She could not keep the heat from her voice. "I know not whom you speak, but I am a Princess of Sparta. Disparage my honor at your shame!"

A stunned silence followed her words. Too late Helen realized she had exposed herself. She was not supposed to claim her parentage. A royal woman traveling in the company of foreigners was highly suspicious. No one would think twice if she were some minor noble seeking her future fortune in Troy.

The vicious harpy, Helen simmered. The vizier meant to insult, or he would not have switched to Grecian tongue. So unsettled was she at the man's actions, Helen had forgotten about Bay.

The sickly chancellor, already standing so close it bordered on impropriety, gaped openly at her. *"Princess?"* His face reflected his horror, and he backed away, finally embarrassed by his indecent behavior.

A loud clap broke the tension, followed by several more. Seti lounged in his throne, clearly entertained by the drama unfolding around him. "Of course she is a princess!" He laughed, also switching to Greek. The cutting note in his mirth was directed back toward the chancellor. "You are a fool if you did not see it, Bay. And I thought you more clever than most." When his attention turned back to Helen, his eyes lingered appreciatively as he studied her up and down.

Helen stiffened under the scrutiny. She could always tell when a man desired her. It was in his eyes. His pupils would constrict and his breath became heavy as though the lust-filled thoughts fought for control. Before he could act on those impulses, however, the Egyptian princess stepped forward, a restraining hand placed on Seti's shoulder.

"What is it, Twosret?" He simmered over the interruption.

"Such fire and grace," the princess whispered in awe, her hazel eyes locked on Helen again, soaking in every detail. "If Hathor took human form, I would swear it were She. Nemhet has wronged our guest, Husband. We must make amends."

Helen studied Twosret with equal amazement. She was the beauty of a starlit night and spoke with a courage uncommon in women of the Hellas.

Seti waved her back with an imperious gesture. "My wife speaks true, Princess. Please forgive the brash words of my vizier." He stared crossly at the scowling official, the disapproval evident on his pinched face. "Ask what you will of Egypt, and we will do our best to comply."

"Thank you, Your Grace." Helen blushed with discomfort. "I require nothing. We came to marvel at the splendors of your Temple. That privilege should suffice."

But Seti was not a man one refused. He leaned forward, a mischievous glint to his dark eyes. "Surely there is something you desire?"

Helen turned to Paris, trying to get some guidance, but his face was a blank slate. Her mind racing, she hunted for a response. "Well, there is one thing..." The admission fell from her tongue before she could think better of it.

"Yes?" Seti pressed.

With the undivided attention of the court upon her, she had no choice but to proceed. "Prince Paris spoke to me of a purification ritual," she stammered. "If it is not too much bother, I would like to undertake it."

Shocked dissent broke out amongst the nobles. Even the priests were affronted by her request, their complaints piling on top of one another:

"Preposterous."

"She's a woman!"

"Would you offend the Gods?" One priest's shrill voice pierced through the others. "She's a foreigner!"

"The Gods of the Two Lands are the Gods of All." Twosret shot back at the thin man. "A truth, as Second Prophet, you well know, Penanukis!" But the princess' argument only sparked further protest. The dais quickly resembled the atmosphere of a tavern brawl. Fists shook and angry slurs filled the air.

"Quiet!" Seti screeched the command. He waved down the other protestors until order resumed on the dais. Slowly, while his advisors quietly begged his forgiveness, the wild affront melted from Seti's stiff posture and his indulgent smile returned. He shifted his focus to Helen, lifting the decorated crook and flail from his lap, rubbing the objects suggestively. "By my eyes, Helen of Sparta, you *are* perfection. What need have you for purification?"

She stiffened, knowing she was being mocked. Though her pride flared, demanding these insults be challenged, she heeded Paris' warning for caution. "You flatter me, Your Grace." She nodded to Seti and the other nobles on the dais, locking eyes with the only sympathetic face before her, that of the Egyptian princess. "I did not mean to offend. Had I known the ritual was forbidden to women, I would not have asked."

"But it is not!" Twosret objected, drawing the angry mutters of the gathered priests. Again, the princess' courage amazed Helen. She could never have spoken so openly in Agamemnon's court. The Mycenaean king made it abundantly clear how he dealt with unwelcome outbursts from his queen and royal sister.

Twosret stepped forward, her proud stance silencing her detractors as much as Seti's demands. "If the need is great, Pharaoh can approve your petition." With a delicate gesture, she dipped her head respectfully to her husband. "Pharaoh, or his Prince Regent."

Seti's eyes narrowed. He had the look of a man weighing his options. He glanced between his wife and the priests, his mischievous smile returning. "State your case, Princess," he urged her, "and know that Egypt will treat you fairly."

Helen hesitated, her heart hammering in disbelief. Was it possible? Could all she had suffered in Mycenae and before, all the guilt and shame, be washed away? That possibility took hold of her, and a flare of hope blossomed in her chest. She found herself desiring this ritual with a desperation that frightened her.

Before she could answer, Paris stepped beside her. "*It's not safe, Helen. Withdraw the request. Tell him you made a mistake,*" he whispered urgently into her ear.

But it was not a mistake. She wanted a future in Troy, not

just a chance to live. Just as leaving Mycenae required a leap of faith, so too did this. Helen pushed him away. Steeling her nerves, she approached the throne. "I have lived my whole life along the western frontier, Your Grace. Our ways are brutal, cruel." She poured all her hurt into that plea, allowing her hope to show naked on her face. "I wish to be cleansed of it before I travel to more... civilized lands. Please, grant me this boon."

She could see Seti waver. He stared deeply into her eyes like one struck. Helen did not blink. Nor did she turn her head. "Please," she pleaded again and dropped to her knees. She prayed it was enough to sway the prince.

Paris had to fight himself from rushing to her side. He hated seeing Helen humble herself before any man. He had no idea what possessed her to ask for the ritual, or why she petitioned for it so fervently, but there was something compelling about her honest plea. Seti would be a man made of stone to deny her.

Unfortunately, despite what Twosret claimed, Seti's authority only went so far. It was a matter for the Temple, and the decision did not rest with the crown alone. The five priests crowded about Seti and began bickering amongst themselves in Egyptian.

"*She's a woman. It's never been done before.*"

"*Perhaps, but we should consult with the First Prophet.*"

"*Impossible, we can't let a foreigner into the inner sept! Her pagan blood will offend Amun. The First cannot change that.*"

"*We must refuse.*"

Paris' heart sunk as he listened. Helen had not stirred from her respectful pose. She was fortunate not to know what they said. Her courage, which so clearly captivated Seti, would evaporate with that knowledge.

But Helen was not blind. She could sense defeat in the air. Seti said something sharply to his advisors in Egyptian, and they answered back with similar bite. The sterile priests studied her with heavy frowns. There was no question of their position on this request.

I tried. She tried to console herself, but all the anxiety and frustration of the past two weeks overwhelmed her. Her shoulders sagged and she dropped her gaze to the floor, cursing herself for her naiveté. From the moment Paris spoke of the ritual, she felt drawn to it, as though the Gods were speaking to her, showing her the way to reclaim her honor, to prove that her rash decision to run away with Paris was right.

You naive fool, she chided herself. She was too old to cling to such foolish hopes and dreams. Her tenure in Mycenae should have taught her to be wary of that nonsense. She raised her head, determined not to let her hurts show on her face.

What awaited her was far more upsetting.

Every person on the dais, *in the entire throne room*, was staring at her, eyes wide with disbelief. Too late she realized their heated conversations had come to an abrupt halt. In its vacant place, a gasp echoed down the hall. She lifted her head, curious to discover what new drama this foretold.

A soft touch on her elbow jolted her from her thoughts. The warmth of hot breath tickled her skin and was soon followed by a kiss from a slimy, rough tongue. Helen turned, surprised to see the young calf nuzzling at her side.

The Mnevis Bull had come to comfort her.

Chapter 14

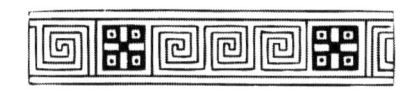

The Foreign Aphrodite

PARIS COULD SCARCELY breathe. The entire court watched in shocked silence as the Mnevis, the sacred calf imbued with the living *ka* of Amun-Re, nuzzled at Helen's side. She placed her arm around the small creature, scratching him affectionately beneath his chin.

No one dared moved. Touching the Mnevis was forbidden; he was a conduit to their Great God. The bull's actions were prophetic and could determine the fortune, for good or for ill, of any who petitioned him. There was no doubt they were witnessing a miracle. And Helen, in her ignorance of Egyptian culture, blasphemed the cult with her profane touch.

Paris exchanged a worried glance with Glaucus. They were all in danger should the priests decide to take offense.

"Marvelous!" A melodious voice echoed throughout the silent hall. "Our guest has wooed Amun-Re Himself! There is your answer, Seti. Deny her nothing."

From the eaves of the hall a graceful and aged queen entered. As one, the gathered nobles dipped their heads in respect as she glided on soundless feet across the tiled floor. Paris flushed with unexpected pleasure, instantly recognizing the beloved wife of the late Rameses the Great.

Nefertari Merytmut was a beauty without equal in Egypt. Her prominent cheekbones drew sharp lines to a swooping forehead where sat the flat topped, blue crown of Upper and Lower Egypt. The queen wore a sheer, pleated gown with loose sleeves along the elbow. A multi-colored belt ran beneath her bust and trailed down the front in two long tails. Her face was painted to recall the beauty of her youth, a fantastic illusion since the queen was far into her third score of years. On her crown, the cobra-headed uraeus reared over a band of gold. She was an elegant, and intimidating, sight.

"Alexandros," Nefertari greeted him with a pleasant smile. "Mut has blessed my eyes that I see you again." The queen glided to his side and placed a chaste kiss on his cheeks.

A flush of warm memories flooded Paris with her kind words. Nefertari, amongst all the royals he had met on his last visit, had impressed him the most with her insight and charm. He dipped into a swooping bow. "It is I who am blessed. Your beauty is eternal, Lady of Grace."

She smiled sweetly, and a twinkle lit up her eyes, hinting at a mind unsoftened by years, one that comprehended much more than flattery. She turned to Helen next, every member of the court watching her breathlessly. "And who is this young lady who travels in the company of our beloved prince?" She offered her hands to Helen, a firm note in her gentle voice.

Helen gazed up at the queen, mesmerized by Nefertari's effortless grace. From the moment she walked into the room, it was as though a spell had been woven, commanding every person to pay her the respect a regal queen deserved. No courtier sneered behind her back. No maid whispered in the eaves. In fact, many watched Nefertari with an open expression of awe, as though a legend walked the halls of the palace. Even Seti, the pampered prince, gazed upon the queen in ernest.

Helen took Nefertari's proffered hands, amazed at the tenacious grip the elderly woman possessed. She brought the queen's hand to her lips, shocked at how natural the gesture of deference felt. "I am Helen, Your Grace, a Princess of Sparta, your friend and neighbor to the north." That last comment drew a cross glare from Nemhet. Fortunately, the vizier held his tongue.

"Helen," Nefertari repeated, her foreign accent making the name sound exotic. She glanced Helen over, pulling her to and fro to see her from all angles. Strangely, the scrutiny stirred greater nerves in Helen than Seti's lustful stare had.

"Such beauty," the queen mused. "It is no wonder you charmed the Mnevis with your grace." Though her smile was pleasant, Nefertari's tone gave no indication which direction her favor swayed. "Princess Twosret is right. Surely the light of Hathor flows through your veins."

"Hathor?" Helen asked as the queen spun her around again, her chiton flowing about her like a banner in the wind.

"*An Egyptian Aphrodite,*" Paris whispered to her softly.

Helen almost laughed. Marked by the Goddess... It was as much a blessing as a curse. If the Egyptians were as religious as she suspected, perhaps that association would also provide a small layer of protection. "So I have been told, Your Majesty." She dipped into a curtsy and found herself hoping she met this regal woman's expectations.

"Grandmare," Seti interrupted, a pinch of irritation on his face for having been ignored for so long. "Have you any counsel to share before I pass my judgement?"

Nefertari beamed at the young man, love apparent in her dark and heavily painted eyes. "It grieves me that Pharaoh will soon make his journey to the underworld, but you will make a splendid king, Seti." The prince straightened under her praise, adopting a more regal position on the throne. "This princess has been chosen by the Mnevis," the queen continued. "You should accept her petition or risk offending Amun-Re."

The priests stirred with upset, clearly at odds with the queen's pronouncement. Penanukis finally stepped forward, the priest a cadaverous-looking man with the red flush of too much drink on his cheeks. "We offend them if we conduct this ritual! No woman has set foot in the inner sanctum."

"Untrue," Nefertari countered, turning sharply on the priest. Her sweet manner evaporated into a harsh tone of command. "I assure you there is precedence. Just as Hatshepsut, *a woman,* once sat upon the throne as Pharaoh."

"Yes, but...," Penanukis stuttered. "That's not—"

"Nefertari is correct." Twosret stepped forward, her presence every bit as mesmerizing as that of the queen. The priest found himself caught between the two imperial women. "Your protests have no merit, Penanukis. You cannot deny the petition based on gender. The Mnevis has spoken. Will you defy the Gods' will?"

Helen watched the exchange with awe. She had never seen a woman, queen or not, address powerful men with such liberty. There was no illusion about who held the real power in this room. Nefertari and Twosret cowed the temple leaders, standing side by side like the godly images that decorated the walls. They commanded with an ease that would make Clytemnestra envious.

"Silence!" Seti rose to his feet, forcing his non-royal attendants to adopt a position of deference. "The Mnevis may have spoken, but I have not!" His tone was one demanding respect instead of possessing it. Helen squirmed. She recognized the madness behind Seti's eyes, the madness of a man desperate to prove his worth. It was the same madness Menelaus effused to dangerous effects.

The priests, however, seemed confident, certain the crown prince was an ally in their debate with the royal women. As Seti turned to Penanukis, the sterile man smiled in anticipation of his pronouncement. "Omens and signs are not my talent to interpret," Seti continued. "Nor are they yours. This is a matter for the High Priest."

"Yes, My Prince." Penanukis shuffled back amongst his brethren, his protest dying on his lips.

Seti slowly turned back to Helen, his eyes drinking in her

full form. "Fret not, dear Princess. My Grandmare is correct. The Gods have clearly favored you." His breath thickened with double meaning. "But your request requires due consideration. Only the Pharaoh or the High Priest of Re can decide the matter. In the meanwhile, I insist you accept my welcome to the Two Lands." He gestured imperiously to the other nobles behind the throne. "Show Princess Helen and Prince Paris every courtesy of Pharaoh and the realm, *or answer to me.*"

Soft assurances followed his command, but Seti ignored them all. Leaping to his feet he descended from the dais, his advisors close on his heels. "I must see to my father." He paused beside Paris. "But we will dine together tonight after you have rested." It was not a request.

Paris smiled pleasantly. "I would be delighted, Your Highness," he said, hoping the response would help sooth the tense royal.

"Setnakhte, see they lack for nothing."

"Yes, My Prince." The general snapped his heels together as the royal entourage passed.

With Seti gone, a more casual atmosphere filled the hall. The musicians began again, and the steady drone of conversation afforded some minor privacy for Paris and his company. He turned to Helen and shared her stunned look. Navigating the royal court was every bit as harrowing as he remembered, but they had somehow managed to enter it safely.

"Don't be afraid." He took her hand in his, conscious of the numerous eyes that watched them. "The ritual is steeped in tradition, but they won't hurt you."

"Enough of that, Alexandros." Nefertari stepped between them, pressing him back with a firm hand on his chest. "She is to be purified and must prepare. Do not soil her with your devilish charms."

"Prepare?" Helen cast a wary glance toward the priests, the thought of being left alone in their company sending shivers down her spine.

"You must fast, silly girl," Nefertari studied her. "To enter the temple, you must abstain from appetites of the flesh, both food and... *other pleasures*." The queen cast Paris a covert wink.

"Oh." Helen blushed.

Paris tucked his hands behind his back and cleared his throat, drawing the queen's attention back onto him. "And how long will that take?"

Nefertari laughed. "So eager, Alexandros?" Her soft voice echoed throughout the hall like a musical chime, but it was a passing pleasantry. Her expression quickly turned from mirth. "What troubles you, young man?" The queen caressed his face tenderly. "You carry more burdens than the boy I once knew."

Paris cursed his carelessness. This was precisely the sort of attention he had been trying to avoid. If anyone suspected their true relationship, Helen and he would find themselves in the midst of a scandal. He pulled the queen's hand from his cheek, lifting it to his lips. "The world has many burdens, Nefertari, and I am the poor messenger who must deliver those tidings. Please, do not think poorly of Helen. The haste is my own. I am under oath to my king to make a swift return."

"We would not dream of delaying you," Twosret chimed. Her hips swayed gracefully as she stepped down from the dais, and a sweet smile lifted her features into an alluring display. "King Priam is rightly eager for a speedy return. You carry precious cargo." She linked arms with Helen, tenderly tucking back a strand of Helen's hair as though her fingers lifted spun gold.

Paris took an unconscious step back from the mixed-blood princess. *She is not what you think*, he scolded himself and tried to correct the move. "Forgive me, Princess. I don't believe I've had the pleasure...?" He gave her a courtly bow, waiting for her formal introduction.

But Twosret turned to Helen, one eyebrow raised playfully. "Has he always spoken so formal?"

Helen blushed, returning Twosret's warm smile with one of her own. The Egyptian princess was of an age similar to her, and for a brief moment, Twosret stirred happy memories of time spent in gossip with Helen's twin. "He is a prince," she stated plainly as if that simple fact explained it all. Twosret laughed, an infectious act that Helen could not help but join.

"Princes come in many shapes and sizes." Nefertari severed their light moment, her studious frown for Twosret and Helen alike. "I have yet to meet one that is all that he seems." She stepped uncomfortably close to Paris.

Helen's smile vanished, a vein of protectiveness arcing through her blood. "His character has been beyond reproach, Your Grace." She mimicked Nefertari's aloof manner. "Of the finest quality I have ever met. I could not ask for a better chaperone."

"Is that so?" The queen folded her arms, one perfectly sculpted brow arched high at Helen's unexpected outburst.

"I pray that is true, My Queen." Chancellor Bay wormed his way into their company, his voice oozing with insincerity. The remaining nobles and officials gathered close behind him. "These are dangerous times for an unattached woman to travel without proper protection."

An unattached woman... Helen tensed, her heart skipping a beat, the threat of exposure pulling at her nerves. If not for Twosret's strong hold on her arm, she feared she'd burst apart.

"Dangerous indeed. Pirates and mercenaries roaming our borders?" Nefertari leveled her dark gaze on the chancellor, her nose crinkling as though she caught scent of something unpleasant. "Isn't it your responsibility to safeguard those roads, Bay?"

"Yes, well..." He flinched at the queen's harsh tone. "I do what I can, Your Grace."

Twosret laughed again, the throaty sound diffusing the tension between the monarch and the simpering official. "Do not trouble our guests with your tales of woe, Chancellor." She patted Helen's hand softly. "You'll be safely back to your travels in no time, Princess. I am sure the temple will not keep you waiting long. A few days at most."

"That is yet to be certain," Penanukis interjected, the priest growing their small company to an uncomfortable crowd. "I have yet to speak with the High Priest. We must consult the Gods. If they allow this flippancy to proceed, surely they will insist we wait until the Inundation—"

Nefertari cut off the irate priest with a graceful wave of her long hand. "Do not concern yourself, Penanukis. *I* shall speak with Meryatum." Even her commands sounded musical.

Penanukis' face puckered with unspoken insult. "As you wish, Great Queen." He ducked his head in deference and backed away, snapping orders to the other priests in Egyptian as he left.

And the jackals lie in wait. Paris grit his teeth, knowing they hadn't heard the last complaint from the Temple. Already his mind ached from keeping track of the various players in the Egyptian courtly game of intrigues. He was fortunate Glaucus was near. His captain was often more observant than he.

But Paris didn't need special skills to recognize the danger at his side. While some jackals chose to scavenge, others were ill-content to wait. "Is there something you want, Chancellor?" He turned expectantly to Bay. "Why do you linger?"

"Seti's orders, Your Highness." Bay wrung his hands suggestively. He eyed Helen like a man savoring a meal. "I am to see the princess to her chambers."

Paris gripped his sword and advanced on the loathsome man. "Hades Hounds, you will not!" The words ripped free of his throat before he could think better.

Bay backed off, his eyes wide with fear. "*I am a servant of Egypt! Do you defy your host?*"

Paris pulled his hand from his weapon, those sober words dousing his anger like a chill rain. "Of course not," he stammered. "But surely there must be someone other than you." He did not trust the lecherous official, and he was not going to sit idly by while a man of questionable morals made familiar with the woman whose life he held more dear than his own.

The insult was not lost on Bay. The chancellor simmered with repressed anger, and Paris knew he'd made his first enemy at the Egyptian court.

"Boys! *Boys!*" Nefertari raised her voice, commanding them with the firm tone of a mother. "Unruffle your feathers. This is not the stockyard where cocks rule the roost. You are in Pharaoh's house!" She chastised them both. "Chancellor, your services are unnecessary. You are dismissed. The princess will be lodging with me and the other wives of Pharaoh."

Paris whispered a silent thanks for Nefertari's foresight. Bay had no option but to do as she bid. The official turned to go, spinning on his slippered heel, but not before shooting Paris a venomous glare. He was relieved when he saw the man disappear down the palace corridors.

Nefertari also followed the chancellor's retreat, her aged eyes narrowed shrewdly. Paris took a deep breath, reassured he was not the only one to consider the man a threat. Others, however, needed to be warned. He took advantage of that awkward moment, while his royal hosts were preoccupied, to pull Helen aside.

Helen could tell the pressure was wearing heavily on Paris by the tightness of his grip. A portion of her could not help but feel responsible. These lies and maneuverings were all to keep her safe, and now her impulsiveness had forced undue attention upon them. "I'm so sorry." She blurted the words as soon as they had achieved a safe distance. "About the ritual. I should have asked you first."

"That doesn't matter now." He waved down her apology, his eyes filled with worry. "These walls have eyes and ears, but I promise you, some of them will be mine. I won't be far. You won't be alone."

A small smile tugged at her lips. How did he know exactly the right words to calm her? "I know." She wanted to touch him, but it was impossible now that they had returned to life at court. "I... I love you."

"And I, you." His eyes teemed with emotion. He stroked the back of her hands with his thumbs, the only contact that seemed safe. "You have to be careful, Helen. Do what they ask of you, and it will all soon be over. Our future awaits us in Troy."

Their absence had not gone unnoticed. A chill ran down Helen's spine when she realized Nefertari watched them closely. "Setnakhte," the queen called to the general, her lips pressed into a thin frown. "Will you see to Prince Alexandros and his men? I am sure he is weary from his travels."

"It will be my pleasure, Great Queen." The general bowed. "Right this way, Your Highness." He motioned Paris to follow him out.

As he took his leave, Nefertari leaned in close to Paris and spoke softly, "Have no fears, Alexandros. I will take care of your treasure." If she wished to evoke a response from Paris, she was pointedly denied. He left with the general, his royal guard trailing after him.

Twosret and the queen waited patiently as Helen watched them go. For the past few weeks Paris had never been out of her sight for more than a few hours. She didn't want to be alone in this strange land. Now, more than ever, she felt the need for his strong presence. She knew her longing must be evident on her face, but she could mask her feelings for her prince no longer.

Courage, Helen coached herself. If parting for this short time caused her such pain, how would she manage in Troy?

It was difficult to know the correct course to follow. So many of her decisions of late had left her filled with guilt, abandoning one duty to follow another. But she and Paris belonged together, *the Gods foretold it*, and this purification was a vital step towards proving the purity of that love. Deep in her heart she knew that without this cleanse neither she nor Paris could live up to their true potential. They'd always be haunted by the stigma of events that brought them together.

It has to work, she pleaded with the Gods. Helen could not bear to bring further shame upon him. She would face whatever challenges the Gods chose to put in her path if on the other side she could emerge a woman worthy of the great love and destiny Aphrodite had foretold. For the promise of a lifetime with Paris, she would endure anything.

Behind her, the temple attendants led the Mnevis calf out of the hall to his new life in the Temple stables. He struggled against their bonds, his little legs trembling in fear, totally unaware of the privilege and luxury that awaited him. Helen shook her head in quiet disapproval. An animal treated as a God, pampered and worshipped until it scarcely resembled the creature of its birth...

And when it is a man on that pedestal? What greater abomination is that?

Helen's gaze lingered to the empty throne and a chill ran down her spine. She had suffered the vagaries of powerful kings, and even mad kings, but never a *God-king*.

The Mnevis mewled. It was a pitiful cry that pierced Helen's heart. She felt a kinship with the beast. They were both marked by the Gods. But where the Mnevis would live his days in peace, she couldn't shake a feeling of foreboding, that she was a pawn maneuvered by the Immortals for greater purpose. Was the path she traveled predetermined, set by Divine Will?

As the hall emptied, Helen turned to join the other wives, an ominous feeling rooting itself in her gut. Time would tell, but she sensed this foray into Egypt would affect far more than just matters of her heart.

CHAPTER 15

THE WIVES OF PHARAOH

THE PRIVATE QUARTERS of Merneptah, Pharaoh of the Two Lands, were as beautiful as the rest of the palace. Helen walked down the long corridors in amazement, soaking in every detail. Every inch of vertical space was covered in colorful paintings. In Sparta the halls of Helen's father were decorated with tapestry and fresco, the Greek artisans of her homeland taking great liberty to showcase their individual style. But in Egypt, the art was etched in stone, and one image flowed perfectly into the next. The Egyptian artisans adopted a uniform style, a strict standardization of form that was as grand as it was intimidating.

"The Petitioner's Hall." Twosret pointed to another exceptional piece. Arm-in-arm with Helen, the princess pulled them to stop. Both Nefertari and Twosret watched over her and Aethra, acting as guides as they strolled the palace halls. Often Twosret paused to highlight the architectural details, dazzling Helen with stories of the Two Lands.

Helen suspected the princess' true purpose was not to impress her visitors but to allow Nefertari to rest. It was quite some distance to the royal harem, and the exercise took a toll on the aged queen. Like the other nobles, Twosret doted on the matriarch and made special efforts to see to her comfort.

Nefertari, however, never voiced a complaint. She leaned heavily on the arm of Memnut, the tall Egyptian manservant who assisted her, seemingly as formidable as a woman in her prime.

"Do you like what you see?" Twosret prompted her.

Helen studied the hieroglyphs. The hall they now entered was dominated by life-sized paintings displaying domestic scenes of women. In a long procession, a line of female petitioners presented themselves to a seated Pharaoh. Some carried urns and plates of food, some danced while musicians played harp and double flute. Great detail was given to the last panel of women who knelt before Pharaoh, their faces turned to each other with hands upheld as though the painted ladies "whispered" to one another. It was a playful scene, and for Helen it felt like the events were unfolding before her.

"It's beautiful," she answered honestly.

"The artists try," Twosret sighed, "but it is a pale shadow to the beauty that surrounds us. There is nothing between the heavens and earth as exquisite as a woman in possession of her true self. Men may claim to rule the world, but it is an illusion. They are all made helpless by our charms." She turned to the bench where Nefertari rested her legs, a pupil seeking the approval of her master tutor. "Isn't that right, Grandmare?"

Nefertari pressed herself up, an unreadable expression on her ageless face. She studied Helen intently as she answered, "For some." She motioned Memnut onward and they continued their march.

Helen resisted the urge to shiver, fearful that this powerful woman saw right through her. She felt naked before Nefertari's knowing gaze, her secrets exposed. She was grateful, in those moments of scrutiny, for Twosret's amiable presence.

Trust no one, Paris' warning flared strongly in the back of her mind.

THE PRINCESS OF PROPHECY

But Twosret seemed genuinely fond her, and Helen felt strangely at ease in the princess' company, her carefree manner a welcome contrast to the soldiers and officials who had recently dominated Helen's life.

"Perhaps such is true for the Two Lands," Helen conversed cordially with the dark-haired beauty, "but the men of the North care little for love. They dream of battle, not beauty."

"Is that so?" The queen seemed amused by the prospect. "And what of Alexandros? Is he not also of the North?"

Helen exchanged a tense look with her matron. Nefertari was prodding for details of her relationship with Paris, to which the answers presented the biggest danger she and her Trojan faced in Egypt. If anyone suspected what they had done...

Twosret's husky laugh pulled Helen from those dark thoughts. "Something tells me the only battles that prince dreams about are in defense of your honor."

"You flatter me, Princess." Helen forced a laugh, mimicking Twosret's playful manner. "If only I had that power. I would have spared myself no end of trouble."

"But you do have that power, child," Nefertari added, the knowing glint in her eyes hinting she was not fooled by the deflection. "Any woman who could bend that stoic Trojan's reserve must have a natural talent."

Twosret nodded with agreement. "Your skill is raw, but if you had been raised like a woman of the Two Lands, you would be a force to be reckoned with." Her eyes lit up with sudden inspiration and she turned to Nefertari excitedly. "You should teach her, Grandmare!"

The queen did not respond right away. She took in Twosret's eagerness and nodded to herself as though making some internal decision. "Why not you, Twosret? You are, after all, my finest pupil."

The princess' cheeks flushed from the praise, and she dropped her head demurely. "You honor me, Grandmare."

Some prospect of the offer tantalized Helen. She made a

habit not to envy other women, but seeing Nefertari and Twosret cow their detractors, the women a vision of grace and power, made Helen wish she could command a similar respect. "Can you show me?"

"That depends," Twosret eyes narrowed mischievously. "How pure do you hope to be when you exit this land?" They both laughed, and for a moment Helen felt like she was back in her girlhood apartments gossiping with her handmaidens.

They entered the royal harem, one room of many lining Pharaoh's private chambers. The tall ceiling was supported by fluted columns carved into the shape of palm trees. An open portico faced the Nile, and a lovely afternoon breeze fluttered the gossamer curtains that lined the portal doors.

The main hall of the harem was essentially one large room. Several of the wives had curtained off sections for private use, but the majority of the space was left open. Scented oils burned in bronze braziers, the smoky tendrils thickening the air and making it harder to breath. Dozens of women sat upon decorated cushions covering the floor, visiting with one another. Helen passed one such gathering where six young ladies, all within an age of her, lounged.

She tried not to stare, but they were exquisite creatures. Their eyes were heavily painted with kohl and pigments, the sculpted designs lending an exotic aura to the women. And their dresses! The sheer wraps could scarcely be called material as far as Helen was concerned, and their nubile bodies were easily visible beneath the ivory fabric. They sat in positions that accentuated their lovely curves.

"Hup, Hup!" Nefertari clapped her hands sharply, drawing the attention of all the women in the harem, both inside and out. "Daughters, we have a guest. This is Princess Helen of Sparta, Beloved of Hathor and Chosen of Amun-Re."

The air filled with soft murmuring. Helen could not follow their foreign dialect, but she knew she was the object of their curiosity. Like in any court situation, they were determining her standing. She smoothed her chiton down around her hips, ruing the harsh conditions of weeks spent on the high seas. She wished she could present a more regal appearance. One of the wives even touched her soiled dress, pulling back as soon as Helen shot the woman a stern frown.

But nobility was not skin deep. Helen tossed her hair back, the blonde strands a stark contrast to the hues of brown and black around her. These women were exotic to Helen, but she was equally exotic to them, a flower of a different breed. She would not be found lacking to these foreign princesses and queens. She met every eye that dared study her directly, challenging any notion that she did not belong. This flower had thorns.

"She travels with Prince Alexandros of Troy," Nefertari added, and excited murmuring erupted from that announcement. More than one heated whisper of "Trojan" broke out through the room. "On Pharaoh's honor, make efforts to show her the beauty and grace of Egypt."

The room became a buzz of activity as the ladies giggled and whispered to one another. Perhaps it was her stillness that drew Helen's attention, but one princess stood apart, her smoldering eyes ablaze.

"Shoteraja, my sister-wife," Twosret whispered softly in her ear. Helen frowned at the unfamiliar term and suspected the two women were related by marriage.

The older princess wore twice as much jewelry as any other wife, and exposed twice as much flesh. It was a pathetic attempt to draw attention to a body that was lacking. With an ample bosom and hourglass curves, Twosret was a rose in full bloom compared to Shoteraja's wilted flower, a fact the other princess clearly resented. She glared at Twosret and Helen alike, a bull defending its territory.

"Follow me." Twosret tugged on her arm, and she turned away from that baleful glare to the portico where the princess led her out into the sunshine.

The large patio fed to the Nile, ending in wide stone steps that descended into the river. More women lounged beside the water where lilies floated by and lush foliage of reed, palm and grass provided shade. Two young girls, no older than six and ten, splashed in a pool, their wet gowns plastered to their skin. Beside them, a grey heron pruned its feathers and a pair of bitterns cooed from inside the brush. It was a garden paradise.

Helen sighed, wishing she could join the girls. She had spent the majority of her childhood summers in a similar fashion, playing in the Eurotas river. In Mycenae, Agamemnon forbid the members of his household from such frivolity. It had been ages since she last swam, and she ached to wash away the salt from her long voyage at sea.

Twosret cast her a knowing smile and untangled herself from Helen's arm. "Prepare a bath for the princess," she called over to a servant. After a sharp sniff she added, "And fresh clothes. We'll wait for you along the river."

Helen almost groaned her appreciation. The princess was surprisingly observant. "Thank you, Your Highness." She dipped into a short curtsey.

"Twosret, Helen." The princess tucked a lock of Helen's hair back, a gentle smile curving her lips. "We are not in court. Here, in the seclusion of these halls, we women may be at ease with one another."

Helen tensed. Could she? She looked to Aethra, her matron's raised brow warning against the wisdom of lowering her defenses. But Helen was a guest in Pharaoh's house, and she would not dishonor her host. "Thank you, Twosret."

They took a seat beside the river, the queen retreating to a shaded alcove where a pair of servants propped the matriarch up on colorful cushions. She watched over the gathered wives with observant eyes, presiding—while not participating—in their youthful activities.

Helen sat beside a pair of young women cooling their ankles in the water. She unstrapped her sandals and joined them. The foreign beauty nearest to her grinned, the colorful beads woven into her many braids jingling as she inclined her head.

"This is Talia," Twosret introduced the woman, "and beside her is Merit. They are both wives of King Merneptah."

Helen's eyes shot wide, suddenly understanding the term Twosret used in the hall. *Queens sharing a husband?* Clytemnestra would kill any woman who thought they could steal her position. Yet here these women sat, the braided beauty and the timid woman beside her, holding hands and seemingly as close as sisters. "Are they all wives of Pharaoh?"

"Wives to one Pharaoh or the next." Twosret plucked a lily from the water and tucked it behind Helen's ear. "Some were wife to Pi-Rameses, like Nefertari. Others to Merneptah. And some are queens in the making, since Seti has not yet ascended his throne." The other wives tittered playfully, acknowledging Twosret with many nods of respect, a strange gesture of deference from queens to a princess.

Helen shared a look with Aethra. "So many..." she mused, her small gasp the only indicator of her shocked sensibilities. Three kings claiming over three hundred women? She could not imagine sharing Paris with a single person, let alone enough to fill an entire court. The thought of him in the arms of another was enough to make her stomach twist. "Do you not worry which one he loves best?"

Talia giggled, hiding her laugh in her hands, and Helen spun to her. "Did I say something funny?"

The Pharaoh's wife looked to Nefertari, a shade of embarrassment on her face. "Speak your mind, Talia." The aged queen motioned over a servant who began to cool the queen with a woven fan of ostrich feathers. "We are all *dying* to know what you are thinking."

Talia giggled again, a flush heating her cream-colored cheeks. "Pharaoh is Horus incarnate, Princess. We must all serve our God as best we can. If he is best served in the arms of another, we should rejoice that he is satisfied and not worry about the petty concerns of our heart." Her eyes lit up with a fervor Helen had only witnessed in temple priests and priestesses. It seemed Talia did not think of her husband as man of flesh and bone, but a revered deity she was honored to serve.

Duty without love. Helen knew only too well the hollow existence that sort of relationship boded. That was her fate until Paris awoke her to something better. These women, at least, did not have to suffer that duty in solitude. They had each other for company.

"But what of succession?" Aethra prodded the queen. "How do you determine which prince inherits the throne?" The sharp look her matron shot to her told Helen to pay attention. Understanding the power structures of one's host could not only spare her future humiliation, but potentially save her life.

"Pharaoh selects his crown prince," Twosret answered, taking a seat beside Helen at the river. The other wives instantly made room for the princess. Though not yet a queen, Twosret had certainly carved out her position amongst her sisters. They looked to the stunning beauty with as much awe as they did Nefertari. "The Crook and Flail pass to the strong. It is not set on birth rank or sentiment of heart."

"It is true," Talia added, her sweet voice so small Helen had difficulty hearing her. "Pi-Rameses sired 96 princes. Merneptah is the son of Nefertari's sister-wife. He was chosen by the Gods to outshine his many brothers."

Perhaps she imagined it, but Helen swore a pang of sorrow creased Nefertari's face. She suppressed her urge to question further, sensing the matriarch did not welcome the conversation. Egyptian hierarchy seemed amazingly complex.

Not all present were as sensitive to the queen's desires. "Odd, is it not, that our Grandmare's boys were not destined to rule?" Shoteraja strode into their gathering, a pale and sickly toddler balanced on her hip. "Oh Nefertari, Great of Praises, Sweet of Love, Lady of Grace, Great King's Wife, His Beloved, Lady of the Two Lands, Lady of All Lands, Wife of the Strong Bull, God's Wife, Mistress of Upper and Lower

Egypt. The One for Whom the Sun Shines."

The entrance of the Egyptian princess was like a frost on a spring day. The other wives silenced immediately, their festive mood gone. Shoteraja seemed to enjoy their fear and she cast an evil eye on Twosret as uttered the next, "Pharaoh has many wives, but only one *Great Wife*."

Nefertari acknowledged the title with a twisted smile and rolled her eyes, the first sign of irritation Helen had spied on the composed woman. "A distinction I earned because I loved *Pharaoh* best. I gave him no reason to doubt my love. Remember that the next time Seti calls you to his bed, child."

The other wives giggled loudly before Shoteraja's stern glare silenced them again. "I'm afraid my skills pale in comparison with yours, Grandmare," she cooed, her sultry tone oozing with falsehood. "They say in days gone by, a man would kill to possess your beauty, and Pharaoh most of all."

Helen tensed, inching closer to Aethra. She had seen Shoteraja's type before: jealous and eager to tear down friend and foe alike so she would seem to stand taller. She hoped the power exchange they witnessed was innocent and not something more sinister.

Twosret stood and raced to the shaded corner where Nefertari sat. "For shame, Sister." She placed her hands on the queen's shoulders protectively. "Why do you stir those unpleasant memories? Men did not just say they would kill for Grandmare, *many acted on those passions*. It is a terrible thing to be lusted after so powerfully. You cannot begin to understand those dangers."

Helen shuddered, understanding intimately the dangers the princess spoke of. All of her life she had been preyed upon for her beauty. From the haunted expression on Twosret's face, it was clear the princess was no stranger to those dangers as well. Helen locked eyes with Twosret and they shared an understanding that went far beyond words.

The moment of accord was not lost on the other princess. Shoteraja refocused her attention on Helen and let loose a sharp laugh. "What terrible hosts we've been," she chastised Twosret with mock sincerity, taking the princess' former seat beside Helen. "Prattling on about our Grandmare while we have a guest." She bounced her son on her knee despite the fact the young prince looked ready to sick up. "Do tell, Helen. What of Sparta? Do you have a Great Queen like Nefertari? Or is the land truly as brutal as you claim?"

For the women not in the main hall, details of Helen's arrival were new, and they leaned in closer, hanging on her next words. Only Twosret hung back.

Helen schooled her face to blankness, knowing she had somehow become immersed in a feud among sisters. She did not need Aethra's tense look to know to proceed cautiously. "We do not have sister-wives in the North." She met the wives' curious faces with a raised chin. "Though you are certainly without equal, Nefertari." She made sure to pay the monarch the respect due a queen. "In the Hellas, every wife is considered great by her husband."

"And were you?" Shoteraja fluttered her eyelashes, a false show of confusion tensing her face.

"Was I what?"

"Considered great by your husband?"

Helen stiffened, the color draining from her face.

"I assume he must be dead," Shoteraja continued, her sweet tone belying the dark intent behind the question. "Why else would a woman require purification? Why else would a princess your age travel to Troy?"

Helen's heart hammered against her ribs. This woman was a danger to her, and not just with subtle shaming and innuendo. There was something darker afoot. She could feel it in her bones.

An instinct to survive took hold of Helen. Perhaps the Egyptian way was to play coy and speak in riddles, but Helen was Spartan, and like the hardy warriors of her motherland, she was taught to face her foes head on. Ignoring a potential threat would only encourage it to return in strength. She grit her teeth and glared at Shoteraja. "You assume much, Princess. My future husband awaits me in Troy. And my reasons for purification are mine alone."

Aethra cleared her throat. Helen knew she was treading on thin ice by addressing a royal in such a tone, but she was finished with letting powerful people abuse her with impunity.

A twisted grin crept over Shoteraja's face. Helen suspected few dared to directly confront the woman, and the princess seemed to enjoy the spirited encounter. "Of course you travel for marriage. Please, pardon my confusion, Princess. I am ignorant of your Northern ways. In Egypt we would never send a princess for a royal wedding with no honor guard save a single maid. Sparta must truly be as brutal as you say."

Aethra placed a steady hand on Helen's arm, keeping her in place. Her pride burned, and she longed to show the brazen woman just how brutal Spartans could be.

"My Queen?" Memnut stepped forward with caution. He approached the river, his eyes darting nervously between the royal women. "The bath is ready." A few paces back a copper tub had been placed on the patio. Steam rose from the scented water that reached its brim.

Helen rose to her feet, locking eyes with Shoteraja. Without thinking why, she plucked the pin from her shoulder and stepped out of her clothes. Memnut inhaled sharply, averting his eyes from her naked body. If the grace of the flesh was all these Egyptians valued, then Helen would show them she was as well endowed as they.

The other wives gasped, but did not shy away. They gaped openly, taking in their fill of her. Even Twosret stared, her eyes as hard as fresh cut emeralds. Soon, their girlish giggles morphed to soft murmurs of approval.

"You seem overly concerned with beauty, Princess." Helen began unweaving the small braids in her hair, completely at ease in her nudity. "In Sparta, we believe true beauty cannot be measured by the eye. It is ethereal, the spirit of Aphrodite that all must worship and adore. It is not something men can kill to possess. True beauty is what they die to defend."

Shoteraja's eyes flashed hot, and a small glimpse of the bitter nature beneath shone through. "If that is true, then I weep for the poor dead souls that will fall in your wake. For my part, I will take my men strong and breathing." She rose hastily to her feet and fled the yard, her son crying bitterly as they exited.

A tense silence lingered in her wake. The young wives looked to each other, eyes wide. Their lack of response was an indicator of the influence Shoteraja held over their sisterhood. She was an agitator, one they stepped carefully around, and now many watched Helen with that same unease.

"Our sister acts more like a man every day." Twosret shook her head, her gentle sigh breaking the tension on the patio. "The day is young. The sun is shining. Do not let Shoteraja's shadow cloud your fun."

Talia giggled softly at the jest, her chiming laugh like the trickling of water that precedes the thaw. Soon the other wives joined her, and the patio became a place of joy again.

The rush of adrenaline drained from Helen's body, and the sour grip of remorse took its place. *What have I done?* Her behavior was atrocious! Brazen! But Shoteraja's had been far worse. With a flush of embarrassment, Helen realized she had let the princess bait her. She berated herself, feeling as she had in Mycenae when at the mercy of Agamemnon and his belittling comments. Like her former king, Shoteraja wanted to make her feel small, and Helen had just shown her how. She turned to her bath, channeling all her frustrations inside. She could not succumb to such obvious ploys.

Helen cursed her prized beauty and the jealousy it inspired. She had warned Paris that others would try to claim her, that he would spend his life defending her against lusty men, like Bay or Seti, who sought to make her their prize. To her folly, she had forgotten about the more insidious danger of the fairer sex. While some desired to possess beauty, worse were those who sought to destroy it. Shoteraja was of the latter sort.

"Forgive my sister's insults, Helen." Twosret stepped to her side. "It is me she hates. Seti loves me best, even though she gave him a son. Now she strikes at anyone she considers a threat." She guided Helen to the tub, a twinge of embarrassment on her delicate features. "It is petty and cruel what she does. We are all sister-wives here, but some of us will never truly be family. I fear for Egypt if she gains the power she seeks."

Shoteraja as a Great Wife? Helen shuddered at the thought. She glanced over to the shaded alcove where Nefertari watched over the harem with regal detachment, her narrowed eyes studying the two princesses as they conversed.

"There is nothing to forgive." Helen lowered herself into the steaming water, letting the heat soak into her clenched muscles. "I've faced worse dangers. Words and veiled threats do not disturb me."

"As well they shouldn't," Nefertari added, the queen, surprisingly, crossing over to the tub. "Especially when a woman is protected with charm and grace." Memnut rushed over with a stool and the queen took a seat beside the tub. "Do you still wish to learn the secrets of Isis, Princess?"

Twosret stiffened with confusion. "But I thought I was—"

"I changed my mind." The queen shushed the princess' concerns. "Our Spartan is a special case. Since her time is limited, I will see to Helen's care. You may attend to your other duties, Twosret," she added blithely as way of dismissal.

"Of course, Grandmare." Twosret composed herself. With a gracious smile, she turned to Helen. "Welcome to the Two Lands, Princess. I hope we will be good friends." She curtsied to the queen and left the portico.

Helen exhaled deeply, trying desperately to relax. As Great Wife of Egypt, Nefertari was quiet possibly the most powerful woman in the world. She did not inherit that power with the title, she *exuded it* like one born to rule. As a guest in her house, Helen owed her courtesy and respect.

Instead I offer falsehoods and lies.

Though the shame of those lies bore down on her with the weight of a mountain, Helen mustered her courage. She needed this instruction more than ever. She could not rely on Paris to fight all her battles. Where they were going, Helen needed to be stronger than she ever thought possible.

"I am ready when you are, Lady of Grace."

"Then let us begin." The queen leaned forward, her dark eyes seeming to glean as much information from Helen as she promised to impart. "A king may rule with iron fist, but a queen's power is like the desert wind. Gentle when occasion calls, and scouring when events deem necessary..."

CHAPTER 16

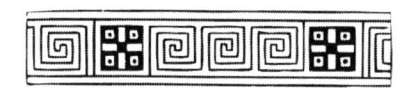

THE ROYAL HEIR

"YOU HAVE CHOSEN the perfect time to visit the Two Lands." Setnakhte informed Paris and his guards as they strode down the long and empty corridors of the palace. "The river will soon inundate, and the Temple will host the annual fertility festival." The general had warmed to him considerably after their audience in the royal hall. His behavior morphed from guard into guide as he lead them towards the guest quarters, his confident step pulling the Trojans deeper into the labyrinth of halls and courtyards.

Paris feigned interest; there was no way he was going to still be in Egypt when the Nile flooded. As they walked, he secretly studied every junction, memorizing landmarks that would assist him in retracing his steps. He swore to Helen he would keep her safe, and he was not going to leave her unprotected, even if Nefertari was near to look after her. An unwary man was a dead man in the Two Lands, and Paris hadn't survived this long by not crafting an exit strategy.

The Egyptian guards marched alongside his own, the butts of their sickle-tipped staves beating a rhythmic tempo as they marched. He knew the guards were meant as a display of honor, but when they enclosed around him in rigid formation, he felt more their prisoner than guest.

He was not alone in his concern. Glaucus' eyes were alert, although his stance reflected a man at ease. He engaged the general in light conversation, the two grizzled veterans taking an instant liking to one another. "I am not certain we are fully welcome. There were some who seemed displeased to host foreign guests. Who is this Chancellor Bay?"

Setnakhte grimaced, a guttural growl escaping his lips. "*Irsu.*" He spat onto the floor.

Paris blinked back his confusion. "I'm sorry, General. I'm not familiar with that word."

Setnakhte flushed an angry red. "Forgive me, Your Highness, but that carrion feeder boils my blood. *Irsu* are self-made men, graspers and schemers. They can't be trusted. Pharaoh has not been well for some time, and where death is nearby, the vultures do gather."

They turned toward another courtyard, this one twice the size of the smaller annex halls. Benches lined a garden setting where small fountains trickled. The far side of the court was set up for arms practice, complete with a set of targets for knife tossing and archery. The Egyptian guards marched ahead of them and took positions along each opening into the central court.

Before stepping out into the open, Setnakhte halted. He grabbed Paris by the elbow and pulled him aside, speaking with a lowered voice. "Egypt is not as vast as it once was," the general offered with slight hesitation. "Our frontier once spread to the very boarders of Anatolia. Thutmose the Great had outposts as far as Carchemish to the north and the Euphrates river to the east." His eyes burned with the shade of that lost greatness. "But we dwindle now. Bay was an administrator at a Mitanni post. When it was lost, he wormed his way in here with nobles sympathetic to the plight of peoples from the North."

He didn't have to say another word. *Sympathizers with the North.* Mitanni was a border kingdom between the empire of

Hatti and the coastal regions of Canaan. If Bay lived in close proximity with such a powerful neighbor, Paris was certain the chancellor compromised more than just his post. He suddenly understood why he detested the man.

"Need I be concerned?"

Setnakhte shook his head. "His power comes from others. So long as you support our true king and heir apparent, you are safe from his webs." He straightened himself, his dark eyes watching every corner as though expecting something—or someone—to emerge. Paris quickly stepped out into the courtyard, also feeling they had dallied too long in the shadows.

"And what of Helen?" Glaucus asked the general, expressing the concern Paris knew better than to espouse. After his foolish display with Bay, Paris was determined not to draw further attention to her with any of his ill-begotten actions. "The welfare of the princess is our primary concern. Any man in my company would lay his life down for her."

Setnakhte cast a quick glance to Paris, a dozen unspoken questions in those observant eyes. "She is the chosen of the Mnevis. The Gods protect their own."

Paris steeled his face. He trusted the Gods' favor as much as he would a starving thief.

"You need not worry, Your Highness," the general continued. "My son commands the guard protecting the royal harem."

"I do not question the honor of your son, General." Paris met the man's firm stance with one of his own. "But I would rest easier if I had one of my own in his ranks."

Setnakhte tensed, but when Paris held his ground, he nodded his consent. The general turned to Glaucus. "Name your man. I will see it done."

They continued into the courtyard and Paris took a moment to reflect on the events that had unfolded. From the moment they had stepped on Egyptian soil, all of his fears had come true. Pirates, corrupt officials, quarreling nobility... Each obstacle increased the odds they would not escape the Two Lands before news from Greece followed after them. It was his cursed luck working against them. He had led Helen into this mess and was unsure if he had the ability to pull her out of the quagmire if events unravelled.

On the surface, they were welcome guests in a proud and majestic realm. As the longest lasting Old World Empire, Egypt's accomplishments were unmatched throughout the world, and that legacy made them arrogant. They truly believed they were Gods amongst lesser men.

As a diplomat, Paris had learned to walk carefully around his Egyptian hosts. Now that his royal status was known, his every action represented the honor of Troy to Egypt. Any mistake on his behalf would dishonor his father and cause serious damage between their two lands. He could not offend his hosts, no matter how much he wanted a swift exodus from the Two Lands. Teeming with frustration, Paris shook his head. Their future departure would be determined by the crown, and that lack of freedom made his skin crawl.

"Your quarters are directly ahead of you. Barracks for your guards are to the left." Setnakhte gestured, moving toward the practice area that feed into the main portico.

Before the general took a second step, half a dozen men spilled out of the guest chambers and filled the remaining space in the courtyard. Dressed like Egyptian servants, these men were not of the Two Lands. Their skin was a paler hue and covered with numerous cuts and welts from their master's whip. They dropped to the ground before Paris, foreheads pressed to the soil.

He inhaled sharply. *These men were Greek.*

An Egyptian noble sauntered through their ranks. He had the look of the Hatti in his features and was so close in appearance to Twosret, he must surely be her brother. Paris resisted his natural urge to cringe.

"Prince Amenmesse," Setnakhte dipped his head respectfully, "may I introduce our honored guest, Prince Paris of the royal house of Troy?"

So this is Seti's rival. Paris smiled, recognizing the name from Seti's tirade in the throne room. This younger prince was at least a full hand shorter than an average Egyptian, and to Paris—who was tall even for a Trojan—the difference was immense. The prince came only to his chin. Amenmesse puffed up his chest, trying hard to negate that shorter stature.

"Prince Paris," Amenmesse dipped his head with the formal greeting. "Did you have a lovely stroll through the palace?" He crossed over to where Paris and Setnakhte stood, lowering his heavily-painted eyes as he studied him.

"Your Highness," Paris inclined his head, a gesture of respect but not deference. Egypt had many princes, but only one *crown prince.* Paris was only required to defer to Seti. Amenmesse held no more power than any of Paris' twenty illegitimate brothers. "To what do I owe this unexpected display?" He waved towards the men at his feet.

Amenmesse gripped a decorated flail in his right hand. He snapped the whip, and the prostrated slaves began to tremble. The item was too pretty to be intended for real use, and Paris couldn't help but notice it seemed a pale shadow of the kingly regalia Seti bore. "A gift. To make you feel more at home." Though the prince spoke respectfully, Paris somehow doubted his sincerity. In diplomatic endeavors, gifts were never given without reason.

"It must strain your stamina to speak in Egyptian all the time," the prince continued. "Pharaoh thought it best to give you servants of your own tongue." He barked an order at the Grecian men, kicking the sandy-haired man nearest to him. They jumped to their feet, their faces blank of expression.

"Servants?" Paris toyed with the word, not believing for an instance these men were free-workers.

"*Meshwesh* slaves." Setnakhte grimaced with disapproval. "The prince should not mingle with these pirate scum, Your Highness. I can make other arrangements."

"You will not," Amenmesse snapped back. "Take your

womanly concerns elsewhere, Setnakhte. Our guest has no fear of pirates. He vanquished a whole band of them just yesterday morn." Setnakhte stiffened from the insult, but did not budge.

Amenmesse turned his back on the general, the simple move filled with dramatic flare as he put his full attention back on Paris. "This lot is tame. My father broke them himself, just as he broke their military lines when they attacked our borders. They belong to Egypt now."

Paris studied the slaves, his gut twisting in disgust. *Broken...*, how aptly stated. The men were well cared for, their bodies clean despite their many wounds, but their eyes were vacant as though the spark of life that made hope possible had long died out. He could not refuse this gift, however much it sickened him.

"Are you what he says? Pirates and mercenaries?" He switched back to his native tongue. At the mention of 'pirate' all save one of the slaves dropped their eyes to the ground. The last, the man Amenmesse had kicked, had ice-blue eyes that showed no such broken spirit. Paris paused before him. "Are you men with no honor?"

The slave flinched, his gaze darting to Amenmesse and the flail in his hand. "What honor we had was taken from us, Noble Prince. We live only to serve, now." He then dropped his eyes to the floor like his brothers.

"What is your name?" Paris prodded.

"He is a slave," Amenmesse scoffed. "He has no name."

Paris ignored the prince. Lifting the Greek's chin, he forced the captive to meet his gaze, commanding him to answer.

"J... Jason, Your Grace. I am from the western isles." He swallowed his words as though he questioned the wisdom of speaking even as the words left his lips.

"And have you lived in Heliopolis long?"

"Five years, Your Grace."

Paris turned to Amenmesse, switching back to Egyptian,

THE PRINCESS OF PROPHECY

"*These will do. Please thank Pharaoh for this kindness.*"

"I am sure he will be pleased that you are pleased." Amenmesse brightened. "These pirate scum are a danger all nations must address. A threat to one sovereign is a threat to all." He stalked around the helpless men, tapping the flail in his left palm. "The peasant who takes up arms against his king is a pestilence that spreads like the desert winds. Egypt will not stomach it. Should Troy wish to pursue this enemy, She will find allies here. We *must* take a firm stance against those who mean to do us harm."

Paris glanced over his shoulder to Setnakhte, the general bristling with unleashed tension. Amenmesse wasn't asking for Troy's support for Egypt, but for himself. Not once did he mention Pharaoh or Seti.

"I see you have a military mind." Paris clasped his hands behind his back, making sure he appeared aloof and disinterested. "I wish you could speak with my brother, Hector. He, too, has an eye for defense. I am only a diplomat and am not destined to rule."

"Neither am I," Amenmesse rose an eyebrow at the curious statement, "but that does not absolve us of our duties to protect." He held the flail out to Paris. The heavy object slid into his hand, as uncomfortable as the obligations it imparted.

"Indeed, Your Highness."

"Use it well, Trojan." Amenmesse switched back to the northern tongue. "Remind theses animals what happens when they fail to serve their masters." He spun on his heel and disappeared down the dark corridor.

Paris watched him go, a knot of tension easing in his gut. These sorts of plots and intrigue were precisely why he wanted to avoid the Two Lands. His hand itched for his dagger. But, knowing Egyptians the way Paris did, the dangers he faced could not be quelled with metal.

Fortunately, he knew to keep his guard up. Others in his party were not so lucky. He felt a raw tugging on his nerves as his thoughts strayed to Helen. He had left her alone in the viper's den. "Glaucus," he hailed his captain. "Send that guard to Helen immediately. She's never to be alone. Understood?"

"Any preference who draws the lot?"

Paris turned to inspect his royal guard and paused, surprised to discover Iamus amongst his brothers. Brygos, Dexios and Ariston locked eyes with Paris, each man seemingly eager to fulfill their prince's request. The disgraced soldier, however, stood apart, his hands tucked behind his back. Iamus did not try to elicit Paris' favor, and his eyes were downcast just like the slaves beside him.

Paris stalked over to him. "Do you want your place back at my side?"

"*More than anything,*" the silver-kissed man answered fervently.

"Then keep her safe. Protect her as you would me. Do that, Iamus, and all is forgiven between us."

The soldier snapped a curt salute and followed Setnakhte out of the courtyard. After they departed, Glaucus turned to him, an amused twinkle in his eyes. "Curious," the captain mused, adjusting the balance of the sword on his hip.

"What?"

"After all our years together, you still have the ability to surprise me."

Paris rolled his eyes. "I'm touched." He hoped his old friend was not going soft on him. Surrounded by enemies, he needed his Trojan guard in peak performance.

He turned back to the Greek servants, the cowed men still awaiting his orders. With a flick of his wrist, he motioned them to lead on to his new apartments. They scurried like animals shying away from a cruel master. Paris grimaced at the scarcely human behavior. These men were a product of Egyptian justice, and a telling reminder of the lack of value his hosts placed on human life. Their presence here was more warning than gift.

"Keep your eyes open, Glaucus," Paris warned. "I want to be the only thing that surprises you."

Scylax scurried away with the other *meshwesh* slaves, careful not to study the prince too closely. He had played his role perfectly, adopting the broken mannerisms of a man in chains. He did not want to tip his hand with suspicious behavior.

Grabbing an urn of fresh water, he lingered near the soldiers, ready to serve. His keen ears picked up the last bit of conversation between Paris and his men. The prince was clearly a man conflicted, and, as Scylax well knew, such men were easily manipulated.

A sour grimace tugged at the corners of his mouth. The next portion of his plan would be tricky. The queen wanted the Trojan dead, and dead he would be, but Scylax was not going to start a war on her behalf. The deed would have to look like an accident.

It was unfortunate the princess was being held in separate quarters. He could not move until he was certain he had access to her. But, with the right pressure, the Trojan would be Scylax' unwitting ally in that effort.

He need only be patient. It took time to lull a prince into confidence.

Twosret paced Seti's private chamber, twisting her hands as she waited. She grit her teeth against the mounting pain lacing through her head.

Countless hours spent in the company of the vapid beauties in Pharaoh's harem were starting to get to her. Their mindless chatter and proclivity for laughter belonged in a menagerie, not beside the greatest seat of power in the world. Many days, she longed to wear her disdain for their behavior as openly as Shoteraja.

Twosret leaned heavily against a colorful pillar as another wave of pain arced through her head. Her sister-wife was as clumsy as she was obvious. Shoteraja's brazen behavior made as many enemies as it quelled. She would never be a Great Wife. She would never lay claim to Nefertari's legacy. Only Twosret knew how to harness the power of beauty the Gods graced her with. The *real* power. And with Their blessing, she would restore Egypt to its former glory.

She paused alongside Seti's medicine chest, pulling out several glass vials. Twosret had long ago memorized their contents by the markings etched along the rim of the glass vials. The powdered ingredients, so similar in grain and scent, could be deadly if mixed in the wrong combination. She plucked out a jar with an iridescent shine on its surface and measured a few heaping spoonfuls into a glass of water. The mixture instantly bubbled and she downed the tonic quickly. Wormwood left a bitter taste in her mouth, but it did wonders to quell a splitting skull.

"What is taking him so long?"

Time was running out. Soon her father would be dead and her fop of a husband would be crowned king. If such a weak man sat the throne, the realm would split into pieces. Already there was dissension in the Lower Kingdom. With each new pirate raid, their enemies were emboldened. In time, they might strike at the heart of Egypt itself.

She spat on the ground, ruing the Fates that decreed she be born a woman. Amenmesse wasn't the only one to criticize Seti's reluctance to defend the realm. Had she a set of stones between her legs, she would raise her own army and meet the enemy in the field. These peasants turned mercenaries would tremble at the might of the Two Lands. She'd flay the flesh from their bones and display their rotting corpses along the Delta for any would-be challengers to contemplate. No one would dare challenge Egypt again.

Alas, it was not to be. Her precious husband, the infamous

Crown Prince of Egypt, sat in his gilded palace, refusing to lift a finger. Her stomach rolled at the thought of her pampered prince. Seti lacked the spirit to rule. He'd rather indulge his selfish appetites than establish a legacy of strength worthy of the Two Lands. He didn't have half the courage of their brother, nor a quarter of Amenmesse's keen intellect.

The chamber doors swung open and Bay marched in, his cream-colored robes swishing about his ankles as he walked. Twosret glanced irritably at the sun dial on the portico: a full mark past midday. The chancellor was well over an hour late.

Bay took too many liberties. Even the way he walked smarted of insolence. He bowed low before her, his eyes caressing the body his fingers dared not touch. "Your Highness. You called for me?"

"Leave us," she commanded to the guards at the entrance. They bowed sharply, closing the doors behind them as they left. "Where have you been?" She laced her words with all the aggression she had suppressed since the Mnevis ceremony.

"I have been doing as you commanded," Bay stuttered, wisely sensing now was not the time to challenge their relationship again. "Watching over the marshlands and keeping our enemies near."

"*Shhhh.*" There was a time to talk of such things, but it was not at midday in the palace. The walls had ears, a fact she typically used to her advantage. "I meant this past hour, you imbecile. Why have you kept me waiting?"

Bay took the insult in stride. He had suffered many a worse lashing from her tongue. The ambitious climber knew better than to bite at the hand that kept him fed. "Your brother had need of me. We were seeing to the Trojan." His face twisted with disgust. "I distrust the prince, Twosret. He is as slippery as an eel. I would not believe a word he says."

She scoffed at the chancellor. It was more apt Bay disliked the man for having made him seem a fool. "Forget the Trojan. I know what manner of man emerges from the Troad. They are arrogant, defiant, and sow dissent with the air they breathe...

but above all, they are predictable. The prince will not lift a finger without the say of his king." She renewed her pacing, the pressure building again in her skull. "The woman, Bay. She's a northerner. Have you forgotten what treachery those island scum are capable of? Why is she here? What do you know of this Helen of Sparta?"

Bay blinked, taken aback by her question. "The princess? There is little to say. She was quiet mostly. Hardly the sort to conspire with criminals."

Twosret rolled her eyes. Of course he hadn't considered Helen to be a threat. The chancellor was blinded by the false superiority of his sex. A woman could not be a real danger in a man's world. Twosret swore that blindness would prove to be her greatest asset.

"You're taken with her..." The accusation hung like a death sentence between them.

"I am not!" Bay responded forcibly, his eyes wild and darting away from her unforgiving glare. "She is practically a barbarian. What beauty she holds is perverted. The Spartan is the flickering light of a candle beside the blazing heat of your sun, Your Highness." He fell to his knees, this time with the full respect deserving of a future queen of Egypt.

Twosret buried the spike of hate growing in her heart. Bay was loathsome, but she needed him. His network of spies and underlings was unmatched in the Lower Kingdom. And while his lustful nature disgusted her, the thought that he might desire another disturbed her more. She wanted this Spartan out of her country. Like ripples in a pond, the effects of her beguiling presence were already felt. The other wives whispered of Helen's courage and strength, and her exotic charms lowered the defenses of the men sworn to Twosret's purpose. She could not afford the distraction the princess presented. Not when her plans were so close to fruition.

She gazed down on Bay, the man still prostrated before her. She'd beat him to her will, if that was what it took. But such brutal methods were best used by men.

"Am I still the beauty that stirs your heart, Bay?" Her question drew his head up in a flash. "Is this the temple you wish to adore?" She pulled the string holding the top of her gown in place, exposing her bosom to the balding official. Bay's eyes bulged in his head.

A wicked grin spread across her face. She let her hands trail over her breasts, savoring the hunger reflecting back at her from his eyes. "Do you desire me?" The question dropped like honey from her lips, and she trailed her fingers down her abdomen, one hand slipping beneath the hem and grabbing her sex.

"Princess?" his breaths were coming in quick gasps.

Twosret delighted in teasing the man. Bay was a simple creature, but he was *her creature*. And he best not forget it. She pulled her hands free and planted a foot on his shoulder, shoving him down on his back. As he gazed up at her, she let her dress fall to the floor.

"Have you any idea what Pharaoh does to men who dare touch his property?" She moaned as she continued to stroke herself, Bay's hunger and fear arousing her far more than the touch of her experienced fingers. "They slice off his manhood and feed it to the crocodiles while he is forced to watch," she continued, the words rolling off her tongue like poetry.

She straddled Bay, lowering her body over his with the serpentine grace of a cobra. His stiff erection pressed against her throbbing sex, the thick material of his robes denying him real satisfaction.

Bay quivered, his eyes darting nervously to the chamber doors and the imminent threat of exposure. She had only to raise her voice and his life would be at an end. She could almost taste his fear.

"After the beasts have been given a taste, the infidel provides the main course." Twosret rubbed against him harder, her words rising and falling with her heavy breaths, her chest heaving with the effort. "Jaws snap, bone splinters, and the man's screams are drowned in the thrashing, until he is pulled into pieces. They don't like to share, you see. And neither does Pharaoh."

And neither do I...

She kept her breasts maddeningly out of reach, his lips bare inches from her taut nipples. With one last thrust, the sweet shivers of orgasm swept over her, and she cried out softly.

Twosret closed her eyes and moaned with pleasure, the sound catching in her throat with a guttural purr. It never ceased to amaze her that she could please herself far better than Seti could.

Unfortunately, her sexual appetites were sometimes as much a weakness as a strength. She had let herself get distracted, and Bay took advantage of the slip. The chancellor wrapped his arms around her, stroking her naked backside and pressing his lips to hers, his tongue forcing its way into her mouth.

Twosret shoved him off, kicking the impudent man roughly as she stood over him. "I am King's Daughter, and King's Wife," she sneered at the chancellor. "Such ambrosia is not for the likes of you. You may watch, Bay, but no more!"

"Forgive me, Princess," Bay blubbered, regaining his standing. "I did not mean to offend."

"Oh, shut up," she groaned with displeasure. She slipped her dress back into place, his covetous gaze dampening as she covered up the temptation. "I do not care that you desire more than the Gods have given you, but do not fool yourself that you will receive it without my blessing. Now, swear you will do as commanded."

He bent knee again and his eyes lit up with fear and awe, the hunger returning with that small promise of reward. "I am yours, Princess. Body and soul. In this world and all those to follow."

Twosret almost laughed. Nefertari and all her talk of grace and charm... The matriarch was a legend in her own time, but Nefertari only scratched the surface of what she was capable of. The true power of beauty did not lie with purity and coy behavior but in harnessing the desire it created. Amenmesse could rally all the troops of Upper Egypt, but one did not win a throne by strength alone. Twosret would find a way to restore power to the realm. *Her way.*

"Follow the prince. Find me some way to discredit him and bring shame upon Seti. Do this, Bay, and I'll give you his Northern bitch."

The chancellor's eyes lit up with a fevered gleam and he began to sweat. "It will be done, My Princess."

"Queen," she snapped as he rose to leave. He hesitated, flinching at the heat of her command. "I am your queen, Bay. And you will have no others before me. Now go and serve me well."

Chapter 17

A Boy and His Master

MENELAUS WAS DREAMING. He could always tell when he dreamed. The tense knot of emotions that resided in his gut, that sharp edge that made him battle-ready, disappeared. In its place a soothing calmness resided. For a man with one eye ever in search of enemies, dreaming was a dram of smooth spirits for a weary soul.

As usual, his dreams returned him to the memories of his youth. He was young, barely six and ten, and half the size he was now. Menelaus had been late to grow, and when he did, height came before girth. He was on the plains of Thessaly in a camp of exiles. His father, Atreus, had been slain three years prior. After their Uncle Thyestes had usurped the throne, Menelaus and Agamemnon barely escaped the capital with their lives. The fifty men left in the encampment were all who remained loyal to the true princes of Mycenae.

Finding refuge had been a complicated affair in those early years. Many neighboring kingdoms turned them aside in fear of Thyestes' new reign. Menelaus had lost count how many moons had passed since he had last slept inside walls. Those rough military encampments had become more home to him than the palaces of his childhood.

He sat before a blazing bonfire, the night heavy with the scent of horse and sweat. Smoke stung his eyes, but he continued to stare into the smoldering embers. Menelaus liked the pain. It reminded him that he was still alive, despite all the powerful men who wished otherwise.

He glanced across the camp to where his brother, with his inner circle of advisors, plotted their next movements. Since the day their father fell to the traitor's dagger, Agamemnon had changed. He surrounded himself with brutal warriors and veterans of their father's many bloody campaigns. The crown prince was fixated on securing his revenge, and he and Menelaus had become strangers virtually overnight.

Not that they had a warm relationship prior. Agamemnon tended to treat family like competition he needed to obliterate.

Four other boys on the verge of manhood surrounded Menelaus' fire. Like he, they were exhausted from a day spent in training. Aniketos was Menelaus' age, but appeared older with signs of facial growth shading his broad cheekbones. Dolops and Dieneces, brothers and jokesters, dominated the conversation as they did every evening the boys gathered for meals. The brothers were adept at getting under Menelaus' skin, and though there were two of them, he often boxed their ears to the point where both boys begged for mercy. The last boy, Cisseus, was a year older than him, and because Menelaus was prone to long bouts of silence, he became the de facto leader of their small band.

Only one recruit was missing from their entourage: Sabineus, the best fighter of the entire group.

Menelaus settled into his dream. He remembered this evening vividly. The chirping cicadas in the summer grass drowned out the raised voices from a dozen other campfires — heated voices that spoke of imminent war. The stars burned bright in the night sky like the celestial hearth fires of deceased heroes who had transitioned to the Isle of the Blessed. Their brilliance, along with a waxing moon, lit up the encampment to great detail. From the tents on the outer perimeter, the private quarters of Agamemnon's high-ranking officials, Sabineus stormed toward their camp.

The conversation died off immediately as their friend took a seat on a nearby log. His face was a bloodied mess, and the boys stared openly at him. The gash over Sabineus' eye trailed blood, and a vicious bruise discolored his throat, the markings a perfect outline of the fingers that must have constricted his breath. His lip was split, a nasty cut that would require stitching if he didn't wish to be an oddity for the rest of his life. But Sabineus didn't move to see a healer. He just sat by the fire and bled.

"*What did he do to you?*" Menelaus broke the silence, a cold fury building within him. Sabineus refused to answer. He stared blankly into the flames like Menelaus had but moments before.

"You need to report him," Cisseus added, shock lending him gravitas.

Sabineus shot an angry glare to the elder boy. "To whom? He is the general of our forces. Who am I compared to him?"

The other boys shared nervous glances, knowing Sabineus spoke true. Greek boys were required to submit to their masters. Their chosen elder tutored the boy in lessons of society, higher learning and sexuality. The pairing was one of instruction, never meant to last longer than a few years and never to harm. But Xanthos, the general of their exiled host, had always been a cruel master, and when his king was slain, his appetite for causing pain increased. It was this sadistic nature that made him such a valuable asset to Agamemnon.

Menelaus' friends turned to him, wrongfully hoping he could intercede. Agamemnon didn't give two shits what happened between a boy and his master. Menelaus knew it.

And so did Sabineus. The raven-haired young man stared at him from across the fire, a sad resignation in his dark eyes. "I'm not going to report him." Bitterness seeped from Sabineus' voice. "I won't give him the satisfaction."

After ten minutes of silence, Cisseus could bear it no

longer. "Damn it, Sab. At least request a new master. You have to do something—"

"LEAVE HIM BE," Menelaus snapped. "He doesn't need you pestering him like a harpy."

Cisseus sniffed, taking some offense. Gathering the other boys, he exited the camp, leaving Sabineus alone with his prince.

For a while they sat in silence, the crackle of the night fire thundering in his ears. Across its orange haze, Menelaus could not help but stare at his wounded friend.

"Does it hurt?"

"No," Sabineus lied, but there was a crack of vulnerability behind his facade of strength, as though he unconsciously relived the moments of what must have been an epic beating.

"He deserves to die for this." Menelaus growled, a dark resentment growing inside him.

That minor compassion only provoked Sabineus to further ire. "Ah, to hell with you, too. I don't need your pity." He kicked a smoldering log, sending flurries of burning ash into the sky. Before the smoke cleared, Sabineus had stormed off to his tent.

Menelaus followed his friend without thinking. Not even the muffled sobs from inside the tent deterred him from entering. He tossed aside the hide and stalked over to Sabineus' huddled back, pulling the large teen around to face him.

Tears streamed down Sabineus' dirty face, laying tracks between the blood and soot. He tried valiantly to keep his nerves together, but it was a losing battle. "Don't look at me like that," he begged. "Not you, too, 'Laus."

Something primal took hold of Menelaus. He felt protective in a way he'd never experienced before. He trailed his hand over the wounds Xanthos had inflicted, a burning fury mounting. "You deserve better than this." Without thinking, he took Sabineus' face in his hands and pulled his friend to him in an impassioned kiss, tasting the blood on

Sabineus' lips, its metallic tang tinged with salt.

Sabineus froze at his touch, shocked by the embrace, his back stiff as though fear rooted him to the ground. Menelaus pulled back, and the two boys stared at each other with wide-eyed confusion. The only sound in the tent was from their heavy breaths.

Menelaus couldn't move. What he was feeling was wrong. Physical acts between men were restricted to a boy and his master, an endeavor of study never conducted with amorous intentions. His arrangement with his own master had been short-lived, the prince having a deep aversion for anyone who tried to control him. But when he kissed Sabineus, Menelaus was powerfully aroused. He felt himself drawing closer to the larger boy by a force he could not resist. When Sabineus took hold of him, wrestling him to the ground, he did not resist.

Hungry lips pressed hard against his own, and he tasted blood again. They tore at each other's clothes until they were both naked, the hard outline of their manhood barely visible in the dark tent. In the absence of light, Menelaus' other senses took over. He let himself become inundated with the taste, touch and scent of the young warrior. In that moment, Sabineus, his life-long friend, became more real to him than any person had ever been before.

Wrong. So wrong.

Menelaus knew he should not crave the succulent flesh of another man. *It is unnatural,* his mind screamed at him, though his body acted of its own accord. He savaged Sabineus' chest with his mouth, moving across the taut skin of sculpted muscles, down his abdomen, and circling lower. He took Sabineus' phallus in his mouth, suckling him. When the larger boy groaned in pleasure, Menelaus no longer cared what others thought right or wrong. He needed this release. *They* needed it.

The following few hours were the most erotic moments of his life, and the boys exchanged pleasures until utterly exhausted. Sabineus was fast asleep when Menelaus finally left his tent.

When the night was at its darkest, Menelaus visited the tent of the cruel Mycenaean general. In the morning, Agamemnon conducted a search of the entire camp in a vain attempt to discover who had killed Xanthos in such a brutal manner. The murderer had severed the general's stones and shoved them down his throat. Tied to his bed, Xanthos choked to death on his own blood.

Agamemnon never found the culprit, and from that day forward Menelaus never spoke of his first kill.

⁂

Menelaus woke from his restless dream, one arm draped over the back of his male lover. It took him long moments to realize his surroundings: the familiar contours of the servant's quarters adjacent to his royal apartments, and the person sleeping soundlessly by his side. Not Helen, but Sabineus, as he preferred. Past and present merged. He was home — as much as Mycenae would ever be home — newly returned to the Capital and to news of his wife's abduction.

A screech owl hooted outside the balcony, its piercing cry ripping through the fog of Menelaus's mind. It was early still, the night watch had not yet been changed, and aside from a few broken moments, sleep had fled the Mycenaean prince.

He shifted on the lumpy mattress beneath him. At one point around the Hour of the Wolf, he considered retiring to the soft, and now empty, bed of his marital chambers, but Menelaus had never felt comfortable with the pampered luxuries his royal birth afforded him. He preferred the privacy of the windowless stone walls of Sabineus' room. In this simple, unadorned space, hidden from the scrutinizing eyes of the Mycenaean court, he was free to live as he chose.

He shifted again, trying hard not to disturb Sabineus with the restless activity. It was a pointless worry, however. The veteran warrior was able to find rest even on the eve of battle.

No so for Menelaus. Ichor boiled in his veins preventing him from any real rest.

That treacherous Trojan. A cloud of red-hot rage tinted his vision, as it had when he first heard news of Helen's abduction. *How dare that perfumed lordling take what is mine?!*

When the messenger delivered the dark tidings on the Mycenae dock the night prior, Sabineus had been forced to physically restrain him. Menelaus had tried to board a ship immediately, to sail in pursuit. Fortunately, the raven-haired warrior saved him from the folly of that rash action. Though Menelaus longed to skewer the Trojan thief and bathe in his blood, a greater opportunity had presented itself. An opportunity he had sought for far-too-many years to count.

After all these years, Sparta can finally be mine...

He could almost feel the awesome power of that throne and the freedom it represented. Only one man stood in his way, a man Menelaus could not defeat with strength of arms. If he could set aside his pride and play these events to his benefit, the Spartan crown would be Menelaus' for the claiming.

This has to work. That plea sounded desperate even to his own ears. Despite half a night spent in counsel, Menelaus was unsure he was up for the task. Politics was not a sport for a soldier, it was a skill he had never mastered, and the stakes of this battle were no less dangerous than those of leading the vanguard.

If I fail now, I will never get another chance.

The owl let loose another forlorn cry as though in agreement. Menelaus crossed himself to ward off the bad omen.

The chamber door to his apartments slammed open with an ominous thud. Menelaus jolted upright, his hand instantly searching for the dagger alongside his bed. The barest hint of morning light filtered in from the balcony, just enough to make out the hulking figure of his brother, the king.

"Get out here, Menelaus! Lest you want the world to know

you are as depraved as you are useless," Agamemnon hissed.

Menelaus inched toward the edge of the bed, watching his brother as closely as he would a buck that was about to bolt before the arrow. It was impossible to predict the king's moods, and Menelaus had long learned to approach his brother with caution.

"*'Laus?*" Sabineus stirred awake, the linger of sleep doing little to affect his alertness. The raven-haired warrior was always quick to recover, a trait born from the many campaigns he had survived in the Mycenae blood-guard.

Menelaus placed a calming hand on his lover. *"I know what to do,"* he grunted softly between clenched teeth. He didn't bother to dress. Naked as a newborn babe, and with one eye locked on the king, he rose to his feet and crossed the distance to the main chamber.

Agamemnon glared at him. Though the king made a pointed effort to not look into the darkened chamber, a sneer of disapproval still crossed his face as Menelaus joined him.

"What do you want, Brother?" Menelaus returned the glare with equal disgust. He detested when his brother barged into his private space.

Agamemnon towered over him, using the few extra inches of height he possessed like a platform of superiority. "Your wife is missing, and you spend your first night home in the arms of another? If our liegemen knew of this depravity, they'd mock us in the streets."

You wouldn't dare... Menelaus' stomach rolled as the sour scent of beer wafted over him from Agamemnon's spittle. He puffed up his chest, his pulse hammering against his throat. Though his pride flared, he forced his fist to unclench. He would not let Agamemnon provoke him to violence again. Taking a deep breath, he reached back and resolutely closed the inner door, blocking Sabineus from sight, a line in the sand his brother had best not cross.

"No one will mock me." Menelaus simmered with that threat, eager to crush any man who dared mock him, even his regal brother. He was careful in his nocturnal activities and quick to give injury to any who sought to snoop into his private affairs. There were only a few souls who knew about his... preferences, and that was how he was going to keep it. "No one."

He pushed past his brother, strutting across the room towards his chamber pot, showcasing his muscular physique. Though Agamemnon had inherited the right to rule, there was no question which brother was superior in terms of battle. Menelaus shot his brother a steely glare as he pissed.

The king's face flushed from angry-red to a vivid-purple as Menelaus continued to relieve himself. These small disrespects were petty, far beneath a prince who should be king in his own right, but it was all Menelaus had. They were sons of Atreus, and a long and tragic family history bemoaned the dangers of taking the life of a sibling. Neither Menelaus nor his brother, though they detested each other, wished to invoke the wrath of the Furies. He shook himself dry and pressed past Agamemnon, grabbing a wrap off the stone floor to cover himself as he took a seat in the antechamber.

The main chamber was in a state of distress. The scattered remains of Sabineus' and his nightly meal lay about the small table, along with several empty skins of wine. The implication was not lost on Agamemnon. Menelaus had not seen his bed until late into the night and the thought of his activities twisted his brother's face with disapproval. "The keys to the Golden City lie with a stupid, lecherous fool." He groaned with frustration. "How the Gods punished our House when they allowed such a baseborn cur to be born to the royal line!"

Menelaus reclined against the embroidered cushions of his bench and grabbed a half-filled goblet of spiced wine, lifting the vessel to hide the frown tugging at his lips. He had stopped trying to curry favor with his sibling years past, but still the insult hurt. How many years had he looked up to the man on the throne, trying desperately to do as he pleased, only to be met with those black eyes of disapproval?

"Aberration," those eyes shouted. *"Perversion."* After years of hearing such barbs, he almost believed it true.

But Sabineus' sage words buoyed his spirits. *He cannot make you less than the man you are simply by opinion alone. Your legacy is determined by you, and you alone.*

"Which is worse, Brother? The love of one's subjects, or the love of one's Self?" He gripped his goblet tight, the jeweled facets cutting into the flesh of his palm. "Look to your own sins. The Gods do not humor a mortal whose hubris rivals their own."

"Do not lecture me on how I choose to rule. It is a sacred duty that I, at least, give its proper respect." The king struggled unsuccessfully to school his face back to a place of calm. "If your lust for male flesh distracts you from your duty to your family, I *will* remove the temptation from you once and for all."

Something snapped within Menelaus, and the goblet slowly bent beneath his crushing grip. He launched himself to Agamemnon's side faster than his brother could anticipate. Standing toe-to-toe, they seemed like dark reflections of one another. *"Try it,"* he growled, "and we'll see how Mycenae likes a new king."

A wicked grin crept across Agamemnon's face. "Watch yourself, Baby Brother." The king held his ground, unfazed by the display. "If you become too attached to your toys others will use them to hurt you." There was no mistaking which "others" he meant.

Menelaus cursed his weakness. It was not the first time Agamemnon threatened the life of his lover, nor would it be the last. Had Sabineus not been the most feared soldier in the Mycenaean ranks, Menelaus would have more cause for concern. Sooner or later, however, the king would make good on his threats, and not just with taunts and jabs. The nearing certainty of that moment exposed something raw within Menelaus, something primal, and his inability to control it shamed him. It took several, terrifying moments for him to

THE PRINCESS OF PROPHECY

take hold of himself.

"What do you want, Agamemnon?" He grabbed another goblet, pouring himself a healthy dram of spiced wine. The tart fluid burned against the acid in his throat. "Say it plain."

"*What do I want?*" Agamemnon nearly choked on the words. "It is what you should want. That bastard prince has shamed you. And through you, he has shamed Mycenae. Is it your intent to sit by and do nothing? Shall I tell our banner men that Prince Menelaus would prefer to live out his days a cuckold, too fat and lazy to protect what is rightfully his? *That Trojan has taken your wife!*"

A low growl escaped Menelaus' lips. He fought to control himself. *Do not let him bait you. The Trojan will pay... in time.* Turning to his brother, he shrugged, feigning disinterest, knowing he was driving Agamemnon near mad. He retook his seat, letting his brother bellow on. If he waited long enough, the king usually ran out of steam.

"You need to rally the kingdoms." Agamemnon began pacing, spittle collecting at the corners of his mouth. "Make the men who swore before Tyndareus to honor their oath, and then go after Helen. We unite the Hellas and storm the gates of Troy in force!"

Menelaus drank deep from his goblet. When he was sure Agamemnon's patience was threadbare, he delivered his response precisely the way he had practiced the night before. "What is Helen to me but a barren wench with no dowry I can claim? If you want her back so badly, you go get her."

Agamemnon smoldered at his defiance, the spark in his jet-black eyes the first indication that Menelaus was finally breaking through. "*You know it has to be you.*"

And there it was, the linchpin in his precious brother's designs. Agamemnon had spent years manipulating every event in the Hellas to secure his seat of power over the other Grecian kings. That "Grand Destiny" was all that mattered to him. In that pursuit, his brother trusted the spineless bootlickers at his side but not his own flesh and blood.

Menelaus was a knife to be feared, a nascent threat that must be subdued. Never his equal.

Until now...

"You are right." Menelaus grit his teeth in a wicked grin, knowing he held his brother by the stones. "The oath they swore was to ME. The kings of the Hellas will unite *in my defense, not yours.*" He rose to his feet. "The war you have long desired is within reach, but not without *my say!*"

Agamemnon paused, his shock writ large on his face. Menelaus nearly laughed, his brother's thoughts all-too-apparent. Menelaus, the derelict prince, displaying *guile*? The boy he called a "wild rampaging animal" who wrecked everything in his path? *That man* gave no thought to strategy and command. This was a calculating side to Menelaus that Agamemnon had not thought possible.

"You have terms." It was not a question, but a realization, and the king approached him with the same cool wariness he did when probing an uncertain ally.

"I do." Menelaus nodded. "Many kings and princes swore that oath, but not all. Tyndareus and his Spartan hoplites remain unencumbered. Only a Spartan king can rally that army, a title I do not hold because of you."

Agamemnon had no answer for that. It was true Tyndareus bore the House of Atreus no love. The Spartan king turned his back on Mycenae after the bad blood of Clytemnestra's courtship. Agamemnon preached patience to Menelaus, his strategy was to wait until the old man passed to the next world before allowing Menelaus to pursue his familial claim to the throne. That cowardly plan was the source of their most heated arguments. Menelaus could not afford to wait until that distant day, and now, neither could Agamemnon. No Grecian army was complete without Spartan warriors.

"You would have me sue for peace with Tyndareus." A flare of resentment flashed on Agamemnon's face confirming all the worst Menelaus suspected. It was pride, not strategy, that kept him from his Spartan throne. Agamemnon would never debase himself before Tyndareus, the self-righteous King of Sparta, least of all for Menelaus' benefit.

But if placing his pride aside aligned with his own self-interests?

"The Oathmakers' army for a throne." Menelaus' lips pressed into a grin as he savored this small victory. "Secure Sparta for me, Brother, and I promise you a war for the Ages. I will kill every last man, woman and child in Troy. Women shall weep over their fate long after our bones turn to dust." A darkness took hold of him, that shroud of anger that made Menelaus so terrifying in battle. "For the honor of our house and the glory of Greece, I will make the Trojans suffer. Zeus strike me blind if I prove false."

Agamemnon paused as he considered the offer. There was very little to consider. Menelaus had effectively backed his brother into a corner. He studied the king carefully. Experience had taught the Mycenaean prince this was when he should be the most wary.

"Done." Agamemnon nodded to himself, the eager look emblazoned on his face stealing away Menelaus' thrill of victory. "Deliver me the Oathmakers' army, and I will see you sit Tyndareus' throne. Together, we will crush Troy."

They shook hands on the unlikely alliance, the moment of accord a miracle itself. The sons of Atreus, who had made a life's mission to undermine one another, had found common purpose.

Agamemnon turned to go, but before he exited the chamber he paused, his hand hovering over the latch. "You best not fail me, Little Brother." He turned back to Menelaus, madness lighting up his stress-lined face. "Or Hades himself will envy the tortures I devise for all that you love."

※

"He is gone." A sour grip of bile grew in Menelaus' throat as his chamber door slammed shut.

Sabineus slid out of the second chamber, quiet as a ghost. "You played that well, 'Laus. Every day you prove to be a finer king than he." Pride shone on his lover's face. Though Sabineus had heard every word of Agamemnon's threats, it was characteristic of the raven-haired warrior to spare no thought for his own safety, to waste no time on hurt feelings.

"Are you sure this is the best way to handle it? *That Trojan...*" Again Menelaus struggled for control.

"Absolutely." Sabineus nodded with iron-clad certainty. "If you are of one mind about this transgression, you lose your leverage. This war is what Agamemnon desires. Use it against him and you will have all that you desire."

"And if he comes after you?"

Sabineus frowned, the dark specter of violence shimmering in his eyes. "Then let him come. A king who attacks his own protectors will soon find no shields to guard his back." When those words were not enough to sooth his misgivings, the soldier took hold of Menelaus' hand, the only form of contact they allowed in daylight hours. "Do not worry about me. I will be fine. You must focus on securing your crown."

Menelaus shook off his doubts. Sabineus was right. Risk was inevitable. They were soldiers and their battle was just beginning. It would take a king to make sure Troy fully paid for this crime, and he would never secure the Spartan crown if he did not first emerge from the abnormally large shadow Agamemnon cast. For the promise of that freedom, he could put his pride aside.

But still he shivered, sick with the pressures of deceit. "I just want to be free of him."

"Follow the plan, and we will be."

CHAPTER 18

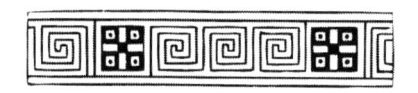

THE HIGH PRIEST OF AMUN-RE

"HOLD STILL!"

MERIT slapped Helen's hands away as she continued her ministrations. Helen, surrounded by the most important women of the harem, had been sitting for hours as the young queen toiled to make her presentable to the High Priest. After two days of anxious waiting, Meryatum was finally leaving the care of his idols to others to make time to meet with her.

"Take heart, Helen." Twosret advised from the corner where she stood attentively over Nefertari. "She is nearly finished. You will see why all the other wives treasure Merit for her skill." She leaned back against the cool stone of the wall, the charismatic princess exuding the timeless elegance of the statues surrounding the palace, clearly a recipient of Merit's talent, herself.

Normally Helen hated the fuss her chambermaids made over her when dressing her for royal functions, but for some reason, on the arid banks of the Nile, she felt differently. The primping and efforts of beauty were not a tedious affair here but some form of magic whose secrets these women, and Twosret in particular, possessed. She wanted to learn it all. Unfortunately, as Aethra loved to remind her, she was a slow learner.

Helen squirmed again, uncomfortable in her new garb. After one look at the sorry state of her Grecian dresses, Twosret insisted she accept a new garment. Helen tried to refuse, imagining the scandalous gowns the other wives favored, but the princess persisted, and when Twosret revealed the dress Helen now wore, she was grateful she did.

The pleated gown was covered in strands of multicolored faience, the glazed ceramic beads sparkling iridescent in the torch light. The light linen fabric fell perfectly over her curves, neither too snug nor too loose. The final touch was the jewelry. Bands of electrum, sculpted into the shape of serpents, wove around her upper arms, and a golden sun disk with two wings spread wide sat across her chest, the necklace decorated with beads of turquoise, garnet and malachite. The wealth of a minor household rested on her body, a fact that made her skin itch.

Merit plucked a hair loose from Helen's brow and she let fly a curse. It was a particularly fowl utterance, one she had picked up from the Trojan sailors. Helen did not need to see Aethra's stern glare of disapproval to know how inappropriate those words were in a royal palace.

While Merit blushed, Twosret laughed a throaty chuckle that shook her amble bosom. Helen resisted the urge to join her. The two princesses had become fast friends over the past few days. Their late night conversations often outlasted the banked coals of the harem's braziers. But friend or not, Helen swore Twosret was enjoying this painful beauty routine. The twisted smile on her lips reminded Helen painfully of her youth when her twin gloated her superior knowledge over Helen's naiveté.

"Discomfort is fleeting," Nefertari commented from her cushioned stool. "A first impression, however, lasts forever." She stroked a large, spotted cat that reclined on her lap. The feline was one of several that called the royal harem home. The women doted on the furry creatures, and the most social cats were granted greater privileges than the servants who clean up after them.

"*Another lesson*, Grandmare?" Twosret raised a delicately pained brow.

"That's logic," the queen stated point-of-fact.

Helen sighed and readjusted herself with regal poise. Of the many hours she had spent with the aged monarch, Nefertari had still not warmed to her. She used every moment to instruct, a rigid taskmistress hellbent on shaping Helen into a model of Egyptian nobility. Twosret glanced discreetly to Helen, her dark green eyes sparkling with sympathy. In their nightly conversations the princess confided it had been the same for her.

"Meryatum is not a man easily moved to favors," the queen added. "He has an affinity for cleanliness and order, and any efforts you make on that behalf cannot hurt your chances."

Nefertari had been dropping several pearls of wisdom on dealing with the infamous priest. Half the time, the queen spoke with deep affection, the likes of which she reserved only for the capricious felines she so loved. The other half, she spoke with caution, giving light to how powerful the high priest truly was. If queens stepped lightly in his presence, how could a foreign royal expect to win his favor?

Which was why Helen accepted Merit's offer to help her appear more Egyptian. She fidgeted again, dying to see the results of the young queen's efforts. "May I see?" she asked eagerly. After this much time with paints and dyes, Pharaoh himself would surely be impressed. Nefertari smiled and motioned over a servant with a bronze mirror.

"Patience is the root of serenity, Princess." Aethra murmured quietly to her as she passed. "Heated blood is the fire that has caused empires to topple. A wise queen strives for calm."

Helen didn't know whether to laugh or cry. Nefertari was one of many queens trying to shape her into their image. She decided to show her matron—and Nefertari—that she was not a hopeless pupil. She took her time rising to her feet before inspecting Merit's work.

The woman staring back at her from the hammered sheet of bronze seemed an altogether different person than the one who had left Mycenae. Green malachite, powdered and mixed with water, became the pigment Merit painted over Helen's eyes. Those eyes were sculpted with black kohl into an alluring and tapered form. Red ochre was used to brighten her cheeks and lips, and henna to dye her fingernails. Her hair fell loose around her shoulders, the locks interwoven with strands of gold rosettes that dangled from a diadem along her brow. She felt exotic and beautiful like the little birds of Pharaoh's atrium.

Even Aethra was impressed by the results. "You have outdone yourself, Your Grace."

Merit acknowledged the compliment with a nod. Like all the Egyptian royals, she was uncomfortable with a servant speaking informally in her presence.

"And what do you think?" Helen spun towards Iamus. Over the past two days the Trojan guard had watched over her as assiduously as a falcon defending its chic. His attention was never far from where she stood despite the many temptations the harem provided.

"You make the dawn envious, Princess," Iamus stuttered, taken off guard as usual when she addressed him directly. "Your light is limitless." He ducked his head respectfully and resumed his alert stance along the wall.

Helen sighed. His response was terse, but it was far more verbose than when he had first arrived. She had thought a man whose reputation with women was envied by his fellow soldiers would have settled into a post guarding the royal harem like a hound with endless bones. The wives of Pharaoh spent their idle time fawning over the solider, trying to thaw his icy demeanor. But Iamus proved a man made of stone; he was utterly focused on reclaiming his honor. Helen could not help but admire his discipline even as she delighted in testing its resolve.

"Do you think my future husband would approve?" She spun around in a circle, the strands of beads along her dress fanning around her as she twirled.

"He would be a fool not to," Iamus grunted.

"Alexandros chooses his guards wisely." Nefertari shooed her cat away and rose to her full height. "This one watches over your honor more closely than the prince himself."

Helen cast the queen a nervous smile and gave the dress another twirl, trying to distract Nefertari. She made a concentrated effort not to speak of Paris in front of the Egyptians, making only vague references when necessary. Ever since the queen learned Helen was traveling to Troy for marriage, she had not ceased with her subtle prods.

"Forgive me, Your Majesty," Aethra interjected. "You seem so familiar with the prince. Do you know Prince Paris well?"

"I make it my business to know *any* handsome man who visits our shores." The queen lowered her voice, leaving Helen to only guess at her true meaning. "Regrettably, most are quite forgettable." That earned her a round of giggling agreement from Merit and the other wives. "Alexandros was *different*. Priam is fortunate to have a son so well versed in international relations. I would have claimed him if the Gods had not tied his loyalty so firmly to Troy."

"*Claim?*" The word escaped Helen's lips before she could censor herself.

Nefertari laughed at the outburst. "Not for myself, silly girl. But one of my daughters, certainly. Egypt would have prospered from a stronger alliance with Troy." A dark shadow crossed her eyes as she sighed. "But it was not to be. Other alliances came first."

Helen spun in the direction the queen looked. Just over Twosret's shoulder, Shoteraja approached. The pale-skinned princess swayed with a rhythm any dancer would envy, an obvious attempt to overcome the lack of curves in her lanky body.

"Helen," Shoteraja leaned in to kiss her on each cheek. "The Nile has washed away the grime of the North and revealed a lotus hiding within. You look marvelous."

"You are too kind." Helen forced a grin and strained to fill it with a genuine grace that escaped the Egyptian princess. She shook out her golden hair, happy to provide a contrast to Shoteraja's shades of black. "To what do I owe the favor of this visit?"

The princess released her and sauntered over to Iamus, her dark eyes narrowed as though they saw through the soldierly facade the man presented. She ran a finger down his chiseled abs while Iamus did his best not to look directly at her. "I passed the high priest on his way from the temple," she added as an afterthought. "Since this meeting is of such importance to you, I thought to bid you good fortune."

Helen stifled a terse response. She scarcely believed Shoteraja wished to bid her anything except goodbye. Still, if the princess thought to see her squirm, she had best hold her breath. "How considerate of you."

"Do you know that Meryatum is a powerful magician as well as prophet?" Shoteraja spun to her, her interest in the Trojan guard vanishing like smoke on a windy day. "They say he can tell when a man speaks falsehoods or truth." Her smile gave away to a malicious grin. "*Or a woman.* I suppose you will be spending quite a bit of time together."

Better with him than you. Helen bit her tongue.

"I best be on my way. Far be it that I distract you..." Shoteraja turned to go. At the last moment, she swung in close to Helen to impart another wisdom in private. "The Gods have a perverse way of granting us the things we seek. Good fortune, Princess. You're going to need it."

Helen forced her face to reflect none of her rising anger. As she watched Shoteraja's diminutive form disappear down the corridor, she commented to Twosret, "She will be a Great Wife one day, won't she?"

THE PRINCESS OF PROPHECY

"*Not if I have any say in it,*" Twosret whispered fiercely. The heat in her voice was startling, and Helen took an unconscious step back. The break in composure was short lived. Twosret's serene smile returned, Shoteraja's disturbance seemingly no more bothersome than a gadfly.

Nefertari, however, was not content to let the matter lie. "It is possible." She crossed the portico, picking up a bottle of perfume from a tray and pressing a few drops of the fragrance to Helen's lobes. "Should anything happen to Seti after he claims the throne, she could become regent for his heir." The comment was meant for Twosret more than Helen, and the princess spun away from the queen, her face a blank slate as she collected her paints. "But you need not worry about that. You and Alexandros will be long returned to Troy before that could occur."

Mighty Aphrodite, let it be, Helen whispered the prayer and tried to ease the tension out of her muscles. She inhaled deeply, the perfumed scent of cinnamon and myrrh steeped in sweet wine filling her nostrils. Surprisingly, it helped her to regain a sense of calm.

"Why do you call him Alexandros?"

Iamus's comment stunned Helen. First, that he was speaking without being prodded, and second for the deep disapproval in his voice.

"Because it was given to him, Soldier." Nefertari's amused smile lit up her graceful features. "A man wears many names throughout his life. In Egypt, Pharaoh assumes a new appellation as he assumes the throne, one that reflects the manner of ruler he is destined to be. Alexandros is no different."

Helen shared a wary glance with her Trojan guard. *Alexandros* meant "protector". It was a kingly name. Nefertari couldn't possible mean... "The prince is a second son," she began with caution. "In the North that means he will not inherit. Paris is the only name he will know."

"Is that so?" Nefertari raised a sculpted brow in silent

disagreement, her knowing gaze suggesting she didn't consider for a moment that Helen believed it either. "Perhaps it is too early for him to claim his royal titular, but he will. I have a sense of these things. Call it a mother's intuition."

A wave of realization washed over Helen and she had to stifle a gasp. All of Nefertari's probing questions... they were not to decipher her relationship with Paris, but to seek after Paris himself.

Nefertari cared for him.

The doors of the harem swung open behind them and a herald stepped forward, his baritone voice silencing the hum of conversation in the hall.

"Meryatum, High Priest of Re, First Prophet and Chief of Seers, Pure of Hands in the House of Re, He Who Beholds the Great God."

A bout of nerves seized hold of Helen and all thought of titles, princes, and crowns fled her.

The high priest had arrived.

Meryatum, High Priest of Re was unlike any man Helen had ever met. Everything about the man screamed austere, from the lack of hair on his entire body, to his serene, wide eyes that never blinked. He wore the same archaic white robes as his brethren, made of the finest linen and tied at the waist with a simple cloth belt. His hands were folded into the billowed sleeves, and he stood pillar-straight with a self-control a soldier would envy — a feat for a man well past his second score of years. He was a man etched in stone.

"Your Holiness." Helen dipped into a curtsey, lowering her eyes from Meryatum's dark inspection.

"The Gods saw fit to name me Meryatum. Men declared the rest. You may call me Meryatum, Child."

She righted herself, taken off-guard by the priest's gruff manner. A quick glance to Nefertari helped to set her nerves straight. An almost unnoticeable flutter of the queen's hands encouraging Helen to proceed.

Disarm your opponent with charm and grace. Nefertari's teachings floated through Helen's mind. *With defenses down, they are far easier to persuade to the position you most desire...*

"I am Helen, Daughter of Tyndareus, and Princess of Sparta." She forced a tender smile. "I thank you for coming to see me, Meryatum."

It did not escape his notice that she did not tout her other superlatives. *Beloved of Aphrodite, Chosen of Mnevis...* Aethra and the royal wives had drilled those words into her mind for the past two days. If the high priest placed no value on his titles, then neither would she.

"So, Daughter of Sparta, in you I discover the source that has my *pastophoroi* up in arms. Many of my priests fear you like a second coming of the ten plagues." He studied her, a hairless brow arched high. "And now I see why. Amun-Re himself would be tempted by your beauty."

Helen was unsure if Meryatum meant the comment as a compliment. There was no warmth in his pallid skin nor demeanor. She took a deep breath and forced herself to relax.

"It grieves me to have caused you such troubles. That was never my intention." She looked up at him through dark lashes, pouring distress into that gaze. She hoped it was enough to melt the man's stony defenses. "When I persuaded my Trojan chaperones to bring me to Heliopolis, I only wished to marvel at the splendors of your temple. To be blessed by your Gods would be a great honor."

The priest rolled his eyes. "Sweet words, Princess. But they will not purchase you entrance into my temple. We have much to discuss."

Helen pulled back, an unconscious shiver running through her body from the icy aura the man projected. "Yes, sir."

"Meryatum," Nefertari stepped forward confidently once their introductions concluded. "You bring the light of Re with your welcomed presence. It pains me that I cannot bask in it more often."

"Lady of Grace." The priest, stiff as a plank, bent at the waist. "Though the pleasure of your company is an elixir of the Gods, I cannot neglect my duties. Forgive my absence."

"Of course." The queen pulled his arms free from his stance. "Your service to Re is unparalleled, as are the gifts He has bestowed upon you." She stroked the back of his hands with her thumbs, the expression on her face one of pure love. "Few are as fortunate to share in the favors of the Gods, but our guest is one of them. I pray you give her equal consideration you would a lector priest requesting the same ritual." There was a hint of challenge behind Nefertari's words, as though Helen's innocent request had inadvertently aggravated a festering sore between the royal women and their male counterparts.

"I promise you that I will." Meryatum bowed again, replacing his hands back into his sleeves. He turned to Helen, a hint of thaw in his stoic facade. "Walk with me, child. I tire of being surrounded by stone. We can conduct our business while taking in the bounty of the gardens."

Nefertari placed a soft kiss on his smooth cheek. "I will send a repast to your favorite pool."

Meryatum murmured a quick word of gratitude and began a measured pace out the portico. Helen was forced to keep stride. "The queen is quite taken with you," he commented as they stepped onto the rough earth of the garden pathways.

"Is she?" Helen blinked back her confusion, wondering if the comment was some form of test. "Nefertari is a gracious host. I am fortunate to have her favor."

They walked further into the gardens until they were quite some distance from the palace. Papyrus reeds lined the path, stretching high into the heavens. Within a few short steps, the sounds of the marshland emerged: cicadas chirped, frogs croaked, and the trilling song of swallows serenaded their walk. The air grew uncomfortably hot, and Helen began to regret her decision to let Merit cover her with paint.

"If I am to fairly consider your request, I will need to know the reasons why you have requested it." Meryatum began in a hushed whisper, his lips barely moving as he spoke.

Helen tensed, the priest's apprehension leaking into her as she prepared herself to lie. Typically, Helen scorned those who concealed their intent behind falsehoods. A virtuous person spoke forthright without fear of the repercussions. Unfortunately, that was no longer an option. If lie she must, then her words would be peppered with shades of truth. "A new husband awaits me in Troy. I...I wanted to be cleansed of all that came before and enter this new chapter of my life renewed."

Meryatum cast her a harsh glare, his dark eyes filled with scorn. "Prattle that nonsense before the court all you like, *girl*, but not to me. No one comes before the temple for such symbolic gestures. Did you kill a man?"

"What?" Helen choked. "No, of course not!"

The priest wove down her anxious cry, placing a finger to his lips to shush her. Only then did Helen realize the towering reeds, while great in providing shade, were as useless as the palace walls from deflecting unwanted ears.

"Do not look so surprised," Meryatum continued, his small measured steps making the priest seem to glide on a pocket of air. "Murder is the most common reason a man asks to be purified. When the ritual is complete, the crime is no more. That is why I conduct these interviews in private. Now I'll ask again, why do you seek to be purified?"

Helen suppressed the ball of tension growing in her stomach, unsure how to respond. Nefertari would coach her to act demure, to elicit his sympathy by provoking a man's protective nature. But some nagging fear gave her pause. Meryatum was not a man to manipulate in such a manner.

Perhaps it was Shoteraja's backhanded warning. If the high priest was as powerful as she declared, then Helen was best served telling the truth. She took a deep breath, gathering courage to follow her instincts.

"All my life, men have lusted after me, trying to claim me for their own." The words stuck in her throat, but she forced them out regardless. "I have been powerless to stop them. I go now to Troy, to a new life, a chance for a fresh start. I... I just want to be whole. I can't enter that life burdened by the past. I need to erase the stain of the things they did to me."

Meryatum ceased his steps. "Things?"

Helen faltered, the courage to speak those atrocities out loud evaporating on her tongue. She looked up at the priest, embarrassed in her helplessness.

"I see." His eyes widened softly with understanding. "There is no greater sin than a man forcing himself on a woman. It is a heinous crime that disrupts the flow of *ma'at*. Women are the font of life, and those who seek to profane that altar are doomed to the eternal pits of night." He lifted her hand, patting it gently with his own. "But those predators are the ones who should seek purification for that foul deed, not you."

Helen shook her head, understanding what Meryatum was trying to impart. "It does not feel that way to me." Laying blame at the feet of those who wronged her did not absolve her of shame. Nor did it absolve her of the atrocities they committed while in pursuit of her. She needed to wash it all away. Perhaps Meryatum believed that to be a symbolic request, but to Helen it was anything but.

Something odd happened. Like the man himself, Meryatum's touch was icy cool, but, as he tightened his grip on her hand, a flush of warmth spread through her. His eyes dilated and he gasped. It was a small articulation, but for a man with little expression, it resounded as loudly as a deep-chested cry.

"You are no ordinary woman, Helen of Sparta." His voice tinged with latent power. "The Mnevis chose you. *Amun-Re chose you*. The burdens of your past will burn away like tinder in the inferno of your future."

"I..." she responded lamely. *Inferno?* How could he know

the dreams that plagued her? She pulled her hands away, deeply disturbed by his words.

Meryatum shook himself, pulling away from the prophetic spirit that gripped him. "You're trembling." He tried to soothe her shaking arms. Wrapping his arm around her shoulders, he guided her down the path. "Come with me. Rest is not far."

A sharp bank in the trail led to a clearing where a natural pool sat beneath a grove of palm trees. As promised, two stools and a small repast awaited them, along with a servant carrying a skin of wine. Meryatum set Helen down and immediately dismissed the servant, chastising the poor woman not to dally on her return. After the sounds of wildlife replaced the woman's frantic steps, he finally spoke again.

"You should eat. It will help."

"I am fasting," Helen refused him. She could still feel the tremors of shock from his prophetic words coursing through her body.

"If I conduct the ritual, it will not be the first tradition we ignore." He loaded up her plate with fruit and cuts of dried meat. "The procedure will tax your faculties, both body and spirit. You will need sustenance."

Helen accepted the plate but did not touch the food, her stubborn pride refusing to relent. "Do the men fast?"

"Yes."

"Then I will as well." If the Gods wished to test her, they would not find her lacking. No prophecy or dire warning would send her cowering from the future she desperately sought. She was born of stronger blood than that.

The priest laughed at her stubborn antics. Though he seemed genuinely amused, his laugh did not spread beyond a smile. He reached over and plucked away the fruit and meat, leaving only a crust of bread.

"Then eat as I do. Ingest not the flesh of animals, nor spirits which cloud the mind. Grain is of the earth, grown from the rays of Re. In this holy food will He sustain you."

Helen took a small bite of the bread: barley with a hint of honey. She almost groaned with relief. She knew she was deeply malnourished from her time at sea. Over the past two days her pangs of hunger had faded to a numb ache. Loath as she was to admit, the lack of food had made her grow weak in the knees. She devoured every last morsel of that bread, deciding it tasted better than the finest feast.

"You are no stranger to prophecy." Meryatum handed her his share of the loaf after watching her lick her fingers clean.

"What makes you say that?" she managed between mouthfuls.

The priest smiled, amused by her weak attempt to evade his question. "It is in your eyes. That was not the first time a servant of the Gods spoke of your future. It is typically so for those with great destinies."

Helen swallowed painfully, a hard knot of bread sticking in her throat as she collected herself. "The rumors must be true, you have the All-Father's sight." When he did not respond, she continued. "My... union with Troy was foretold in the Temple of Aphrodite. I go now to fulfill that prophecy."

It seemed a lifetime ago that the high priestess tantalized her with vague promises of a powerful destiny and an even more powerful love. Her mad dash to Troy was a blind leap of faith in pursuit of that destiny with as many dangers as it held promises. The Goddess did not speak directly of Troy, but Helen was convinced she followed Aphrodite's divine plan.

Meryatum studied her for an agonizingly long moment, as though puzzling out the truth of her words. She shifted nervously on her stool and wondered if Shoteraja was right, that he could sense when a person spoke falsehoods.

"You are a child of prophecy?"

Helen nodded, surprised that was all he questioned. "I am blessed with that privilege and duty."

He folded his arms back into his sleeves, the reserved aura of his position returning to him. "I have many titles, Princess. The High Priest of Re, Chief of Seers... but to those who know me best, I am First Prophet, One who Beholds the Gods and Hears the Whispers of Their Hearts." His pressed lips spread into the first genuine smile she had seen him produce. "Omens and prophecy are my special talent. I look forward to a deeper discussion about your foretelling. Perhaps your foray to Egypt was not quite as happenstance as it seems."

Helen's breath caught. She was no sage. She had no insight into the plans of the Gods, nor her place within them. Could Meryatum, this austere and foreign priest, provide her with the answers she desperately sought? Dare she trust him?

For a moment, there was a crack in Meryatum's rigid armor. She saw the man beneath, an aged spiritual leader balancing the great duties of his office. He was a hard man, but one of compassion and reason—not unlike her father.

She laid her hand on his forearm, the icy cool of his touch burning away in the heat of her enthusiasm. "I... I would like that very much." She surprised herself with that desire.

"Meryatum. Princess." Chancellor Bay stepped through the reeds, breaking their intimate moment. "I am glad I found you."

Helen yanked her hand away from the priest, a flush of embarrassment on her face. Meryatum, however, was unruffled. He studied the oily chancellor with a calm that Helen could only envy. "You have some urgency, Bay? I pray you are not disturbing temple business flippantly."

"Of course not, Your Eminence." The chancellor snapped a curt bow for the high priest. "Penanukis sends word from the temple. Your presence is required there post haste."

"You were in conference with Penanukis?" Meryatum raised a hairless brow, his eyes boring into Bay. "Why?" He did not need to raise his voice, but the simple question set the chancellor's knees to shaking.

"I was reporting on the construction of the temple in Heracleion," Bay stammered. "A bird arrived from Thebes. That is all I know, Your Eminence." He dipped his head in deference, but not before Helen saw his cheeks blotch in angry spots.

"So be it." Meryatum sighed and rose to leave. "You will see the Princess back to the palace?"

"It would be my pleasure." Bay grinned, his face twisting from fear to a sick pleasure that turned Helen's stomach.

"Pleasure is for the weak." Meryatum held Bay's gaze with unflinching eyes. "You should avoid its excess, Master Chancellor, lest you wish to be its slave." Once he was fully satisfied that Bay was subdued, he turned to go.

"Meryatum?" Helen rushed after the priest, a deep anxiety gripping at her. "Will I see you again?"

The priest's brow furrowed as he considered. "Now that we've met, I will submit your request before the Gods. Once I have consulted the omens, you will have your answer."

Helen cursed Bay and his poor timing. This would cost her time she could not afford. Some of her disappointment must have given him pause. The high priest hesitated at the trail head and turned back to her. "Tomorrow. Come to the temple at sunrise and participate in the salutations to Re. We will study the omens together." He delivered his instructions with a curt perfunctory. Dipping into a bow hinged at the waist, he said his goodbyes and retreated down the path.

Helen watched him go, one hand lifted in farewell. So many of her hopes rested with that man. "Thank you." She knew her words were too soft to carry, but she said them anyway.

Bay crept up to her side, standing far closer than custom should permit. "So, you are to study at the temple?" His voice thickened suggestively. "You must have impressed the high priest for him to take such a risk. He should worry your presence will tempt his 'Pure Ones'."

Helen bristled, pulling away from the chancellor. *"Pure Ones?"* A sudden realization hit her and she gasped, understanding the predicament she presented to Meryatum. "Are the priests celibate?"

"Did you not know?" Bay twirled the long hairs on his

chin with delightful glee. "Truth told, some priests take their vows more seriously than others, but your virtue *should* be safe in the temple, Princess." He emphasized the word, giving Helen reason to doubt. "I could help you, if you were so inclined. Make certain only the most trustworthy priests were assigned to your care..." He held out an arm for her, a gallant offer if it had come from any other man. Bay, however, was delighting in the discomfort it caused her.

She refused him an answer and sped down the trail towards the palace, eager to spend as little time as possible with the slippery chancellor. With each step, her nagging doubts grew, and she prayed Meryatum would prove a man above reproach.

Her life, and Paris', depended on it.

Chapter 19

A Den of Thieves

AN EGYPTIAN PATROL marched down the street of Heliopolis' slums, the workers' village comprised of narrow alleys and mudbrick hovels. Scylax took cover beneath a wooden cart carefully stored by its owner in the shadowy recesses alongside his shop. He waited for a count of ten as the heavy footfalls of the guards receded, the twinkling light of their oil lamps disappearing into the night.

It had taken some effort to infiltrate the royal palace and get placed as a Trojan servant. He was not about to risk that advantage by getting caught in the open. This trip into the underbelly of Heliopolis was necessary, but it had best be brief.

He pulled a length of cloth over his head and hunched over, taking care to stumble every third step so as to appear a sickly drunk, the sort of character Egyptians frowned upon but did not find suspicious. While Egypt was no stranger to international relations, it was unusual for a foreigner to travel openly so deep in the Two Lands. He kept his head low and moved as quickly as he could without drawing attention.

He wasn't the only one seeking anonymity this night. Scylax passed several gatherings of men huddled in darkness, their heated whispers silencing when he stumbled too near. Hands quickly tucked inside their dark robes, hiding powders, weapons and purses of silver and gold. He made a mental note of the alley these black-market dealers traded in. He might have need of their products before his task was complete.

A torch burned in a sconce outside his destination. The mudbrick hovel had no windows or decorations. There were no markings along the lintel, like on the homes of the Israelite slaves. The unremarkable dwelling was virtually identical to the units to either side, and the only sign of occupation was the fat drunk snoring on a barrel beside the door.

Yet the place *was* unique, even if only a master builder could notice the difference. Situated at the division line of the north-east-south-west axis, this house was at the heart of the worker's village. It sat atop the sewage canals that channelled refuse down to the marshland of the Nile — canals that many a mercenary had used to make his escape from the City of the Sun, Scylax included.

He stepped before the wooden door and waited. Only a fool would knock. If his brothers of the sword did not already have an arrow aimed at his back, he'd cut off his own manhood and declare himself a *meshwesh*. He waited for the signal to be given that would grant him access.

It was not a hidden bowman, but the drunk beside the door who barred his entrance. His snoring did not stop even when the tip of the man's dagger pressed against the tender flesh of Scylax' gut.

"Go find your own kind, Northerner," the cutthroat growled, speaking in a pidgin language that was part Egyptian and part Greek. "Only dead men enter here."

Scylax moved his left hand wide, showing he meant no harm. While the guard was preoccupied following that motion, his right moved swiftly to the man's throat, a hidden dagger springing forward from the latch on his forearm.

"But in Death we are equals." Scylax grinned at the sloven

man, giving him a covert wink. "And you *are* my own kind. Now be a good boy and open this door." The guardsman made quick work getting to his feet, as eager as Scylax to avoid a public encounter. The door swung open, and he pushed the man in before him.

The acrid stench of opium smoke filled the air. In the dim light, Scylax could just make out the room's half dozen occupants lying around a hookah pipe, their eyes glazed over from the drug.

"Where are the masons?" He tightened his grip on the guard's throat.

"In the back. To the right." The guard struggled against his hold. Scylax planted a hand in the man's lower back, shoving him to the floor with the other degenerates.

"My thanks." Scylax holstered his dagger. "And try not to piss yourself. I *am* expected."

He sped down the short hall feeling more than a little disturbed. The Brethren had lowered their defenses if they allowed undisciplined boys to guard their backs. It had been years since Scylax left Egypt for Mycenae, and it appeared Pharaoh's wrath had truly broken the spirit of the men who once dared to defy the God-King.

He strode across the room, tossing open the door to the back. Four men, dressed in finer clothing than the lost souls who frequented their common room, sat in a circle around an agitated asp. They took turns snatching pebbles around the serpent, their hands darting in quickly before the venomous fangs could find purchase. It was a clamorous affair, and, as Scylax entered, a Nubian tribesman with skin as black as obsidian nearly lost a finger.

"Sloppy, Taharqa. Have you grown so fat and lazy these past years you cannot tame an asp?"

The Nubian glanced up at the disruption, his eyes widening with joy. "Ah, ha! Scylax, you salty dog! Is it true? You've returned to the Two Lands?"

"Afraid not." He shook his head. "I have business to

conduct and will soon be on my way."

Taharqa wrapped his arm around a young concubine reclining in the corner beside him. She was naked save for the henna designs painted over her lithe body and ropes of gold draped across her chest. "You see this man, lovely girl? He is the most vicious killer north of the cataracts. I once saw him gut an Egyptian overseer and strangle the man with his own entrails. You should make love to him and brag to your sisters that you lay with a Titan."

"Oh," the girl's eyes widened. She placed a finger in her mouth and moaned suggestively as Taharqa bounced her on his knee, her perky breasts wobbling ever-so-slightly with the movement.

For a moment, Scylax found himself tempted, but only because the girl reminded him so strongly of Heliodora. With her long black hair and even darker eyes that sparkled with secrets no man would ever possess, it was impossible for him not to see signs of his wife whilst traveling in her homeland.

"I haven't much time, Taharqa. May we speak in private?"

The other masons voiced their disapproval loudly, with many upset gestures pointed to the unclaimed purse of their gambit. Taharqa rose to his feet, flexing his thick muscles with an imperious glare. Before the seven foot might of the Nubian warrior, they quieted their complaints. Gathering the serpent back into a reed basket, they collected their women and left Scylax and Taharqa alone.

"I thought your messenger to be touched by evil spirits." Taharqa poured two glass drams of a bitter tea, handing one to him before retaking his seat. "Scylax would never return to Egypt, I say, but here you are, in the land you swore in vengeance to destroy. Should I be worried, old friend?"

You should... Every day spent in the company of Egyptian royalty seared at his soul. He was sorely tempted to renew that ill-fated quest. If not for Heliodora and the sacrifices she made, he feared he'd stray down that dark path again. He owed her his heart, and more so, his courage to stay true to the life they had built together. "I am that man no longer."

"I know that I am pretty." Taharqa smiled, his perfect white teeth flashing dangerously. "But you have not come all this way merely to bask in my presence. Some great need must fuel you, Scylax of Sparta. What is it you need of me?"

There was no man Scylax trusted more than Taharqa of Punt. His sword arm was more true than a God's Wife's virtue. But most friendships were enriched with mutual profit, and it provided his silence as well. Scylax tossed the man a heavy purse. The Nubian untied the leather drawstring and murmured appreciatively, surprised to see the glint of gold instead of silver.

"I am on a mission for the crown of Mycenae to kill a murderer and thief and return the woman he abducted."

Taharqa whistled. "And so they send you, also a known killer and thief? Perhaps it is they who are touched with spirits, 'eh?" They both shared a brief laugh, but when Taharqa's died off, he watched Scylax with unease. "It is unlike you, old friend, to take a bounty for the crown. I pray your time in Mycenae has not compromised your allegiance to the cause."

Scylax glowered, the curl of his lip telling Taharqa just how unpleasant that conversation would prove to be if he chose to pursue it.

The Nubian's prodding was not unexpected, however. Taharqa was *Medjay*, of the nomadic clans along the Second Cataract. His people suffered greatly from the Egyptian military campaigns to expand their kingdom. He had lost mother, sister, brother and son to Egyptian swords. For Taharqa, his fight against the God-King was personal.

For Scylax that ill-fated quest had begun as one of desperation. A man must eat. In the powerful grip of hunger, Scylax discovered there was not much he was unwilling to do. It was only when he discovered the *true* lives of their noble rulers, of their vanity and waste that beggared the common people, did he dedicate himself to balancing the scales of injustice. He was a soldier in that righteous army, a fighter who always triumphed because he had nothing to lose.

Until now...

"My reasons for accepting this bounty are none of your concern. I do not need to know why a mark is set. And neither do you."

Taharqa reclined in his seat. Though his eyes sparkled with curiosity, he held his tongue. He rolled the purse of gold in his hand and considered his next words carefully. "How might I help you, old friend?"

"I need access to the escape tunnels and your fastest barge to take us back to the Delta. I will make my own way from there."

"When will you need these services?" The Nubian plucked a nugget from the purse, testing the yield of the soft metal with his teeth.

"That part is uncertain." Scylax rose to his feet and began to pace. "My thief has taken refuge inside the royal palace. And my access is... restricted. Until I can arrange for the right conditions, I cannot act."

"I have a man on the inside who might be of some value," Taharqa offered, the hint for more gold as blatant as the nose on his broad face. "A chancellor of questionable morals."

Scylax' stomach churned and he spat on the floor. "I don't work with Egyptians!"

Taharqa laughed. "Fortunately for you, he is not of the Two Lands. Shall I introduce you?"

He considered the offer for a moment, but then shook his head. The fewer people who knew of a task reduced the chances it would be exposed. Moreover, Scylax did not want to reveal his true identity to anyone who colluded with Egyptian royalty. "I work alone."

"Like old times, 'eh?" Taharqa leapt to his feet and took Scylax' hand in his. "It will be done. My tunnels, my silence, and passage for two."

Scylax grimaced, that last item reviving the nagging question that gnawed at his angst-riddled nerves. Killing a Trojan prince on Egyptian soil invited the wrath of two kingdoms. Scylax had no wish to draw the evil eye upon himself again. He had barely survived the last time. If he could not arrange an "accident" for the Trojan in due time, he would have to complete the task elsewhere. "Best make it for three."

They exchanged information on how to reach one another, and Scylax was soon back into the night skulking through the empty alleyways of Heliopolis' slums, more uncertain than when he first set out.

One thing *was* certain. The Trojan prince was not the thief the queen had portrayed. Something deeper, more sinister was at play here. If that Mycenae bitch-of-a-queen thought to use him as her weapon and toss the blade aside, she was in for a reckoning. Yes, the sands of the hourglass were running out— for Paris and for Scylax, and when the last grain fell, Heliodora and his girls had best be returned or there'd be no kingdom on Earth where his wrath would not follow.

Chapter 20

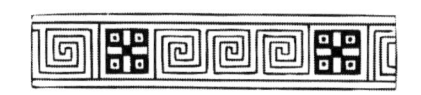

Entertaining Seti

"SHE SPENDS HER mornings in the temple cloistered away with the high priest," Ariston reported to Paris.

Seti and a pack of his supporters enjoyed a leisurely afternoon of sport in the field behind them. Paris had spent the whole morning, and the six before that, in the company of the crown prince. Only during the cool hours of twilight, when Seti was forced to attend to his father, did Paris get a moment's rest.

Each day passed much like the others, with sunshine, frivolity and hours of empty conversation. Seti was a man who enjoyed his entertainments, and Paris was quickly coming to realize that included him. If he was forced to play another frivolous game of Jackal and Hounds or another temple servant tried to press a date or fig upon him, he was likely to scream. When he spotted Ariston returning from his rendezvous with Iamus, Paris quickly took advantage of the distraction and begged leave from the crown prince.

"Has he set a date for the purification ritual?"

Ariston shook his head. "Not yet. But the princess says to be patient. She is certain he will declare it soon."

Paris began to pace. Patience was a luxury they couldn't

afford. An entire week had passed while they waited for Meryatum to 'prepare' for the ritual, which was more than enough time for a Mycenaean response to follow them to the Two Lands. The only thought that gave him relief was that no one, not even Paris himself, had reason to believe they'd travel to Egypt.

"Anything else?"

"She sends more warnings about the Canaanite princess." Paris nodded, having heard those warnings before. Shoteraja was an angry tribute-bride stirring up trouble, but her influence paled in comparison with the children of Rameses' Hittite bride. Twosret and her brother, Amenmesse, were the bigger threat. The young prince had been hounding Paris' steps, keen to secure Troy's alliance for his imaginary war.

"Oh, and one more thing," Ariston added, blushing a furious red.

Paris missed the young soldier's discomfort and waved him on impatiently. "And that is?"

"...Her love. She wants you to know she misses you."

Paris stopped mid-step, a pervasive guilt flooding him that he had not sent her similar sentiments. "Did you see her this time, Ariston?"

"Yes, My Lord. She was a distance away, by the Nile, but I could see her."

He didn't need to ask; Ariston's softened expression spoke volumes. Even at a distance, Helen captured the hearts of those who had come to adore her. For Paris the loss of her presence was felt ten fold. Their first night apart, he had felt as though a piece of his soul had gone missing, and he spent the remaining time from that day forth on the edge of civility, desperate for even one glimpse of her lovely face.

But he would never risk exposing her for his own selfish desires. He kept his distance. "Thank you, Ariston. Report back to Glaucus. Make sure he knows all that you know." He waved over one of his *meshwesh* servants to show the soldier where Glaucus had set up the Trojan field drills for today. The captain changed the location every morning as a general precaution.

Jason was the closest. The sandy-haired servant was typically the most alert whenever Paris required service, but when Paris made his request, Jason relayed the message to one of his brethren in a guttural language that Paris was not familiar with. A short and curly haired man with only one hand stepped forward and led Ariston onward while Jason elected to remain by his side.

Paris had made a concentrated effort to get to know his *meshwesh* servants. Though Greek was their common tongue, they were a diverse lot. Their members were comprised of Shardans from Sardinia, men renowned for their tactical skill in battle; Tusci from the Thracian steppes north of Troy, whose endurance bards praised in song; Sikels from the western isle of Syracusa, men so coarse of hair and manner they resembled the beasts that roamed their homeland; and Achaeans from the mainland of Greece. Jason was one of the latter, a privileged ranking among his fellow pirates. The Achaeans were the ringleaders of their failed attack, a position of leadership Jason apparently did not lose in captivity.

"Can you see what other nonsense Seti has in store for the rest of the afternoon?" Paris struck up conversation as they headed back to the courtiers.

"Hoops and Reeds, Your Highness." Jason shielded his eyes against the glaring light of the midday sun. "Unless I am mistaken, that is a game best played drunk. I suppose the nobles will have been well watered by the time we return."

For someone held in captivity for years, Jason a was surprisingly likable man. He had a sharp sense of humor and his piercing ice-blue eyes never missed a detail. Paris could only surmise what his skill on a ship might be—certainly enough to cow his fellow prisoners.

"If they're drunk, I might stand a decent chance this time. Do you have any pointers?"

The Achaean smirked. "I am hopeless, Your Highness. The

only sport of Hoop and Reed I excelled at was between the sheets."

Paris laughed, very much in agreement. "A much better sport than wasting away in this heat."

A breeze picked up along the Nile, helping to remedy the powerful rays of the desert sun. The relief was fleeting, however. Heat waves radiated from the sun-scorched earth, and even the oasis where Seti's pavilion was stationed shimmered.

Paris had to adopt Egyptian dress to manage the long afternoons of the crown prince's entertainments. He was stripped to the waist and wore a similar pleated *shendyt* as Seti. It was important for a diplomat to never go fully native. Paris' power came from the unique stature of being foreign. Assimilating into the local culture put him under its rules and obligations. His host, however, seemed to feel anything foreign was akin to barbary, and persuading Paris to appear more Egyptian was an attempt to 'civilize' him.

"How fare you, Trojan? Are you enjoying Seti's little distractions?" Amenmesse emerged from the shaded portico behind them, nearly causing Paris to jump out of his skin. How long had the prince been nearby and listening to his words?

"Ah, Amenmesse. Good to see you again. Have you come to join the festivities?" He paused to let the prince step in pace beside them. Amenmesse cast a scornful glare at Jason until the man receded to a respectful distance. Over the past week, the Egyptian prince had made his hatred for the *meshwesh* invaders abundantly clear.

"Since our father fell ill, Seti has held three score of these absurd gatherings," Amenmesse scoffed. "He has become very popular with the local governors and noble houses."

While Paris agreed with the disdain Amenmesse effused, he could never admit it to the young prince. No king, or king-in-waiting, was ever all he claimed, but power dynamics and jealousy inevitably swayed public opinion on a ruler. In Paris' experience, the truth was usually somewhere in-between. Plus, some of the prince's complaints about his brother bordered on gossip that would have made a ribald chambermaid blush.

"Seti is fortunate to enjoy a secure land." Paris fell into a comfortable pace with him. "Peace promotes pleasure. In Troy we are often preoccupied with the safety of our realm and those of our sworn vassals. I wish we could devote more time to leisure like you do here in Egypt."

Amenmesse rolled his eyes, frustrated again that Paris evaded giving a real answer. "If you lack pleasure in your life, I am sure Seti will see you have your fill," he arched a brow, a hint of challenge in his dark green eyes, "but when you tire of these boyish games, perhaps you would like some real sport?"

Paris could not help but mirror Amenmesse's eager grin, praying for any excuse to recuse himself from Seti's tedium. "Such as?"

"Do you fancy a bit of archery?"

Seti immediately agreed to Amenmesse's request for a change of venue. The young prince rounded up a pair of chariots while Paris retrieved his bow from his apartments. Word spread throughout the palace, and the archery court quickly filled with royal administrators and staff. Even the wives of Pharaoh left their garden paradise to watch a sporting challenge between princes.

"Where is your bow, Seti?" Paris asked as he strung his own. "Are you not joining us?" Sitting below the filling arena, he tried his best to concentrate, but with the women so near, his eyes constantly scoured the crowds for any sign of Helen.

Seti preened before his guests, as though to let the multitudes bask in his regal presence. The leather pleats of his kilt were studded with gold filigree, and his skin shone with a scented ointment that surely had gold foil blended into the mixture. His smile was one of utter indulgence as he soaked in their whispers of awe and admiration. Though he was not yet Pharaoh, he certainly conducted himself as though he were already a God.

"This is my brother's sport." Seti sniffed, his words coming with a bit of a slur. He gestured wide with the goblet in his hand, wine sloshing dangerously over its sides. "I'll act as judge and arbiter in the event of a tie."

Paris inclined his head. "As you wish."

The crown prince, unsurprisingly, was more spectator than player. Not so his brother. Amenmesse had stripped down to the waist and was performing stretching exercises in the section partitioned off for the competitors. The prince was incredibly lean, and though he was small in stature, his frame was limber. Paris suspected he dedicated himself daily to the strengthening and toning of the body he was born to.

"Your bow is too small, Trojan." Amenmesse teased him as he completed his set of stretches. "You'll never hit a flying target with a bow meant for a child."

Paris took the taunt in stride. Amenmesse did not seek to belittle him but jested in good spirit. Though his ego made him overconfident, the prince nevertheless behaved with the regal decorum expected of one of noble birth. After the madness of Agamemnon's court, it was a welcome relief to Paris.

"I'll take my chances," Paris quipped back. "Besides, I prefer this bow. It has the familiar grip of an old lover." The bow, like Paris himself, had several surprises in store for the Egyptian prince. The bone handle at its center had molded over time to Paris' hand. Supple lengths of yew made up the core, and the ends were tipped with sinew that bent away from the archer. It was an elegant design he had picked up in Assyria, one that allowed his arrows to fly with greater power than those fired from larger, more cumbersome bows.

Glaucus paced the perimeter of the practice grounds, his arms clasped behind his back. As he passed Paris on his return he muttered down to him, "You should let him win."

Paris bristled, "I hardly think that's necessary."

"Whomever you are trying to impress will understand," the captain persisted. "We hardly need the irate attention of a sore-losing prince."

He cursed softly, knowing Glaucus was correct. Paris had been looking forward to a fair game with Amenmesse and the chance to compete with his full skill. A lifetime of deferring to others, of being told his life was without value and worse, had built up like acid eating away at his soul. Perhaps Helen's faith had gotten to his head, but he wanted to prove he was more, that he could be all that she imagined.

"Understood." He nodded to his old friend. He knew the folly of overreaching. Now was not the time to step on toes. The last thing he needed was for Amenmesse to consider him a threat. Paris finished the final knot on his now strung bow and gave it a practice pull, the gut-string releasing with a vigorous twang. Inside, he was as taut as the weapon. He turned to Amenmesse, his joy of the upcoming event evaporating.

"Shall we begin?"

※

Helen and Aethra walked back to the palace after another morning spent in study at the Temple of Amun-Re. The standard her matron hoisted blocked out the most intense rays of the unforgiving Egyptian sun but did little to cool the pair as they journeyed across the desert plain towards the acropolis.

"You must press the high priest for a swift answer." Aethra stressed to Helen, the urgency of her matron's tone increasing each day they lingered in the Two Lands.

"*I'm trying.*" Helen grimaced, the pressure of the delay adding to her sensation of being smothered. "But Meryatum is not a normal man. One does not press a priest of his stature for anything."

Under constant scrutiny, and judged by queen and priest alike, Helen was having difficulty holding up under the strain. For every question the elites asked her, her answers created a dozen more. At times, she had become dizzy with her efforts to satisfy them without revealing too much. If only she could see Paris—simply talk with him—a few words would buoy her spirits more than a week of rest would.

As they neared the palace walls, a throng of minor nobles and royal staff exited the gates heading west toward the river. By their excited chatter, something big was underway. Helen paused to let them pass, taking advantage of this last opportunity to speak candidly with her matron.

"Is it selfish of me?" Helen voiced the guilty thought that kept her awake at night. "Am I putting us in greater danger by hoping for this ritual?"

Aethra lowered the standard, her hard eyes softening as she turned to her. "Danger is a fickle mistress, child. It follows no matter how well you safeguard against it." She sighed heavily. Raising a hand to her brow, she gazed across the desert to the north towards their former home. "The stain of the crimes against us lingers far longer than the crime itself. I know why you seek this ritual. Purity is a blessing the Gods grant to children. If it frees you to follow your heart, for my part, it is worth the risk."

Helen placed a hand on Aethra's arm, touched by the woman's loyalty. "Thank you."

The stodgy matron shifted under Helen's heartfelt gaze, uncomfortable with the attention. "Yes, well, that does not mean we should dally. The sooner you get that priest to commit, the better."

Helen suppressed a laugh and smiled. Ever since their arrival in Egypt, her world seemed in a constant state of flux. With so many personalities and intrigues at hand, she had no idea whom to trust. In that whirlwind, Aethra, was an anchor. "I miss our talks."

"As do I."

As the last courtiers disappeared down the western bank, Helen motioned to Iamus to continue onward. The Trojan guard stood a good ten paces ahead, his hawkish eyes scouring the terrain as though they walked in the midst of a battleground. Helen often wondered what possessed the man to remain so vigilant. Surely they were safe from attack in Heliopolis, a high seat of power in an internationally feared empire, but Iamus remained as disciplined as ever, hand on sword and shield in position, approaching each junction as though an army waited on the other side.

They did not make it past the first pylon, however, before being surrounded by a massive force. Two dozen wives of Pharaoh, and their collection of royal guard chaperones, crowded the gates, their eager chatter and rushed footfalls a practical stampede. Iamus pressed Helen and Aethra to the ramparts to avoid getting separated in the mix.

"Helen!" Twosret hailed her, a graceful weave to her steps as she walked down the stone rampart. "I'm so pleased I found you." The princess hooked an arm through hers, pulling Helen outside the palace grounds and joining the other wives.

"Where are we going?" Helen craned her neck over Twosret's shoulder, making sure Aethra and Iamus followed after.

"To the archery fields!" Merit clapped her hands together excitedly, her eager expression shared with the other wives.

Twosret quickly informed her about the princes' competition, a less-than-amused roll to her eyes as she spoke, "Your Trojan protector against Prince Amenmesse. A proper use of their regal vigor, wouldn't you say?"

Perhaps it was the way Twosret phrased her comment, but Helen found herself at a loss on how to respond. It felt like a question worthy of Nefertari, laced with double meaning. Helen scanned the crowd, looking for the elder monarch. "Where is the queen?"

"Resting, the poor dear." A crease of sadness marred

Twosret's pale brow. "It's amazing she can rise at all most days. Traveling outside the palace grounds taxes her strength. It's best she stays behind. Our dear matriarch won't last forever."

That thought made Helen's blood run cold. She could not imagine Egypt without Nefertari. Her aloof but calming presence was the glue that held the royal women together. If something were to happen to her, Helen feared the fallout would be immense. She hoped that whatever ailed the queen was not serious.

Twosret set a good pace. Her hand was painfully tight around Helen's arm as though she thought her guest might escape. So it was, half-dragged and surrounded by giggling young wives, that Helen arrived at the practice grounds.

The yard teemed with courtiers and palace officials. There was a strum of excitement in the air. Everywhere Helen turned, painted faces stretched wide with eager grins. The nobles chatted gaily in Egyptian about the coming match. Their dress was elegant, and man and woman alike wore carefully tailored wigs with a cone of scented wax atop the crown, a perfume that would mask their body odor as it melted in the heat of the day.

After spending the morning in the austere halls of the temple, surrounded by those devoted to understanding the Mysteries of the Gods, these giggling nobles seemed empty vessels to Helen, garish in their self-indulgences. Thankfully, Twosret ignored them all, weaving between many well-wishers and not stopping until she reached the raised pavilion where her husband waited.

The crown prince was a shimmering sight, so covered in gold that it hurt Helen's eyes to stare directly at him. She dipped into a curtsey, thankful for the excuse to lower her gaze.

"You are looking well, Wife." Seti wrapped his arm around Twosret's waist. Even at a distance the prince's wine-soaked breath washed over Helen. She covered her nose with her shawl, pretending to ward off the heat.

Twosret also grimaced but did not pull away from her husband's touch. "The occasion calls for it, My Prince."

"It does indeed." Seti caressed her hip in a suggestive manner, a man lording over his prize. Soon his lusty gaze slipped from his wife and over to Helen. "You have blossomed before our eyes, Princess." He pulled Helen's hand to his lips, his hot breath raising the hairs along her arm. "The clime and garb of the Two Lands suits you. Are you sure you must travel to Troy?"

"I am expected, Your Grace." She pulled her hand back as soon as was socially acceptable. "We can scarcely afford the delay as it is."

He stepped aside, helping both Twosret and her onto the pavilion. The four-pillared structure, with its rose colored canvas draped from each corner, was the only bit of shade in several hundred yards. It also boasted the best view of the practice grounds, a massive open field half reclaimed by the desert. The spectators faced west where the sun glinted off the distant waters of the Nile. Helen took her seat, searching instantly for Paris.

Her Trojan was some distance away. He stood beside a chariot, stroking the neck of his lead horse. Naked to the waist, his lean chest was bronzed from the sun, his hard muscles glistening with sweat. She could just imagine him whispering to the animal in a soothing tone, cajoling the beast to perform as he commanded.

Helen sighed with longing. She wanted those hands on her body with a power that frightened her. As though he could sense that, Paris looked up, his eyes riveted on her. The space separating them did little to dampen the passion she felt pouring in her direction.

"Wine!" Seti bellowed to a passing servant.

Helen politely refused when the woman offered her a bowl of the ruby dark fluid.

"Are you not thirsty?" Seti prodded, taking a generous

swallow from his own vessel.

"I am fasting," she replied with a note of apology, giving the prince a sweet smile. Helen had been around enough men possessed by spirits to know almost anything could set them off. It was best to give them no provocation.

"It seems a ridiculous tradition." Seti gestured as he spoke, his wine sloshing dangerously close to the rim of his bowl. "Why should one purify herself before a purification ritual? Isn't that the point of it all?"

"I... never thought about that." She turned back to the field, hoping to draw Seti's attention elsewhere than on her.

The crown prince was not to be deterred. He laughed, a wicked grin spreading across his inebriated face. "In fact, this would be the perfect time to indulge in all manner of devious behaviors, Princess. You could embrace your darkest fantasies and have them wiped clean before leaving the Two Lands." It was apparently clear that was not an observation but an invitation.

Helen blushed furiously. She and Paris might have come to Egypt requesting favors, but that did not mean she would grovel before distasteful behavior. Fortunately, an unlikely defender was not far away.

"Seti," Shoteraja purred with disapproval, taking a seat behind them. "You should not jest. You know Meryatum would never allow that manner of person to abuse the mercies of the Gods." Her eyes narrowed and she gave Helen a knowing stare. "His wrath would be unimaginable if someone came to him under false pretenses."

She is trying to provoke you. Helen schooled herself to calmness. *She doesn't know anything. If she did, we'd all be in chains.*

A horn blast rang out, and soon Shoteraja and her troubles were far from Helen's mind. The crowd erupted into cheers as the princes mounted their chariots and began a short practice lap around the grounds. Dust rose in small clouds from their wheels as they spun around each other, each man showcasing his deft skill in maneuvering their carts.

The targets were somewhat large: clay plates three hands across. A vaulter launched the disks into the sky and the princes had to aim and shoot while their chariots were in motion.

Paris went first. He moved with a fluid grace, his tactic of releasing his arrow almost as soon as he drew made his skill seem effortless. The plates he fired upon shattered with a loud crack from the impact, and an excited audience rewarded him with massive applause. By the time he finished, he had not missed a single target.

As they waited for the dust cloud to settle before Amenmesse would start, Helen could not help but long for her prince, to tell him how proud she was. She could show him no special favor, though, not if she hoped to uphold the fiction that circumstance had forced them to adopt.

Helen turned from the pavilion, the falseness of that pretense eating at her like a parasite. Stuck with a woman who despised her and a prince half-crazed with drink, she longed for just one person she could share her true feelings with. Catching a slight movement from the corner of her eye, she realized relief was near. She had Iamus.

"He's amazing," she whispered down to the Trojan from the pavilion. "Did you know?"

Iamus glanced out to where Paris parked his chariot, a hint of pride on his usually somber face. "He is like Apollo, Himself." Iamus nodded. "There are none in Troy who can match him with a bow."

Helen settled back into her seat as Amenmesse took to the field. He carried an elegant longbow, and when the string was taut, he presented a regal profile much like the hieroglyphics lining the temple walls. His skill was equally impressive, and measure for measure, he matched Paris' score.

"Your brother is quite talented," Helen offered to Seti, the prince's face red from alternating cheers and jeers for his sibling.

"Yes, he is," Twosret answered for him, frowning at her husband. "He brings much honor to our house."

"You mean to himself." Seti's lips twisted into a growl. He raised a white flag, signaling the vaulter to change targets. They began another round with smaller disks, again with the same, tied results.

"Oh, get on with it," Seti grumbled, the mixture of wine and sun making him cross. "Bring out the swifts!"

Palace servants ran across the field carrying several large crates, the flurry of wings against the reed slats indicating the next targets would be live.

"Amenmesse, you go first," Seti commanded imperiously. "The first unanswered hit wins." He reclined in his stool, wrapping his arm around Twosret and fondling her breast. He leaned in to her ear and spoke in a husky whisper, "Your brother always did have trouble following a fowl. Let's see how he does before the entire court." He lowered his lips to nuzzle at her neck, groaning as his erection grew noticeably beneath his kilt.

Twosret stiffened like a plank. She made no move to counter her husband as Seti continued to make free with her body. Only the dark spark of hate in her eyes gave light to her true feelings beneath.

Helen watched the exchange with growing unease. She had known the matrimonial ties in Egypt were complicated, but if what Seti had said was true, then Amenmesse was brother to both the crown prince *and* Twosret. Which meant Seti was equally Twosret's brother as he was her husband.

Helen's stomach rolled. *What horrors the woman must have endured!* Like she with Menelaus, or Clytemnestra with Agamemnon, Twosret had no choice but to suffer her husband's abuse. A wave of sympathy washed over her for the Egyptian princess, and Helen could not help but feel sorry for another woman forced to deal with an amoral husband.

She must have made some sound. Twosret's eyes snapped to Helen, the dark hate the princess reserved for her husband unleashed on her. This woman was not helpless. This woman had no need for pity. Helen shirked back in her seat.

"Later, Seti," Twosret purred, shifting her body further *into* his embrace, her face ablaze as though daring the man take his depravations deeper. "We'll miss the winning shot."

That factor seemed to sober Seti a bit. He resettled back in his stool and raised another flag to signal the contestants. The first bird took to air and Amenmesse whipped his chariot in pursuit.

The swift was an amazingly fast bird with great dexterity. Its crooked wings allowed it to make sudden changes in mid-flight. If Seti had planned to challenge his brother, he could not have picked a more troublesome bird.

Amenmesse whipped his chariot around and nocked an arrow. The swift folded its wings alongside its body, setting into a dive. The prince tried to readjust, but his bow was too long, and the butt end hit the edge of his chariot as he let loose his arrow. It flew harmlessly wide, and a stunned gasp went through the crowd.

"One point down!" Seti shouted, a malicious glee lighting up his face as he signaled for the next release.

Helen turned to where Paris mounted his chariot. Glaucus was beside him and they seemed to be in the middle of a heated exchange. When the horn rang out, the captain walked off, his rigid stance one Helen had come to recognize for when he thought Paris was being overly unreasonable.

The second bird took to the air. It made a meandering path across the sky, dipping into free-fall then darting forward as quickly as any horse. Paris gave chase, setting his chariot on an intersecting course before he dropped the reigns and reached for his bow.

It should have been quick work for him. In every other volley, he nocked an arrow and immediately released. But not this time. He held his bow, arrow taut, for agonizing moments. When his chariot hit a rut in the road, his arrow shot forward. It came close to the panic-driven bird but did not hit. The crowd howled with displeasure, and none so much as the crown prince.

Seti held up a new flag, one that signaled the riders to return. Both Paris and Amenmesse guided their chariots before the royal pavilion, each man short of breath with chests covered in dirt-tinged sweat.

"Marvelous!" Seti hailed them both. "Truly marvelous. You are a born marksman, Trojan!"

"It was not exactly perfect," Paris offered an embarrassed glance to Amenmesse. "I missed the last mark. Perhaps we should call it a day? I think both the prince and I are feeling the affects of your Egyptian sun."

Amenmesse remained silent in his chariot, but his face spoke of welcome relief. He nodded his consent to Seti.

The crown prince, however, was not quite so content to call the match a truce. "I have yet to declare a victor."

"But neither one of us—" Paris began.

"Your arrow was nearer the mark." Seti spun to the waiting crowd. "The Trojan wins!"

As expected, the courtiers exploded with applause. Ironically, neither contestant seemed pleased. Amenmesse, in particular, took the news poorly, his face twisted with the bitter taste of defeat.

"Do not look so sour, Brother," Seti crowed, raising another bowl of wine in salute to the winner. "You can redeem yourself on the morrow. We'll have a rematch in the marshlands."

Paris shot a wary glance to Glaucus, this revelation settling over him with deep unease. "The marshlands? Why do we have to travel so far?"

"Because," a wicked grin spread across Seti's face, "I wish to hunt bigger game."

Bigger game? Helen swallowed nervously, wondering what greater danger the crown prince would demand in pursuit of his entertainment. She waited breathless for Seti to continue.

"Hippo..."

Chapter 21

Lessons of the Vanquished Foe

PARIS STORMED OFF the field after Seti's announcement.

A bloody hunt. What next? Am I to perform like a monkey in his court?

The crown prince was establishing a suffocating hold over his life. He needed to get away, even if for only a moment. Giving no thought to the direction, he let his feet carry him where they saw fit, and soon Paris left the palace grounds and headed into the less populated terrain to the south. Ahead of him, the enormous limestone walls of the Temple of Amun-Re dominated the horizon.

Jason rushed to keep pace, though he remained a respectful distance behind Paris. Glaucus, too, tried to join, but the furious look on his face was enough to keep the Trojan captain with his troops. Paris did not fancy another of Glaucus' lectures on the wisdom of winning and losing. Not now.

Seti was making good on his promise that the Trojans would provide him a much needed distraction. The crown prince demanded his entertainments like a child glutting itself on sweetmeats. Wasting Paris' time with foppish games and drink was not enough for the God-king-in-waiting. Now he thought to use Paris as a tool to humiliate his brother.

Amenmesse was an arrogant toe-rag as well, but, as a second son who strove to do something more with his life than sit on the sidelines, Paris could not help but sympathize with the man. He did not relish being used in the petty feud emerging between the princes.

He kicked a pebble out of his path, venting his frustrations on the innocent rock. He should have lost outright to Amenmesse, as Glaucus suggested. His foolish pride had gotten in the way, and now that he had proven himself capable, Seti was not going to give his shiny new toy a moment's rest.

A bloody hunt!

It was abundantly clear that Seti didn't give two shekels about the urgency of the Trojan quest. He cared only for himself and his pleasure, and Paris wouldn't put it past the prince to assert pressure on the Temple to delay their departure.

There was only one way to know for sure, and Paris had subconsciously chosen this path wisely. He needed to speak with the high priest.

A long ramp led to the temple gates where square pylons rose into the sky. The processional walk was lined with seated rams, carved of stone. At the entrance, two guards stood, their sickle-tipped staves crossed.

Paris paused, allowing Jason to fully catch up with him. The poor Grecian was trying not to show how the heat taxed him. The collar around his throat was of thick leather, and the metal ring in the center looked equally heavy. In this heat, it would have made the man struggle for every breath, and yet he uttered not one word of complaint. Jason watched Paris with alert, ice-blue eyes, ready as ever to serve.

"Have you been inside the temple before?"

Jason shook his head. "They do not let profaners on sacred ground."

Paris expected as much, but now that they had come all this way, he was not going to send the man back. "Keep your head down. Try not to look too closely at any of their artifacts. If they catch you staring at an idol, they'll probably execute you. I won't be able to stop them."

Jason seemed surprised by the warning. It was probably more consideration than the slave had ever received from a royal. But Paris wasn't trying to win the man's loyalty; he did not want a dead man's spirit weighing down on his conscious.

He marched up to the temple guards. They were hairless, like the priests, but the similarities ended there. These men were born warriors, their pectoral muscles clenched tight as they glared down on him from their higher position. Behind them lay a long corridor, its inky blackness magnified by the brilliant speck of light at the far end of the tunnel.

"Who dares to enter the House of Amun-Re?" said the guard nearest him.

"I am Paris of the royal house of Troy. I have come to speak with the high priest."

The guards exchanged a quick look, but were otherwise expressionless. "He is not expecting you, Prince of Troy. You should wait for his invitation."

Paris grimaced. He was not going to be deflected again. Every day, *every minute*, he wasted waiting on Egyptian pleasure, was another opportunity for Agamemnon's wrath to catch up with them. "Then I will wait, *but inside*. You can at least extend me the courtesy of the shade of your court."

The two guards conversed in urgent whispers before the first came back with a rueful expression. "You may enter. But the court only. One of the *pastophoroi* will see to your request."

Paris nodded his agreement and stepped into the dark corridor, the sudden drop in temperature making the hair rise on his neck. The tunnel seemed to radiate a celestial cool from its thick blocks of perfectly shaped stone. Raising his hand against the blinding light at the opposite end, he stepped out into the main court of the temple.

The grounds were enormous, the outer gates encompassing over 150 acres of land. The paved court where he now stood was some 500 feet long by 350 feet wide. It was lined on each side by colonnaded stoas, long walkways with roofs that reached only halfway up the massive perimeter wall. Ahead of him sat an enormous rectangular building that sloped up to a flat roof. At the very center of that roof, a squat, square-based obelisk made of red-granite stretched into the sky like the finger of a God. A capstone of electrum decorated its tip, the silver/gold metal catching sunlight with a gleaming spark. A second set of pylon gates framed the building, hiding the rest of the temple, and its secrets, beyond.

Paris watched as one of the guards sprinted across the court and into that inner sanctum. He suppressed the urge to follow the man. Now was the time for patience. Turning to the shade of the walkways, he began a perimeter stroll, Jason trailing behind him.

Every inch of temple wall was decorated with hieroglyphs. From what Paris remembered of his education in Egyptian religion, the pictures dealt mostly with the Ennead, the Egyptian origin myth where the creator god, Atum, emerged from the primordial waters of nonexistence and begat the nine other deities who made up the core of the Egyptian pantheon. The temple at Heliopolis was dedicated to Re, God of the Midday Sun, the most influential deity in the Two Lands. The temple artisans had outdone themselves in their many colorful representations of the powerful god.

He continued down the path, refreshing his skill of reading the Egyptian script. It was not until he was halfway down the length of the court that he realized Jason was no longer with him.

"*Jason?*" He raced back down the walkway, searching the open court for any hint of the sandy-haired man. The open-air space was not devoid of activity. Several temple workers went about their business scrubbing floors and refreshing paint on the western wall. Many cast him disapproving looks as he raised his voice.

He took a sharp corner that lead back to the temple gates and almost tripped over the man. If not for the steady rise and fall of his chest, Paris would have sworn Jason was a dead man standing, his face was that pale. His eyes, however, sparked of life, staring daggers into a freshly cut black granite stele before him. At nearly ten feet tall, it was an imposing sight, and Paris was amazed he had missed it.

"Are you all right?" He approached Jason cautiously, but the man did not stir. What was it about this object that had possessed the man so?

Atop the stele, King Merneptah—shown as a vigorous Pharaoh—received a sword of power from Amun-Re. The inscription beneath read:

"In regnal year five, on the third day of the third month of the period of Inundation, under the Majesty of Horus Re, King Merneptah, the Strong Bull, the King of Upper and Lower Egypt raised the victorious sword of power, smiting the Nine Bows until their seed was no more.

"Great fear of Egypt was in their hearts. Their legs did not stay firm, but fled. Their archers threw their bows away. The wretched conquered Prince of Libya fled, his brothers plotted his murder, his officers fought with one another, their camp was burned and made to ashes."

On and on it went, detailing the brutal victory of Merneptah over the Libyan revolt and their hired Grecian mercenaries. The land was laid waste where "nothing would grow for generations." The king destroyed his enemies, "enraged like a lion", and captured some 9,000 prisoners that he had castrated and their hands removed like damaged livestock.

Jason stared at the hieroglyph showcasing that mutilation, his expression unreadable. The enemies of Pharaoh were shown in a line, some cowering beneath his boot, others manacled and chained together, and more still dead and pierced with arrows.

It was typical for rulers to tout their victories in battle, and the Egyptian kings had a flair for exalting their deeds into grandiose spectacle. For the people of the Two Lands, it reinforced the notion that their God-King was infallible, but for the vanquished foe? Paris studied Jason, his quiet rage and simmering control, with a new appreciation. There were countless disgruntled men, like the former pirate, spread across the world. How long would they be content to wear chains?

"Can you read?"

"I don't need to read to know it lies." The words rumbled from Jason's throat like a pending avalanche. "The king never set foot on the battlefield. He had his generals set fire to the grass. *He burned his own men to achieve his victory.* What manner of person does that?"

Paris was surprised to hear such candor from a slave. The complaint was valid, however. Many kings, empowered with extreme hubris, committed cruel and profound injustices to secure their seat of power. In his tenure as a Trojan diplomat, it seemed the number of those rulers had increased over the years. There was little a commoner could say or do to change that, however. The Gods had placed noble men in power. Voicing opinions to the contrary could only send the unwary protestor to the execution block.

Jason must have come to the same realization. His ice-blue eyes spread wide and he dropped to his knees. "Forgive me, Your Highness," he begged. "I did not mean to speak so disrespectfully. Your host is a righteous man. The Gods favor his sword. His retribution on those who defy the Laws of Man should be terrible. My brothers thought to steal from a king. We deserve all he inflicted upon us and more."

Steal from a king...

Paris stiffened. By taking Helen from her homeland, that was precisely what he had done. He swallowed hard, at a complete loss of how to respond. In the dark nights when he could not sleep, he had tried to convince himself that a person was not property, but he was sure Agamemnon would not see matters that way. In the eyes of Western law, and perhaps even Egyptian, Paris was a thief no different than the slave prostrated at his feet.

"You deserve to be treated like a man, not a piece of meat," Paris grimaced, his stomach churning with those dire thoughts. "All men, even slaves, have a right to an opinion, whatever opinion that may be. But be wise when you voice it. Now get up." No man should be made to grovel, and before him least of all.

Jason scrambled to his feet, the disbelief etched on his face a small indicator of the oddness of Paris' reaction. "I... I will, Your Highness. Thank you." He seemed genuinely touched. Paris wondered how many horrors the man had endured under the Egyptian lash that such a small act of human decency could have that profound an effect.

"You should not be afraid to speak with me," Paris said, knowing it was a small gesture. "I will help you, if I can."

"...Thank you."

They were no longer alone. Paris heard the slippered steps of the approaching priest, even though the man did well to mask them. Taking a deep breath, he prepared himself to deal with the temple servant and whatever new deflection the *pastophoroi* had come to impart.

Paris was not, however, prepared for what awaited him. The man standing before him was no mere temple priest, but Meryatum, the High Priest of Re.

"Your Excellency," he dipped his head with respect. "Thank you for making the time to speak with me. I have no right to expect such a quick response."

"No, you do not," Meryatum snapped, his dark eyes showing the agitation that lay beneath, "but you are here now, so let's away with these pretenses. Why have you come, Trojan?"

Paris cleared his throat, trying to recapture the earlier frustrations that had led him to the temple. He motioned Jason to give them some space and stepped beside the priest. "I am here to inquire about Helen. Do you—"

"I remember you." Meryatum inhaled sharply with recognition. "You were barely a man at Merneptah's coronation, still filled with the curiosity of youth. You asked to study the Mysteries at the House of Life, if I recall."

"I did." Paris stiffened with surprise. Their encounter had been a chance meeting ten years prior. He had spoken a mere handful of words to the high priest. Hardly memorable. "A petition you granted. A privilege for which I am eternally grateful."

Paris had been young and unfamiliar with the nuances of international relations when he first traveled to Egypt. Those long hours of study in the House of Life, surrounded by the wealth of Egyptian knowledge, were a godsend. It created a thirst in Paris that he carried into each new kingdom he visited.

"You granted me that petition long ago, which led me to believe you would approve another," he continued, determined to get answers. "Why is there no date set for Helen's purification?"

Meryatum studied him, a hairless brow arched high. His face was unreadable. If he withheld the ceremony on order of Seti, or if he stalled for some other purpose, Paris would never know save his confession... and the High Priest of Re confessed to no man.

"You have some learning in you." Meryatum folded his arms into his sleeves and began a measured pace along the stoa. Paris was forced to keep stride. "You will understand the importance of consulting the Gods and interpreting their omens."

Paris cast a dubious look to the priest. "Yes, but—"

"For example," he interjected, "consider this omen in which your untimely visit interrupted from my contemplation.

THE PRINCESS OF PROPHECY

This morning, as I finished my salutations to Re along the western desert, a single locust lit upon my arm. It was unremarkable, as far as locusts go, green and average in size, but as I lifted my arm, it spread its wings, displaying the most incredible colors—a vibrant tapestry I had never seen before. It lifted into the sky and was joined by a thousand more, the swarm spiraling together and collecting into a perfect circle before blotting out the sun. For a moment, I stood in shadow, certain I was witnessing a message from Amun-Re. Then the swarm dispersed, a thousand insects traveling in a thousand different directions. Odd behavior, wouldn't you say?"

"Indeed." Paris nodded.

"So, what does it mean?"

He almost laughed at the irony. Paris was the last person who should be consulted to interpret omens and dreams. In his view, temple officials took perfectly explainable phenomena and laced it with whatever meaning they wished. "I doubt I am qualified..."

"If you can puzzle out the meaning of Re's message, perhaps you will find the answer you came here seeking."

He sighed. There seemed no alternative than to play along with the high priest's wishes. A blotted out sun could mean a bad harvest, or a lackluster foaling. He almost said as much, but his last conversation with Jason had filled his head with other concerns. "A single locust becomes a swarm. The one become many. Together they are strong enough to rival the sun, the greatest power of the land."

The wrinkles along Meryatum's eyes tightened with approval. "My acolytes could not fathom the importance of that omen." He paced sedately around Paris, inspecting him from all sides. "Perhaps, when you tire of travel, you might find a future in service to your Gods."

Not likely... A bitter irony surged within him.

"I thank you for your wisdom, Your Excellency. It is not my future, however, that concerns me, but that of my charge. We cannot afford a long delay in our journey. Do you intend to perform the ritual for Helen or not?"

The question stumped the high priest and he ceased his walking. His face tensed and he seemed a man conflicted. "I am unsure. The omens are misleading. They speak of great favor *and* woe. The princess is no ordinary woman. I... I need more time with her, to see Amun-Re's plan."

The desire in his voice... *More time with Helen?* For the God's purpose or his own? Paris tensed, a spark of violence inside him begging to be unleashed. He prided himself on his self-control, but danger to Helen struck him deeper than threat to himself.

Though he did his best to recover from the slip, Meryatum missed nothing. The priest inhaled sharply like a man sensing danger. Lightning quick, he grabbed Paris' hand, flipping over his palm to study the criss-crossing pattern of lines. The priest's touch was icy cold, and to Paris it felt like the piercing sting of nettles arcing through his arm.

Meryatum took a large step back. He dropped Paris' hand and stared at him as though he were a specter made flesh. "It appears I am mistaken. The Gods have a special purpose for her." His voice rumbled with a cold power. *"And for you."*

A familiar emptiness flooded Paris. He had seen that cold look of disapproval before. The priests of Apollo had looked upon him with similar disfavor, calling for his death since he was a child. Meryatum's scrutiny was no different than theirs. That dark gaze had one purpose: to seek some flaw, some sign of impurity in him. In Paris' experience, if one searched hard enough, he inevitably found what he was looking for.

Paris stood tall, battling the judgement that would surely follow the only way he knew how... with cool indifference. "The Gods' ways are mysterious. For my part, I strive to honor them. The rest I leave to the Fates."

"Fate..." the priest murmured, a prophetic gleam shining in his eyes as his face drained of color. "We are all slaves to Her merciless pull. I take comfort that She is but a handmaiden to the Gods, a tool they use to balance the scales of *ma'at*.

THE PRINCESS OF PROPHECY

Though Meryatum spoke with conviction, he nevertheless tightened his grip on the Eye of Horus amulet around his neck, a medallion meant to invoke protection from malicious forces. "Be careful, Trojan. No man can escape his fate." He bowed stiffly at the waist. "May Re's light shine upon you."

Humiliation surged within Paris as he watched Meryatum retreat back into the temple. Had he done something, *said something*, to set the priest off? He quickly regrouped with Jason and headed back to the palace at a fast pace, wanting to put as much distance between himself and the judgement of the Gods as possible.

Escape my fate...?

Those words sent shivers down his spine. The high priest did not strike Paris as a man without wisdom. He spoke of *ma'at*, the cosmic order of light over dark, of good over evil. Of life over death. A chill settled into his bones despite the heated air, and he felt the dark shadow of his birth omen return to haunt him again.

But the omen was false... He hoped against reason that that was true. Deep down inside, however, in the broken corners of his soul, he still doubted. A lifetime of being told he was the herald of woe could not be erased in the span of a few weeks, no matter how strongly Helen believed.

The darkness of that fate surrounded him. He suffocated beneath its massive weight. The thought that it could bring danger to Helen as well was beyond his endurance. They needed to leave Egypt. *Soon.* He was no longer going to wait on Seti and the temple for permission.

As they entered his guest apartments, he grabbed Glaucus by the arm, towing him to a quiet corner where no one could overhear.

"How well do you know the streets of Heliopolis?"

"About the same as you." Glaucus shrugged. "I don't."

Paris cursed, spinning away from his captain. It would take time to infiltrate the black market of the city and secure their escape, and time was one commodity that was running scarce.

A soft noise drew his attention from those dark thoughts. Jason stood a short distance away, a fierce look of determination dominating his features. "I know Heliopolis."

Paris exchanged a quick glance with Glaucus, the captain sharing his misgivings. "That won't be necessary—"

"Please, Your Grace," Jason pleaded, in fact begged. "You said before that you would help me if you could. *But I can help you.* Let me be of service."

He hesitated. Paris needed help, and Jason certainly held no love for the Egyptians... but could he trust the man? The Greek's crystal-blue eyes said that he could.

"Please, My Prince. I will not fail you."

Chapter 22

Honor and Oaths

"FROM THE MOMENT the Trojans arrived, there was something false about the prince." A light rain fell on the acropolis as the queen shared her tale before the near empty megaron. Achilles paced along the portico, his eyes locked on the Mycenaean king who sat on his throne beside his wife. A handful of noble stewards, the king's *lawagetas* military advisors, and three royal visitors were all that stood in attendance: a dozen men in a space that could hold over two hundred, a fact the king seemed less-than-pleased about as he shifted in his seat, his eyes darting with a manic energy over the assemblage.

Achilles shared a look of concern with his fellow royals. He had travelled to Mycenae at the king's invitation. As did Diomedes, King of Argos, and Palamedes, Prince of Nauplia, both neighboring realms to the south. They had come to the capital with promise of feast and games — games *honoring* the Trojan delegation. And now they were witness to an act of war? It was a convenient twist of fate that raised the hair on Achilles' arms.

"He offered veiled insults in court and a cool arrogance when shown the splendors of Mycenae," Clytemnestra continued. "Helen bravely volunteered to act as Prince Paris' guide, to spy on the Trojans and discover the true purpose of this unannounced visit." The queen's eyes darted nervously to her husband and she tightened a shawl around her neck, wincing in pain. She hid the bruising well, but not as well as she thought. Achilles had noticed the dark marks when Clytemnestra first entered the hall.

What sort of beast tests his strength against a woman? Achilles glowered at the king. How the Gods tormented him when Phthia had been forced to pledge fealty to such a man.

"The more Helen reported, the more it became clear," the Mycenaean queen continued. "Paris was not here to establish bonds of friendship between nations but to remind Mycenae of the greatness of Troy, of Her military and economic might. To remind us of our proper place before the Golden City — on bended knee."

The nobles broke out into heated commentary, each man trying to outdo their rivals with declarations of Grecian valor, their angry murmurings the sort one would expect from trained dogs performing on cue. Achilles scoffed at the vainglorious men. These sycophants administered Agamemnon's rule in the provinces. While they held the power of life and death over their subjects, they inspired no love in their people. They had no concept of how to rally warriors to their cause. They preened with self-importance, nothing more than mongrels fighting for scraps from their master's table.

He continued to watch on in silence, rainwater sluicing down his matted blonde hair to the stone tiles of the portico. It splattered against the rock with a rhythmic pounding, pulsing like a finger on an exposed nerve. It was not so long ago that Achilles had stood on opposite sides of a battlefield from these Mycenaeans. How they got the best of his father was beyond him, but best Phthia they did, or he would not be forced to stand here and listen to this drivel.

The queen was not finished. She waited with regal cool

until the outburst wore down to a manageable murmur and continued, "Before we could conclude our negotiations, my husband and Menelaus were called away with news of their Grandsire's murder. Once gone, the prince showed his true nature." A dark shadow crossed over her lovely face, and she shook with a barely contained anger. Even the maids who simpered and cooed at her every word took a noticeable step back. "With the cloak of night to hide his depravity, he raided the royal treasury and kidnapped Helen. His galley slipped anchor with the midnight tide, and we did not discover his foul deeds until the following morning when they were long set to sea."

Agamemnon gripped his scepter with a death lock, his knuckles so tight they drained of color. He tipped the royal regalia toward his brother, and Menelaus stepped before the central hearth, the burning coals hissing from the steady drip of water leaking down from the oculus above.

"That bastard of Troy will pay for his crimes." The orange flames danced in Menelaus' eyes with a wildness that matched the prince's reputation. "I don't care how many men he has to hide behind. I will find him and slice his throat for this insult."

The Mycenaean king rose to his feet, his dark gaze leveled on every man in attendance. "This insult is not borne by Menelaus alone. As diplomat, the prince was acting on behalf of Troy. King Priam treats the Men of the West with no honor, and if we do not answer this treachery forthwith, then we have none as well. You all swore the Oath. It's time the kingdoms of the Hellas united!"

Cries of allegiance filled the air. There was no end of nobles eager to swear their swords in the powerful king's service. Not a single one of them had the wits to question the fanciful tale, to question Agamemnon's battle lust. Even Palamedes joined their heated cries, his call for Trojan blood ringing out across the megaron and bouncing off the stucco walls and high timber ceiling.

Only Achilles and Diomedes stood apart. The Argolian

king clasped his hands behind his back, soaking in every word Agamemnon uttered. From the tight expression on his face, he did not favor this turn of events any more than did Achilles.

Troy, the golden gateway of the Hellespont, one of the mightiest empires of the Old World, a kingdom that had stood for a thousand years. A sovereign nation whose armies greatly outnumbered their own. And Agamemnon wished to attack them based on the words of a woman...

Achilles leaned over and whispered fiercely into Diomedes ear, "If Troy was truly behind this incident, would not the prince have taken the queen?"

Clytemnestra was an alluring woman, her beauty like that of the massive ice crystals that formed on the high reaches of Mt. Orthrys, as awe-inspiring as it was deadly. She and Helen were identical. Kidnapping the queen would have satisfied any man's lust-filled fantasies *and* have been the act of war Agamemnon claimed.

Diomedes nodded, his dark eyes narrowing as he silently considered Achilles' argument. Like his collected appearance and short-trimmed beard, Diomedes espoused care and reason in all his actions. Over the years of his kingship, he had earned a reputation for fairness. He was not one easily manipulated. If Diomedes found merit in Achilles' concerns, perhaps others would as well.

"Convenient, isn't it?" he pressed on. "The Trojan takes the *one* woman we all swore to defend? The only person who could unite the Hellas."

The prince had to have known about Tyndareus' oath. It was common knowledge throughout the Hellas. To have taken Helen smacked of either arrogance or idiocy, neither of which were words he'd ever heard describe Troy.

Perhaps Troy didn't care whom they offended. Perhaps they hungered for war and thought shaming the West good sport, that the death toll sure to follow would earn them infamy the bards would sing about for all the Ages. But Achilles doubted it. There was only one man he knew who fit that description, and he was standing in this room.

"Who's to say the Trojans even have the princess?" Now given ear, Achilles could not stop his restless thoughts from flowing. "Agamemnon is hiding something, Diomedes. Mark my words."

"Have you something to say, Son of Peleus?"

Achilles lifted his gaze to meet Agamemnon's, the spark of fury on the Mycenaean's face taunting him to speak his mind —a temptation Achilles could not answer without causing the people of Phthia to suffer the consequences.

The other kings of Greece did not allow Agamemnon to claim Phthia as a vassal state, but he might as well have. After the Mycenaean host spread across southern Thessaly, a great famine followed in their wake. The "peace" treaty between kings only further strained Phthia's dwindling resources. Their once mighty nation withered like grapes left on the vine. Those who survived were grief-tested, hardened by their struggles, and the Myrmidon soldiers who emerged from the ashes were as fearsome as they were few.

Achilles gripped the hilt of his sword, those dark days of battling a foe who had no face made him itch to thrust his sword into someone's gut. Unfortunately, the man he most wanted to gut was also a king. He buried those dark memories away, determined to show no sign of weakness before this detestable man. "We did swear an oath," Achilles grit his teeth, allowing his defiance to ooze through every pore of his skin, "to defend *Menelaus* against wrong done to his marriage, but how do we know he has been wronged? You were gone when the Trojan envoy left your shores. What proof can you offer the other kings that Helen is even with them?"

A long moment of silence greeted his words, the king glaring at him all-the-while with hate-filled, inky black eyes filled. "I have never known you to back away from a fight, Achilles." Agamemnon seethed. "Have you grown craven during the quiet years of peace?"

"If you think me craven, then you are blind enough to

believe the other kings will hand you an army to do with as you please." Achilles' hand strayed down his side to the hilt of his sword. He prayed the king was fool enough to challenge him publicly.

The nobles broke out in angry rumbling, shocked by his brazen words. In theory, he outranked the commanders at his side, but many of those grizzled veterans considered Phthia a conquered territory and treated its prince with similar disregard.

"They *will* hand me an army." Agamemnon waved down the courtiers. "And when they do, you best be careful that I don't march on your homeland first, Son of Peleus."

"Which is precisely why they will never hand you those reins."

The shouting became deafening. Achilles did not respond to it, standing silent as their empty threats rained down around him. There was one voice in the din, however, that gave him pause. The dulcet cry of a child...

"STOP IT!" Iphigenia shouted out over the megaron.

Achilles turned to the princess, stunned by the breathtaking vision of beauty that awaited him. This was no child. While new to her maidenhood, Iphigenia was every bit as regal as her mother. Her honey-brown hair was braided with ropes of pearls, and her elegant chiton clung to her curves. A gentle innocence, as fresh as dew on a spring morning, surrounded her. She seemed a pure creature in a world surrounded by darkness. How could something so beautiful come from a man so detestable?

"Stop it!" Iphigenia pleaded again. The princess trembled with unspoken panic, her soft brown eyes teeming with unshed tears.

Achilles flushed, ashamed of his conduct before the royal woman. "Princess?"

"All your squabbles of oaths and allegiance! Where is your honor? He *took* Aunt Helen. What horrors is he subjecting her to while we fight over petty nonsense?" Her voice cracked and a tear trickled down her cheek. "We have to save her. Please.

THE PRINCESS OF PROPHECY

She needs our help..."

The men fell silent following the princess' impassioned plea. Even Agamemnon watched his daughter with a new appreciation. "You require proof, Achilles? It so happens I have some." He turned to his wife and Clytemnestra stepped forward, leading a curvaceous raven-haired maiden out of the crowd of women behind her.

"Astyanassa is one of Helen's handmaidens. Tell them." The queen stroked the woman's back. "Tell them what you witnessed that night."

Astyanassa took a timid step forward, the gentle prodding of the queen seeming to buoy her confidence. "That night the prince was lurking around the palace grounds. My mistress was suspicious of his odd behavior and demanded we follow him, her elderly matron and I. Despite my protests, she insisted on accompanying us. They broke into the treasury. The princess was outraged, and she confronted the Trojans, demanding they stop their theft."

The maid shivered, evoking murmurs of sympathy from the gathered men. Only Achilles was not fooled. The vixen feigned coy, yet in her eyes was the quiet control of a warrior who knew precisely what she was doing. "*He mocked her*, claiming her courage naive. He then bound her hand and foot, bragging he would claim another treasure of Mycenae, taunting her with claims of all the horrible things he would do to her once they left. Placing a gag in her mouth to silence her screams, he took Aethra and my mistress captive, leaving me locked inside the treasury to 'tell the Mad King what happens when he thinks himself better than Troy.'"

A stunned silence followed the maiden's words. Achilles stood as one struck. Had he heard the woman correctly? "*Aethra?* The disgraced queen?" He turned to Agamemnon. "They took her captive as well?" Lusty, treacherous thieves left a tasty morsel like Astyanassa behind while taking a woman well into her third score of years?

The lie was writ all over the king. He glared at Achilles

with the heat of Hephaestus' furnace. In the absence of his response, other voices filled the hall. Palamedes strode forward, grabbing Menelaus by the forearm. "Nauplia stands with you, Menelaus. Invoke the Oath. The other kings will come, or I will make them come. All of Troy will pay for this insult."

The announcement was met with applause from the court, a palpable air of relief spreading amongst those gathered. The peace that presided over the Hellas was tenuous at best. No one looked forward to shedding Grecian blood. None, that was, save the king.

"Achilles," Agamemnon descended from the throne. "A word in private, please."

Against his better judgement, he joined the king. Agamemnon led them out the portico where the earthy musk of rain-soaked soil greeted them as they walked down a set of stairs to the courtyard beneath. The rain had stopped falling, but the pooling water made the steps slick. Achilles never wavered. He had long learned how to stay on his feet.

"You do not like me," Agamemnon spoke as they stepped off the landing. "No, do not deny it." He waved down Achilles' protests. "You are a mighty warrior, Achilles. The other kings rightly fear you. *But I do not.*"

The king's sudden change in tone took Achilles by surprise. Lightning fast, Agamemnon gripped him by the throat and slammed his back against the foundation of the palace. It took little effort to withdraw the dagger at his hip and press the tip into Agamemnon's side.

"If you value your manhood, you will release me," Achilles hissed. It was an empty threat. Achilles could not harm his host without Phthia suffering the consequences, and by the callous glint in Agamemnon's soulless eyes, he was well aware he had nothing to fear.

"*You are no king,*" Agamemnon hissed back. "You are a mixed blood mongrel. Why your father would take a barbarian as wife is beyond me, but I see the wrath of her tribesmen in you, Beggar Prince." Spittle foamed at the king's mouth and he spat on the ground. "If you *ever* question my leadership in front of another man again, I will leave Phthia without an heir."

Rage clouded Achilles' sight. The blood-vision, he called it. The world tinted red, and he twisted his blade, placing enough pressure on the massive king to make him relinquish his hold. He dropped into a crouch, a lethal energy tensing his muscles.

"*Others have tried,*" he growled. "None have succeeded. It will take a mighty warrior to grant me Death's final blessing. Are you that man, Agamemnon?" He jostled the sword at his hip, praying the king was that foolish.

Agamemnon was no fool, however. He backed off, a twisted smile pulling at his lips. "I don't want you dead, *Myrmidones*. I want you fighting at my vanguard. Honor your oath, or Zeus help me, every street brat in the Hellas will know you for craven, Achilles, just like your dear, dead father."

Achilles holstered his blade, his racing pulse still thundering in his skull. He would not let this hated man bait him. It was clear the Mycenae king longed for an enemy to test his prowess, a military target to prove his worth to the other Grecian rulers. Phthia could not afford to draw his wrath again. He stood down, his gut twisting with the sour grip of bile. Agamemnon got precisely what he wanted, and some part of him smarted over that fact.

"I am glad we have an understanding." Madness laced through Agamemnon's eyes, the menacing brute gloating in the humiliation Achilles was forced to bear. "And one more thing."

Achilles whipped his head up, defiant.

"Stay away from my daughter. She is the Crown Princess of Mycenae, a far greater prize than you will ever enjoy."

The king spun on his heel and raced back to his throne room, taking the steps of the portico two at a time. In his haste to return, he failed to see Iphigenia standing at the base of the stairs.

"I..." she stuttered, a flush of embarrassment coloring her cheeks a rosy red. She carried a plate filled with berries and fresh bread. "I brought these for you." Her eyes darted in every which direction save at him.

Humiliation flooded Achilles that someone would see him so debased and incapable of defending himself. *Not incapable, but unable.* The futility of his position frustrated him all the more.

But to the princess, his prolonged silence signaled something else: that she was unwelcome. She placed the plate on the ground for lack of a better solution. "I should go..."

Achilles grimaced. This was all wrong. He shouldn't even be here, kowtowing to that arrogant piss of a king. But standing before the princess, her beauty the crisp colors of a spring morning, he couldn't imagine being anywhere else. It took all his strength to muster his voice. "Stay."

Iphigenia hesitated but obeyed, her desire to remain overwhelming the impulse to flee. He took the princess by the hand, leading her to a bench beneath the viewing window off the throne room. Should anyone choose to catch a fresh breath of air, they would not see the two of them together.

"My father should not speak to you like that." Her face creased with unease. "You are our guest. He should not disparage a man so greatly admired."

"Please, Princess, do not speak of it."

She bit her lip, "Of course not. I mean, I won't. I wouldn't want to shame you further." She yelped, turning her head away and hiding her face in her long tresses of honey-brown hair.

Her words were innocent, but they made him relive those bitter moments. Achilles clenched his jaw, a fire burning within him. "It does not matter how greatly admired a man might be. Your father cares only for the amount of swords he can command. In that endeavor, Princess, I have little to offer him."

And little to offer a wife, in that Agamemnon was correct. A first born princess of the wealthiest kingdom of the Hellas was far beyond his reach.

Iphigenia smiled sweetly, as though those trifles mattered not at all. "'A shepherd who defends his flock, knowing the odds are against him, is far more courageous than a captain leading a great host,'" she chimed. "A large army does not make one great."

He could not help but smile. It was precisely what he needed to hear. "Not one of yours?"

"No," she gulped, her eyes dropping to her lap. "My aunt Helen's. Or Grandfather's. Most of her lessons were really just his in disguise."

He wondered about the missing princess. He had met Helen of Sparta just once, back at her betrothal. She seemed an honorable person, one who inspired great loyalty. A quality her niece had inherited, he supposed. "You miss her, don't you?"

"Yes." Her voice cracked with the admission. She twisted her hands as though she wished to say more, and when Achilles did not interrupt, she continued on. "When I was little I fell ill. Mother was thick with child, with my sister Electra, and could not care for me. Even our maids refused to enter my rooms, claiming the malady was inflicted by the Immortals, recompense for Father's latest conquest. I was only four and knew the cold grip of certain death." Her eyes swelled with unshed tears making them shine all the brighter.

Achilles restrained an urge to reach for her, to comfort the princess against that dark memory. What horrors had she endured from her kinship to that hateful man?

Iphigenia smiled, mistaking his movement for encouragement to speak on. "Aunt Helen was the only person who did not fear. She moved into my quarters to see to my recovery and did not leave my side for two months. When someone saves your life, you are bound to them, are you not?"

Achilles could not help but nod, amazed someone so young would know the complexities of a life's bond. Then again, he had not been much older than she when Patroclus pledged him fealty for a similar cause.

"Helen looked after me my whole life," the princess continued. "When things were... dark... at home, she was always a source of comfort." Her voice broke and a slight tremble shook her body. "I think of what the Trojans must be doing to her, to Aethra... It's just wrong. She deserves better."

Her heartfelt sorrow touched him, as it did in the hall. In all the rattling of swords it was easy to forget an innocent person stood at the heart of this tragedy. He lifted Iphigenia's chin, forcing her light blue eyes to meet his own.

"I do not question your father without reason. War without cause is never glorious. It is a bloody affair, a rampaging fire that burns the innocent and guilty alike." Bile burned in his throat. Achilles knew that cold truth intimately. While he hungered for battle like every true-born man of the West, he only took to field against a worthy foe, and certainly not for the purpose of enriching Agamemnon. "If I am to lead my men in battle, I need to know the cause is just."

"I understand." Iphigenia gazed up at him, her gentle expression evoking an unfamiliar ache in his chest. It was a shame she was so young. A few more years and Achilles might defy the wrath of her father for the promise of something so pure. It was for the best he did not. Iphigenia did not deserve the attentions of a man as brutal as he. The only maiden Achilles courted was Death, and one day She would come to claim him.

Though the story of his life might be writ in blood, it did not make him a monster. He raised the princess' hand to his lips, a courtly show of his respect. "I promise you this, Princess. If your aunt is truly in danger, the Hellas *will* unite. And there is no force on earth that will stop my armies from reclaiming her."

A hopeful smile spread across Iphigenia's face, and for a

moment, he wished the matter were that simple. Something was brewing in Mycenae, something that stunk of lies and deceit, and Achilles had a feeling he knew its source. Before a single ship sailed, he was going to get to the bottom of the muck.

Chapter 23

In the Marshland

THERE WAS NOTHING quite as spectacular as the dawning of a new day over the Egyptian marsh. The perfectly smooth waters of the Nile reflected the pale-pink light like a plate of glass. River-land creatures stirred, waking with the sun. The melodic call of aquatic birds merged with amphibious croaks, and the air was filled with song.

Paris stood in the center of a papyrus boat, harpoon in hand, soaking in that majesty. The small craft was an ingenious design, some fifteen feet long and five feet wide, constructed of tightly bound reeds water-proofed with bitumen. He held his footing with relative ease, his years at sea having blessed him with an instinctual sense of balance.

Others on the small boat were not so skilled. Seti reclined comfortably on a set of cushions at the bow as though this excursion were nothing more than a pleasure cruise. Save for Glaucus and their pole-man, they were the only occupants on the boat, meaning Paris had been subject to the prince's incessant chatter since the first hint of light spread over the horizon.

"My father despised the hunt." Seti's fingers trailed the in river, the small waves rippling through patches of lily pads and blossoming lotus flowers floating on the surface. "He said the only sport worthy of a reigning monarch is that of expanding the realm. He reclaimed much of the land usurped by the Semites to the east."

Half a dozen other boats dotted the Nile around them, each one with a pair of hunters on board and a slave kneeling at the back steadily poling the craft deeper into the wadi. Setnakhte rode in the vessel closest to Paris and the prince, his steady gaze never far from his monarch.

The other huntsmen, however, were not so enamored with their liege lord. They cast anxious glances to Seti, a valid concern growing that his jabbering might scare off game. Fortunately, the thick patches of reeds and protruding palm trees reduced how far the prince's words carried.

"Yes, Your Grace." Paris lowered his voice and kept his attention on the thick cover, his spear gripped tight. Both he and Glaucus tensed with unease at the dangers it could hide. These shallow pockets of the Nile, with dense vegetation for cover, were favorite habitats for all manner of deadly creature, including the elusive hippopotamus. Working together, the hunters planned to channel the animals out of the water to a cove where they could not escape a bombardment of spears and arrows.

"Grandfather should never have ceded so much land to the Hatti," Seti sighed. "It emboldened the slaves and wrecked havoc in the Levant." He plucked a lotus and inhaled deeply of its sweet bouquet, his words as casual as if he spoke of a poor breakfast.

Paris desperately wished Seti would stop talking. He was sick of the caravan of comments that flowed from the prince. He praised the conquests of his fore-bearers, touting other kings' accomplishments, yet had no example of his own. Paris suspected the prince suffered from an inferiority complex, a ridiculous notion considering the pampered life Seti insisted upon.

"I suppose it will fall to me to right these wrongs." Seti

cooled himself with a reed fan, using the object to bat away mosquitos. He leaned forward, staring intently at Paris. "Some treaties will need to be broken, and others forged..."

"What was the prince's signal if the beasts had been spotted?" Glaucus shaded his eyes against the rising sun, every fiber of the captain's body on high alert.

Paris could almost kiss the man and his well timed deflection. Trying to spear an enraged animal that weighed nearly 90 talents, had skin as thick as cured armor, and was armed with thick ivory teeth was dangerous enough without adding politics. Besides, one look at the effeminate prince was enough for Paris to know he was an unreliable ally.

"I shan't be surprised if we hear nothing from Amenmesse." Seti's angular features tensed at mention of his brother. "When we were children he got lost in the palace trying to find his way back from the kitchens. He has a terrible sense of direction."

Paris chose not to comment. He was determined not to pick a side in this growing feud, but when Seti had refused to let Amenmesse on the water this morning, that position was growing harder to hold. Seti had commanded the younger prince to lead the scouting party, the select handful of men who rode along the frontage road in chariots in search of their prey. Their task was to herd the animals down-river into the waiting spears of the huntsmen. It was an important role, but one that deprived Amenmesse from any glory of a kill.

"Surely, we will hear something—" Paris began, his words cut short as the reeds directly in front of them began to shake violently. The huntsmen fell silent, muscles clenched and ready for whatever would emerge. Even Seti had flipped over to his stomach, the soft linen of his robes tangled in his legs, preventing him from rising further.

As suddenly as it had begun, the movement stopped, and the river became eerily silent. Seti turned to him, his eyes wide in confusion. "What was that?"

The reeds erupted as a flock of ducks took to air. Paris

dropped to his knees and covered his head as he was surrounded with the flutter of wings and feathers. The other hunters were quicker to recover. Several throwing-sticks found their marks, the fowl dropping into the marshland with resounding splashes.

"Ha, ha!" Seti laughed. "Marvelous! Well struck, Setnakhte!" he shouted to the general.

Paris collected himself, disturbed by his defense behavior. His time in Egypt was making him jumpy. He normally would never spook so easy.

In the disturbance, their boat had floundered closer to land, a patch of reeds now within an arm's reach. As Paris raised his head, he came eye to eye with another marshland inhabitant: not the colorful fowl that took to air, but a grey heron. The elegant bird waded through the shallows, its tapered bill stirring up the silt of the river bottom.

"*Bennu!*" their pole-man exclaimed. The slave dropped his oar and pressed his forehead to the deck.

Bennu? It was an unfamiliar word for Paris. He shot a questioning glance to his host, surprised to see Seti had crept silently to his side.

"The *Bennu* holds the *ba* of Re. He is the spirit of the Great God as he flies daily across the sky in his solar barque." Seti stretched out a hand to the animal. "Salutations, Brother. May your journey remain eternal."

The bird ignored Seti, ignored them all in fact. When the crown prince shoved his hand even further toward its head, the heron drew back with a sharp cry, fanning its wings.

Paris rose to his feet, amazed at the power of the thin bird. It hung in the air before him, its wings spanning six feet across.

For a moment, time stood still. All sound of the marsh dropped out, save the thunderous pounding of those enormous wings. The heron tucked its long neck back into its body and issued a deep croak, a sound so guttural it seemed to rip from the belly of the creature. Paris felt its pull tremble in his bones. He stared in awe at the majestic bird, understanding why the Egyptians had come to revere it. Tapering its body, the heron took off with powerful speed, narrowly missing Paris' head.

Slowly the sounds of the marsh came flooding back to him, and with it, utter chaos. Huntsmen were shouting, the waters of the Nile were churning, and the pounding beat of hooves on soil greeted his ears. The scouts had returned, and with them their prey.

It was impossible to hear instructions through the clamor. Paris grabbed his spear and took a defensive position. Two dozen hunters surrounded him, anxiously awaiting the herd, each man with spear or arrow nocked and ready to let fly.

Within seconds the hippopotami showed their heads, the cows bellowing their displeasure loudly with heavy snorts, their massive bodies churning the still waters of the Nile into a boiling cauldron.

Something tugged at Paris' nerves. With so much activity it was almost an unnoticeable sound. But as a bowman, it was one he associated with danger: the unmistakable twang of an arrow released, too soon, from its bow.

"Paris!" Glaucus shouted, his captain pointing behind them. A single bolt shot through the air, not at the hippopotami, but directly where he and Seti stood. There was no doubt in his mind it was a killing blow.

Glaucus barreled into him, shoving him to the deck. Paris tried to wiggle free of his mountainous bulk but was hopelessly pinned. And then his captain screamed in pain, a sound so piercing it hollowed out Paris' heart. The arrow had sunk deep into Glaucus' back.

"NO!" He found a strength previously unknown to him, and he pushed the limp soldier over on his side. The activity proved too much for the small boat, and the craft flipped over, dumping everyone overboard...

Into the path of the rampaging hippos.

Broad faces with nostrils flared wide bore down on Paris.

Their black eyes, like pools of bitumen, dilated wide with fear. Thirty animals filled the river, both adults and their young, an avalanche of blubber and teeth. The dominant bull, a beast noticeably larger than the females surrounding it, took aim on Paris. To a man struggling to stay above water, it seemed like a mighty titan, a remnant of monsters from a forgotten era. He clung to Glaucus' arm, careless of his own safety. Kicking as hard as he could, he dragged the unconscious captain out of the hippo's path butting up against the other reed boats.

"SAVE THE PRINCE!"

Paris whipped his head around in response to Setnakhte's call. Seti was further downstream. He had caught a finger of current and was battling to stay ahead of the enraged hippos. As Paris watched, the crown prince dipped below water and did not re-emerge.

"Take him!" Paris shouted to the general, tossing Glaucus' arm over the hull. Without a moment to think, he took a gulping breath and grabbed hold of a passing hippo, his arms scrambling madly until he found purchase on the beast's tail.

Water spilled over the heaving back of the animal, flooding Paris' face. He could not see, let alone breathe. When the beast had carried him a good distance and he could no longer make out the Egyptian shouts behind him, he finally let go.

"Seti!" he cried out, spinning in a circle and scanning the shore for the crown prince, but there was no sign of him.

Paris dove into the river, forcing his eyes open despite the burn from the murky waters. It was a hopeless task. The hippo charge had turned over the silt, and visibility was nonexistent. Paris could see no further than an arm's length.

He tried to feel about. The waters were shallow. If Seti had been knocked unconscious, he could be laying on the river bottom. He alternated, shouting Seti's name at the surface before diving down and performing search patterns, letting his fingers see for him. On the fourth trip to the surface, the crown prince finally answered.

"I'm here!" Seti called, clinging to a floating log stuck in the foliage. The prince looked utterly exhausted. A gash above his eye trickled a trail of blood down his face. Paris reversed his stroke and was by his side in an instant.

"Are you all right?"

Seti nodded, too tired to speak. His cumbersome robes were plastered to his legs and arms, making it impossible for the prince to swim. Paris flipped over on his back, hooking his arm through Seti's, and towed the prince back to shore. Together, they crawled the few short feet through mud and grime to be clear of the water, and collapsed.

Paris filled his lungs with heaving gulps of air. His pulse was racing. He wanted nothing more than to just lay there, in the filth, until someone carried him off. Seti appeared to be in no better condition.

A nagging thought forced Paris to action. Someone needed to alert Setnakhte, to let the general know the crown prince was safe. Groaning from the effort, he lurched to his feet and waded back into the river to flag down the boats.

The huntsmen weren't far. Paris blinked, trying to clear the silt from his eyes. With each blink, the papyrus boats went out of focus, and in his exhaustion, they morphed into that single arrow arching in the sky towards him.

His cry for help froze on his lips. *Someone had tried to kill the crown prince.* And that "someone" was still out there. He splashed back to shore and shook Seti roughly. "We aren't safe here. We have to go."

Seti groaned, barely coherent. Paris cursed his frustration. They were too exposed on the shore. He lifted Seti's arm over his shoulder, prepared to drag the man to safety if needs be. Digging his feet into the soft mud, Paris heaved, inching closer to the cover of the thick brush.

But the brush began to quiver, the reeds bending forward as something rustled inside. There was no place to run. They could be surrounded for all Paris knew. He dropped the prince and took a stance before him. Reaching down his leg, he grabbed a dagger strapped to his calf, a whisper of relief coursing through him that he was not completely defenseless. Holding the small weapon before him, he waited for his assailant to show himself, his muscles burning with the effort to stay upright.

"Come on!" he shouted as the long moments wore on, his nerves as tense as his trembling body. "You want him? Then have the courage to face me, you coward!"

The attack came quickly. The beast came crashing through the undergrowth, its massive snout gaping open, displaying a long row of thick teeth. Paris had heard tales of the Nile crocodile before, but nothing could prepare him for its sheer size. Fifteen feet long and massively thick, the croc looked fierce enough to try its hand at a hippo. It snarled at him and Paris froze. In this fight, he was woefully outmatched.

A peaceful inevitability flooded over him. If he was meant to die this day, he would meet his end with dignity, but if the Fates wanted his blood, there'd be a price for that reckoning. He held his ground, staring the baleful monster in the eye and reversed his hold on the dagger, ready for a killing blow.

"No," Seti cried out behind him. "Re-Horati, spare me! I am your Chosen!"

Paris had no time to warn the prince before Seti shuffled away from the creature, scrambling backwards on hands and feet. The crocodile, drawn to the movement, darted around Paris, crawling over the ground in a zig-zag pattern. Its jaw snapped down on Seti's leg, and the prince screamed.

"Don't move!" he shouted to Seti, racing after them.

The beast dragged the prince into the river. As soon as they hit the shallows, it began to roll, pulling Seti below water.

For a moment, Paris hesitated. That was twice in a short span of time that he had stared death in the face. That was twice the specter of Hades passed him by. He was armed only with a small dagger. He could do nothing to stop that creature of the abyss. He would be tossing his life away. It was futile to keep fighting.

Paris could not help himself. He had been born fighting

futile causes. He leapt into the water and plunged his dagger down, praying he did not hit Seti by mistake.

The crocodile thrashed, bucking violently. Paris tried to reverse his blade for a second strike, but it held fast, embedded in bone. The croc twisted, diving deeper. Paris straddled the beast, his thighs pressed firm against its scaly hide as he held on to his weapon with a strength born of sheer desperation.

And then the water went still. The croc ceased its rolling, only its tail continuing to twitch sporadically. Paris struggled to the shore, dragging the croc out of the water behind him by its tail. His dagger was planted squarely into the creature's skull.

Seti bobbed to the surface, coughing violently. He seemed to expel half the Nile from his lungs. His eyes, once filled with fear as he spied the crocodile, morphed to awe as he regarded his rescuer.

"Please," he begged, pointing to his still-pinned leg in the monster's maw. "Take it off."

Paris shook his head. "You'll loose too much blood. We need to wait for the others." He settled down beside Seti, shielding the prince's body as best he could. "Don't worry. It won't be long now."

He did not bother to scan the perimeter for danger. He did not care if a hundred arrows were aimed at his back. He knew this land was dangerous, and he had come anyway. He had brought this reckoning upon himself.

A bitter bile burned in his throat. He should have known better. A lifetime of experience should have prepared him for this inevitability. Every time he tried to forge something pure, to claim a better life, it was denied from him. Like the high priest had said, the Gods had other plans and would grant him no clemency. It seemed Egypt herself was giving breath to that dire warning, trying to expel him from her shores.

The moments that followed passed in a blur. Setnakhte jumped free of his boat, shouting a dozen commands to his troops. Paris heard not a word of it. He sat in a daze, staring at the lifeless corpse of the crocodile at his feet.

Let them come... That challenge simmered in his gut. *I don't care if the Gods try to take me themselves. I will face them all. I'll die spitting in their faces.*

It wasn't until they were well on their way back to the palace that he thought to inquire after the assassination attempt. Setnakhte's troops had done a sweep of the marshland, but it had been too late. The culprit was long gone.

Chapter 24

Royal Reports

A HUSHED SILENCE permeated the stone enclosure of the House of Ails. Once, only the lector priests roamed the narrow hall, their slippered feet walking soundlessly across the tiled floor as they darted between beds to check on patients. Tonight, however, a full regiment of Egyptian troops guarded each entry, and the general of the Lower Egyptian forces himself kept watch.

Meryatum stood with Setnakhte, both men keeping a vigilant eye over the infirmary. News of the crown prince's accident proceeded the hunting party's return to the capital. As high priest, Meryatum was next in command if neither Pharaoh nor his crown prince survived the night. An inherently dangerous position he neither wanted nor knew how handle, especially if what the general said was correct.

"The arrowhead is an older Egyptian design, primitive but deadly." Setnakhte held the item in question, a wickedly barbed piece of slag ore the surgeons had removed from the Trojan's scapula but an hour ago. "It's a common item in back alley trade, virtually untraceable."

Perhaps that was true of the weapon, but not the poison laced on its tip. Only Egyptian royalty and those inducted into the Mysteries had access to those deadly agents. If the back-alley traders had somehow infiltrated those stores, no man or woman in the capital was safe.

If not for the tell-tale scent of almond in the wound, the Trojan might not have survived his encounter. For all the world, he would have appeared to have suffered a blood infection from a flesh wound, an unfortunate accident in a hunting excursion gone wrong. He was lucky the doctors of Heliopolis were well versed with the silent killers.

"And you believe this arrow was meant for Seti? Not the Trojan ambassador?" He tried to not influence the general with his suspicions, but ever since the Trojan delegation had arrived in Heliopolis, the temple had been awash in dark omens. A spiritual storm was brewing, and he was certain the Trojan stood at its center.

"Untraceable weapons? Venom tipped arrows? Who here could want the Trojan dead so badly?" Setnakhte frowned. "But Seti... I can think of two right now with the desire *and* the access to perpetrate this crime."

A sharp cry echoed down the hall. Meryatum resisted the urge to race to the crown prince's bedside. Crocodile attacks were common in Egypt. Most men never survived the bone-crushing first strike. It was a testament of Amun-Re's favor that Seti still drew breath.

He wished he could do more for his prince, but in battles of the flesh, Meryatum was as useless as a child learning his letters. His tenure as high priest had been one of exploring the Mysteries of the Gods, of philosophy and magic. Treating the ailments of the body was left to the lector priests, the tacticians of herbs and poultice.

He scowled as one of the physicians passed by them. Like all his brothers, the lector let his hair grow wild and wore colorful robes that caught the eye. Two feathers woven into his hair, the mark of their brotherhood, was the only feature that distinguished him from a common street performer. Lector priests bore no resemblance to his *pastophoroi*.

But they will save our future-king, he reminded himself, schooling his face to blankness.

The healer caught sight of him and quickened his steps. The lectors might not be under Meryatum's authority, but they nevertheless feared him. If his prince died on their watch, he'd make all their worst fears a reality.

"Will Seti walk again?" The general's heartfelt question denoted much more than the concern of a loyal citizen. A Pharaoh who was not whole signified an Egypt of similar distress.

"It is uncertain. The wound was deep."

A poultice of raw meat was applied to the gaping wounds in Seti's thigh. He was doused with a tonic of hemlock, just enough to dull the pain shooting through his body. Meryatum presided over his treatment. Hemlock could be lethal, if administered in the wrong amount, and, if access to the poison storehouses could be bought, then the men who administered them were most likely available for purchase, too.

He swallowed a lump in his throat, fighting a sense of helplessness at the events spiraling around them—a feeling as unfamiliar to Meryatum as the embrace of a woman. "Tell me again how it happened."

Setnakhte grew pale. The mountainous man was a veteran of many brutal campaigns. He had spilt oceans of blood in defense of the Two Lands. He had also witnessed the counter-stroke, knowing what Meryatum and few other Egyptians were privileged to share—how close Egypt, and Pharaoh, in their illustrious history, had come to defeat.

The favor of the Gods balanced on a teetering scale, and the loyal general was a God-fearing man. When he spoke of the day's ominous events, it was with the tremor of one haunted. "A Nile croc, as massive as Sobek himself, took aim on the Trojan. He said something to it... I could not hear... and it *passed him by*, racing around the prince and straight for Seti. I... I cannot explain it."

But Meryatum could. The multitude of omens manifesting

in the past fortnight spoke of calamity. It could not be coincidence that the foreigners arrived at the same time.

Paris of Troy was an enigma to him. When the prince first visited Egypt, Meryatum had sensed nothing special about him. He was a bright young man with a keen intellect. But now? There was a darkness in the prince, as black as the forces of Chaos Incarnate. It was as though the path he walked had corrected itself, that some crucial event had set him on a new course. Danger to Egypt, and perhaps even the world, surrounded him, and the Gods were screaming at Meryatum to pay heed.

"It seemed like the prince commanded the beast," Setnakhte continued, the general still gripped by his powerful vision. "Had he not saved Seti, risking his own life in the effort, I would have brought him back to the capital in chains. Egypt owes him a debt of gratitude."

That sobering fact gave Meryatum pause. The Gods gave him conflicting omens. Sobek, in sparing the Trojan, acknowledged some greater purpose in the man, choosing to attack Seti, the Defender of Light, instead. Yet, without Paris, Seti would have died. It was a riddle Meryatum could not fathom.

Why would the Gods spare an agent of Chaos? It troubled him. Meryatum could feel the world shifting beneath his feet, moving inescapably toward ruin. The scales of *ma'at* were unbalanced, and it was his job to set them right. Should he aid the Trojan, or send him far from Egypt's shores? It seemed the Gods wished both. He had no clear mandate in either direction.

"If someone is trying to kill our crown prince, we have larger issues to contend with than the presence of one Trojan prince," he reasoned, speaking more to himself than to the general.

"He is a distraction," Setnakhte agreed, his dark eyes hardening as Seti's cries died off in the distance. "A dangerous one."

THE PRINCESS OF PROPHECY

A gong pealed out from a distant portico, signaling the midnight hour. Setnakhte turned to go, his habit of conducting a full perimeter check on the hour predictable but strangely comforting. Before his heavy boots took two steps, he turned back to Meryatum, his hand held beseechingly over his heart.

"Forgive me if I trespass," he hesitated as though he knew his next words would do precisely that, "but you should complete the ritual with due haste. If the Trojan prince is not directly responsible for this attempt on Seti's life, then his presence here only complicates my efforts to find the culprit... and if something should happen to him, I don't fancy facing the swords of a Trojan army in retaliation."

Meryatum studied the general, a man who defined the world in the absolute terms of enemy and ally. He liked Setnakhte. He liked the solid pragmatism the solider effused. Setnakhte sometimes saw details that Meryatum's spiritually-aimed mind missed.

"Egypt, and Seti, are fortunate you are their vigilant protector." He nodded to Setnakhte, knowing the man was eager to be on his way. "I will consider your advice, General. The sooner the Trojans leave our land, the better for all."

※

Helen stared at a speck in the ceiling above her bed, unable to sleep. The soft breath of the women sharing her blankets should have lulled her into dreams long ago, but with all the events of the day she could no more sleep than grow wings. Glaucus almost died today, and Paris with him. It could have happened in an instant, and she was powerless to stop it.

Perhaps it was her imagination, but the speck seemed to grow larger, a black spot that threatened to consume the white plaster surrounding it. She took a deep breath and tried to center herself, her mind racing back to her morning lesson with the high priest. Meryatum was teaching her about the foundations of destiny before news of Seti drew him away. He spoke of the patience of the Gods, how a thousand years would pass, and a hundred-thousand men would live and die before one was born who could shake the foundations of the earth.

She knew he meant the lecture as a means to delve into Helen herself, to understand the prophecy Aphrodite revealed at her womanhood ritual. What he did not know, what he could not know, was that it spoke of Paris. *Her love* would shake the foundations of the earth, that was what the Goddess had foretold.

He cannot die without me knowing. I would feel it...

A small sob escaped her lips. She had never felt so alone as in these past few days without Paris. She cursed her weakness for the pathetic display that it was. She was surrounded by people morning, noon, and night. Her host saw she lacked for nothing, but the company of beautiful Egyptian women was a pale candle to warmth she felt in Paris' presence. She was complete with him, and without, she felt like an empty shell of herself, walking through the world with no purpose.

She must have disturbed the bedding. Merit rolled over, wrapping an arm around Helen's waist. The young queen was fast asleep, but her grip was surprisingly strong. With only one husband to satisfy their needs, the wives had grown accustomed to finding comfort in each others' arms. Some even went further than that. Her first night in the harem, Helen had been shocked to encounter their amorous advances.

She pushed Merit off her, and the girl slid back into Talia's arms on the other side of the bed. Settling back into her pillow, Helen took to gazing at the speck again, the jumble of emotions boiling within her refusing even a moment's peace.

A dark shadow, the unmistakable shape of a man's head, blotted out her view. She nearly screamed, but a rough hand pressed over her mouth, silencing the attempt. The man lowered himself over her face until the dim moonlight lit up his features. It was Iamus.

Helen sighed, her muscles unclenching as she recognized

her guard. He slowly removed his hand, raising it to his lips to signal her to keep quiet, then waved for her to follow him.

The bulky Trojan had the agility of an alley cat as he led her between pillars, always keeping to shadow. His caution bled into her, and she crept forward on tip-toes, using every bit of skill her father had taught her in approaching prey. The soft moans echoing throughout the harem indicated not all were at rest, and Helen doubled her efforts to remain silent. It seemed best not to draw the women's attention from their nocturnal pleasures.

They crept out onto the empty portico and into the moonlight-dabbled gardens along the Nile. "Iamus?" Helen's heart thundered in her chest, her mind racing with a hundred dire reasons the Trojan would seek to converse with her in private. "What is it? What's happened?"

He stepped aside, and the reeds parted behind him as Paris stepped into the path. She nearly cried in relief and threw herself into his arms.

"You are safe? Unhurt?" She pressed her lips to his neck, his cheeks, his lips... any piece of exposed flesh that she could reach.

Paris clung to Helen with equal fervor. The long hours on the road back to Heliopolis, and those spent in the infirmary beside Glaucus, had done little to settle his nerves. His muscles refused to unclench, and any sudden movement was apt to make him jump. He hadn't felt this exposed since he was a child and at the mercy of the Apollonian priests. "I'm fine." He tried to reassure her, pulling her hands down between them, kissing them tenderly. "But someone is trying to change that."

A deep fear took hold of Helen and she gripped his hands tightly. "Paris, what happened? The rumors at court are horrible. They say someone tried to kill Seti!"

Paris cased out the portico, his eyes darting across the empty space, alert to any movement or shift in shadow. Once, he might have thought this behavior paranoid, but not anymore. He pulled Helen deeper into the gardens, wrapping his arm around her protectively.

"I don't know if the arrow Glaucus took was meant for Seti," he added after telling her of the events in the marsh. "It could easily have been meant for me. Whatever forces are at work here would think nothing of killing a Trojan diplomat simply to send a message to the crown." He began to pace, his feet moving with a manic energy, as though his body begged to be set in motion, to not provide a sitting target. "If they succeed, I need to know you will be safe."

Helen watched Paris with growing alarm. He was clearly in shock. His closest friend had nearly died for him today, and now he spoke of his own death with casual ease. "What are you saying?"

Paris paused mid step, the panicked note in Helen's voice piercing the chill numbness that had been his constant companion since childhood. People had been trying to kill him his entire life. To let fear take root would have ensured they succeeded long before now. He knew one day their blades would strike true. It was inevitable. But standing before Helen, her face tensed with worry, he could not claim indifference. He had never wanted to live more.

That desire, however, did not dissolve the danger around them. He made a promise to Helen, one he intended to keep, dead or alive. "If something happens to me, go to Iamus. My men have standing orders to see you safely out of Egypt and on to Troy." He swallowed hard, trying to soothe over his raw nerves. "It's imperative you seek out Hector. *Hector alone.* Tell him everything. What happened in Mycenae and here in Egypt. He is the best of men. He will believe you."

Helen shivered, her thin nightdress doing little to stave off the chill that soaked into her bones. *Leave without Paris?* A fire burned in her breast, defying that dark possibility. "No." He tried to reach for her, but she brushed his hands aside. "We are going to Troy together. It does not end here."

Paris shook his head. "And if that's not possible? If I'm

lying in a sickbed like Glaucus? What happens to you?" He grabbed her arms, the pressure to protect her mounting in his chest. "I cannot leave you alone in this pit of jackals. *You must escape Egypt.*" His voice broke with the power of that need. "Please, Helen, promise me. If danger comes, you will save yourself."

Helen was speechless. Paris trembled before her, his dark eyes begging for her to place her life above his own. How could she explain that without him she had nothing to live for? There was no future for her without Paris. His request was honorable, but it could never be.

On impulse she threw her arms around him, crushing herself against his chest. "I knew the dangers we would face when I came with you."

"But if you were harmed—"

"I will defend myself." She grit her teeth, clinging to him with a strength she did not know she possessed. "You mustn't give in to this thinking. Whoever tried to harm you is a coward, striking from shadows. *You are stronger than he is.* Whatever he tries next, we *will* survive it."

Paris tightened his arms around her. Her courage amazed him. He pulled back, lacing his fingers through her golden hair and caressing her cheek with his thumb. How many men looked upon her and saw only a beautiful face? They were blind fools who failed to see her greatest asset. She was so much more than the sum of her parts. She was a warrior princess, a vision of tenacious strength and fortitude.

And she's given her heart and soul to me.

He almost shook with disbelief. A cursed prince was not worthy of such devotion, but, as she gazed up at him with utter faith, he vowed he would be. He cupped her face between his hands, his chest constricting with emotion. "*I love you, Helen.*" He kissed her, pouring a lifetime of longing into that embrace.

Helen melted into his arms, returning his kiss with ardor. It had been too long since she last felt his touch. All the sweet wine in the world could not quench the thirst she had for this man. As he wrapped his arms around her, the kiss became deeper, pulling at her loins, awakening a hunger within her.

Paris responded in kind, lifting her from her feet, his hands moving over her body as though they had a will of their own. The past week had felt like an eternity, and he desired her with a power that frightened him. When she pressed her body against his, he lost his ability to think. His phallus bulged beneath his kilt, and he gasped, the surging power pulling inside him nearly bringing him to his knees. If she touched him again, he would not be able to contain himself.

One look into her lapis-blue eyes, eyes clouded over with desire, he knew they were both beyond that. Swooping an arm around her waist, he lowered her to the ground, the stone tiles of the garden path a welcomed cool against his heat-flushed skin.

He lifted up the skirt of her night dress, lowering his hand between her legs, her soft folds tightening around his fingers. She moaned deeply as he caressed her, and he pressed his lips to her throat, savoring the vibration.

"Please," she moaned over and over again, her hips pressed delectably tight against his pelvis. He fumbled at the strings of his loin cloth. In his haste he pulled them into knots.

"Damn it." He sat up, tearing at the bothersome garment.

From the corner of his eye a sudden flare caught his attention and he froze. Someone was on the patio.

It was a small flame, certainly shielded and almost unnoticeable behind the lush foliage of garden plants between them, but Paris had been trained to spot such disturbances. Good reflexes were the best defense against silent killers. He knew too well that one man could be more deadly than ten.

He pressed Helen behind him and crept back into the reeds. He thanked the Gods she did not question his actions. She moved as quietly as he did, her eyes wide with alarm. They waited for several tense minutes as Paris watched the portico from between the stalks, his hand clenched on the hilt of his sword. Only when the soft chatter of female voices carried across the distance, did he lower his guard. "A false alarm." He turned to Helen and forced a smile. "Are you all right?"

Helen nodded, a blush of embarrassment creeping over her cheeks. Her eyes dropped to the ground as she dusted off her dress.

Paris' gut twisted with shame. This behavior sickened him. Lying about his feelings for Helen, stealing kisses when no one was looking—it all felt wrong. This past week apart had been intolerable for him.

What would it be like in Troy? Would it be a year or more before he dared to publicly seek her hand? He could never last so long, and each time he snuck into her bed, he would risk tarnishing her reputation.

Paris buried that angst deep inside. First they had to reach the Golden City. He took Helen's hands in his, lifting her to her feet. "We're leaving Egypt as soon as I can make arrangements. I'm not going to wait for the Temple's permission. In the meanwhile, you must be extra careful. Trust no one."

Helen nodded. She understood the need for urgency, but still her shoulders slumped with disappointment, her traitor heart reluctant to go. Did they really come all this way, risking their lives and those sworn to them, for nothing? After all of her preparations at the temple, surely Meryatum was ready to grant her petition.

But was he really? Helen shook her head, unsure. She could not bet the lives of others on vague feelings. Nor the man she loved more than life itself.

"When must we go?"

"When Glaucus is released from the infirmary. The healers want to observe him another day to make sure he doesn't relapse." Paris prayed for a swift recovery. The stoic captain had earned a long and luxurious retirement, and Paris was going to make sure he got it. "I have a man who can get us out of the city. The night after next, we're leaving this cursed place. *Xenia* be damned."

For Helen, that delay was an unexpected surprise. *Two days.* Surely it was enough time. She gathered her courage as a spark of hope kindled in her breast. "If I can sway the priest, if he agrees to perform the ritual immediately, you will wait?"

"Wait?" Paris paused, taken aback by her question. He had thought this ritual a passing fancy, a request she had made in error, but one glance into Helen's hopeful eyes, and there was no mistaking how desperately she desired it.

Guilt swelled in his chest. He had asked so much of his princess, and every time she asked for something back, he preached caution and compromise. Time and again, she placed the plight of his mission above the desires of her heart. His resolve softened, and he studied her with quiet understanding.

"You need this, don't you?"

"*Yes.*" The single word felt raw, as though the confession exposed her heart. She tried to turn from him, to hide behind a curtain of her golden hair, but he lifted her chin, pulling her back.

"Why is this so important to you?"

Helen hesitated, unsure of how to answer. Paris had sworn to protect her. He stood ready and willing to risk his life on her behalf. How could she explain that she longed to do the same? Her enemies were not flesh and blood, but something intangible, and this ritual was the only way she knew how to fight back.

"If I do this, I start over. Everything that happened before would be wiped away. *Menelaus will have no claim to me,*" she voiced the hope that before Egypt she scarcely dared to believe possible. "If the Gods purify me, I can come to you clean, unburdened by a sordid past. I'll belong to no one but you." Tears leaked from her eyes, and a small sob escaped her lips. "If I'm pure, you won't be ashamed to love me."

Paris was stunned beyond words. *Ashamed to love her?* Was

that what she thought? "Helen—"

"Please, don't." She shied away from his touch, knowing he would deny it, but the awful truth of their flight from Greece could not be denied. It was a dark cloud that hung over any future they tried to forge. Paris was prince of Troy, a proud and mighty empire. He deserved more than the love of another man's wife. He deserved something pure. The Gods owed him that.

Helen steeled her nerves. *The Gods owe us both that.* "If Meryatum agrees, will you wait for me?" she asked again, her resolve building.

Paris stared deeply into Helen's eyes, amazed again at her courage. She risked her life to be with him. He could do no less. "Of course I will." He tightened his arms around her, pressing his forehead to hers. "For you, I'd wait through eternity."

They had dallied for too long. With a few more words of caution, he urged Helen to return to the safety of the harem. It pained him to leave her, but he trusted Iamus to keep her safe. For now, anyway.

After she disappeared behind the curtains, he stepped back into the brush, a new determination lengthening his stride. Ritual or no ritual, he was going to spend the rest of his life with Helen. He only prayed they could escape Egypt before the next arrow flew.

Chapter 25

The Heifer or the Lioness

HELEN RETURNED TO the harem, concealing herself in the long curtains along the portico as Iamus conducted a perimeter check. She steadied herself against a pillar, her head still woozy from her encounter with Paris. *Two days.* She had two days to persuade Meryatum to her cause, a man so entrenched in his dogma she doubted even Zeus could force him toward a verdict he was disinclined to follow. But the priest had never stood between a Spartan and her intended target. She crossed her arms beneath her breast, a surge of stubbornness fortifying her spirits.

He will listen to me.

Iamus waved to her from across the hall, and she stepped out of hiding, a nagging sense of caution tensing her nerves. The harem had gone silent. It was unusual not to hear the soft moans of women coupling even at this late hour.

"Having trouble sleeping?" Nefertari stepped out from behind a pillar, her arms folded across her chest.

"Your Grace." Helen spun to face the queen, her words falling awkwardly from her tongue. "You startled me." What was Nefertari doing up at this hour? Helen tried to collect herself, masking her fears behind a weak smile. "Did I wake you?"

"In a fashion." The queen seemed mildly amused by that statement. Her amusement did not pass her lips, however, and when she spoke again it was with the tone of command. "Come with me, child."

She led Helen to the far corner of the harem, to the wall facing the Nile and the garden beyond. When there was no further they could go, the queen pulled back the thick curtains lining the wall and revealed a false door built into the rock. She waved Helen through first, and slid the door shut, the thick stone moving soundlessly on well-oiled hinges.

The secret chamber was nothing more than a small bedroom lit by oil lamps. Helen had suspected Nefertari had her own quarters. The space was snug but cozy. A small brazier at the center of the room radiated warmth, its orange-red coals banked low. Two dozen glass vials and jars sat atop a long table against the far wall, holding—Helen supposed—the medicine the queen required for the frequent aches and pains of her aging body. Her bed was made, the first indicator the queen had not slept this night, and an empty decanter of tea sat beside two used glasses.

Helen swallowed hard, wondering who the queen's guest had been. She turned to ask, and saw the wall facing the gardens for the first time, the question dying on her lips.

Large folding doors lay open to the night breeze. Tall lengths of papyrus hid the door from the gardens, but Helen was more than sure the queen had an excellent view of the spot where Helen had just met with Paris. A cold knot of dread settled into her stomach.

Nefertari crossed the room, the sly smile on her face suggesting she knew what Helen feared. She took a seat beside the table and motioned her to do the same.

"It seems our time is running short. Before the Fates separate us, there is one more lesson you must learn."

There was a difference between learning a lesson and being taught one. If Nefertari suspected she had lied to her...

Helen's gaze dropped to her lap, a wave of guilt silencing her tongue.

"Thus far, you have been an apt pupil, learning the ways of Gentle Hathor, but beauty such as yours can destroy as easily as it inspires." The queen's dark eyes bore into her, as though that sentiment were an accusation. "A weak woman denies that power. She clings to innocence, ignorant of her other half, ignorant of the dual nature of the Goddess herself. And in doing, she becomes its victim."

Helen trembled, too afraid to speak, afraid she would reveal herself. She had heard those words before, a long time ago. Nefertari spoke of the shadow faces of Aphrodite, of lust and jealousy and all the foul deeds they inspired. If this was the lesson the Egyptian mysteries wished to impart, then Helen wanted no part of it.

"Beauty is inherently dangerous." The queen twisted in her stool and began to sort through the vials on the table. "Men will always see you as a prize and try to possess you. There is only one way to protect yourself." She pulled out a clear bottle with a seal of black wax and gave its liquid contents a swirl. "You must become Sekhmet, the fierce lion goddess, She of *terrifying beauty*, whose thirst for blood is only matched by Her thirst for justice. You must embrace your dual nature. That is the only way you can become its master."

The change in Nefertari's behavior frightened Helen. There had been hints of a metal core beneath the queen's graceful exterior, but witnessing the shift filled Helen with unease. This was a monarch whom others would dare not cross.

"Nefertari... what is in the vial?"

"An equalizer." The queen frowned. "The Gods saw fit to grant men strength of arms. We women must rely on beauty and charm. As I'm sure you already know, beauty is sometimes not enough. There are times when that beauty must *bite*. For that, Isis granted us the wisdom of poison."

A chill flooded through her. Glaucus had been poisoned

this very day, by an arrow, Paris said, that was possibly meant for him. She studied the contents of the queen's table with dark foreboding. Why would Nefertari reveal she had a plethora of the toxins herself? What was the queen trying to tell her? Had she taken part in that crime?

"This one here is made by distilling the leaves of a laurel tree." Nefertari swirled the vial again. "In small quantities, it can produce confusion in an enemy and drive them mad. Much more than a drop would paralyze the strongest of men, inducing coma and death."

She handed the vial to her, and Helen held the glass between two fingers, reluctant to place even that amount of flesh in its proximity.

"This one," the queen continued, pulling forth a blue tinted bottle with a glass flower for a stopper, "quells all sorrows with forgetfulness. Useful for an aching heart or if one wishes to erase a single act from a person's memory." That, too, went in Helen's hands.

"Your Grace—"

"Here we are." Nefertari picked up a gold band, a thick bracelet forged in the shape of a serpent with a head on each end: one with fangs bared, the other at rest. She secured the bauble to the table with a vice clamp and twisted off the ends, revealing a hollow center down each side.

"Do you know why I vouched for you that day in the throne room?" She plucked the opaque bottle from Helen's hand and proceeded to break the wax with a small knife.

"Because the Mnevis had chosen me?" Helen answered, feeling more unsure of her safety than ever. She watched as the queen measured out a lethal dose of the poison. "You said Amun-Re had spoken."

"Don't be stupid." Nefertari poured the liquid into the hollow end of the bracelet and replaced the cap. "The Mnevis is nothing but a scared calf. It sought comfort in the arms of the one person not fawning all over it. That is not why I chose to help you, nor why I continue to help you." She reached for the other vial. "Now speak the truth. I'll know if you lie."

It was one 'lesson' too many for Helen, and she blurted out the first answer she could think of. "Paris. You are helping me because of Paris. You love him."

That was not what the queen expected to hear. She froze, a stopper filled with serum poised above the bracelet. "What makes you say that?"

"The way you speak of him, with such esteem and regard. No one speaks that way of Paris." She squirmed back in her stool, inching away from that dreadful substance. Would Nefertari dare to use it on her?

The queen laughed, the musical sound doing little to put Helen at ease. "I do care for him, but not in the way you think, you lovesick girl." She finished her doctoring of the bracelet and gave Helen her full attention. "I was once very much like you, a beautiful little creature thrust into a cruel world. Young and naive, and unable to see my true potential. I made many mistakes, ones I hope you do not replicate."

Helen shook her head, wary to trust. "But why do you care? I'm a complete stranger to you, a nobody. I'll never be a queen." In Egypt, status meant everything, and Nefertari had given no indication that she thought differently.

The queen rose gracefully to her feet, her unblinking eyes making Helen feel ignorant as well as foolish. "You have the potential to be great, Helen of Sparta," the matriarch towered over her, "but not until you wise to the ways of the world."

Helen shirked back in her stool. To hear one speak so blatantly... it was as rare as it was uncomfortable. No one spoke to her like that, save for Aethra and her father.

Nefertari removed the bracelet from the clamp and crossed the room to the patio doors. She spread the reeds apart and moonlight flooded into the room, cascading down her face. She seemed to bathe in it, as though the celestial orb imbued her with a strength beyond her years. Lifting the jewel, she began a soft incantation in Egyptian that Helen could not follow.

"Turn your face to me, My Lady Isis. I know thee, I know thy name. The power of your magic flows through my veins. Make me your vessel of ma'at."

Perhaps it was an illusion, but the golden bauble gleamed white as Nefertari whispered her spell. It was a harsh light, imbued with the silver power of the moon, an illumination devoid of life.

Nefertari released the reeds and the magical light vanished, taking with it Helen's breath. The queen glided back to her. Lifting her arm, Nefertari slid the bracelet onto Helen's wrist. It hung there with dire purpose, with the power of life or death. It was a priceless gift, and Helen gaped at it with wonder.

Why me?

"I was very young when I was taken from my mother." Nefertari retook her seat beside the brazier, staring into the coals as though reliving that fateful day. "I lived in a village outside Thebes, a child of a poor farmer. A temple overseer took a fancy to me and insisted I be raised in the purity of Isis." She gave Helen a telling glance. "He had other plans for me, I was soon to learn."

A wave of sympathy rushed over Helen. The unbidden memory of her own abduction rushed to her, the terror of the night raid on their camp, of being snatched away from her sister. She trembled with the force of that long distant fear. Now was not the time for such distractions. She steadfastly ignored that memory, locking it away in a corner of her mind.

"It almost destroyed me," the queen continued, watching Helen's tiny reactions with observant eyes, "but I always had more hope than fear, even when there was no cause to believe anything would change. Until one day, it did.

"When Rameses came to the temple he was already a king. I was nobody, a peasant servant in the House of Isis, yet when I saw him I knew. My soul would not be at rest unless I was at his side. His presence struck me like a bolt of lightning from a clear sky. I was powerless in his gaze. What I didn't know, *what I could not know,* was that my presence struck him as well." Her eyes shone with love as though the specter of her late husband walked before them.

"'My Nefertari', he called me, 'The One for Whom the Sun Shines', and for me he would do anything, including marrying a commoner just to keep me safe." A single tear rolled down her cheek.

"My sister-wives were not pleased. Many whispered that I seduced Pharaoh, charmed him with my 'unnatural' good looks. Phaw." Nefertari laughed softly at the foolish thought. "*I did seduce him.* Not with promises of the flesh, but by inspiring the valiant spirit within him. I loved him the way a great man deserved to be loved. Others sought to use him, or gain power through his favor. I thought only of Rameses, and in doing, I became his Great Wife."

Helen marveled at the tale. It seemed impossible Nefertari had known such tragedy and blossomed into the graceful queen before her. Yet, the queen had found her salvation in love. Helen prayed she had half of Nefertari's fortitude moving forward with her own journey.

"When Rameses died," the queen choked on the words, her eyes swelling with unshed tears, "I lost half my soul. Half the light of the world vanished." She seemed to sink into herself, the formidable Great Wife exposing her vulnerable core. She was simply an elderly woman whose body was failing, a collection of bones whose vital life-force was as much an illusion as the paints on her face.

"Part of me died with him," another tear ran down her cheek, "and there were none who recognized my sorrow. Save one. A young prince of Troy, who, unlike the vultures swarming over my dead king, cared naught about who next sat the throne. He comforted a grieving wife and pulled me back from joining my love in the afterlife."

Helen studied the queen with new understanding. Nefertari did love Paris, but not as a lover. She owed him a debt of kindness. Helen cursed her stupid pride. The queen was not a danger to her. If there was one person in Heliopolis she was sure she could trust, it was Nefertari.

"I... I love him," Helen confessed, some part of her needing to proclaim that fact with pride. "Paris was born for me. And I for him. We belong together. I will marry him, if the Gods allow it." She paused, taking a heavy breath. The queen deserved to hear it all. "But there are many people standing in our way."

Nefertari took her hand in hers, giving it a gentle squeeze. The look on her face said it all. This news was no surprise to her. "If you love him, then you must defend him." She let her fingers trace over the golden band.

Helen looked up to the queen with surprise. Was she suggesting...?

"Great men always need protection," the queen continued. "While Rameses lived, I vowed no one would do him harm. Men are short-sighted. Always in search of a hidden blade, they fail to hear whisper and rumor, the shadow powers that wait silently for a person to relax their defenses. That is the world of women, and I excelled at keeping those powers at bay." She gripped Helen's hands, helping her rise from her seat.

Can I do the same? Helen eyed the golden band on her wrist, a gilded shackle if anyone discovered what was inside. *Will I kill for Paris?* As much as she didn't want to face that dark truth, she knew the answer was yes.

A shadow crossed over Nefertari's face as the queen guided her back to the false door. "A reckoning is coming. The high priest is not the only one who sees it. There are signs of it everywhere. I fear we will need more men like Alexandros before long." She tightened her grip on Helen's arm almost to the point of pain. "You must keep him safe, Helen." She leaned in to kiss her on her brow. "By any means possible."

Helen nodded, understanding the heart of this last lesson. Hathor or Sekhmet, the heifer or the lioness, the virtuous beauty or the bloodthirsty seductress... She had to embrace her abilities, *all her abilities,* to keep Paris safe.

By any means possible. She bid Nefertari goodnight, and returned to her bed, the power of that vow coursing through her veins.

※

Amenmesse stalked the dark corridors of the palace back to his private rooms. For the second time that night he tried to visit his brother in the House of Ails, and for the second time that prat of a general had turned him aside. If Seti was on his death bed, then his next of kin deserved to know!

It frustrated him to no end that the laws of their kingdom did not honor the status of his birth. There was room for only one God-King, and the remaining royal children were but sad reminders of the mortality of man. They lived in Pharaoh's giant shadow, and soon Amenmesse would live in his brother Seti's as well.

He entered his darkened chamber, kicking the doors shut behind him. His frustrations bled into his moves as he tore the golden breastplate from his chest, tossing it to the ground. He fumbled for the leather guard underneath, stripping down to the waist, nearly colliding with a small table holding a half-empty decanter of wine.

Why was the room so cursedly dark? He'd have the house staff whipped for this oversight. Of course, he should have suspected the truth. He was not alone.

"I thought you'd never return."

Twosret stretched out on his bed, the luscious curves of her naked body catching the moonlight. His earlier frustrations vanished in an instant.

His sister, his sultry, mesmerizing sister, whom every Egyptian secretly desired but Seti had claimed as his second wife, was his to savor. Twosret, the cool dram of water to a man dying of thirst. After the exertions of this day, Amenmesse was incredibly thirsty.

"Come here," he growled.

She flipped over onto all fours, crawling to him like a cat in heat. "Yes, My Lord." She pressed her lips to his flesh, looking up to him under her kohl-black lashes, her hands roaming over the taut muscles of his abdomen. Her eyes, so similar to his own, were like pools of green fire, commanding him to ravish her. He ran his hands over her backside, slipping his fingers into every crevasse.

Suddenly she was everywhere, pulling at the ties of his belt, pushing up the fabric of his kilt. He groaned as her delicate fingers encircled his phallus and began to stroke. He had to brace himself against the post of the bed as she rose to kiss him, the force of her pounce stealing his breath away.

"I love when you come to me from the field." She pulled his lip between her clenched teeth. "You smell the way a man should, of sweat and blood."

Dirty words from a dirty mind. Twosret had the habit of saying the most inappropriate things, making him desire her all the more. She was wild, untamable.

He slapped her on her rump and she gasped in pain. "Do you tire of our perfumed brother? Does he not satisfy you?" He thrust his hand between her legs, pealing away the petals on her moist core.

She groaned with pleasure arching her back at an impossible angle, giving him access to her voluptuous breasts. He dove right in, lifting her erect nipple in his mouth as he stroked her.

"He is nothing compared to you." She wrapped her hands into his hair, shoving his head down to please her. "*Nothing.*"

Amenmesse was mad for Twosret, the one insatiable hunger he could not control. She belonged to Seti, a treasure his brother was incapable of savoring. Seti lorded his ownership of her, yet another item he possessed that Amenmesse never would. Or so the pampered fool thought. It took a real man to please this woman, and there was a reason Twosret returned to his bed.

He pressed his face between her legs, sucking and pulling the hard nub until she cried out with pleasure. She tightened her legs around his head, the pressure exquisite. "I want to feel you inside me." She groaned with that command.

He stripped off his remaining clothes and climbed on top of her, thrusting in deep. They both cried out with intense joy. Harder and harder, he pumped, until she screamed, her body convulsing in orgasm. He instantly came with her, his body shuddering in small spasms.

Collapsing on the bed beside her, a tingling calm washed over him. "That was a pleasant surprise."

Twosret laughed, a throaty sound that almost stirred him to arousal again. "It was a day worthy of celebration. How fares our brother? Is it too much to hope for an infection?"

"Yes." He spat his disapproval. "What possessed the Trojan to act the hero?" Paris had no great love of Seti— he was sure of it. The Trojan should have let the crocodile take its meal and spare Egypt the horror of having such an ineffectual fool sit the throne.

Twosret rolled over, trailing her fingers along his chest. "You should not have left the deed to the croc. Why did you miss? You never fail at that range."

He sat up, confused. "What are you talking about?"

She sat up, too, equally confused. "The arrow. Like we discussed. Kill Seti and place the blame on the Trojan."

Amenmesse shook his head. "That was not me. Seti forced me into the scouting party. It was too obvious a position for me to take the risk." With Setnakhte acting as guard dog, Amenmesse had been forced to make other plans, ones less conspicuous than outright murder.

He did not bother to tell Twosret that he preferred the new plan to the old. He liked the Trojan and did not see the benefit of making a new, and potentially powerful, enemy. His sister, however, was touchy when it came to trusting others.

"Horus smite them dead!" she cursed. "Whoever shot that arrow did us no favors, Brother. Security will tighten around my precious husband, if it hasn't already. We will not get another opportunity like today."

He hated seeing her so distressed. She wore the burden of their plots more heavily than he. Twosret desired a clean transition, one unsoiled by mutiny however justified. But Amenmesse craved the valor of the sword. He would prove to Egypt, by force if necessary, who deserved to rule the Two Lands.

"It is too late. Setnakhte guards Seti himself. I could not even get in to see him."

Twosret buried her face in her hands, wringing her hair as she cried out her distress. "He cannot be crowned," she moaned, rocking on her heels. "If he sits the throne, the Crook and the Flail will fall to his children. Not to you. Not to me. *We will be nothing.* This cannot be."

He took her into his arms, trying to soothe away her fears. "Shhhh." He stroked her back. "I won't let that happen." He slid his hands down her hips with that caress, her perfect, shapely hips. He immediately grew hard.

"Promise me!" She shoved him down on the bed with a strength that surprised him. Her long black hair hung loose around her head like the hood of a cobra. He was mesmerized by the vision of her terrible beauty.

She straddled him, pressing her lithe body down on his, mounting him. "Before Pharaoh departs this earth, Seti will be dead," she commanded, riding him violently. Every thrust sent shivers through his body. *"Promise me."*

"Yes." He pressed his lips to hers, delirious for more. "Anything you say," he swore, knowing he was enthralled in the spell she wove. Knowing and not caring.

"It will be done."

CHAPTER 26

SALUTATIONS OF RE

MERYATUM'S MORNING BEGAN much as any other. In the pre-dawn darkness, he rose from the stiff cot in his chambers, donning his simple robes and plain sandals woven of palm fiber. He joined the *stolist* priests at the sacred lake to cleanse himself, wading into the tepid waters and scrubbing away any hint of impurity with fists full of sand.

At this hour, the temple was a hive of activity. While the cult officials purified themselves, the regular staff prepared for the awakening ritual. Kitchen fires had blazed for hours, and the final touches to the culinary offerings were completed. Two dozen hearty loaves of bread, still steaming from the ovens, joined trays ladened with dates and figs. A haunch of roast ox, taken from an animal raised on temple grounds and fed a diet of fresh grass, sat on a spit. It was a feast that could feed a small village, and the *stolists* would carry it before the golden idol of their God, as they did every morning. They would bathe and clothe the idol, and beseech Re for His continued blessings.

But not the high priest. Meryatum left the tedium of cult duties to his lesser *pastophoroi*. He presided over the greater Mysteries, delving into the very nature of the Gods themselves. Those hefty contemplations included performing the Salutations of Re. He headed out the temple grounds, a solitary man crossing the desert, until he hit the eastern facing bank of the Nile.

She was waiting for him, the beguiling Princess of Sparta. Since he had arranged for her education in the temple, she had never once been late. While Helen was not allowed access to the sacred lake, she was nevertheless clean. After seeing the results of his meticulous preparations on their first day, she made efforts to mimic him. It was another example of her careful consideration that almost made him forget the purpose of these meetings. He was meant to observe the princess with impartial eyes, a task that grew harder as he warmed to her presence.

"Meryatum." She dipped into a curtsey, removing a light scarf from her head. The warmth of her smile rivaled the sun, a blasphemous thought if Meryatum had not known she had charmed Re Himself.

But how could one person embody the elements of both life *and* death? He felt drawn to her presence even as he felt the earth tremble in her wake. The princess was equally dangerous as her Trojan companion, if for no other reason than the temptations she aroused. In helping her, he could not help but feel he was indirectly helping the other—a terrible prospect if what he suspected about the Trojan prince was true.

They took their positions kneeling in the sand, hands held high. The sky shifted in color, moving from a muted pale grey to a blushing pink. Like a corpse taking on new life, the world soaked in the encroaching rays of light, reflecting a vibrancy of color where before there had been none. The burning mass of the sun peaked over the horizon, and he began his Salutations.

"Greetings, Re, at Your rising,
Amun, Power of the Gods!
You rise and illuminate the Two Lands!

THE PRINCESS OF PROPHECY

Nut greets You, *Ma'at* embraces You always.
You cross the sky in peace,
Sitting in the morning barque,
Traversing the primeval ocean,
Transforming into Khepri in the morning,
Re at midday,
Atum in the evening,
Until You appear in the House of Shu,
Opening the western gates to the netherworld,
And battle the Great Serpent before rising again."

Meryatum pressed his head to the sand, prostrating himself before the majesty of his god. He felt the *ba* of Re wash over him, the electric tingle of energy that made flowers blossom, wind stir, and all life possible. As the solar rays flowed through him, Meryatum took comfort that the power of Re was omni-present, even in the diminutive form of the princess beside him.

Helen followed his lead, bending at the waist, and staying low as Re emerged from His sojourn in the netherworld. Meryatum strayed a glance to her as the sun fully rose into the sky, the golden rays dancing over her high cheekbones and picking up honey highlights in her long hair. She was a vision of beauty, and certainly the most exquisite creature Meryatum had ever encountered. In his heart, he knew she walked in Light. The enemies of *ma'at* would feel more false, their appearance would be less fair.

But omens never lie, and she brought darkness in her wake.

"We must discuss your purification ritual," he told her immediately after they rose from the Salutations.

Helen blinked back her surprise, a pleasant smile growing with his announcement. "Of course. I wanted to talk to you—"

"I cannot do it."

Her smile vanished. "What?"

"It is nothing personal," he tried to reassure her. "I consulted the omens, as promised, and they were unfavorable. The Gods are in flux, striking indiscriminately. We would invite their wrath if we tried to force their hand." It was the most succinct answer he could give Helen without delving into too many of his suspicions.

The princess held her abdomen, as though he had impaled her on a blade. He had to fold his hands into his sleeves to fight the urge to comfort her. Though he was curious how the Gods would respond to her incendiary presence, this refusal was for the best.

It was the princess' reaction, however, that peaked his interest now. She moaned a weak protest with inarticulate words, her face alternating between utter shock, mournful sorrow, and bitter anger. At the last, her hand tightened around a gold bracelet, and her face stilled to an unreadable calm.

"No."

He was shocked by the quiet power in her voice. "What did you say?"

Her eyes narrowed to hard little rocks that refused to soften. "I do not accept your answer." Again she spoke with utter calm, the still center in a storm of emotions that surely raged within. "If you are going to refuse me, I would know the reason why. *The real reason.*"

The High Priest of Amun-Re was beholden to no man. Not even Pharaoh could command him. He did not explain himself to anyone, not even a foreign beauty who captured his imagination. He almost turned from her to return to the temple, but the absurdity of that act struck him. She was only a woman making a request, and Meryatum would not run from *a woman.*

"You are not prepared to face such truths." The cold edge of his fears seeped into his voice, but still she did not flinch.

"I am stronger than you give me credit." She lifted her chin, defiant. "Whatever I have done to dissuade you, I would know what it was. Tell me."

She blamed herself? This vision of grace that even the Mnevis sheltered in her light? "It is not you. It is the company you keep!" He finally gave voice to the dark rumblings on his mind. "A darkness follows your Trojan protector, and I want no part of it."

Those stark words shocked her. Again, he watched the hope drain from her face. When she stumbled away from him, he finally allowed himself to reach out to comfort her. "I am sorry, Princess. You have a powerful destiny awaiting you, one I am sure the Gods watch over with interest. I hope you move out of his shadow, and soon."

True to her claim, she was stronger than her delicate frame suggested. Her eyes flashed like blue fire and she batted his arm away. "Paris is an honorable, noble prince of Troy. By what right do you accuse him of wrong doing? He saved your prince!"

Meryatum shook his head, wracking his mind on how to break through to her. "He is much more than that." For her own safety, the poor girl had to listen to reason. "I would not be High Priest if I could not see hidden dangers. Dark forces shadow him. The prince is dangerous. You need to be careful."

"You don't even know him." Helen refused to back down. As the sun rose steadily in the sky, the heat waves shimmering up from the ground seemed to come as much from her as the sand below. "You are wrong about Paris. He is the best of men."

The way she defended him... she was as fierce as a lioness defending her pride. Meryatum swallowed his surprise, a sudden realization flooding over him. He was a blind, stupid fool.

"You love him."

She did not deny it. Arms folded beneath her breasts, she glared at him as though she were the master and he the pupil. "*He is my destiny.* All your silly omens and you cannot see that?" She stepped forward, gaining confidence as his wavered. "If your Gods approve of me, then they also approve of him. Our paths are entwined."

Was it true?

He stumbled back from her, his vision going out of focus. She became a silhouette against the brilliance of the sun, its rays casting a halo around her. What was Re telling him? That there was dark within the light? He had spent his whole life seeking purity, fighting the dark forces that sought to engulf Egypt. He had always known his enemy...

He held a hand out to the princess, warning her to keep her distance. "I cannot take the risk," he bemoaned, his confusion threatening to break his priestly composure. "What if you are wrong?"

Helen sighed, her shoulders slumping as the fight drained from her. "I could be. I am no prophet or seer. I have no divine powers to see into the hearts of men. I know only what I have witnessed, and Paris is a good, *moral*, man."

She turned to the north, her eyes—and thoughts—gazing off into the distance. "If a man is told he is a criminal his entire life, and in the end he becomes one, was that fate inevitable, or did he walk the path others set for him?"

She did not move a step toward him, but her anguish found its way to his heart nonetheless. "A wise king once told me we sometimes create the outcomes we fear." She turned to him, her eyes swelling with tears. "And the ones we desire. Both are equally possible, depending on our actions. You have the power to shape our destinies, for good or for ill. To show us a kindness or turn us away. The Gods have placed that sacred trust in you." She gazed up at him, her soul in her eyes. "So Meryatum, High Priest of Re, the question you must answer is this: which path will you set us on?"

He did not answer. For the moment, he had lost the capacity to speak. Her plea was as heartfelt as it was insightful. Did he truly have the power to shape the destiny of others? Was that the answer to the riddle that plagued him? Were the Gods warning him about the consequences of inaction, that this danger needs must be confronted and, with his help, purified?

As the minutes trailed on in silence, he watched the hope drain out from the princess' lovely face once again. She slowly wrapped her scarf around her head, a sad resolve informing her every move.

"I am sorry to have bothered you, Meryatum." She turned to go. "May Re's light shine upon you."

And upon you... The familiar incantation came unbidden to his mind. But it was not the princess who needed to be cleansed in the light of Re. Purifying one half of a fated pair was not enough. A sudden warmth burned in his chest, and he knew what he must do.

"Princess."

She stopped in her tracks, turning back to him with a timid hope.

"Tonight, after Re has returned to the netherworld, I will open the temple to you. You will face not only the daemons of your past, but those that await you. If the Gods find you unworthy, you will not leave the temple alive. Knowing this, do you still want to undertake the ritual?"

"*Yes,*" she answered without hesitation.

"Then await for my summons." He felt the first certainty he had in months. The Gods would decide which path the lovers would take, *both of them.*

For Helen's sake, he hoped it was a good one.

Chapter 27

Proof of Conflict

ACHILLES SHOVED ASTYANASSA against the wall of his bedchamber, the feisty vixen squealing with glee as he pressed his lips to her throat. It had been harder than he had expected to get the maiden alone. The queen watched over her more carefully than a she-bear with her cubs, but even a queen must sleep, and one wanton look from Astyanassa told Achilles exactly how to tempt her.

He lifted her hands above her head, narrowly missing the torch burning in an ornate sconce beside them. The rooms Agamemnon had offered Phthia's heir were sparse, but somehow Achilles had upended every bit of furniture in their foreplay.

"I've never been with a prince before," Astyanassa purred as he pealed off the corners of her chiton. The flimsy material fell to her waist, exposing two perfect breasts the color of fresh milk. She glanced down at what was quite possibly her finest feature, inviting him to enjoy.

But Achilles was not here to enjoy himself. He had no illusions about women. The weapons they used were just as deadly as his. This maiden was no juicy morsel to be savored. Astyanassa was a ferret, a spy for the queen, and he had no intention of letting her weave her charms over him.

With a wicked grin, he spun her around roughly, pressing her to the wall. She gasped as her heated flesh met cold stone. "And what about a king?" he groaned in her ear, pressing his stiff phallus against her backside. "Have you been with one of those?"

She responded instantly to the touch and lifted her hips, wiggling against him. "A lady never tells," she laughed, the throaty sound hinting at all manner of sinful behavior.

He released her, taking a few steps back to study his opponent. Astyanassa was too crafty to interrogate in the usual manner. This woman needed... persuasion. And there was only one thing a lusty siren like this desired.

"Come here," he growled the command.

She obeyed immediately, stepping out of her chiton as she sauntered to his side. He locked eyes with her, watching her movements with cool detachment. Whatever she saw in his hazel-green orbs only ignited her passions more. Her mouth hung open expectantly as she clawed at his garments, her hands pulling at the bindings of his tunic, snatching at the knots of his belt. He remained stone-still as she savaged him. When he finally stood bare before her, she ran her hand down the length of his phallus, her eyes widening with appreciation.

"My Prince," she purred as she stroked, beginning a trail of kisses that ran down is navel. "Whatever you desire, ask it. Let me serve you."

He wove his fingers through her silky black hair. Right when she pressed her lips to his shaft, he pulled her upright, her mouth inches from his. "Wine," he rasped, letting the heat of his breath linger between them like an imminent promise. "Bring me wine." He gave her rump a none-too-gentle slap.

The look of frustration on her delicate face was priceless. She poured a goblet of tart, blood-red vintage Achilles had brought with him from his homeland and offered the vessel with a flustered hand.

"Not like that." Achilles pulled her before the bed,

positioning her like a statue adorning a temple. "Here." He lifted the goblet to her breasts and then knelt before her, pressing his mouth to the folds of her cleft. The lascivious smile returned to her lips as she poured the liquid down the valley of her breasts to his awaiting mouth. He made sure to lap up every drop, and she shivered with delight at the stroke of his rough tongue.

"I've been thinking of what you said in the throne room." He rose to his feet, pressing her back on the bed. "Of how the Trojan prince 'bound her hand and foot' and made off in the night to have his way with her." He spread Astyanassa's legs apart, teasing her flower with the tips of his fingers. She moaned and arched her back. "Powerless and at the mercy of his sick desires," he continued, snatching up the length of rope from his belt. "Would you like to know how that feels?"

Her eyes popped open and she responded with a heat that surprised him. "*Yes.*" Astyanassa wiggled into position beneath him, a wicked grin on her face. "Don't hurt me," she pleaded, her eyes telling him to do his worst.

His stomach twisted with disgust. He had no place to question what carnal pleasures others enjoyed, but if her mistress had been treated in such a manner, this fantasy bordered on treason.

"Was it like this?" He grabbed her ankles and wrapped the rope around them. "Or was he behind her?" He flipped her over. The lithe little maid was light as a feather in his arms.

"Yes," she moaned again as he trailed his hand along her backside. She arched her back, rubbing into his groin.

"Which was it?" He pressed into her gyrating hips, teasing her.

"Behind. No, in front." Her words came in heavy gasps, and he knew he had her on the edge of reason. Just a taste more and his little bird would sing her song.

He flipped her over again, and bound her hands with a sash. She struggled against the bonds with mock urgency, her legs parting, inviting him in.

He lowered himself, hovering mere specks above her, sharing her body heat but not touching her skin. "And did he toss her over his shoulder? Or did he take her right then?" He stared into her dark eyes, eyes heavily laden with desire. She tried to kiss him, but again he denied her. "Well?"

"He took her," she blurted out, lifting her hips against his, the suggestion blatant.

He pinned her to the bed by her throat and thrust himself into her. The sultry siren was ready for him, her moist core taking in every inch. "Like this?"

"Yes..."

He thrust again and again, until she was moaning incoherently, her mewls rising with intensity. And right when her thighs tightened around him, he pulled out, keeping her dangling on the edge of ecstasy.

"I thought you said he taunted her, 'with claims of all the horrible things he would do once they left Mycenae.'"

"Yes. No. Please, don't stop," she moaned, in fact begged. She lifted her hips, trying desperately to get to him, but he kept himself frustratingly out of her reach.

"It never happened, did it?" He lowered his lips to her ear, twisting her nipple in his fingers, eliciting another groan. "Don't worry, sweet thing. I know what you need, and I'm going to to give it to you." He slapped the greedy mouth between her legs with just enough sting to make her gasp in pleasure and pain. "But first you are going to give me something."

"Anything," she promised, bucking at her bonds.

"The truth." He slapped her font again, letting his hand linger long enough for her to press into it for relief. "And not some hawker's tale about a prince who snatches crones and leaves an exquisite treasure like you behind."

The maiden was mad with her need for release. Like clay to be molded, he knew she was his. "I wasn't there," Astyanassa confessed, her eyes rolling back as he rewarded her by stroking her throbbing flower. "No one saw them leave." She rubbed against his hand with rhythmic thrusts. "The Trojan was craven, not bold like you, My Lord." A moan escaped her lips. *"Please..."*

He continued to stroke her, the familiar thrill of victory surging in his veins. "Tell me everything." He pressed his lips to her quivering breasts. *"Everything, Astyanassa."* He mounted her again as she cried out his name. "And I'll show you why every king in the Hellas fears my sword."

※

"Agamemnon has lied to us all!" Achilles paced around the bonfire of the Argolian courtyard. An owl screeched overhead, darting through the starlit sky, spooked from its perch by Achilles heated tone.

Diomedes and Palamedes sat before him, wrapped in the thick folds of their woolen cloaks. His fellow royals were not pleased at being wakened at such a late hour, but Achilles was beyond such considerations. After Astyanassa sang her tale, he stormed down the acropolis to the private annex housing Agamemnon's honored guests and their retinue.

"For all we know, he might have killed the Spartan princess himself and placed the blame on the Trojans." Achilles was working himself into a fury. He could feel the cold grip of reason slipping away from him. That lack of control was doing little to sway the minds of the two men before him, and they shared an uneasy look as they listened to all he discovered. "He hungers for glory and doesn't care whose men he slaughters to achieve it!"

"Think on what you say." Palamedes grimaced, his eyes darting nervously to the palace on the hill. "You are a guest in Agamemnon's house. You cannot go about accusing the man of treachery without proof."

Achilles glared at the prince, unsurprised to find Palamedes' courage lacking. Naupalia was a small principality in the shadow of Mycenae's might. From his courtly dress and the fashion of his coiled beard, Palamedes was Mycenaean in all but name. He had spent every minute of his time at the capital currying favor. If he had not also shown a mind of great cunning, Achilles would have left the prince out of his findings altogether.

"I have proof." Achilles lowered his voice and strove for calm, forcing the words out through grit teeth. "Their 'witness' confessed that her story is a complete fabrication. There was no raid on the treasury and no witness to Helen's abduction."

"*The words of a whore,*" Palamedes countered, raising to his feet in agitation. "Will you stand in the megaron and denounce a king on the confessions of such a base person? Are you mad?"

"*Yes, I'm mad.*" Achilles gripped his sword and took a menacing step toward the offensive man. "And you should be as well, unless you enjoy dancing for your master when he pulls your strings."

Palamedes' face constricted in near panic, and he took an unconscious step back, gripping his cloak tightly about his neck.

"Peace, Achilles." Diomedes stepped between them, a steady hand pressed against Achilles chest to keep the men at bay. "Palamedes speaks reason. Agamemnon is a powerful man. His lands greatly outsize any other kingdom in the Hellas. The prosperity of Mycenae's trade ensures the wealth of the entire West. He is not a king you cross lightly. Now, think. If the events behind Helen's abduction are a lie, what purpose do they serve?"

Achilles released his hold on his weapon, Diomedes' deliberate words soothing his heated blood. *Think, do not be Agamemnon's pawn.*

"He seeks to invoke the Oath, to unite Greece." He took a measured breath, his hawkish eyes still locked on Palamedes.

"And is that such a terrible thing? To come together under bonds of fellowship?" Diomedes guided him back over to the fire, pushing him down on the log Palamedes had vacated.

"Should we not answer the Trojan's insult with an iron fist?"

"But if they don't have the princess—"

"Oh, who cares?" Palamedes kicked sand into the fire, cutting Achilles' words short. The coals sparked and embers jumped into the sky, punctuating the irate stance of the prince. "Troy has long stared down their nose at Greece. Agamemnon is right to desire redress for their arrogance. What does it matter if they hold the princess?"

"Because it matters!" Achilles shot back. Was the man willfully ignorant? Respect earned with the skulls of the innocent was not glorious; it was tyrannical. The Gods punished such hubris with terrible consequences.

"I've heard enough." Palamedes turned to go. "I suggest you bury the hatchet you bear for our host, Achilles. The tide of war approaches, and you'd best get comfortable with your allies." He straightened his shoulders, attempting to look confident in that decision. "Are you coming, Diomedes?"

The Argolian king did not stir. He twisted the short hairs of his beard with his thumb and forefinger, studying Achilles with a thoughtful expression. "In a moment. Rest well, Palamedes." When the prince was gone, Diomedes extended his hand to Achilles, offering his help up. "Will you walk with me?"

Achilles nodded, his frustrations mounting. The proof of Agamemnon's wrongdoing was right before their eyes, and they cared not. Was it futile to even try? Was Agamemnon truly that powerful?

Diomedes led him out of the small courtyard he shared with the Naupalian delegation. They followed a small garden path made of river rock until they reached the perimeter wall of Mycenae. The thick, defensive barrier towered fifty feet above them where Mycenaean guards patrolled along the walkways. Even in times of peace, Agamemnon safeguarded against attack.

"You have every right to hate Agamemnon, Achilles. His treatment of your father has not been forgotten." Diomedes clasped his hands behind his back as he walked. "Phthia might not be as strong as it once was, but her legacy lives on. You are an honorable man, and your sword is invincible because it is always swung with righteous purpose."

Achilles tensed under the praise. One did not offer compliments unless unpleasantness was to follow.

"The other kings respect you," Diomedes continued, "but this is not the battlefield of your experience. Politics is a king's game. It is not a simple matter of true or false. It is a negotiation of power on a delicate scale, unbalanced by the smallest defector. You *must* put these dark feelings aside."

Achilles held his tongue, his thoughts simmering as the trail came to an end. Before them, a massive tumulus rose from the ground, a covered limestone circle that housed the ancient dead. Achilles turned his back on the monument, feeling as trapped as the corpses rotting beneath those stones. "So I am to suffer my disapproval silently? He has bled Phthia dry. Am I honor bound to also give him my life?"

Diomedes shook his head, placing a calming hand on Achilles' arm. "No one said you had to serve him, Achilles, but you did swear the Oath, and Helen *is* missing. If we unite, it is to reclaim her only. Agamemnon will not renew his campaigns in the West. Put your fears to rest."

Put my fears to rest? Fire burned in his belly. Only fools turned a blind eye to danger. "You think me paranoid." Achilles grimaced, understanding Diomedes' reluctance all-too-well. Acknowledging the unsavory nature of a man you broke bread with was inconvenient. It was easier to turn one's head from their crimes than to admit you were powerless to stop it. "My father once thought as you did, that Agamemnon was a man of his word. If you play the courtly games and offer him no insult, the specter of Mycenaean death will pass you by."

He glanced over his shoulder at the tomb again. Inside rested the forefathers of the House of Atreus, men as mad as they were ruthless. Men who once toppled an empire...

THE PRINCESS OF PROPHECY

Imperial Crete had been the strongest power in the Mediterranean but two centuries hence. If that mighty nation bowed its head before Mycenae, was it so terrible if Phthia joined that esteemed alumnus?

Achilles' stomach twisted with defiance, refusing defeat. "You know not the powers you meddle with, Diomedes. Agamemnon is not a king. *He's a conqueror.* He does not play your game of kings, not unless it suits his purpose. His ambition knows no bounds. He won't be satisfied until every king in Greece bends knee to his rule."

Diomedes opened his mouth to protest, but the effort died on his lips. Some portion of his words must have rung true.

Sadly, it did not matter if Diomedes believed him. His hands were tied, the same as Achilles'. Protest all he like, he could not defy his host—at least not openly. He strutted over to the tumulus, to the men who had sired that beast of a man. Tossing his cape over his shoulder, he lifted his tunic to relieve himself. Phthia may have fallen, but her spirit would remain unbroken.

"Mark my words, Diomedes. He *will* try to claim your lands, and the lands of those of whom you love. And when he does, the reigns of power you grant him might just be the rope he hangs you by."

Achilles shook himself dry. He returned to the palace, leaving Diomedes alone with the inglorious dead to ponder that dark and future day.

Chapter 28

A Poisoned Offer

"WE COULD LEAVE tonight," Scylax prodded the Trojan prince again. Paris paced the tiled floor of the guest apartments, a man on the edge of good reason. If he continued his stride, he was likely to carve rivets into the ground. "There is a team of smugglers at a hidden wadi north of town. They can carry us to your ship in Heracleion."

Just one more push and Scylax would net the queen her prize. Just one more step and the Trojan and his Spartan captive would be irrevocably in his clutches. He'd have the means to get his family back. And once Heliodora and the girls were safe again, he'd carry them far from Greece and the royal scum that always managed to ruin his life.

"We wait," the prince bristled with the command. "I will not leave Glaucus behind."

In the dimming light of twilight Scylax had difficulty reading the man's expressions. The prince was frustratingly loyal. In Scylax' experience, when pressure ran high, a royal would always save his own skin over his bondsmen's. He just needed the right motivation.

Scylax motioned to Yuli, one of the other *meshwesh* servants, and he quickly set about lighting the evening candles. His former swords brothers, still shocked by his arrival in their prison, were quick to respond to his commands. Though he had known none of them by name, they had all heard tale of *him*. Yuli, like many others, believed he had come to rescue them. Scylax sneered at the thought. Such fantasies were for children. The only respite a man could expect from this living hell came when the cold earth embraced you.

"My Prince, we may not get another opportunity like this." He adopted the timid speech of his assumed character. 'Jason' was a mixture of many captives he had taken over a long, and illustrious career. Fear and desperation was what fueled those facing their end. They clung to a false hope that there was some way out, some chance their miseries would end. That tiny spark of hope never ceased, even when his sword came down on their necks. "Surely your captain can follow after?"

"No!" Paris kicked a three-legged stool, sending the item crashing across the room. Sandarvo, a Sikel, had to jump out of the way to avoid getting hit. "Glaucus is family. He would never leave me behind, and neither will I him."

Scylax cursed internally. If reasoning would not sway Paris, then perhaps fear could. "I am sorry I upset you, My Prince. I meant no disrespect. It is only that I fear for your safety. And the princess'. A poisoned arrow could easily become a poisoned cup."

The princess... that was his angle into the Trojan. Paris' face creased with deep pain. He crumbled onto the cushioned bench in the center of the room, the manic energy of his pacing vanishing.

Scylax raced to the bench, kneeling beside him. "Your Highness? Are you all right?"

Paris' gaze was far away, a palpable sadness surrounding him. "Have you ever loved someone more than life itself?"

Scylax stiffened. It made him uncomfortable when Paris spoke so openly.

"A person," the prince continued, "who when they look at

you, cuts straight to your soul and makes you want to be a better man? A man even a fraction of what they think you can be?"

Scylax fought to control his reaction. Paris was on the edge, ready to succumb to the right pressure. His mission was within his reach...

Heliodora came unbidden to his mind. His Egyptian healer had mended so much more than his broken body. She took a tortured soul, unworthy of even an ounce of compassion, and reshaped him. He understood, intimately, what the prince was experiencing.

"Yes, I have." He surprised himself by answering honestly. For a moment Jason's mask vanished and he knelt before Paris as he truly was.

The Trojan clasped his shoulder, a friendly act between equals. "Then you have an inkling of what I feel for Helen."

The calculating portion of his mind screamed at him to act, the portion that had crafted and enacted cruel acts of brutality. Paris was vulnerable. The time to strike was now!

But he was utterly confused. The Trojan was not the cowardly prince the queen had led him to believe. He had not hidden behind others but had shown considerable skill in battle, a commodity that would have swollen the ego of a baser man. Yet Paris was modest. He treated all men, whether high or low born, as his equals. In another life, Scylax would have admired him.

Even his crime of abducting the princess was more complicated than it had originally seemed. Helen had come willingly, a fact the queen must have known. The princess was being hunted, persecuted, simply for having fallen in love with the wrong man.

Was he feeling... *compassion*? Scylax sneered at himself, squelching those weak inclinations. He did not care how deeply the lovers felt for each other. It did not make him love his family less. He would not sacrifice their lives for a pair of royals, no matter how honorable the prince might prove himself.

He cleared his throat, forcing the words across a heavy tongue. "If you love her, then you must protect her." He could hear a tiny portion of his soul cry out against his actions, a voice that sounded surprisingly like his missing wife. "Your captain would tell you to do the same. We should leave immediately."

Paris was on the verge of saying yes. He opened his mouth, the guilt of forsaking his comrade writ large on his face.

A heavy knock came from the chamber doors, the thunderous pounding reverberating throughout the room. Paris shot a quick look to his Trojan guards and they immediately flanked him, their casual stance belied by the speed in which they moved. The prince turned to him, any trace of his earlier vulnerability gone. "Jason, will you see to that?"

Scylax almost cried out his frustration. He couldn't afford another delay. The queen had been explicit about the cost of failure. He had these few precious days to do as she commanded while no kingdom interfered. If he failed, Heliodora would pay the price.

The knocking continued, and Paris was waiting. Scylax had no choice but to comply. Buckling his shoulders, he scurried to the door in the manner of a frightened slave.

Paris waited anxiously as Jason opened his chamber doors. His feet itched to be gone from this place, but he had promised Helen these last few days to secure the ritual, and he would not rob her of that chance.

Every minute they remained he felt more and more like bait dangled before the mouths of those who wished to consume him. The fact that he had no inkling who those forces might be, frustrated him to no end. How can one fight an

THE PRINCESS OF PROPHECY

enemy who did not show his face?

Jason stepped back from the door, the servant surprisingly speechless. His shock should have warned Paris what was to follow. Meryatum stepped into the room, a half-dozen of his *pastophoroi* trailing behind him.

Paris rose to his feet, a deep dread gripping his heart. "Glaucus? Is he...?"

"No." The high priest crossed the room to him, stopping just out of his reach. "Your man recovers in the House of Ails. The last I saw of him, he was conscious and asking after you."

Paris took a deep, shuddering breath, releasing a tension he had not realized he carried. He had told Jason that Glaucus was family, but the captain was much more than that. He was friend and father, the most loyal companion a disgraced prince could hope to find. That he might die trying to protect him stirred more guilt than Paris knew how to bear.

"I must see him." He raced to the door. He did not make it past the priest, however. Meryatum clasped his arm with an iron grip.

"He must wait. I have come to speak with you about Helen."

Paris' earlier dread paled before the icy bite of terror he experienced now. "What about Helen? Is she all right?" He unconsciously clung to the priest, gripping the man with greater force than the priest had him.

The *pastophoroi* muttered in alarm at his behavior, a few looking over their shoulders as though to call for help. Meryatum, however, was less concerned. The high priest stared at the offending hand until Paris released him.

"The princess will face the Gods tonight. They will judge her soul on the scales of *ma'at*, and if she is found lacking, she will not return to the realm of the living." He spoke that dire possibility without an ounce of emotion.

Paris's blood ran cold. He never, in his wildest imaginings, thought the Egyptian temple to be a danger. A purification ritual was a simple matter, a procedure the high priest had probably presided over a thousand times. Death was never a possibility.

I should never have brought her here. This whole visit has been a colossal mistake. He decided then and there to take Jason's offer. Helen would be heartbroken, but she would understand. He would not risk losing her for the privilege to love her with divine permission.

"Cease your preparations. She will not participate."

"Helen has already agreed. It is too late to stop the ritual. By now, she is in the House of Re." Meryatum stood firm, his face a mask of indifference. "And where she goes, so must you."

The *pastophoroi* broke out into grumbles again, clearly at odds with the high priest's decision. Brygos and Ariston formed ranks behind him, hands gripped on their swords. Even Jason looked deeply distressed. He motioned secretly to Paris from the door, urging caution.

"You want me to undergo purification?" The request was beyond suspicious, especially after the deadly stakes the priest had just declared. "Why?"

Meryatum cast a single glare at his priests to silence them. "Your fates are linked. Do not deny it!"

"I... don't." Paris' protests died on his lips. His soul was bound to Helen's, and he was exhausted from his efforts to hide that. A strange relief flowed through him hearing another acknowledge that as fact.

"The Gods may have blessed the princess, but they have shown you no such favor," Meryatum simmered with disapproval. "She goes before them, not to purify herself, but to challenge the omens against you, to prove you righteous. *She risks her life for yours.*" He directed his anger squarely at Paris, shaking with the effort to control himself. "Will you do no less?"

Paris could not tell if he was more touched than he was shocked. *Helen, you precious, crazy fool...* He could not fathom the faith she placed in him, nor the courage she continued to show in his defense. In some small measure, he understood Meryatum's anger. He was unworthy of her sacrifice.

"May I have a moment to consider?"

Meryatum nodded and withdrew a respectable distance as Paris turned to his guards.

"*You cannot be considering this!*" Brygos spoke in a heated whisper.

"*It could be a trap,*" Dexios quietly agreed. "*They could kill you both, or keep you captive behind that fortress of stone.*"

And what of Mycenae? Glaucus' responsible voice lectured him despite his absence. *What of the danger it presents to Troy? We have a responsibility to warn the king.*

Paris had sworn an oath to king and country, but he had also sworn an oath to Helen. He promised to follow her to the ends of the earth, and if this was the path she chose to take, he would go, regardless of his misgivings.

"I know the dangers," he tried to console them, sounding more confident than he felt. "If I am not back by the time the sun sets again, find Glaucus and get out of Egypt." Brygos tried to protest, but Paris silenced his guard. "*That's an order.* Jason knows the way. Work with him and get back to Troy. Make sure my father knows everything that happened. *Everything.*" He did not envy the man who must hold that conversation in his stead.

He turned back to Meryatum, the unblinking man studying him as though he were an aberrant piece of a puzzle. "I will go with you," he told the priest, a cold vein of fury burning inside him at this manipulation. "Not because of your threats, nor out of fear for your Gods, but because it is what she would wish. I do this for Helen."

The declaration meant little, there was nothing he could do if this man wanted him dead, but he felt stronger for saying it, nonetheless. Meryatum nodded as if he expected nothing less. The *pastophoroi* filed out the door with Paris at their center.

For Helen, he pledged to himself, and prepared at long last to face the Immortals who had cursed him.

Chapter 29

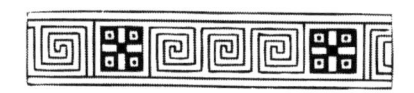

Sacrifices to the Gods

HELEN PULLED THE hood of her cloak over her head as the *pastophoroi* led her to the temple gates. Six priests marched in step around her, the fiery brands they held aloft gleaming off their hairless heads. Her heart hammered against her ribs when they came to collect her from the harem, each man, like a stone-cut statue, frowning down on her in mute disapproval. Not one word had they uttered in the long walk from the palace to the temple. Nor did they give hint or gesture that might shed light on the deadly ritual she had committed herself to.

Courage, she coached herself. Her heart's desire awaited after this test of spirit. For Paris, she could endure. Yet every step she took increased the angst-filled hollow within her, and courage seemed an empty hope for a young girl in an alien world.

They passed the outer pylons, entering the dark walkway that led into the temple complex. Over the past week, she had been permitted no further than the courtyard on the other side, the last boundary of the profane world before entering into the sacred. Tonight she would pass into the inner sanctum itself, a place only priests of the highest order were permitted to approach.

Moonlight bathed over her as she stepped into the court, the silver glow reflecting off the sand-swept floor like the facets on a jewel. The vibrant colors of the inner walls and second pylons were a muted grey now, as though all life in the House of Re had retreated with him into the netherworld. Helen pulled her cloak tightly around her, a chill running through her that came not from the air.

The *pastophoroi* led onwards. An alabaster altar sat before the temple doors, square and tapered inwards, a micro replication of the temple itself. Penanukis awaited them, one hand held forward, barring the priests further entry.

"I will take her from here." He dismissed the others and motioned Helen to follow him.

As Second Prophet, Penanukis was Meryatum's second in command. He wore the same archaic robes as the other priests, with a single amulet draped around his neck to signify his office. Helen had had several occasions to get the know the man better, none of which had impressed her. He considered any intrusion into the peaceful world of temple life as unwelcome, and watched those of greater authority than he with hawkish eyes. He reminded her of the nobles in Mycenae, eager to tear down those around them so they might seem taller.

"The First Prophet has decreed that you will complete the full induction tonight." He walked the temple perimeter on soundless feet, leading her down the covered walkway to the priests' private quarters. "The one our acolytes perform when they are raised to *pastophoroi*." His nasal tone declared his resentment loud and clear. "Why is that so?"

"I don't know," she answered honestly. Helen had no idea why Meryatum insisted she endure the lengthy ritual. She had no desire to become a 'Pure One', but if the high priest deemed it necessary, she was not going to argue.

"He has taken special efforts for you, Princess." Penanukis grimaced, the first mar on his otherwise still face. "No foreigner has ever been inducted to the Mysteries. You owe him a great debt."

A greater one than you can ever know. To no longer be bond to Menelaus and his brother was a freedom she could not fathom. A tingle ran through her spine at the thought that moment could be near.

The priest opened a wooden door to a preparation chamber, the room a scant fifty feet from the temple proper. Inside, the candlelit room boasted a single stool and a table holding bowls filled with water, powders, and ointments. She stepped into the room and stood lamely by the stool, unsure what was expected of her.

Penanukis shut the door behind him, a hint of anticipation gleaming in his eyes as he held a candle high to inspect her. "Remove your clothes."

"What?" She backed away from him, stumbling against the stool. "Why?"

"You must be cleansed, the filth of this world removed." He rolled his eyes, his tone that of an impatient elder speaking to a child. "You go into the God's world as one newly born. Now remove your clothes."

Where was Meryatum? Why did Penanukis bring her to this tiny room where they were alone? Helen's mind screamed at her to run. The four walls of the windowless room seemed to close in around her.

Courage, she tried to buoy her spirits again, *this is not Greece. He is not Agamemnon.*

Helen lifted her chin, forcing her daemons to keep at bay. She had nothing to fear from this man. The priests were celibate. She removed her cloak then pulled her dress up over her head, doing her best to ignore the hunger reflecting back from Penanukis' eyes. Standing naked before him, she imagined this discomfort as her first trial. If the sins of her past were to be absolved, then fear of the flesh was the first item she'd sacrifice on that altar.

"I see." He lowered his candle and picked up a bowl of

clear water, approaching her. "Perhaps Meryatum's favor is no mystery after all." He dipped a cloth of wool into the bowl, and began to bathe her. He pressed the sodden rag to her thighs, his fingers squeezing her tender flesh as he sluiced away the dirty water. The bathing continued for long, agonizing minutes. She tried to pretend this was any other bath, that the hands cupping her breasts were Aethra's. She closed her eyes, retreating into her mind.

I am not afraid of this man. Nor any other man. Her body was no longer a toy for others to abuse. Those words became a mantra she repeated to herself over and over again. She was not the gentle calf forever a victim to her powerful masters. She could be the lioness. She could take back the power she had given over to them.

Helen opened her eyes, a dark fury burning inside her with that promise. She did not strike the priest, but her bearing said all the words she elected not to speak.

Touch me, you cretin, if you dare.

Penanukis froze, his hand suspended above her chest. "That should be enough." He put the bowl down with a shaky hand, picking up another filled with the light green powder of henna. Mixing water into the bowl to create a paste, he approached her with a wooden stylus in hand.

"What are you doing?"

"Markings..." He motioned to her body, his nervous gesture responding to the command in her tone. "For protection. So the Gods will recognize you as one of their servants."

She nodded, letting him proceed. Cowing the man was a small victory, but one she desperately needed, especially if she would prove herself strong enough to face the Gods.

Penanukis was a masterful artist. Over the next two hours, he painstakingly painted intricate patterns over her body, the henna fading to a rich orange-red, the color of banked coals. The Eye of Horus was drawn on each arm. Over her chest went the winged solar disk of Re. Many others she did not recognize covered her belly and legs. By the time he was finished, her body resembled the temple walls, every inch below her neck covered with protective spells. Written, so the priest told her, in the magical language of the Gods.

She wrapped her cloak around her shoulders as they prepared to leave, wondering about the one spot he had left untouched: the oblong section directly over her heart. If the designs were meant as armor, then the priest had left her most vulnerable spot exposed.

A breeze had picked up from the east, carrying with it a low hanging mist. The moonlit clouds swirled as she stepped through it, making the air itself seem to breathe and vibrate. The altar before the temple was now lit, the flames carving out a section of color in the pale-blue night. Standing before that flame was the High Priest of Re.

Meryatum was resplendent in his ceremonial robes. He held the staff of his office: a wooden rod equal in height to his tall frame, its golden solar-disk headpiece complete with a crystal center. It reflected both the light from above and below, pulsing like the north star, guiding her toward him.

Helen stepped up to the altar, her mind ablaze. She wanted to ask him so many questions. Where had he been? The solemn cast to his face, however, told her to remain quiet. He was in communion with his Gods. Now was not the time for idle tongues. She let her cloak drop to the stone beneath her feet and lowered her head.

Meryatum reached for a tray held out by his *pastophoroi*, lifting a jewel-encrusted censor. He shook it, sprinkling water over her head, as his resonate voice rang out across the courtyard. "Helen, Daughter of Sparta. You set forth into the realm of the Gods so you might be reborn an innocent to this world. But to live again, you needs first must die. You must pass into the netherworld and welcome the embrace of Nun's soothing waters. Inside this temple, the enemies of *ma'at* will seek to destroy you. If your heart is pure, if your destiny is great, you will prevail."

He lifted a stylus, one forged of electrum, the tip a finer edge than the wooden instrument used by Penanukis before. With it he drew a cartouche over her heart, sculpting the hieroglyph of a grey heron, the *bennu* bird, the spirit of Re himself.

"The Gods test those they have chosen for great purpose. In meeting their challenge, we prove ourselves worthy of that honor."

Again he turned to his priest, this time to procure a chalice of incredible beauty, the work of a master goldsmith. Bloodstones as large as eggs lined the cup, the gems glinting from the bonfire like fiery daemon eyes. He pressed the chalice to her lips and she drank deeply, the bitter tonic burning her throat as she swallowed.

"Go now, Daughter of Sparta, Beloved of Aphrodite, Chosen of Mnevis. Go now and face what was, what is and what will come, not in fear, but with courage. Prove yourself worthy of their divine protection."

The dulling of her senses was almost instantaneous. Meryatum's rigid face began to blur, and she could not feel the stone beneath her feet. She would have fallen to the ground if she had not formed a solid image in her mind of remaining upright. Still, Meryatum had to hold her arm to guide her across the courtyard to the temple doors.

Strength and Honor. Her father's voice echoed across the distance in her mind. Spartans always faced their fate with an unconquerable spirit. She let that heritage fill her.

The doors of the temple swung open as if by some mysterious force. A mist billowed out as though trying to escape the yawning abyss inside.

Courage, strength, and honor...

She cast one last look at Meryatum, releasing his arm. The priest's face was pinched with concern, but he let her go, nonetheless. Taking a deep breath, she stepped into the temple.

THE PRINCESS OF PROPHECY

Paris entered the temple complex, his mind awash with misgivings. His entire life he had avoided the company of religious zealots, and now he was willingly placing himself in their hands. It had been easy to discount the mad ravings of Aesacus, his father's seer who had a thirst for power unmatched by any holy man in the Old World. But if the Egyptian prophet saw the same darkness in him...? Paris could not help but worry it was true, and so he walked to the temple in silence, his steps weighted with the pall of the condemned mounting the execution block.

His *pastophoroi* guards led him to the sacred lake, the brilliant canopy of stars reflecting in its still waters. That plane of water seemed a window between worlds, one above and one below. They ordered him to strip and wade into the lake.

He hesitated, scanning the surrounding buildings for any sign of activity. "Where is Helen?" He felt a tugging at his veins, an urge he had come to associate with her when she was in distress. He turned back toward the temple, knowing somehow she was near.

"You must be cleansed," the priest insisted, pushing him towards the lake. Paris resisted the urge to push back. Meryatum would take him to Helen soon enough. For what other reason would the priest have brought him here? He removed his tunic and sandals and walked into the cool waters.

Two *pastophoroi* joined him. They pressed him under the surface, rubbing him down with sandstones. For a moment, he nearly panicked. The priests were stronger than they looked and, with little effort, could hold him down until breath escaped him. There were less obvious ways of killing him, however, if that was what they wished. An assassin who employed poison was not likely to show his hand so readily. With reluctance, Paris unclenched his muscles and let the priests do their duty. By the time they finished, he was pink, his new skin raw and highly sensitive to the chill wind that stirred from the east.

Water dripped from his hair and down his back. He was offered no towel, nor was his clothing returned to him. Paris sighed, frustrated at himself for expecting anything different. He shook himself dry like a mongrel, trying to preserve what little dignity he had left. Not waiting for permission, he pushed through his *pastophoroi* chaperones and back to the temple where he could get some answers.

Meryatum was waiting for him, standing beside a blazing bonfire at the alabaster altar. The man was tall for an Egyptian, but when Paris ascended the altar, the high priest was forced to look up. An eddy of mist swirled around them, cutting them off from the dozen other priests standing vigil.

"Where is Helen?" Paris strove for a respectful tone, a difficult endeavor as the pulling in his veins increased. "Is she safe?"

"That depends on you." The high priest frowned, studying him like a man puzzling out a riddle. "Are you the man she claims or are the omens true? The Gods are conflicted."

Were they? Or was that what Meryatum wished him to believe? Empowered with the symbols of his office and in view of the House of Re, the high priest was in his element. Standing naked before the man, Paris felt nothing more than a puppet, his strings manipulated by a master magician.

"I know who I am." He grit his teeth, sick of the pretense. "As do the Gods. I have made my peace with them."

Meryatum looked unconvinced. "Be that as it may," he shook his head, "Amun-Re will be the final judge." The fire crackled behind him, sizzling as a branch crumbled to ash. Paris took an involuntary step back. Meryatum was silhouetted by the angry red flames, the priest seemingly imbued with their fiery power. "Our paths did not cross without reason, Alexandros of the House of Priam. Amun-Re brought you, and your foreign beauty, to Egypt. He wishes to show you something, and I am unsure you will survive the viewing."

There were few things on this earth that struck Paris with fear. He learned long ago that reality held worse dangers than the panicked imaginings of the mind. Yet hearing the tremor in Meryatum's booming voice, he could not help but look to the temple, and the mysteries it hid, with trepidation.

"Has Helen gone in?"

"She has."

He squared his shoulders. "Then so will I."

Meryatum waved over another priest, picking up a small vial the man held on a cushion. "If you are to behold the Great God, you will have to embrace your true nature. Your soul must be laid bare. You will see as the Gods see."

Drugs. At least one thing was consistent amongst the religious practitioners of the world. He nodded and prayed that the effects would not be permanent.

"I warn you, this will not be pleasant." The high priest pulled out the glass stopper filled with a small measure of green liquid.

"I can handle it," he said with more confidence than he felt. Just the sight of the unfamiliar substance made Paris' already sensitive skin itch.

Meryatum motioned forward two *pastophoroi* and Paris was seized from behind. They pinned his arms behind his back, raising his head with a grip on his hair.

"What are you doing?" He flexed against their tight hold.

Meryatum did not answer. He loomed over Paris as the remaining priests lifted their voices in a light hymn, a strangely celebratory song despite the prophet's ominous warnings. He raised the dropper over Paris' face and released a single drop in each eye.

Paris screamed. He had never experienced such intense pain in his life. The drugs seeped through his eyes, seeming to ignite his very skull. The world burned in liquid white pain, and he fell to his knees, still locked in the priests' hold.

"*What have you done to me?*" he yelled between sharp gasps. When the pain did not abate, a new terror took hold of him. *What had he done with Helen?*

"You lying bastard!" He heaved against his captors, fighting to get back on his feet. "You are going to kill her. Like you tried to do with me. And Glaucus..."

His blood pounded in his veins like a war drum and Paris found a strength inside him he had never known existed. He swung his right arm, dislodging one priest. Though his vision had not returned, he heard the man stumble across the altar and scream as he landed in the fire. Another shove sent the other priest to the ground and out into the courtyard.

He was a fool for coming to Egypt. A fool for trusting the good will of the temple. When would he learn? They were all murdering bastards who only cared for their own self-importance. "Where are you?" he shouted, his arms spread out before him, sweeping around to find the high priest.

Something changed. A black blur emerged in the white cloud of his vision. The song of the *pastophoroi* rose to a new level, their chanting building with intensity. In the midst of that noise came a new sound, one much closer to Paris. That black blur took form, and he knew the high priest stood over him.

"*Awake, O Mighty God. Awake Re, and vanquish your enemies.*" A piercing light stabbed at Paris' eyes from the tip of Meryatum's staff, and he covered his head to shield from it. "*Draw out Chaos so that he may be banished in your Light.*"

Protective spells. As the world slowly took form around Meryatum and his awesome presence, Paris realized those spells were not for him, *but against him*.

A resounding boom echoed throughout the courtyard and a cold draft wafted across Paris' legs. He spun to see what new danger the priest had conjured and was met only with blackness. The cold, empty black of the void.

"Go now!" Meryatum commanded, his powerful voice

seemingly inside Paris' mind. "Go and seek out your destruction." He planted his hands on Paris' shoulders and shoved him into the temple.

Meryatum trembled as the priests slid the bolt on the temple doors into place. He had been prepared to face the wrath of the Trojan but had not expected such strength. Fueled with righteous anger, the prince had the power of ten men, a small token of what he might be capable. Meryatum suspected the prince kept those forces hidden, even from himself.

Penanukis stepped up on the altar beside him, the second prophet as disturbed by the Trojan's raw display as he. "Are you sure it was wise to give him the night flower? He could kill her you know."

He could, and the guilt of the princess' death would lie entirely at Meryatum's feet. "I had no choice."

The decision to move forward with this plan had not come lightly. Meryatum baited Chaos in hopes that the Gods would reveal their purpose in the shadow-haunted man. If the Trojan was what the omens decreed, Helen would pay for it with her life.

"If he kills her, it is the will of Re. The root of dark tidings will be revealed, and we can restore balance."

He raised his torch, beckoning the other priests to follow him to the observation chambers. There was no more he could do but wait. Paris and Helen's future rested with the Gods now.

And what if she is right? An unbearable guilt weighted down Meryatum's heavy steps. Can a man overcome his fate and become something more? Or had he sentenced Helen to an early death by the man she loved?

Scylax hurried down the palace corridor keeping to shadows as best he could. The hour was growing late. The insufferable Trojan guards had kept him preoccupied long after the prince had left with priests, plying him for details about their nonexistent escape plan. His skills had been stretched thin trying to find suitable answers.

Why had the high priest picked tonight to change his mind? He was so close to securing Paris and Helen that he could almost hear his daughters' laughter. The Gods mocked him, showing once again how they unjustly favored the noble kind.

He pressed himself flat against the wall as another guard completed his rounds, the metal-tipped butt of his staff beating a stucco rhythm as he passed. It was sheer desperation that forced Scylax to move through the palace so openly. He hoped Taharqa was right about this man.

The temple taking possession of the prince was the worst possible scenario for Scylax. If they killed the princess in their ridiculous ritual, the queen would blame Scylax for failure and take Heliodora's life. If Helen and Paris both lived, they'd no longer need to flee the capital. Seti would fill their empty larders and they'd be back on the high seas to Troy. His mission would be delayed, and the queen would blame Scylax for failure and take Heliodora's life. The sands of the hourglass had run out. He needed access to the fugitive pair, a feat of considerable undertaking considering the fortress that now held them.

Two guards stood vigil outside the chancellor's door. Sell-swords by the look of them: one a Nubian as dark as Etruscan soil and the other the deep brown of a Hyksos tribal man. It seemed Bay did not place his protection in the hands of the Egyptian military. Scylax lowered his guard a bit, which meant he was a tad less lethal than a coiled asp. He stepped out of the shadows, and the guards tensed uncomfortably, stunned by his silent approach.

"What do you want, slave?" the Nubian sneered at him,

brandishing his sword.

"I have a message for Chancellor Bay." He held his ground. It was a rarity for a slave to show a fraction of courage. He hoped it was enough to peak their interest. He did not relish the idea of leaving a trail of bodies in his wake to get to the man.

The guard grimaced and sheathed his blade. "Follow me."

The chancellor's chambers were dimly lit. A few oil lamps burned in niches along the wall, the rancid smoke from their wicks adding to the claustrophobic feeling of the room. Bay sat at a large desk covered with scrolls. He didn't bother lifting his head from his letters as Scylax crossed the room.

Bloody arrogant fool. A man could lose his head being so careless. This was the turncoat Taharqa said he could trust?

"What do you want?"

"I bear a message for you from my Trojan master." Scylax waited for Bay's full attention, but the scratching of his quill continued on uninterrupted.

"Get on with it."

"He said to tell you the springs in Ugarit are fair if you can survive the storms."

The quill dropped. Bay finally turned away from his documents, his beady black eyes narrowing as he stroked the thin hairs on his chin. "It is fortunate we are not in Ugarit. The land of eternal sunshine is a far better place to call home."

"Indeed."

"That will be all, Nobati. You may return to your post."

The Nubian guard bowed stiffly at the waist and left the room. It wasn't until the door clicked shut that Bay finally rose to his feet to inspect him.

"You show too much pride for a *meshwesh* slave," Bay purred, stalking around him in a circle like a buzzard spying a meal.

Scylax grimaced. Why were the weakest men always oblivious when they faced real danger? "And you show too much ambition for a trumped up overseer with eyes on the throne."

Bay stopped in his tracks, a vicious snarl curling his lips. "I could have you killed for uttering such lies."

"*You could try.*" Scylax did not need to raise his voice for the threat to resonate with the puerile man.

Bay backed up toward his desk, his eyes darting to the door, realizing too late the folly of dismissing his guard. "Who are you?"

"Who I am is of no consequence. What I *know*, however, could be of great value to you."

Bay stopped to consider, shifting from fear to suspicion with alarming ease. "I am listening," he said after a lengthy pause, his fingers again finding purchase on his beard.

Scylax almost walked out the door. Joining forces with a court toady... it was enough to make him question his soul. Bay was the sort of creature who would sell his own children for the right price, and Scylax was handing him a prince of the rarest caliber, one who valued the life of his servants over his own. The sour taste of bile crept up his throat.

"I will sing you my song once I am satisfied that you can meet my terms." He pulled free the dagger strapped against his thigh and proceeded to pick his nails with it. The gesture was not lost on Bay.

The arrangement was simple, and mutually beneficial to both parties. Bay readily agreed. He still lacked appreciation, however, for what would happen to him if he thought to double-cross Scylax. In the end, the deal was struck, and Scylax walked back to the Trojan quarters feeling more bound by his agreement with Bay than the collar around his throat.

Dora would forgive him for these crimes he was forced to do in Clytemnestra's service. For the girls, she would understand. Or so he lied to himself as he waited through the long night for the prince to return.

Chapter 30

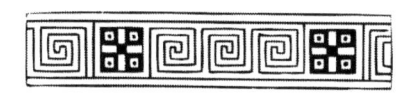

The Swamps of Creation

SHE WAS ENVELOPED in darkness, its crushing weight pressing Helen to the temple floor where she lay for moments beyond counting. Her senses grew dull; she could not taste, smell or feel. There was only the black emptiness, a plane of reality that existed solely in her mind.

And in that world, she was not alone. Helen was a child again, hiding under the furs in her father's tent. Clytemnestra was near. Her twin was not a separate entity, but a part of herself. They shared the same thoughts, the same emotions, and tonight, as the cries of death and battle raged on outside, the only emotion they felt was fear.

Helen tried to raise an arm, fighting for control of her body, to seek some escape. She did not want these memories. They had been banished to a dark corner of her mind where they could never resurface again. In the cavernous night of Re's temple, however, there were no boundaries, and those memories surrounded her.

Hands latched on to her legs, pulling her from her nest of safety. Those meaty palms, sticky with the blood of her fallen people, bound her hand and foot. She was hoisted over her assailant's horse like nothing more than a sack of potatoes, and they rode off into the night.

Don't look. Don't see. He doesn't exist.

The older Helen could squint her eyes and pretend the events that followed were but a dream, but the child had no such luxury. She twisted and looked up at her captor.

No stars shone in the sky, as though the Gods designed to aid the thief with supernatural stealth. His features were obscured in darkness, a black substance that seemed to swallow what little light surrounded it. Twin fires stared down on her where his eyes should be, like hollow furnaces ablaze. He seemed a daemon of the underworld come to snatch her away.

No!

Helen pressed up on her elbows, a surprising anger fueling her body. She reached up to his face, her hands—no longer bound—twisted like claws, and raked the blackness away. It fell in thick tar-like goblets until his face was revealed underneath.

It was Agamemnon.

She tore at him again, his flesh falling away as though sculpted of clay, only to reveal Menelaus beneath.

You cannot hide from me! I will see your face. She ripped at him again, desperate to see the villain who had begun her tortured existence, careless how deep she would have to dig. Her fingers struck something solid. She wiped away the debris and chunky remains of flesh and bone, to reveal the visage beneath. It shone with the burnt-red glow of polished bronze.

The face was her own.

No, it was Clytemnestra's. Helen stretched out her hands to feel for herself, her fingertips tracing the high cheekbones and sculpted brow. The cool flesh radiated evil, and the dark glint of her ice-cold eyes were those of a madman. It couldn't be her sister...

Is it me?

Was this some darker side of herself she had never dared

to acknowledge? The Helen that might have been had she followed Clytemnestra's ways? She removed her hand with a hiss, a deep revulsion twisting her gut. On impulse, she swung her arm, striking the creature across the head. They both tumbled to the ground, the impact absorbed by a dark cloud hanging low over the earth.

Not me. You cannot claim me. Not ever.

She pummeled the creature with fists and feet, each strike breaking loose a bundle of fear that lodged itself into her heart. When the last blow fell, the captor vanished, dissolving into a swirl of smoke.

Helen's chest heaved, drawing in precious air. *What am I doing?* She spun in a circle, the black fog making it impossible to see farther than ten feet ahead. *This doesn't exist. I am in Egypt, in the temple.* She kept that thought firmly in her mind and slowly the stone walls of the temple took shape around her.

She stood in a forest of stone. There was no other way to describe the hall filled with towering columns. A hundred pillars stretched seventy five feet into the air, each one shaped like a marsh reed, complete with a blossoming lotus for its capital. Windows high up on the walls showered moonlight across the hall, the shafts of light cutting through the gloom.

Helen touched the pillar nearest her, a colossal column the width of four men standing abreast. Every inch of it was covered in hieroglyphs with pictures of the Gods leading their chosen ones through the afterlife. As her fingers traced the rigid surface, her vision dimmed, and her precious hold on reality slipped.

A mysterious light filled the room, and Helen saw at midnight as she would at midday. The walls erupted in activity and color, and the figures of the past, carved in such painstaking detail, broke loose from their stone prisons and marched free around her.

A God stood before her. He bore the body of a man, some eight feet tall, and the head of a jackal. His ink black eyes gleamed with power, never blinking. It was Anubis, Protector of the Dead, the God who escorted dead souls to judgement. Helen should have been terrified, but strangely she was not. When he offered his hand, she took it, letting the God lead her through the temple.

The hypostyle hall melted away like a sheet of papyrus curling from the heat of a candle. Behind this plane existed another: the realm of the Gods. Hand in hand with Anubis, she stepped through the embers into it.

The Hall of Judgement was the most dazzling display of grandeur Helen had ever seen. A hundred kneeling supplicants lined the walkway to a throne, their voices lifted in songs of praise. On a raised dais sat Osiris, the God of the Dead, his body completely wrapped in linen like the mummified Egyptian dead. His two wives, sisters of fierce beauty and strength, stood quietly behind him, each one with a hand upon his shoulders.

Before the throne rested an enormous golden scale. Had Helen been a child, she could have easily sat on one of the weighted platforms. No child would play with this toy, however, for a beast with the haunch of a wolf and head of a crocodile guarded it. Its central pillar was formed in the shape of an ankh, and its crossbeam and chains were inverted raised arms, the Egyptian symbol of *ka*, the spirit. Anubis drew her to it, and Helen knew her moment of judgement had come.

A loud crash echoed throughout the temple. It seemed a distant thing, scarcely noticeable in this divine world, but the supplicants' song wavered, leaving Helen to wonder what had caused it. After a moment's hesitation, they began the song again, renewing their efforts with powerful notes that strummed at her soul, lulling her into a peaceful acceptance. Whatever happened in that other place no longer mattered.

She stepped before the scale and was greeted by another God, Thoth, God of Scribes, Arbiter of Justice, Keeper of the Mysteries, and He of the Ibis Head. He held an ostrich feather of pure white in his right hand, one of such singular beauty

Helen had to avert her eyes. He placed it on the scale and it stood upright, balancing on point.

The feather of ma'at. Helen gaped in awe. Ma'at, a symbol of truth, order, and all that is fair and good in the world. Her life would be measured against that cosmic ideal. Helen's pulse raced. She had tried to live an honorable life, but would her deeds be enough to erase the sin she and Paris had committed?

Thoth held her arms, lowering the tip of his thin beak until it touched her lips, forcing her mouth to open. She gazed in wonder into the God's eyes. Like Anubis', they were black as the depths of Hades, but in Thoth sparkled the light of a million stars, his eyes a hidden window to the cosmos. She was clay in his hands, enthralled by the majesty before her.

He spoke. It was a single word, one Helen could not fathom, but in it rumbled the power of a thousand volcanoes. Her chest constricted and a sharp pain stabbed through her heart. Helpless, she trembled as that burning pain rose up through her esophagus and emerged as a brilliant white light from her mouth. Thoth guided that glowing orb to the scale.

The balance tipped with the new weight, teetering up and down in a haphazard fashion. Anubis made small adjustments along the cross arm, as Thoth stood by, quill and scroll in hand. The supplicants had ceased their hymns, every eye riveted to the pronouncement soon to follow. Even Osiris and his wives leaned forward in anticipation.

A thunderous boom rang out, shaking the foundation stones of the divine hall. Helen spun around to see its cause, but there was no one near. It pounded again with demonstrative force, ripping at the very fabric of this realm. Tiles crashed down from the ceiling, and the stone bricks of the wall began to crumble. Beyond, Helen was given a glimpse back to the temple and was stunned to see herself lying prostrate on the ground, her back leaning against a pillar.

The Gods rushed to the opening, blocking her view. Their efforts to mend the rift were too slow, and another shockwave rang out, making the floor leap up and knocking Helen from her feet. The scale crashed down around her, breaking into pieces. She covered her head with her arms and watched in silent alarm as the feather of *ma'at* drifted down before her eyes.

What is happening? Panic coursed through her veins. What calamitous events transpired, events of such greatness they shook the world of the Gods? Helen trembled on the ground, a growing fear that this destruction was in some way her fault. It pursued her, and there was no place of safety, no realm where she could escape it.

A cloud of dust settled from another blow. As it dissipated, Thoth stepped forward, his strong hand helping Helen to her feet. In his other, he held the luminous orb filled with her life-force. It pulsated with each successive blow to the chamber. She looked to the God in confusion.

He spoke again, a word too beautiful, too powerful, for Helen to comprehend, and the orb flattened and grew in size until it was the height and width of a burly man. Through its milky haze, she could just make out the placid waters of the Great Sea on the other side. Thoth had created a doorway, a portal between worlds.

He leaned into her, pressing his finger to the cartouche on her chest, the markings of the *bennu*. Her heart ignited from a warmth within. This fire seared through her bones, painful yet powerful, and she could scarcely breathe. Her body instantly began to change, shrinking down into the form of the elegant bird. Her legs elongated into stalks, her arms into powerful grey wings, and she was filled with an overwhelming urge to fly.

The walls of the chamber cascaded around them. Without a second thought, Helen spread her wings and launched through the portal.

The last thing she heard before the chamber disappeared was a mournful cry of someone calling her name.

Paris fell hard on the temple floor, skinning his hands and knees. His hazy vision took on greater focus, and with it came a dire realization. Luring him to the temple had been a trap, and he had walked right into it.

He spun to the doors just as they slammed shut behind him, the bolts of his stone prison locking into place. *"Why are you doing this? I've done you no wrong!"* he screamed at the priests on the other side. He pounded on the metal panels, knowing his efforts were futile, but he could not stop. His insides burned with the poison they had injected in him. It demanded a release, and so he pounded and pounded, slamming his fists against the doors until his arms ached.

When there was no response, a morbid realization leeched the strength from his body. This was no house of the Gods. It was a tomb, and Helen and he were going to die in here. Slumping against the wall, he slid to the floor.

"HELEN!"

He screamed until his lungs heaved for air. Then he screamed for her again. Where was she? In the mad burning of his mind, she became a phantom, a muse, a tender vision of love that did not exist, an illusion that taunted him with what could never be.

Focus! He forced his mind to obey. Pushing himself off the ground, he lurched to his feet. Helen was near, he could feel it. He just had to find her.

He entered the hypostyle hall, the silhouettes of a hundred pillars towering over him. In his pain-induced haze those stone reeds actually seemed to grow, their roots embedded in the low hanging mist that ebbed and flowed around his feet. He waded through that mist, his legs sluicing through the insubstantial material as though it were bog water and the tiled floor the spongy soil of the marshlands. Each step was considerably harder than the next.

Stop it! He screamed in his head. *They gave you drugs. None of this is real. You have to get to Helen.*

He took a deep breath, but his vision did not alter. Soon even the sounds of the marsh grew around him: the chatter of birds, the chirp of insects, and bats... Suddenly they were all around him, wings slapping against his head, their high pitched squeals piercing his ears.

Focus on your breath. It was a concentration exercise Paris had learned in his time with the Amorite clans of Canaan. Breathe and count to ten. Exhale and count to ten. Repeat. Slowly his hallucinations began to waver and the room took form. He collapsed to the ground, whispering a prayer of thanks to the nomadic priests for their tutelage. They had once been slaves of Egypt. Perhaps they too had discovered its usefulness while combating the toxins of their former masters.

Sweat dripped from his body with his efforts, and yet an unnatural chill coursed through Paris' body. Was this the touch of Death? Had Thanatos finally come to claim him, the Egyptian priests succeeding where Apollo's servants had failed? He easily could have fallen into that deep sleep had something more powerful not compelled him onward.

The cry came from the belly of the temple, into the black depths, far beyond the reach of moonlight from the clerestory windows. It continued with long heartbreaking agony. A cry of a soul splitting apart. That voice was more familiar to Paris than his own. Even through his drug-addled senses, he knew he was not imagining it.

Helen was in danger... and with his last breath, he'd destroy anything keeping them apart.

Chapter 31

The Phoenix Takes Flight

HELEN SOARED OVER the great watery expanse of Nun, the liquid mass stretching as far as her keen eyes could see. Not a ripple marred its perfect surface. No current stirred its depths, yet it brimmed with energy as though all of life pulsed within.

She banked low, the tip of her wing trailing along its surface. With a few powerful strokes, she increased her speed, luxuriating in the utter freedom of her new body. Up ahead, the sun rose, its rays crawling over the horizon and turning the primordial waters into liquid gold. It soaked into Helen's feathers, seeping into her hollow bones.

Those rays were pure ambrosia, the nectar of the Gods. Basking in its warmth, Helen knew she belonged to it. The Light of Life, the solar fire that beat back the dark... it was what she was named for, it was the source of power that made the world of men possible. Her journey through the temple thus far had given vision to her past and present. But this... this was her future: an endless expanse of possibility, the freedom to fly wherever her heart could carry her, and the blessing of the Gods to give her speed.

The sun advanced across the sky. A tiny speck on the horizon rushed toward her with great speed, forming an enormous landmass. She reversed her stroke, arcing back from the city that sprang up from its soil, a rising acropolis of marble and gold surrounded on three sides by water.

From on high, she could see the city and all its glory. Elegant architecture of granite and marble competed for beauty and strength, a blend of Old World classicism and Western experimentation. Down wide avenues, ox-driven carts hauled goods to market, supporting a thriving industry of commerce. Everywhere was peace and prosperity. This was Troy, the city of her dreams. Her future home.

She folded her wings, landing gracefully atop its thick, defensive walls, a barrier so formidable it must surely have been constructed by giants. Inside the inner city, a hundred thousand people went about their business. Children played in the streets, the chimes of their laughter echoing up the acropolis to Helen. There was happiness here, happiness *and* security. She ruffled her feathers, the sun soaking into her and the Golden City alike.

As she watched, a tent city sprung up in the plains outside the defensive walls. Shepherds brought in their flocks, and merchants unloaded their ships from port. As the seasons flowed, their tents were struck, and the plains emptied, only to be filled again at a later date.

To Helen, time sped by, the sun rising and setting in the space of a single blink of her eye. The tent city no longer disbanded. Their numbers multiplied like the cascading flow of ants spilling out of their earthen home. Tents crumbled and were replaced with mud brick structures. Soon it spread as far south as the meandering banks of the Scamander River, and to the very shores of the Great Sea.

And the noise... it drowned out the pleasant sounds and charm of the city of old. It was too fast; there were too many people. Their golden towers grew until they blacked out the sun. Helen ducked her head into her wing, trying to shield herself, but she could not escape what lay inside her.

Cut off from the sun, a fire ignited within her. It licked at her fingertips. It sparked from her eyes. She dared not move in fear that it might escape her, but believing she could control it was folly. The heat dripped from her feathers, scattering over the city like molten raindrops of fire. It poured from her heart, as endless as it was painful.

She lifted her head and screeched out a mournful cry, begging the Gods to show mercy. This future did not have to be. There must be something that could be done. She cried again, calling to Zeus, to Amun-Re, to any deity who would listen. Still Troy ignited in flame, the screams of a thousand children laying bare her soul.

When she thought she could feel no more, an exquisite pain surged inside her and her heart exploded. An incandescent light poured out of her, rising in brilliance, crushing everything in its path.

The world *burned*, as her soul burned, as it would continue to burn. And she was powerless to stop it.

※

Paris stumbled into a narrow corridor, leaving the expansive hypostyle hall behind. With every step he took, the walls blurred, the painted lines on their surface glowing from some mysterious force and burning streaks across his mind. He kept his hands stretched out before him.

In the darkness, his hallucinations intensified. Phantoms with burning red eyes barred his way. He struck at them, his hands sailing through their ghostly forms to no affect.

Focus. But his prized self-discipline was tapering off. He could not tell what was real or imagined. Paris banged into unlit braziers. He hit his head against a stone pillar. One fist crashed through a specter and into the wooden hull of a ceremonial barque, the sacred vessel used to transport the God's idol during cult processions. Pain laced through his arm as he pulled his hand free. Blood dripped from where thick splinters had pierced his skin, the sharp sting momentarily clearing his mind.

Another scream rang out.

"*HELEN!*" he shouted into the darkness, his desperate cry bouncing off the stone walls, but she did not answer.

There was a light up ahead. It was dim, no more than a single candle at best, but in this abyss, it was as brilliant as a bonfire. A hundred feet away, Paris could just make out the borders of a door. A long ramp led up to that small aperture, forcing him to crouch as he entered.

The air was thicker on the other side, stale. He stretched out his hands. One step to his left and he reached the wall. One to his right found its partner. The ceiling also tapered in, nearly scraping his head. Paris cringed away from it, feeling the mountain of stone that surrounded him. His pulse quickened, and he realized at last where he stood. He was in the inner sanctum, the naos, the deepest point of the temple, and before him was the gilded shrine of the God himself.

The craftsmanship was breathtaking. The wooden slats of the coffin-shaped box were embellished with golden filigree. Its double doors where folded open, revealing the Holy of Holies inside, a golden statue of Amun-Re in human form, the twin feathers of *ma'at* protruding over his head. A single, long-burning candle sat before the idol, its solitary light dancing over the unforgiving face of the God. Paris fell to his knees before it.

Something lay in his way: the crumpled body of a woman. With a strangled gasp, he rolled over Helen's slacken form, her vacant eyes staring off into oblivion.

She was dead. Her skin was grey, the pallor of a corpse that robbed her cheeks of warmth. He had been too late.

"*NO!*" he cried, a man possessed. He cradled her limp form to his chest and something broke inside of him.

And he screamed with a terrible rage.

THE PRINCESS OF PROPHECY

The wails of Trojans dying had dampened to a whisper. Crouched into a ball in the city's smoldering embers, Helen cried silently with them, feeling their aching loss. A guilt-ridden sob tore through her. She lacked the power to save them.

Every fiber of her being decried that belief as false. It was as though she were missing some vital element, some piece of her soul that would help her triumph over this tragedy. She waited for the end, shivering in her emptiness.

The earth shook, as it had in the Hall of Judgement. A tiny flame of hope kindled in her breast. Help was coming. She gazed off into the distance, the acrid smoke of burning rubble stinging her eyes, and saw him.

He walked through the destruction, a flaming torch in human form. Stone melted before him, timbers crumbled to ash. Nothing could bar his way. He knelt beside her and lifted her into his arms.

"Paris..." She collapsed into his chest with a cry of relief. It was too late, the world could not be saved, but at least they could spend their last moments together.

His presence soothed her, his flames rejuvenating her wilted limbs. His heat was not the painful ruin of the lost city, but the warmth of Amun-Re's light. It was love, and hope, and the promise of a new beginning.

But something was different. The fire leapt off him like curling tendrils, soaking into her skin, linking them body and soul. Her feathers ignited as he dissolved into flame, dissolving *into* her. He was in her heart and mind, a ball of awareness that penetrated her. It was a merging of the sort she'd only heard tale of in legend, the fire uniting them while burning away their mortal shell.

Her grey heron ceased to be. In its place rose an eagle bearing the colors of Troy and Sparta, a red-gold bird of fire that death could not touch. A raptor imbued with the living spirit of the sun, a creature the world had never seen before... a phoenix.

With a mournful cry, the phoenix launched into the air, souring over the desolation with a few powerful strokes. It flew into the heavens turning south by east to the Old World and beyond. Everywhere was in ruin. There was no kingdom left standing, no nation of man unscathed.

To the west the phoenix flew, over the plains of Thrace and to the Grecian isles and mainland. They too spewed forth the black smoke of destruction, the foul stench of human rot filling the air as it was purged from the world.

Like a bolt set loose from a bow, the phoenix shot forth again. Further west it flew, to the very edge of the known world, the Western Wilds.

Here, it folded its wings, dropping like a rock to the charred branches of a fig tree. Below, small shoots of green poked through a layer of ash where the tree's roots spidered across the topsoil, spreading in every direction.

Once, twice, three times it circled on its perch until new leaves burst forth, the branches entwining to form a nest. At its center were two mewling chicks.

Death had placed its shroud over the world, but it could not conquer all. Here, on the outskirts, there were signs of life.

The phoenix cried, an arousing call filled with defiance, its pitch so perfect the sky shattered from its shockwave. The vision faltered, pieces of the world falling away like shards of glass until there was nothing left.

Nothing but a black abyss. A world without light.

Chapter 32

Rising From the Ashes

PARIS OPENED HIS eyes as the vision broke, a deep shudder convulsing his body. He was back in the temple, Helen secure in his arms. His awareness of her bled out of his mind as the aches and pains of his physical body returned.

What had happened?

The last thing he remembered was rolling Helen's limp body over. As he lifted her into his arms, the world *shifted*.

The things he saw... what he experienced... there were no words to describe it. Was it real, or just a hallucination?

Helen stirred in his arms, and Paris pulled her in closer, crying out in relief. He clung to her with a desperate strength, kissing her fiercely. *She had been dead.* He had felt her die, just as he felt life stir in her again. It was a miracle...

Helen moaned as her body slowly wakened. The past few hours had been the most surreal moments of her life. After the phoenix vision had broken, she had drifted in a haze, trapped between worlds, her physical body refusing to function.

And then there was Paris, no longer in her mind, but beside her. His kiss had been a beacon of light in the void, an anchor that pulled her from the shadow realm and back into the waking world.

How he had found her was a miracle she did not question. Some part of Paris was always present with her, and now she finally understood why. The combining of their spirits, the unification of their souls, was a thing of beauty even the Gods would envy.

She wove her arms around his neck, pressing her lips to his, tasting his salty tears as she kissed him. His body shook as he crushed her to his chest with a sob.

Was he crying?

"Paris?" She cupped his face gently between her hands, pulling back to gaze into his eyes. The light of the single candle was dim, but it was enough to see all that she needed: a soul-shattering love that went beyond words.

With a soft moan, she fell toward him, pulled by a force she could not deny. And, as he kissed her back, a desperate longing overtook her. A longing to reunite that which the Gods had separated. She gave herself to him then, body and soul, just as Aphrodite had foretold.

Paris was beside himself in that moment. All he could think, see, feel and smell was Helen. She was alive and in his arms, so soft and yielding. Nothing else in the world mattered. His fingers locked around her back and he crushed her to him, his mouth pressed to hers with a hunger he did not know how to control.

A million warning bells rang out in Paris' mind, but they were insignificant flea bites compared to the roaring demand building in his blood. With a guttural groan, he pulled her onto his lap, guiding his body into hers. They melded into one other, her moans in perfect rhythm with his own.

Helen cried out as he filled her. She pressed against him harder, taking him in deeper, every stroke reigniting the bonding she had felt in her vision. That blissful fulfillment was so close, yet frustratingly out of reach.

He slid an arm under her leg and flipped her over to her back. The cold stone of the temple floor did little to dampen her ardor, and she pulled Paris to her, wrapping her legs around his hips. As he entered her again, chest to chest, face to face, she could not tell where her flesh ended and his began.

For Paris, their intimate embrace was sweet agony. The lingering effect of the priest's drugs was still clouding his mind, heightening his sensations tenfold. The memory of her cold and lifeless body was still too fresh to be forgotten. As was the devastating loss and blinding rage it had evoked. With every powerful thrust, his body ached for her with a desperation that shocked him. A mounting pressure was building within him, as though his body was no longer capable of containing everything he was feeling inside.

"It's all right," she whispered into his ear and kissed his cheeks, wiping away tears he did not realize he had shed. "I'm right here, Paris. I won't leave you. I promise."

He stared into her love-filled eyes, choking back a strangled sob. Not once in his life had anyone shown him even a fraction of the affection Helen freely gave. He loved this woman beyond reason. If he was destined to be persecuted for the rest of his life for that sin, so be it.

He kissed her tenderly. No matter what future the Gods had planned for them, he was never leaving her side again.

"What are they doing?"

Penanukis was not alone in his outrage. Meryatum had allowed five other *pastophoroi* to watch the ritual in the observation chamber, and he alone was the only man to remain silent.

Blasphemy. That was the answer to the second prophet's question. The Trojan and his Spartan lover committed blasphemy, soiling the inner chamber with their intimate embrace.

Meryatum silenced his underlings, and watched the lovers joining, mesmerized. They were witness to something more than the carnal pleasure of the flesh. Something ancient...

It was called the Sacred Marriage, a celebration of the creation of the world, the blending of the male and female fertile forces. The Gods mated through their human counterparts, and though it was forbidden in Amun-Re's temple, Egypt had once taken part in the archaic practice.

Meryatum's skin tingled as he tried to understand the significance of seeing it enacted tonight. It was difficult to clear his mind. The same spores he had given to Helen burned in two braziers of their hidden chamber. The vapors held only a fraction of the hallucinatory force of the infusion she had ingested, but it was enough to help him enter the world of the Gods, as a spectator if not a participant.

Other prophets claimed to 'share' visions with the anointed, but few truly did. Meryatum was unique in that ability. When a candidate was in acute emotional distress, he could pick up on their emphatic experience, and 'see' as they saw.

As he did with Helen. She wore her emotions about her like a second skin. Watching her commune with the Gods was like watching a masterful dance, but despite the beauteous soul the woman possessed, it did not change the doom that followed in her wake.

She and the Trojan were a spark that would ignite the world. There was no doubt in his mind that the Gods had alerted Meryatum to their danger so he could act. They could not be allowed to leave Egypt...

"Will you do nothing?" Penanukis had worked himself into a fit, his rabid behavior infecting the others. Meryatum found himself facing five alarmed priests.

"Mind your tongue!" he growled at the insolent man. "I am First Prophet, High Priest of Re! I will decide their fate, not you."

Penanukis smoothed his robes, a look of embarrassment on his pinched face for having been chastised before the others. Once he was satisfied the man was subdued, Meryatum turned back to the pair.

Confusion ruled his thoughts. The couple embraced in the dark, blissfully ignorant of the eyes that watched them. In that ignorance they revealed a part of themselves that normally remained hidden: the raw power of their affections for one another. Meryatum was humbled by the display. Was the Trojan nothing more than a man seeking love in a less-forgiving world? A chill ran through him as he remembered his first teachings in the House of Life:

"Nothing is more dangerous than the man who is unjustly wronged. The Gods unite in his defense, to right the world in alignment of ma'at."

There *was* a danger on the horizon, one Meryatum feared Egypt might not survive, but was the Trojan truly its source? He needed time to seek that answer before condemning the man to death.

He spun back to his *pastophoroi*, a harsh glare for each man who'd dare defy him. "Keep them here. Say no word to them save I will be back when the sun rises." He wished there was more time. Their world hung in the balance, and he had only a few short hours to contemplate. "They are not to be harmed or let outside the temple gates. Do you understand me?"

Penanukis nodded, and the others followed suit. With all in agreement, Meryatum left the temple for the palace making all due haste. It was time to share his concerns with the royal family. With their help, he prayed he could make the right decision in time.

Helen and Paris took their time in the inner sanctum, savoring the intimate moment the temple had secured for them. For a while, Helen could pretend the outside world did not exist, nor the host of problems that awaited them. Wrapped securely in her lover's arms, she allowed herself the simple peace she always felt in Paris' company.

But they could not stay in the those cold and dark halls

forever, and when she felt strong enough, Paris led her through the temple and back to the main entrance.

A pair of priests were waiting for them just outside the doors. Penanukis she recognized, and he watched her with a blank face. The other *pastophoroi* held out two linen robes, his gaze held firmly at eye level.

"Where is the high priest?" Paris asked, tying the belt tightly about his waist.

"He did not say," Penanukis frowned, a sharp look of disapproval oozing from the man, one Paris remembered all-too-well before entering the temple. "You are to remain in the temple complex. He will come collect you at sunrise."

"Did he say no more?"

But the priests were already gone, moving off toward their private quarters without further word. Paris watched them go with a sigh. Their stonewall behavior did not surprise him. Although the ritual was complete, it was clear that their ordeal with the temple officials was not over.

He took Helen's hand in his and gave it a tug. "Let's get some fresh air." He led her away from the temple towards the sacred lake, eager to leave the confining walls of that stone tomb behind.

On sight of its still waters, Helen cried out in joy and immediately doffed her robes to take a swim. He almost joined her, the sheen of sweat from his exertions in the temple had left him sticky, but he waited on the shore, savoring the sight of her floating through the reflection of a million stars. The water glistened on her skin, and she shone like a celestial event. Helen was more beautiful to him than any Goddess, real or imagined.

"Do you feel... different?" he asked when she climbed out of the water. He wanted to say cleansed, but after what they had experienced, scoured would have been a more appropriate word. He felt purified in the way a new layer of skin was pure when the old had been ripped away. He had been made raw and vulnerable in the process.

"I do feel different." Helen pulled her robe back on and sat down next to him, leaning into the spot on his chest where his steady heartbeat thundered in her ear.

She was amazed at the clarity the ritual had awakened in her. Her fears had not gone away, but now they were the right fears, not the distant phantoms of her past life. If her visions were true, then there were many dangers ahead, and not just for her and Paris, but for everyone. They sat for a time watching the stars travel across the sky before she found the courage to speak of it.

"Was it real?"

Paris shook his head, unsure how to answer. He was both hopeful and terrified what they had experienced was real. Troy in ashes... it was everything the temple had blamed him for since his birth. But his bonding with Helen—he had never felt more complete than in those moments of soaring over the world with her.

Honesty was a cruel mistress, however, and he opted to tell Helen the truth, no matter how unpleasant. "It was a hallucination," he sighed. "They dosed us with drugs. That is why we saw what we most feared."

Helen sat up, perplexed. "That is not all I saw." She tucked a strand of his wavy brown hair behind his ear, letting her fingertips trail down his chin. Paris had saved her. When all hope was lost, one defender still stood, and he carried her away to a new beginning. Where so many others had failed her, Paris alone remained true. She pulled his face to hers, kissing him tenderly.

"We shouldn't." He tensed, looking nervously over his shoulder and pulling her hands away from him. "The Egyptians are superstitious. I've seen them castrate men for less."

The distress on his face made her laugh and she smiled sweetly at her lover. "Alexandros of Troy, ever the diplomat." His regal name rolled off her tongue with a formality she reserved for great halls. Nefertari was right. Had the laws of inheritance been different in the North, Paris would have made the best of kings. There was a subtle wisdom and strength of spirit in him that Helen had not witnessed since leaving Sparta, a nobility that came from character, not blood.

The uncomfortable look he returned begged to differ.

"What's wrong?"

"Alexandros is the name of a king."

Paris sighed as thoughts of Troy invaded their stolen moment of peace. "*Alaksandu,* King of Wilusa, to be specific, a lifelong friend of my father." Helen's questioning eyes prodded him to continue. "Priam hoped that naming me after a powerful king would strike fear into the court and keep me from harm." The crooked twist on his face spoke of how well that had turned out. "It was a role I was meant to play, the regal son, but no matter how well I played it, I never won their respect."

And I never will. He looked at his beloved, understanding now how little those courtiers mattered. He took a deep breath, marshaling his courage for the first act of defiance he had ever dared against the crown. "I will not ask the same of you."

Helen stiffened with surprise. "What are you saying?"

"I won't ask you to play the victim before my father's court." Paris continued, knowing in his gut this was the right course forward. He was through allowing the people who believed the worst of him to dictate his life. "I will not pretend that I do not love you. Neither will I hide from the consequences of our actions. You are no victim, and neither am I. When we enter Troy, it will be together."

Her tender smile was all the answer he needed. He pulled Helen to him, kissing her passionately, heedless of the danger that earlier gave him pause.

Helen's heart leapt in her chest. She nearly cried with relief. After everything they had experienced in Egypt, the deception in court and the trials of the temple, she had known denying her love for Paris was wrong. To hear him say the same was like the sweet song of the *Nereides*. She laughed with a joy she had not felt since they had first left Greece.

Paris joined her laugh, a stray thought filling it with genuine mirth, of how strenuously Glaucus advised against this rash behavior. Perhaps, had they held to the original plan, they would have gained a strategic advantage in court, but in doing so, he would have lost something far more precious. Paris tightened his arms around his princess, vowing to never let her go.

His captain was right in one aspect, however. When they returned to Troy, Helen would not be his lover.

"Marry me," he said impulsively.

"...That's impossible."

"I don't care." He swallowed his misgivings and continued on, "I don't want anyone to ever doubt my commitment to you. You are my destiny, and I'm not ashamed of who I am, not anymore. Let the others say what they will. *Marry me, Helen.*"

Helen rose to her knees. If her heart had wings, they were beating wildly within her. Was it possible? "A million times, *yes.*" She pulled him into a passionate embrace, kissing him deeply.

Paris kissed her back with force. This was reckless, rash, yet he had never been more certain of anything in his life. This was *right*.

"But how?" Helen struggled to catch her breath. "Where?"

His pulse raced at the innocent question. "As soon as we return to our ship," he promised with a husky voice. "Glaucus can officiate, if he is well enough."

That seemed an eternity for Helen. After all they had been through, she could not imagine any oath that would bind them stronger than the experience they had just shared. In her heart she was already bound to Paris. He had claimed her before all the Gods. It was time for the Kings of Men to recognize they belonged together as well.

"Then I will be yours, Trojan." She stole another kiss from him, feeling his body tense with the same passion coursing through her. "In this life and the next. No man will ever come between us again."

CHAPTER 33

THE ENVOY

AGAMEMNON SAT ON his throne twirling his heavy scepter in his hands. He longed for a skull to crack with it. Of the forty kings and princes who swore Tyndareus' oath, *four* stood in his hall. He had heard no word from the others, and their silence was as telling as open defiance.

Oath-breakers and cowards. They will squander this opportunity squabbling over petty nonsense.

Agamemnon had long ago realized his brother kings lacked the vision to see the true greatness of their peoples. Greece was every bit as powerful as Troy. More so, when taking into account the the Men of the West's cunning and ability to survive. But so long as the Hellas remained fractured, they would never rise to their true potential.

Heat coursed through Agamemnon's veins. He *would* unite the West, and when he proved their empire to be amongst the greatest in the world, the unbelievers would bless his name.

Agapenor, King of Arcadia and Agamemnon's neighbor to the west was the newest arrival to the capital. His chest was as wide as the brown bears that roamed his countryside, and his hair as coarse. He was a strong ally for Mycenae, but even he had taken three weeks to answer Agamemnon's call.

"He waited until my husband and his brother were called away." Clytemnestra regaled the visiting monarch with the circumstances of the Trojan's crime. With each retelling, she seemed to suffer the loss of her sister more. Already the common folk repeated her tale, demanding the throne act to reclaim their favored princess.

The baseborn do not stomach this slight, yet my brother kings linger.

He painted a regal frown on his visage, nodding along as Clytemnestra continued her tale. The heady aroma of war was making him dizzy. Though he longed to take to the field, now was the time for patience. Greece had never been given such an opportunity to prove her destiny—and he his.

"The prince was cruel, mocking Helen's bravery, taunting her with claims of all the horrible things he would do to her once they left Mycenae." Tears overwhelmed his queen and she hid her face in her kerchief, one of her noble women rushing to her side to stroke her back.

Feminine foibles. His wife cried when she should let fury reign. Her tears had the desired affect on their guest, however, and Agapenor paled with disgust.

A slight movement drew his eye to the far alcoves of his megaron where Diomedes walked the hall with that upstart prince, Achilles. *What are they conspiring about?* Agamemnon watched them intently, his eyes narrowing.

"This cannot stand!" Menelaus stepped forward on cue, his wild eyes the picture of outrage. Whether it was real or feigned, Agamemnon did not care.

Unleashing Menelaus on his enemies was a tactic he often enjoyed. The fact that his brother had terms for the deployment, however, was shocking. Menelaus *ruling* over Sparta? He would control the fearsome warriors of Lacedaemonia, a key component in Agamemnon's plans to rule over Greece. Would he be handing his brother a powerful army only to face that host one day on the field himself?

Agamemnon sneered at the thought. Menelaus was no

THE PRINCESS OF PROPHECY

leader. The warrior kings of the Hellas would never follow him. He was too unstable to earn their loyalty. Only a king could command the Hellas.

It was fortunate Clytemnestra's clever lie worked towards that purpose. He had confirmed with his Master of Purse that not a copper was missing from his treasury. But the other kings did not need to know that. That small fabrication ensured that the Trojan offense was one the other kings could relate with. It ensured Agamemnon could claim redress as much as Menelaus. Support would rally around Mycenae. The Grecian kings would place their trust *in Agamemnon,* and once they saw him in his true might, they would recognize his right to rule on high.

It all began with Troy. Against that golden empire, command of their allied forces would fall to him.

And so would all the glory.

"You must rally your banner men, ready your infantry," Menelaus pressed.

"For certain," Agapenor agreed. "I can lend you my fastest ships. Do we know where the scoundrel fled?"

Agamemnon growled. *This again?* "They went to Troy, of course." He slammed his fist on the armrest of his throne, leaping to his feet. "As we should do. With a thousand ships, not just your fastest!"

The king of Arcadia stepped back from the outburst. As did Clytemnestra, his queen sharing a panicked look with her handmaiden. Why were they all staring at him as though he were mad? He was the only one who spoke sense.

The Trojan's insult was not meant for Agamemnon alone. The perfumed lords dwelt in their marble palaces, believing themselves superior to the hardy men of the West. They scoffed at Mycenae's achievements as though proximity to barbarians made the Helladic peoples barbarian themselves.

They think us so weak that they can do with us as they please. Snatch our women in the night. Deny us a seat at their lofty table...

Agamemnon would show the Men of the Troad the

strength of Grecian rage. The gates of Troy would crumbled before that force... Troy and any other nation fool enough to slander his realm.

Blessedly, Agapenor did not chose this time to question Agamemnon's ill mood. "Of course, Your Grace." The minor king swallowed his misgivings with a nervous cough. "I look forward to greeting my fellow rulers on your council."

Agamemnon leaned back on his throne, willing his tense muscles to relax. Building an alliance was more difficult than he had anticipated. Placating nobles and neighboring royals was exhausting. He scratched his beard, wondering if the time had come to make a statement that did not require ink and scroll.

"Your Majesty!" Nextus hailed him from the corridor. His steward scurried across the megaron, a folded scrap of papyrus in his hand. "A raven has arrived."

"Give it here." Agamemnon leapt to his feet, practically tearing the missive from his hand. He scanned the document quickly, his face pinched tight from the effort.

The talent of scripting words and reading them back was not a skill Agamemnon took to naturally. Long hours of study and bloodied knuckles from the cane of his tutor had painstakingly hammered in the ability. He scanned the opening, the standard formalities of one king addressing another. Odysseus was a verbose man, and his letters were the same. He delighted in twisting meaning in a phrase, making the effort of deciphering his true intentions a chore. Unfortunately, what his crafty words hid also made Agamemnon's blood run cold.

"That damned Ithakian!" Agamemnon kicked over a brazier beside his throne, scattering the burning coals across the hall. "He's not coming!"

A stunned silence permeated the room. Diomedes immediately stepped forward, his face pale with shock. "Odysseus would not break his oath."

"Read for yourself." He shoved the missive into Diomedes'

hands.

"'*I am bound between my oath as king to my people and to Tyndareus' child.*'" The Argolian king read out loud, his words carrying across the megaron and echoing off the empty space between pillars. It leant his retelling an ominous pall.

"'*Had last season's harvest not been so poor, I would come in due haste. Surely this matter of state can wait until the fields are sown? Any army that marches must also be fed, so one endeavor relates to another. Who knows? Perhaps this misunderstanding with the Trojan crown can be settled before a single soldier sheds blood.*'"

"What does he mean, 'this misunderstanding can be settled'?" Menelaus growled. "Is Odysseus so craven he would have us treat with a thief?" His other counselors chimed in, their outrage drowning out any chance for true conversation. For once, Agamemnon had no wish to silence them.

"I'll have his head for this!" he shouted above the din.

※

Achilles watched Agamemnon call for Ithakian' blood with stoic restraint. How quickly the beast showed his fangs... He turned to Diomedes, catching the Argolian king's eye across the megaron. He was not taking the turn of favor well. Diomedes had long been friends with Odysseus.

I warned you, Achilles shook his head.

"He'll be branded an Oath-breaker," Agamemnon raged, "a stain his children will bear long after him." His toadies quickly showered the king with their agreement.

The charge of cowardice sat like acid in Achilles' gut. Odysseus dared to defy Agamemnon. It was not outright rebellion, but a display of power, showing the Mycenaean crown that Agamemnon did not command him. For Achilles, who had rankled under that yolk for more years than he cared to admit, Odysseus' actions were as brave as they were wise.

"He is no Oath-breaker," Achilles interjected, glowering at

the gathered nay-sayers. "He has not said he will not come. He merely stated he will not come *now*. Your quest is not a priority to him, Agamemnon. I expect you will hear similar tales of delay from more of our brother kings and princes of the Hellas."

That prediction sat as well as an influx of gout on the king. He grimaced, his lip pulled sharp, exposing the teeth of a predator. "If I have to go kingdom by kingdom, so be it. I will make such an example of this island king that no others will dare mimic his offense!"

"Put a knife to your liege men and watch them do the same to you." Achilles renewed his pacing, frustrated he must act as foil to another of the king's witless suggestions. It was becoming tiresome, this role he adopted.

"Achilles speaks reason, Husband." Clytemnestra placed a calming hand on Agamemnon's arm, which he shoved off immediately. "You should send a diplomat, not an executioner. Give the honor to one of your new generals. Make the others fear that you favor him more than them. That will bring the other kings willingly to our shores."

The queen was wise, Achilles admitted to himself reluctantly. The right messenger could dig Odysseus from his rocky shores, and then this tedious wait would be over.

"I will go!" Palamedes stepped forward, an eager expression lighting up his face. "It would be an honor to act in your stead, Your Grace." His offer was met with applause from the court, a palpable air of relief spreading amongst those gathered.

Achilles rolled his eyes. The Mycenaean king played his role perfectly, reseating himself on this throne as he 'let' himself be appeased. "I accept your offer, Noble Palamedes. Go, and remind King Odysseus that his oath was not to Mycenae, but to *all* his brother kings of Greece."

Achilles stalked over to Diomedes, the Argolian king as pale as a corpse. He stood locked in place as though rigor mortis had set into his legs. "Odysseus will hardly be the last.

How many other kings will need Agamemnon's' reminding'?" he whispered harshly into Diomedes' ear. "Are you still confident about handing this man an army without knowing if his cause is just?"

Something shifted in Diomedes' eyes. His jaw clenched tight, and he pressed Achilles behind him. "Let me handle this, *Myrmidones*. And do me the favor of keeping your mouth shut."

※

Agamemnon twisted on his throne. Why were his brother kings so headstrong? Visiting each kingdom one by one could take months... years if they were uncooperative! The time to strike Troy was now, before they could think better of their folly and prepare for the onslaught.

Menelaus bounced on his feet beside him, as eager to redress this wrong as he. It was odd to have his little brother as his ally in this venture. He had thought Menelaus a curse, the God's sick jest meant to thwart Agamemnon's great destiny, but of late, the two sons of Atreus had seen eye to eye on matters.

"*You should press my suit with Tyndareus,*" he hissed into Agamemnon's ear. "*With Spartan hoplites, we won't need the other realms. We could set out immediately.*"

Agamemnon grimaced. Such an act was rash and misguided, but at least Menelaus was predictable. He waved his brother off with a stern glare and turned his focus back to the assemblage. Now was not the time to speak of those plans. Agamemnon's first goal was to unite the Hellas. Burning Troy in the process was but sweet cream after that feast.

"Agamemnon?" Diomedes stepped forward.

"Yes." He settled back into his throne, picking up his scepter as he eyed his petitioner with curiosity. The Argolian king was a lithe man, fair of complexion and clean of hair, his brown eyes matching the color of his perfectly trimmed beard.

He had been young when he'd come to the throne, but what he had lacked in experience he made up for in temperament. There were none who could draw him to ire if Diomedes did not wish it.

"Palamedes might be successful in his voyage to Ithaka, but I see a bigger problem than just collecting our Brothers." Diomedes paced before the throne, setting a stately stride. "One and all, they will ask the same question that noble Agapenor just pondered. Was this theft an act of war, or did the Trojan prince act alone?"

"He's an ambassador! Everything he does is sanctioned by his king!" Agamemnon clenched his teeth, his hand turning purple from the death grip he put on his scepter.

"I am sure you are right," Diomedes nodded with respect, "but it's best you answer that question outright. Send an envoy to Troy. Secure proof of Priam's involvement. No man of the Hellas would dare dally once that evidence is procured. They will rally to your banners, and any who don't will face the wrath of all the rest, not Mycenae alone."

Agamemnon froze.

"It will not delay our preparations, Your Grace," Diomedes added quickly, misreading Agamemnon's deep shock at the brilliance of that plan as reluctance.

"Yes, an envoy." Clytemnestra pushed her handmaiden away, stepping forward with a wild look emblazoned on her face. "Under the white flag of treaty. Golden Troy would not turn aside a formal request. Their precious pride would not allow it."

Even Agapenor brightened at the suggestion. "And if the prince acted alone, give Troy a chance to answer for the theft, to return the princess and pay recompense."

"You could set our terms," Diomedes added.

"The prince must die," Clytemnestra hissed. "We'll accept nothing less for this insult. Hera demands his blood."

"And by my hands!" Menelaus' rage could not be outdone by the queen. His cheeks flushed an angry red.

THE PRINCESS OF PROPHECY

A smile tugged at Agamemnon's lips. How quickly they united behind the righteous quest, blinded to its futility. Proud Troy would never meet their demands. Yet, at the end of their failed negotiations, the Hellas would stand united, and if Diomedes spoke true, the other kings would legitimize Agamemnon's leadership without a drop of Grecian blood staining his hands.

But whom to send? Diomedes certainly looked eager. The king was a skilled diplomat, precisely the wrong sort of character to start a war. He needed a firebrand, a hornet's nest that would sting the Trojan king into action. The answer was so simple that he almost laughed.

"Menelaus," he called to his little brother. "Your loss was the greatest. You should be the one to present our demands to King Priam."

Menelaus crossed over to the throne, a flash of irritation across his ever suspicious face. "*You promised me an army.*" His heated words did not pass the dais, but his behavior raised more than a few brows. Zeus-help-him, but his brother showed not an ounce of cunning.

"*Unless you wish to wait until Tyndareus is dead, we will have to convince the Spartan you are his worthy successor. What better way than to personally 'see' to Helen's safety?*"

His sarcasm was not lost on his brother. Menelaus' eyes hardened with the threat of violence. "I will go to Troy," he addressed the assemblage. "Priam will return my wife to me unspoiled. If that loathsome prince has harmed so much as a hair on her golden head, there will be hell to pay." He simmered with that vow.

Agamemnon grinned. What better man to pick a fight than his best fighting dog?

Others were not as pleased with the assignment as he. Diomedes stepped forward again, a concerned frown on his noble face. "You have earned the right to face the man who wronged you, Menelaus, but we should show care not to honor him with the opportunity to insult you directly." Many nobles nodded in agreement with the wisdom of his words.

"He speaks true," Achilles finally joined the discussion, folding his arms across his chest. Even the way the man stood spoke of an insubordinate nature. "Greece is not a powerless child demanding our due. If they deny you, it will stain all our honor."

Agamemnon grimaced. Was Phthia ever to be a thorn in his side?

"I will go." Clytemnestra declared, the foolish woman speaking without his leave again. "Helen is my sister. The king of Troy will not deny my right to her, and if he double-crosses our truce, no sword will be lost in the effort."

"My Queen," Nextus gasped, the royal steward reflecting the same emotion mirrored on his fellow soft-bellied courtiers. "Your bravery is an inspiration to all Mycenae."

Agamemnon rose to his feet and their murmurs came to a halt. He joined his queen's side, lifting her hand to his lips. There was an edge of steel in Clytemnestra that would cow the bravest of men. It was fitting she accompanied Menelaus on this task.

"Keep her safe, Brother." He laced his words with false concern. "My queen is a treasure I am sure the Trojans will be tempted to collect."

As the hall broke out into preparation for the envoy, Agamemnon settled back on his throne, contemplating the turn of events. The threat to his queen was quite real, but should Clytemnestra fall, perhaps Tyndareus would be more easily persuaded to join their ranks.

Helen, unfortunately, was doomed. Menelaus would ensure she did not come back alive, even if he had to kill the woman himself. There was no saving her now, but she was a necessary sacrifice in the honorable quest to unite the Hellas. Helen would fall... as many others would fall.

Still, he rued the loss of his Spartan beauty. He had hoped to put a child into Helen's belly long before she outlived her purpose. It was not to be, however. His rise to power required a sacrifice, and Helen was the spark that would ignite the mighty flame of his rule. Perhaps, if the Gods were kind, history would remember her name.

One name, though, would stand above all others, of that he was certain. Before the last throat was slit, before Troy's ashes scattered in the wind, he would carve his mark into the annals of History. When peoples of Ages yet to come spoke of Troy, they would remember the wrath of Agamemnon of Mycenae.

Chapter 34

A Prince's Fate

A WAXING MOON hung low on the horizon when Meryatum finally approached the palace grounds. As the desert sands gave way to the lush landscaping of the royal gardens, his feet veered off course. He wandered beneath the canopy of palm trees, listening to the chorus of cicadas and night wings. Here, surrounded by the teeming life of the Nile, he found a small measure of peace.

The coming of Helen and Paris to the Two Lands was significant. With Pharaoh on death's door and the rising tide of dissension in the masses, the Gods warned of impending catastrophe at every turn. Was the pair refugees from that storm or the first stone that preceded the avalanche?

He knelt beside a reflection pool, studying his careworn face. Did the answer truly matter? Be they the messenger or the source it did not stop the reckoning that would follow. He splashed the water, the ripples scattering his reflection until it was no more than a chaotic mess of color and form. He continued on to the palace at a faster pace.

One thing was clear to him. A dark fate overshadowed the Trojan prince. Meryatum almost felt sorry for the man. He could not fathom what sin would draw the attention of the evil eye as soundly as Prince Paris had done. For one trained to see the Mysteries, his future was set in stone.

Meryatum faltered, a sliver of doubt in that final thought halting his step. There was a moment when he saw a different future for the prince, and it was when he reunited with Helen.

When he had first met the princess, Meryatum had been touched in a way he hadn't experienced since he'd been raised to office. She shone with the light of Re, a dazzling jewel men could not help but adore. In her was beauty, justice... *ma'at incarnate*. She could not help but inspire a path to good. There was only one other woman he knew who possessed that power, and subconsciously, his wandering feet had sought her out.

Meryatum pressed through a patch of reeds and stepped out onto the portico facing the royal harem. The night was at its most quiet, when even the night owl had taken shelter, but the queen was still awake. She stood beside her sally door, a single candle raised high, the watcher in the night.

He went to her, stepping into the small circle of light surrounding her before her aged eyes could see him. Lowering her candle, Nefertari smiled at him with the warmth of a hundred suns. "Meryatum."

"Mother." He collapsed into her waiting arms, holding her tenderly. "I need your counsel."

She stroked his back, the small gesture filling him with comfort. "Of course you do. Come in."

He followed her into her private chamber. A small fire was banked low in the central brazier. He took a seat beside it as she set a kettle of tea in the coals. She always kept a satchel of his favorite blend on hand in case he stopped by to visit, one of a hundred little ways she showed her favor.

"You wear many burdens, my son." She sat down beside him and wrapped an arm around his shoulders, a frail little dove with the grip of a lioness. How many times had she held him so, a young boy plagued by visions and omens, her gentle touch banishing his nightmares from whence they came? Even now, a man in his fifties, her presence still soothed him.

"I fear we are on the eve of something terrible," he confided, careful not to damage her bones as he squeezed her hand. "I have never seen so many signs of *isfet*. Pharaoh is dying. His heir also courts the grave. Our enemies harass us from both inside and outside of our borders. Our world is splitting at the seams and I am tasked with preserving order." He dropped his head into his hands, a sharp pain arching across his mind. "I... I am failing, Mother."

"Shhhh." Nefertari rose to her feet, collecting him in her arms. She rubbed his shoulders and rocked him gently. "Peace, Meryatum. Peace. You borrow troubles you are not meant to bear."

He wished it were that simple, but if he did not keep watch over Egypt, who would? Seti had already proven himself incapable of the task. He tried to push her away, but Nefertari grabbed his chin and forced him to meet her loving gaze.

"Your father was so proud of you. Had you not been drawn to the temple, he would have named you his heir." Her dark eyes teemed with pride. "You would have sat the throne well, My Son—so well, some part of you has taken on that responsibility although another holds the title. *But you must listen to me.*"

It was the urgency in her voice that made him sit up. Nefertari seldom offered direct advice. Her way was to listen, allowing Meryatum a safe arena to explore his thoughts and come to his own decisions. "Yes, Lady of Grace. I am listening."

She released his chin, her hand cupping his face gently instead. "You are very gifted, Meryatum. But sometimes, when the Gods favor us, we forget our own limitations. You cannot control everything. *Isfet* is a part of our world, the same as *ma'at*. One cannot exist without the other. The pendulum swings both ways. Even Pharaoh is hard-pressed to keep balance."

He nodded, hearing the wisdom of her words. Chaos and Order. The light and the dark. Helen and Paris... *Isfet* and *ma'at*, cosmic opposites swirling around each other in their eternal struggle. Perhaps the two foreigners truly did belong with one another. The Gods taught mankind the way of *ma'at*, but the Immortals' actions were oft as violent as they were peaceful. Even Amun-Re burned with his light as often as he healed. The goal, for any who observed the Mysteries, was to preserve the balance.

"Whatever it is that you fear, Egypt will survive," Nefertari vowed. "We are eternal."

That struck a deeper concern in the high priest. If the visions in the temple were true, balance itself would be broken. The scale was tipped beyond recovery. If the world burned, the legacy of his forefathers, the great dynasties of Egypt, would be laid low. Was the life of one man worth that risk?

He rose from his stool, embracing Nefertari with a kiss on each cheek. "Re's light shine through you, Mother. I am grateful for your counsel." He turned to the door.

"So soon?" He hated the note of disappointment in her voice. As his duties increased with Merneptah's illness, these meetings had grown infrequent. One look at Nefertari's careworn face reminded him, she too, was not long for this world. "Stay for a cup of tea, at least?"

"One cup." He smiled, unable to deny her. "I must see Pharaoh. I have another matter that demands my attention."

She poured out two drams of the hot liquid, the scent of mint and rose hips filling his nostrils. The tea did wonders for soothing the burn in his chest. He helped his mother to her seat, the process taking far longer than it had a year ago.

"Would this matter have anything to do with our guests?"

"Why would you say that?" Meryatum tensed, reluctant even now to share his thoughts on the pair.

"You took Helen to the temple tonight." Nefertari's tone was innocent although her dark eyes sparkled with hidden knowledge. "It bears to reason that something happened in her ritual that upset you."

It was a futile practice to keep secrets from Nefertari. The queen, as always, was two steps ahead of the conversation. "It is not just the princess who plagues my thoughts." He chewed the leaves of his tea until they became a bitter swill coating his tongue. "I took the Trojan to the temple as well."

"Alexandros?" She sat up, a line of concern constricting her face.

He shifted in his seat, her reaction taking him by surprise. "Do you know him?"

Her eyes dropped to her lap, a shade of embarrassment shading her face.

"Mother, it is important. I must decide if he lives or dies tonight."

Nefertari's eyes shot wide. "Why must you do that?"

She did know the prince. It was in her bearing. He took a deep breath, determined not to scare her further. No one could make Nefertari talk if she did not wish it. "The attack on Seti, the dark omens I told you of, it all points to Prince Paris, not Helen. He is a cursed man." Nefertari spun away from him, walking to the far corner of her room, as though to remove herself from listening. "Please, Mother, if you know something of his character, I'd have you speak of it. His life may very well depend upon it."

She did not turn but gripped the end of the long table until her knuckles turned white. He feared she was in the grips of another seizure.

"Omens and dark tidings," she finally spat, the first note of disapproval he'd ever heard her utter about his calling. "They said the same things when I married your father. 'A falcon does not lie with a sparrow. The fruit of this union will produce poisoned seed.' Did you know that?"

Meryatum froze, one hand stretched out to comfort her. "What are you saying?"

She turned to him, her eyes rife with pain. "It was against tradition for Pharaoh to marry a commoner. It broke *ma'at*, and the temple priests told Rameses to cast me aside. Such a violation of our established law would invoke the wrath of the Gods. They knew nothing about me, nor our feelings for one another. Such trifles *did not matter* when the good of Egypt was concerned."

Meryatum's chest constricted, and he backed away from his mother. If what she said were true, then his brethren denounced the union of his parents, and the 'poisoned seed' they foretold about was *him*. "*Re save me. Shelter me in your light,*" he whispered the urgent prayer.

His knees buckled beneath him and he fell, his flailing arms knocking a small table over and scattering tea and kettle across the floor. His breaths came in shattering heaves, and he steadied himself on hands and knees. Lifting his head, he gazed up at the woman who had out-shone all others in his life: Nefertari, Lady of Grace, Beloved of Mut and the All-Father, The One for Whom the Sun Shines, the greatest queen Egypt had seen in a century. The queen who should never have been...

"Why didn't you tell me?" He could not help but feel betrayed by her silence.

She watched him with her sad, dark eyes, the shade of her youthful beauty faded but not lost. "Tell you? So you could doubt yourself? You, Meryatum, High Priest of Re, First Prophet, the most talented seer to hold the office since Heliopolis was founded? *The priests were wrong.* Wrong about you, wrong about me. Rameses saw it and trusted his heart to show him the right path."

He shook his head. "But that can't be true, not if there were signs—"

"My Son!" She approached him as fast as her weak legs would allow. "You cannot see with your inner eye alone. If you view the world through visions and omens you will be blinded to the possibilities all around you. A man is not the sum of what others claim of him. What of his actions?" A tear streaked down her lovely cheek. "*Your actions?* Is that not a better way to measure your worth?"

He rocked back on his heels, his heart twisting with the realization of why his mother chose to confide this dark history now. He regained his footing, and stood with her eye to eye. "The Trojan?"

Her resolve weakened and she nodded her head. "Yes, I know him. He is a man with a gentle heart. One of compassion. His noble birth fits him far better than many who claim greater privilege with their title. He respects the power and majesty of our Gods. If he did not, he wouldn't have stepped foot on our soil to seek their aid. No matter how you wish to interpret the events of that fool hunting trip, he *saved Seti* from a horrible death."

A well intentioned man could still heap ruin, but Meryatum had to concede that last fact. Setnakhte claimed as much as true. Still, Meryatum hesitated. Did one good deed wipe away the crimes that would follow? Would he look back on this day and wish he had eliminated this threat when he had the chance?

Did the priests wish the same thing of me?

Some bit of his misgivings must have played out on his face. Nefertari reached for him again, though he rejected her advances. She folded her arms under her bosom, any hint of softness gone. "You are right to fear him. Just as the priests were right to fear you. With your appointment to office you ended their family's long-standing influence over the region. They saw your birth as the end to the world they knew. They lacked the vision to see the good that would come after," she sighed. "The world is always on the brink of ruin, my son, and it will fare far worse if you remove an honorable man who has the power to influence it."

"You do not know that—"

"You are smarter than your predecessors, Meryatum," she cut him off, "but you cannot reason this out. You have to feel it. Knowing what you know now, what does your heart say?"

Meryatum looked away, ashamed. He was about to condemn a man for the very thing his mother claimed he was guilty of. If he, a high priest, could become a vessel for good despite a questionable birth, was a similar fate possible for the Trojan? With the guiding love of his Spartan princess, could he change his fate? Meryatum cleared his throat, finally seeing the truth Amun-Re had tried to reveal to him. "My heart says, 'that which is born of love is inherently good'." He lifted her hand to his lips and was rewarded by her graceful smile. "The Trojan will not be harmed by my hand or by those whom I command."

Nefertari was not one for grand expressions of affection. She held his hands lightly and placed a gentle kiss on his cheek, her eyes teeming with unshed tears. "Your father would be proud of you. You are the child of his heart."

In that moment, he knew those words to be true. Pi-Rameses, Ozymandias, the second of his name, was the greatest sitting Pharaoh in Egyptian memory. He lived and bled for Egypt, shirking custom when necessary.

And his son, Meryatum, the High Priest of Re, would do no less.

The night was at its darkest when the high priest came before Pharaoh. Twosret watched the stoic man enter Merneptah's private chambers with a slight tinge of worry. What could bring the holy man to the palace at this hour? She sat beside her father, bathing Pharaoh's forehead with a cool washcloth, never taking her eyes off the priest. Fever gripped the king and he moaned softly as he slept.

"Good evening, Uncle." Seti rose slightly from his cushioned bench, an awkward move due to the brace binding his broken leg.

"My Prince." Meryatum placed a hand over his heart and

bowed low. "How fares Pharaoh?"

"He wanes." Seti frowned. Like Twosret, he had not slept for fear he would miss their father's passing. Even the injuries he had sustained in the marsh could not keep him from Pharaoh's side. He had a team of slaves carry him in on a litter and another in the eaves waiting on him hand and foot. Two semi-nude Nubian women cooled him with ostrich-feather fans, nary a glance to the dying man in the center of the room.

Twosret hid her scowl behind a curtain of loose hair. Her husband cared little for the plight of Pharaoh save how it affected his ascension to the throne. He did not give their king the love a father deserved. Seti cared only for himself.

She tried to moisten Pharaoh's cracked lips, whispering encouragement to her father to take in a drop of the life-sustaining water. Merneptah's reign had been short, but glorious. He would leave behind him a legacy of strength and conquest, one she meant to protect at any cost.

"His time draws near," Meryatum intoned with prophetic formality. Twosret shivered, turning away from her uncle's unblinking gaze. The Gods could not have devised a man more carved of stone than the High Priest of Re. When he looked at her, she had the uncanny feeling he saw *through* her, that every dark sentiment she ever thought lay exposed.

"I had hoped to speak with him on a matter of some urgency." Meryatum sighed. "It seems the Gods insist I rely on my own counsel. Good night, My Prince. Princess." He bowed and turned to go.

"Uncle," Seti called after him, this time forcing his way to his feet. He shoved off the slave who offered an arm and limped his way forward. "I beseech you. Do not go away so burdened. You have often told me to take greater interest in the matters of the temple, and I ignored you. Let me atone for that now. Offer your troubles and hear my counsel."

Meryatum stiffened. As did Twosret. What inspired this earnest plea? It was unlike Seti. She watched her husband with renewed interest. Had his brush with death sobered his juvenile spirit? Or did Pharaoh's nearing end force his hand to appear more regal? From Seti's puffed up chest and wavering tone, she suspected it was the latter.

"Very well." The high priest crossed back into the room, folding his arms into the sleeves of his robe. "You'll remember that I have been telling you about a looming danger to the Two Lands, that the Gods speak of ruin on the eastern horizon."

Seti nodded, the clench of his jaw telling Twosret all she needed about his opinion on that matter. The priests *always* spoke of danger, insisting on more tribute to the Gods so they might keep Egypt's enemies at bay. She sneered. That tribute was best sent to their armies, to keep their military forces strong. Seti, however, liked having his royal coffers full. He dreamed of monuments soaring to the heavens, monuments bearing his name.

"In light of all we face," Meryatum continued, "and will face in the near future, I believe we should send the Trojan and his princess on their way. Their presence here is a distraction we can no longer afford."

A line creased Seti's brow, that decision clearly displeasing him. Twosret almost laughed. How unlike a king he looked. Their crown prince, a man-child who pouted over the loss of his new toy. Egypt would thank her when she put a knife through his heart.

"I see." Seti gathered himself. "If you think it best, Uncle, I will defer to your wisdom."

That answer surprised Meryatum. He looked to her for some inkling of the sudden change in behavior, but she had none. Again she shivered as his dark gaze bore into her, and she feared he read her thoughts. His eyes turned inward, and he had the look of a man weighing his next words carefully.

"There is more."

Her hand tightened on her sodden rag.

"To combat this looming evil," Meryatum continued, "I believe it is in Egypt's best interest to marry the two before they depart."

"*What?*" The word escaped her lips before she could think better.

Seti shot her a furious glare, daring her to speak again. "Is this what Prince Paris wants?"

"I assure you it is." The priest nodded. "Furthermore, it is what the Gods want. My hesitation rests with their fathers. Without their consent we risk offense."

They risked more than offense. If Egypt wed Helen, a tribute bride, to the wrong man, they could draw the ire of both Greece *and* Troy. She turned sharply to her husband. "You cannot be considering this."

But from the tense pinch of Seti's face, he was. "Silence, Wife," he snapped at her.

She bit her lip, silently cursing Bay and his delays. The man claimed that he owned a network of spies unparalleled in the Two Lands, but he could find no stain on the Spartan princess that Twosret could use to her advantage.

"The Gods have advised you to do this?" Seti asked of the high priest, his skeptical tone indicating how unusual a request it was.

"They have made their will known," came Meryatum's terse reply.

Seti waved over his servant, his pride no longer able to support him on his wounded leg. Together, they limped over to their father's bedside, and he took a seat beside Pharaoh, one hand rested on the king's shoulder as though he wished to claim authority through touch.

"The prince saved my life. Egypt owes him a debt of gratitude. If you are certain, Uncle, you should grant him this favor. Be it not said we turn our face from those who defend us."

Meryatum bowed again, this time with more respect. "As you wish, it will be done." He retreated out the chamber on silent steps, as swift as the wind.

Twosret struggled to regain her bearing. The fools! The pair of them! She cast one last furious glare at her husband and stormed out the room.

Ignoring the questioning looks she received from the palace guards, she rushed down the corridor. They knew better than to approach her when she was in a temper, and no fit she had previously displayed even approached what she felt now.

Seti's naiveté was to be expected. He had no respect for any authority save his own. Why should he care about offending two quarrelsome, and potentially dangerous, kingdoms? What truly alarmed her, however, was the stance of the high priest. Besides Pharaoh, the Temple was the single biggest power in Egypt. On matters of succession, they had remained ambivalent at best. If Meryatum changed that position, if he aligned himself with Seti, there would be no way to sway the court against raising her horrid husband to the throne.

No way that didn't shed blood, that was...

She turned the corner to Amenmesse's apartments, in such a fury she scarcely noted the two guards stationed outside his door. She threw open the chamber and stormed inside.

"I cannot watch it any longer, Brother. If Seti holds the Crook and Flail, he will be the ruin of us all."

She stopped short of his desk. Amenmesse was not alone. His chamber was lit with a score of torches, filling the space with the bright of midday. Beside her brother, hunched over maps of the city, was Chancellor Bay.

"What are *you* doing here?" This creature had failed her, and she had the urge to whip her dog.

Bay grinned, his oily expression one that made her skin crawl. "Princess, I believe I have some information that will please you."

She turned to Amenmesse, noticing now his eager stance. He gripped the hilt of his sword, the usual indicator that he was ready for action.

THE PRINCESS OF PROPHECY

"Go on."

Bay sang his tale. The duplicity, the unholy crime committed against a Grecian host, theft and flight... it was the biggest display of cowardice Twosret had ever heard. And Seti was sheltering them.

A hungry grin spread across her face. Seti *and the temple*. Two powerful birds diminished with one stick.

"You will be rewarded for this, Bay," she purred. "Well rewarded, indeed."

Chapter 35

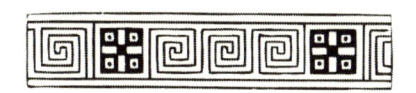

The Joining of Houses

PARIS CRACKED OPEN his eyes an hour before dawn, just as the temple came to life. Priests emerged from their quarters and headed to the lake, cleaning themselves with a perfunctory thoroughness. Those early risers spared him a disgruntled look, but said no word as they completed their morning ritual.

In the courtyard beyond, temple staff led livestock to butcher stations, and the fresh smoke from the cook fires filled the air. It took a moment for Paris to orient himself. The cold stone world of the night before was replaced with the bustling activity of a thriving community, and from the many odd glances in their direction, it was a community that had no place for strangers.

He shook Helen gently. She slept in the crook of his arm, the top of her head nestled beneath his chin. He was loath to wake her, but they both needed to be alert when the high priest came to 'collect' them. With religious folk, Paris had learned the best practice was to present an impeccable appearance.

She yawned and stretched her arms like a cat, settling back into his chest with a sigh. "Helen, it's time to wake." He shook her again, and her eyes fluttered open.

"I thought I dreamt it," her heart filled her eyes as she gazed at him, "but it is done, and you are here. Perhaps this is the dream?" Her generous smile was enough to make him forget his concerns.

"If this is a dream, then never wake me." Her ruby lips begged to be kissed. If not for the nearby splashing of the priests, he would have obliged. "We are not alone, My Love."

Helen collected herself with a practiced ease, banishing her feelings behind a mask of aloofness. Accepting his hand up, she dusted off the dirt from her robes and scanned the perimeter, taking note of the pale hint of light on the horizon. "Where is Meryatum?"

"He awaits you in the temple."

Paris spun to the new arrival, coming face to face with Penanukis. The second prophet wore his sleepless night on his flesh with sallow cheeks and dark circles about his eyes. "He awaits you both."

Perhaps it was the way he looked at Helen, as though she were a forbidden treat too sinful to taste, that made Paris step before her, shielding her from the man's view. "Lead on, then."

Penanukis's mouth twisted with retort, but he refrained, keeping his thoughts to himself. Perhaps he hailed from a noble line, but he was no prince, and Paris towered over the thin man, reminding him of that fact. The priest spun on his heel, walking toward the temple with little of the grace the other *pastophoroi* effused.

Paris followed after him, Helen at his side. Penanukis' behavior was surprising for a temple elite. They rarely showed their feelings beyond a smile, practicing simplicity, restraint and self-control in all things. Why he would look at Helen with such gross familiarity was unfathomable, and it put Paris on guard.

The courtyard before the temple entrance was filled with stolists, the special sect of *pastophoroi* recognizable by the multicolored band at their waists. Some held trays of food, others bolts of fine linen. Even more stood by with nothing in hand at all. Paris thought he recognized a few from the chorus singers the night before. They waited patiently for the sun to rise and their morning salutations to begin.

Penanukis stepped between them and the temple doors, beckoning for him and Helen to follow. They did so with haste. Paris had felt more welcome stepping into an enemy camp than he did in that moment. When Penanukis shut the doors behind them, he almost sighed with relief. That was, until he remembered where they were.

"Meryatum?" Helen called out softly. The priest shushed her, pressing a finger to his lips. He sped past them, and further into the darkened chamber towards the hypostyle hall.

Unlike the night before, torches burned in their sconces, giving definition to the cavernous rooms. With so many pillars and shadowy alcoves, Paris' skin itched, like a soldier in battle with his back exposed. After his treatment last night, he was not convinced Meryatum and his followers did not mean them harm.

Helen, however, walked forward with utter confidence. Her plain *pastophoroi* robes might have been the finest gown in all of Egypt by the way she carried herself, and when she caught sight of Meryatum, *she* pulled *him* forward.

"Be honest with him, Paris," she spoke softly to him, her lips barely moving. "He will treat us fairly, and he will know if you lie."

His stomach churned at that thought. *Trust a zealot?* A lifetime of experience had taught him otherwise. But Helen seemed certain...

The high priest had switched out his ceremonial robes for the archaic white design favored by his brethren. He stood in the center of the pillared hall on the direct axis leading back into the inner sanctum. In his left hand, he clutched his staff, leaning on it heavily as Helen approached him.

"You are well, Princess?" He dipped his head to her.

"I am, Your Eminence." Helen lowered herself into a

graceful curtsey, showering him with one of her rare, heart-felt smiles. He seemed to brighten with the gesture. "I have seen what I needed to see, and it did not break me."

"As have I." Meryatum stood tall, his cryptic words laced with a hint of pride, a man of quiet strength and aged wisdom. How like her father he was! He turned from her to her prince.

Paris approached the priest with far more caution than Helen. He stepped by her side and lowered his gaze, refusing to look Meryatum in the eye. He could not produce the joy Helen effused for this cold man. Clenching his jaw, he chose his next words carefully. "I have seen many things I did not wish to see. Including watching the one I love cross death's door." It took all the restraint in his body not to curse the priest for that bitter moment, and he shook with the effort. "At first, I thought your gamble with her life frivolous, but I understand now why you insisted." He swallowed his anger and retook Helen's hand, the soft touch of her palm both as soothing as it was encouraging.

"Helen has been chosen by the Gods. They wanted to show me that, so I might know my role in her future and how rare and precious this woman is." He lifted his head, locking eyes with Meryatum, willing the man to know his sincerity. "My eyes are open. I will do everything in my power to keep her safe. On pain of death and loss of all that comes after, this I vow." Had he a blade, he would have sworn in blood. Lacking that, Paris dropped to his knees and bowed his head.

"*Paris?*" came Helen's choked reply.

Had she expected something less? She had told him to tell the truth.

A soft touch graced his shoulder. It was not Helen's hand, but Meryatum's. "She is chosen by the Gods, Trojan. *As are you.*" He tapped Paris twice with his staff, the heavy centerpiece pressing into his flesh with the anointing. Paris raised his head, surprised to see the priest, one hairless brow arched high, regarding him with a nod of approval. "Rise. We haven't much time." At that last, Meryatum glanced to the clerestory windows and the ever lightening sky beyond.

"Time?" Helen stepped forward, her heart racing. The single word was the only complete thought she could express after Paris' heartfelt declaration.

"You are departing Egypt tonight, on the evening tide." Meryatum's announcement came as a surprise to them both. Helen shared a questioning glance with Paris as he rose to his feet.

"Tonight? But my captain—"

"Is recovering well and has already been transferred to the ship. Your matron as well, Princess." The high priest sighed, his eyes looking inward. "Egypt must attend to Egypt, now. It is time that we parted paths and your journey continue." He waved someone over from the eaves. "Before you leave, I have one last blessing to impart. Purification was but one step along your path to *ma'at*. If the two of you wish to be wed, I am prepared to bind you."

"What?" Paris nearly choked in disbelief, that offer the last thing he expected the High Priest of Re to utter. "But why?" He did not have to wait long to find his answer.

The queen emerged from the shadows of the temple, her silhouette taking on form as she stepped within the circle of torch light. Her lithe body was draped in the finest linen, a single gold belt beneath her bosom. Across her chest sat a dazzling torque of fine gemstones: lapis-lazuli, malachite, and turquoise, set into a winged solar-disk. Her long neck curved gracefully to the blue crown atop her head, her hair tucked into the rounded cap with a golden uraeus protruding from her brow. Time had done little to diminish the queen's beauty, and his breath caught as it had when he last spied her on his arrival in Heliopolis.

"Nefertari?"

"A youthful boy no longer," she stepped before him, a slender hand uplifted to caress his face. "But a man fully grown. A good man." There was a sad reserve to her tone, much like the queen he remembered from the funeral rites of her husband.

Then she kissed him. It was not a gentle peck on the cheek, but fully lipped, soft and lingering. When she pulled away, there were unshed tears in her eyes. "I wish you happiness, Alexandros, and the love of a woman who appreciates all you have to share."

He was taken aback, stunned by her heartfelt words. "Thank you."

She turned to Helen, and the women shared a look of quiet understanding. She bestowed a kiss on the princess as well, pressing her lips to Helen's forehead. "For my Spartan princess, I wish you wisdom." Nefertari unlatched her necklace and placed it on Helen.

Helen gasped, her fingers trailing over the priceless gift. The metalwork was that of a master, and the detail in the stone was exquisite. The scarab carved from lapis looked ready to crawl away.

"You have the makings of a Great Wife." Nefertari smiled at her. "But like the morning sun, you haven't blossomed into full power yet. You are like Khepri, our Rising God. And, as certain as the path Re's chariot blazes across the sky, your day to shine will come. You must be prepared." The queen produced the snake-headed bracelet from her pocket and slid it onto Helen's wrist. "Go and embrace all the gifts Isis has blessed you with."

The bauble raised the hair on Helen's arm, as much for the coolness of the metal as the poison she knew lay inside. She had left it behind when the priests had come to collect her, partially because of the queasy feelings it stirred in her. She accepted it now with gratitude and made a silent vow of her own.

I will protect him against those who mean him harm. By any means necessary. With Aphrodite's help, they will never see my weapon.

The high priest cleared his throat, and the queen stepped back. "We have no formal ritual in Egypt for the joining of two houses. Once an agreement is struck between father and future husband, the marriage is cemented when the bride moves into her new home." He turned to Helen. "Since we lack the presence of your father, the consent of this union falls to you. As the Gods bear witness, I bid you both to speak true. Are you prepared to bind yourself to one another in the sacred covenant of matrimony?"

Helen waited for Zeus to strike her down with a bolt from the sky. She had spoken her vows before. She was terrified that if she spoke them again, the Gods would know her for an imposter. She turned to Paris, her arms trembling, but one sight of her prince, his almond shaped eyes filled with adoration as he gazed at her, and she knew. The Gods did not bear witness on her last union. That travesty of a marriage was a mistake for both her and Menelaus. By leaving she set him free—she set them *both* free. Paris was her future. He had always been her future.

"Yes," she spoke deeply, her body igniting with that declaration as she soaked in the sheer joy reflected in Paris' face.

"Yes." His words tumbled out immediately after hers. "With all my heart, *yes.*"

The creak of metal pins turning in their joints echoed down the hall as the doors to the temple were pulled open. Music filled the air, the throaty chorus of the morning hymn from a hundred *pastophoroi* outside the temple. It cascaded from chapel to chapel, bouncing off the rock slabs of the ceiling, reverberating through a hundred pillars, and pulsing over them in an harmonic, roaring wave of sound.

"Awake, oh Great God, in peace.
Wake to life, Amun-Re!
The gods rise early to honor your soul, oh august winged disk shining in the sky!
You who break the seal in the heavens and spread gold dust over the earth.

Your eyes spread flame, you light the darkness!
Wake in beauty, oh radiant visage that knows no anger!
Wake peacefully, and let us adore you."

Dust motes danced in the air, glowing orange in the hazy light of the rising sun. The first rays crept over the floor of the entry hall, crawling steadily towards Meryatum and the inner chamber behind him. He raised his arms, staff brandished high, and waved them forward. Paris took Helen's hand, his own trembling slightly, and they knelt before the priest.

"As Amun-Re begins his journey anew, so do the two of you embark on a new beginning. Speak now your promises to one another so all the Gods can hear."

Paris' pulse soared, his mind racing to find the words to express what he felt. The most beautiful woman in the world knelt beside him, prepared to bind her life to his. The morning light washed over her, creating a halo around her golden head. Her beauty ran so much deeper than her skin. Helen was honorable, and honest, and good. He gazed into her lovely face, bursting with pride that he had found her. A vision this bright should not be hidden in a dark corner of the world.

"Helen, Princess of Sparta," his voice rang strong with earnest conviction. "All that I own, all that I am, and all that I ever will be, is yours. I will shelter you, protect you, and defend you. Any who seek to do you harm will die on my blade. You remind me each day of the person I hope I can be. From this day until the end of time, to the Isle of the Blessed and beyond, my heart is yours."

Helen held on to Paris' hand, his solid frame an anchor in the surging ocean of her heart. Her skin tingled, like it had on that fateful night when she had stood in the temple of Aphrodite. Before her was the man promised to her, and he was everything she dreamed he would be: honorable and brave, compassionate and wise. Above all, he *loved her*, truly loved her, and not just as some prized possession. Had they only met four weeks prior? She could not imagine her life without him.

"Paris, Prince of Troy," her heart overflowed with love, and she gazed at her chosen with all of its power, "all that I own, all that I am, and all that I ever will be, is yours. I will defend your honor and good deeds with my dying breath. I will comfort you when you are weary, and care for you when you are sick. In the warmth of my arms, I will banish any memory of neglect *and love you as a noble prince deserves.*" She shook with that promise, its message not lost on her beloved. "From this day until the end of time, I will follow you. To the Isle of the Blessed and beyond, my heart is yours."

The chorus rang out again, this time without lyric, their voices blending in a cascading flow of notes that rose to the heavens. A shaft of light fell across the center axis of the hall, striking the crystal centerpiece of Meryatum's staff. It exploded with color, a dazzling prism of light that trickled down on Helen and Paris.

"Rise and open your arms to one another," the high priest commanded, his powerful voice cresting over all others. "Rise and witness your love before Mut. Embrace and be joined."

Paris lifted Helen to her feet, kissing her fiercely. She wrapped her arms around his neck, melting into that embrace. Her heart felt so light that had he held her less firm, she was certain she'd float away.

A loud clap from Meryatum signaled the other priests to enter, and the hall became awash in the swishing white robes of *pastophoroi* completing their cult duties. Helen ignored them all, pulling back from Paris slightly so she could soak in his radiant smile.

"My husband," she sighed with heartfelt bliss.

"My wife," he spoke with the same awed disbelief. A warmth filled her, the like of which she had never felt before. A warmth that settled into her bones and buoyed her heart.

In that moment, everything was right in the world.

Meryatum stepped outside the temple, squinting into the brilliant light of the mid-morning sun. Temple staff ran to and fro, diligently fulfilling their duties, not an idle body in sight. Hour priests descended from the astronomy deck, conversing in soft whispers. Their step was unhurried, indicating the Keepers of Time spied nothing unusual in their nightly observations.

The lower clergy rustled about as well. The temple was a living, thriving community, requiring the support of over 10,000 souls to maintain the grounds. In his tenure as high priest, the functioning of the cult had flowed as steadily as the Nile. There was no task neglected, no ritual unobserved, no matter how small.

And so, the foreign prince and princess emerging from the temple drew many curious glances, but that was all. The *pastophoroi* continued with their work on what appeared to be a glorious summer day.

Meryatum studied the couple he had just joined. The night's activities had left the pair disheveled, their robes soiled and hair matted. Such trifles were beneath their notice. They held each other close as though the binding had been physical as well as spiritual. He had never seen two people more in love.

"Do you regret your decision, my son?" Nefertari stepped quietly beside him. He held out his arm for her which she readily accepted.

"No," he answered truthfully. "They belong together." Even an acolyte in his first year of learning could see that. "It's just a feeling I can't dislodge. They are children of prophecy. A moment like this should create ripples in the world. I... I didn't expect for it to feel so ordinary."

Your love will rock the foundations of this earth, that was the foretelling surrounding the princess, and there was no doubt in Meryatum's mind that the Trojan was her match.

Nefertari laughed, the musical note chiding his somber mood. "Oh, my son. There is nothing ordinary about true love. It defies all obstacles, refusing to die even when the whole world battles against it." Her dark eyes sparkled with distant memory, and he knew she thought of his father. "You are the first to acknowledge their union. It is a blessing you have given, something pure they can cling to in their journey ahead." She reached up and stroked his cheek. "The path for your father and I was difficult. There were many who wished to keep us apart, but our love prevailed, and it gave the world *you*. Who knows the far-reaches this marriage will effect? Your ripples will come... in time."

He patted her hand, grateful for the long years Re had bestowed upon her and for her steady presence in his life. Nefertari was right. He dwelt too long in riddles and omens that he saw their shadows in the waking world. The joining of houses was a natural event, an expression of the continuity of life. It did not require great fanfare.

He studied Helen from afar, the joy beaming from her sun-kissed face. Surely he had set her on the right path. What harm could result from such love?

A gong rang out across the desert, a ceaseless chain of reverberant peels that were both deep and foreboding. The *pastophoroi* froze, many turning to him for answers. He released Nefertari and strode to the temple gates, a cold dread forming in his chest.

Like black dots on the horizon, a team of horses galloped across the desert. As they neared, Meryatum could just make out the standard of the military guard and General Setnakhte at the head of the charge. They carried the black flag.

He turned back to the courtyard, a quiet pall awaiting his words.

"Pharaoh is dead."

Chapter 36

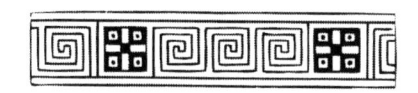

The Claiming of a Crown

SETNAKHTE'S HORSEMEN GALLOPED into the temple courtyard, the animals heaving from their efforts. Paris held Helen close as the guards surrounded them. Each man was armed to the teeth.

"When did it happen?" Meryatum stepped forward, grabbing the reigns of the general's horse.

Setnakhte dismounted, his eyes scouting every corner of the courtyard for hidden dangers. Those eyes widened when they fell on Paris as though he did not expect to find him there. "Some time before the morning staff came in to change his bedding," came his terse reply. "Only the crown prince was with him." His chiseled features furrowed, and he appeared reluctant to continue. "There is more. Amenmesse has accused Seti of treason, and the nobles are picking sides. I need you Meryatum. You are the only one who can speak sense to them."

Paris groaned. Brother fighting brother, a civil war for succession... It was just his damnable luck.

"Paris?" Helen whispered nervously to him.

A surge of protectiveness gripped him. He was not going to risk her in this mess, not again. "It's okay. We're leaving

Egypt. *Now*."

Their movement drew the attention of the general and he stalked over to them, one hand on his holstered sword. Paris stepped in front of Helen, keenly feeling his lack of weapon.

"Trojan." His stony face was an unforgiving blank wall. "Can you account for your whereabouts last night? I know you were not in your chambers." The man bristled with suppressed energy, the muscles of his neck taut. For the first time, Paris appreciated the power this man possessed. If he wanted, Setnakhte could easily cleave a man in two.

"I was here in the temple at the high priest's invitation. There are any number of men who can attest."

"He speaks true." Meryatum stepped between them, his austere presence tempering the general's angst. "What is troubling you, Setnakhte? What aren't you saying?"

The general fidgeted, the sporadic movement turning into a pace. "I smell treason, but not from our crown prince." He spun again to Paris. "Have you aligned yourself with Amenmesse? Are you aiding this effort to put him on the throne?"

"What?" he choked on the word. "No. Of course not. Troy has no interest in who rules Egypt. We profit nothing."

It took long, teeth-clenching minutes for that fact to settle into the general. Paris breathed a sigh of relief when Setnakhte finally turned away and resumed his pacing. This was not a man to cross.

"*Someone is aiding him.* And I aim to discover who. Come, Meryatum. Time is running thin." He moved back to his horse.

"We're coming with you," Paris interjected, following after him.

The general exchanged a wary glance with the priest, both men in agreement of the folly of that decision. "You should stay in the temple," Meryatum advised. "At least until we have secured the palace. It will be safer here."

"We should leave." Paris shook his head, insistent. "I want

no part of your troubles, but if you leave me here, Troy will be embroiled in this mess, whether we want it or not. I need to go. *Now.*"

The general was not a stupid man, and he slowly came to the same conclusion. "Give him a horse." Setnakhte waved over one of his guards. "We ride at once."

They returned to the palace in due haste, leaving their mounts at the royal stables as Setnakhte's men spread out in front of them. Before they could enter the palace, Meryatum pulled Paris and Helen aside, earning the priest an impatient grunt as the general waited.

"I do not think our paths will cross again." His hands twisted nervously inside his robes. "I have no more to say to you save this. The world is what we make of it. Let Re's light guide you and be a force for good."

Helen pulled free from Paris. Goodbyes were never easy for her, and in the few short days she had known him, this stoic odd man had found a way to worm into her heart. "Thank you, Meryatum. I will never forget you or what you've done for us." Rising up on her tip-toes she placed a gentle kiss on his lips.

He pushed her down, a firm but gentle reminder that one should not touch a priest in such a familiar manner. Only his eyes told tale of his affection for her, and their glint of pride made her smile. Turning to Paris, that brief vulnerability vanished from the priest. "Remember your promise." Then he was gone, Meryatum speeding down the palace corridor on soundless slippers.

"Time to go," Setnakhte hailed them from the door.

Paris took Helen by the hand and joined him. "You aren't going with the priest?"

"Meryatum can handle himself, for the time being. I'll see you safely out, then put an end to this nonsense."

Paris gave the man a short nod of appreciation. He supposed this overture was as much of an apology as he could expect from the rigid soldier. "I just need to collect my men and we'll be off to the harbor. I promise it won't take long."

Setnakhte sent three scouts ahead, and they headed out into the palace at a quick pace. In a matter of minutes, they neared the guest wing. The halls were strangely devoid of people. Whenever a servant dared to peak their head out a door, they quickly ducked back in on sight of the military guard. It was quiet, too quiet for Paris' nerves.

"This will all blow over, won't it?" He eyed every corner for hidden blades, his nerves so taut he almost asked the general for one of his.

"With time," the older man grunted. "Amenmesse can curry favor with the nobles all he likes. They will not lift a finger against Seti while my guards patrol the halls." From the battle-ready hardness of the men surrounding them, Paris believed that to be true.

He could not shake an unsettling feeling that something deeper was afoot. It was unlike Amenmesse to declare openly against his brother. Seti would have his head when all the posturing settled down. Paris had thought the prince more intelligent than that. Like Setnakhte beside him, something about this squabble did not sit right with him.

"General!" A guard entered the corridor on the far end, sliding across the tiled floor as he tried to correct his course. Sweat dripped from his brow and his chest heaved as though he had ran some great distance. He collapsed at Setnakhte's feet.

"Hotep?" The general lifted the soldier up by his breastplate, shaking the man roughly. "What are you doing here? Your squadron had orders to secure the city gates."

The guard held to Setnakhte's forearms, scrambling to regain his feet. "We are... I was. General, a great host has been spotted. Several thousand strong. They march from the south."

The other officers instantly surrounded the general and

they erupted in hushed whispers.

"Nubians?"

"It can't be. We're too far from the cataracts. They would have been spotted long before now."

"Then what? Rebels? They march from Upper Egypt!"

Helen clung to Paris' arm. Though she could not follow their Egyptian, she knew something terrible was happening. She found herself battling the urge to run. Where didn't matter, only that they no longer remained still. She felt like a deer in a meadow, surround by a dozen hidden bows.

"Setnakhte," Paris grabbed the general by his elbow. "Go. You're needed with your men." He made to protest, but Paris cut him off. "My rooms are just around the bend. My Trojan guard will see to our defense." He pushed Setnakhte onward. "Go. See to Egypt. She has need of you."

The general backed away, a short nod of appreciation as he went. "Fare you well, Trojan. May the Gods speed your journey and the wind be ever at your back." He lifted a hand in salute and left, the sharp bark of his commands lingering in the hall long after he was gone.

"Paris?" Helen tugged at his sleeve, her face lined with concern. "Shouldn't we leave as well?"

"We will." He cupped his hand over hers, giving it a reassuring squeeze. "It's not far. We just have to get Iamus, Ariston and Brygos." And a few others. He was not going to leave Jason and the other Greek slaves to the cruelty of their Egyptian masters. They had been presented to Paris as gifts, and he meant to call in that ownership and all the privileges it provided. Including setting the men free, a change of status he was sure would not be honored inside the city.

The corridors leading to his rooms were empty, and he sprinted the last few feet to the doors. Flinging them open, his cry to gather died on his lips.

The chamber was packed full of guards, and none of them Trojan. The last thing he saw was the butt of an Egyptian spear as it slammed into his head.

Chapter 37

A Twist of Fate

IT HAPPENED TOO quickly for Helen to react. Paris dropped to the stone floor, and before he hit the ground, four pairs of hands grabbed hold of her, yanking her into the chamber.

"Let go of me!" She writhed in their grips, kicking and jabbing at her captors with all the strength she possessed. It wasn't enough. These were elite Egyptian guards, and they pinned her hands behind her back, shoving her to her knees. She gasped in pain and tried to clear her mind of the specks that danced across her vision.

"Princess..."

Helen strained against her bonds and turned towards the strangled voice. Iamus lay beside her, his hands tied behind his back and blood from a deep gash on his scalp trickling down his grizzled face. Brygos, in no better condition, was also restrained, his face so swollen, his nose must have been broken in two places. Beside them Ariston lay unmoving—dead or unconscious, she could not tell.

"No." She groaned heavily, panic gripping at her chest. Her eyes darted across the room, searching for help, for anything that could be used against her captors. What she saw stilled her blood.

The apartment was completely turned over. Half a dozen Egyptian guards, heavily armed with sword and staff, surrounded them. Chancellor Bay lounged against the far wall, away from danger, and beside him stood an Egyptian princess.

"*You?*" Helen hissed as Twosret crossed into the room. The sway to her hips were no longer graceful, but the sinuous stroke of a serpent ready to strike.

"Yes, me." Twosret's hazel eyes narrowed to dark little slits. "Tribute bride?. What a convenient little fiction," she scoffed. "Lies on top of lies. You didn't think you were going to get away with it, did you?"

The change in the Egyptian princess was startling, and Helen had difficulty forming her thoughts. Gone was the beguiling charm, the friendly demeanor that had lulled Helen into confidence. Before her was the shadow-side of beauty, the fierce lioness that Nefertari had warned her about. This woman was the real danger in Egypt, the *hidden danger*.

"*I trusted you!*" She spat as she lurched to her feet. Her guard had to painfully pinch her arms to keep her from the princess.

Twosret did not flinch. She batted her eyelashes, unfazed. "And who told you to do that?" She moved in close to Helen, uncomfortably close, and dropped her voice to a husky whisper. "I once thought your presence here a danger. How foolish of me. You really are just an insipid, little girl."

A burning urgency filled Helen, washing away any fear she had of her captor. She had brought this evil upon them. Jealousy and misplaced trust had come again to haunt her, this time in the form of an Egyptian harpy. She glared at Twosret, filling her gaze with all the hate she reserved for those who preyed on others and claimed it as strength. "You will *never* be a Great Wife. Poison runs in your veins, and your people will know it."

Twosret stiffed, her eyes hardening. "Is that so?" The coldness of her tone cooled Helen's blood. "I am King's

Daughter and King's Wife. Daughter of Re, Lady of Ta-merit, Twosret of Mut! *I am EGYPT!*" She hissed the word through clenched teeth. "And Egypt does not forgive those who conspire against Her or Her allies." Twosret spun to the guards behind her.

"Bring the traitor in."

※

"PARIS!"

Somewhere in the aching reaches of his mind, Paris heard Helen scream. Slowly, his eyes took on focus and the dark shapes before him merged into men.

Where am I? He tried to get up, only to discover his arms were bound behind him. A guard shoved him back to the floor, and several more laughed at his feeble effort.

"Paris!" Helen called to him again, and he fought to keep his eyes open. She was held, the same as he, by an Egyptian guard.

"*Paris, Paris!*" Twosret stepped before him, her mocking tone followed by a terse laugh. "Would someone please muzzle that bitch?"

A guard pulled Helen up roughly, attempting to gag her. She attacked, her teeth sinking into his hand as he pulled her head back by her hair. The dark man cursed, slapping her hard across the cheek, and she dropped to the floor.

"No." Paris struggled to get to her, but his guard shoved a spear beneath his throat and hauled him to his feet, forcing him to face the Egyptian princess.

"Don't damage her too badly, Chigaru. Her Grecian husband might take it personally when we return her to him." Twosret's lip curled in a vicious smile.

That pronouncement froze Paris in place. *How did she know?*

"Oh, yes. I know all about you, *Prince Paris*," the princess sauntered over to his side, an evil glint to her eye like that of a cat toying with a mouse, "and all of your dirty little secrets."

Twosret thought to intimidate him, but he had been taunted his entire life. He knew how to ignore an instigator. When she pressed into his ear to whisper that last, he looked past her, scouting the room. There were seven guards in total, two at the back near his private quarters, four surrounding them in the antechamber, and the one behind him holding him in place. Twosret stood before him, and on her right was Chancellor Bay, the sick man watching their encounter with open glee. There was no sign of his *meshwesh* servants. There was no sign of any help at all.

A terrible emptiness filled him. They were too many. If he was armed and free, maybe he could take down enough for Helen to escape before he was fatally injured. But he was not, and there was nothing he could do about it.

Defiance burned inside of him, nonetheless, and he glared at the cruel woman before him, pouring out all the injustice he'd suffered from a lifetime of being manipulated by people like her. She felt that force like a heat wave, and her eyes widened in shock. She took an unconscious step away from him.

"You stupid bitch." He spat at her feet. "I don't care what you think you know. I'm an ambassador. Injury to me is an act of war."

She rubbed at her throat, her flash of weakness no more than a fleeting moment. "Spare me. You are no more a diplomat than I am a doe-eyed milkmaid. You're a thief. I've recovered one of the items you stole from your host." She kicked Helen in the ribs. "Now where is the rest? Where's the gold?"

He bucked at his guard, trying again to get to Helen, but the man pressed the spear tighter, constricting his esophagus. "What are you talking about?" he had to gasp out between painful breaths. "I took nothing from Mycenae that did not belong to me."

"Don't think me a fool. Your man confessed to it all." She nodded to the guard at his back. "Tell him, Scylax."

Paris looked up and saw the face of his captor for the first time. He was wholly unprepared for what awaited him.

"Jason?"

Gone was the thoughtful slave, the pensive and conflicted Greek who was so eager to help. The man before him had the eyes of a killer. *I am a fool.* Paris cursed himself. *I should have known...*

"You were welcomed into Agamemnon's home," this... Scylax... grimaced down at him. "Given guest-right and the full hospitality of the court. In return, you offered nothing but insult. You seduced his brother's wife and made free with the treasury while he was away." He spun his spear, flipping it around faster than any man Paris had ever seen in action. The haft slapped against his back, sending Paris back to his knees. "Admit it!"

The theft of gold and a bride... So that was the tale Agamemnon wove to safeguard his precious reputation. Paris would be hunted to the ends of the earth for such a crime. As he looked up at his one-time friend, he knew it was too late. The truth did not matter. If Agamemnon declared him a thief, there was nothing he could say or do that would change his captors' minds.

Knowing there was no way out liberated him to tell the truth. When he spoke it was with cold resignation. "Lies." He shook his head, the word pulled from his chest with a growl. "The insult was all Agamemnon's. I stole nothing."

There was a shift in Scylax' stance, as though some part of the man believed him. It encouraged Paris to continue. "Ask her." He nodded to Helen, his love pressed to the floor under the heel of her guard. "You'll discover the truth about your king."

"ENOUGH!" Twosret shouted at them. "The only lies here are yours, Trojan. Claim your innocence all you want, it does not matter. It is too late for you." She signaled her other guards, and they lifted Helen to her feet.

"Let go of me!" she screamed at the men, kicking any piece of flesh where she could make contact. Two burly guards were more than a match for one princess. They hoisted her into the air and started off towards the bedchamber.

"What are they doing?" Scylax gripped his spear, the deadly note in his voice making the guards pause. "You promised me she would not be harmed."

Twosret batted her dark lashes at the man with false distress. "Of course, but you aren't the only one who I made promises to." She waved the chancellor forward. "She's all yours, Bay. See that you don't 'harm' her too much."

The oily man stepped toward Helen, a sick hunger in his black eyes. She screamed, fighting the guards for every inch they dragged her forward.

"I have to thank you, Trojan." Twosret turned to go. "I had thought an alliance with the North an impossibility, but when I send Agamemnon your head, Mycenae will forever be in Egypt's debt."

A madness took hold of him, and Paris lunged at her, desperation lending him strength. He broke Scylax' hold, and buried his shoulder into Twosret's gut. They tumbled to the ground, Paris atop her. "Let her go!" he snarled at the vicious woman.

Four pairs of hands hauled him off the princess, forcing him to his knees. Twosret scrambled back to her feet, careful to keep a safe distance between them. When he was reliably restrained, her fear turned to gloat, and she laughed at him. "Pathetic. If she chose you for a protector, then she's getting what she deserves."

He envisioned her cold dead body, an ugly corpse that her own people would revile. "I'm going to kill you," he promised. "I'm going to kill you and everything you hold dear."

Her green eyes flashed with anger. "No you won't," she hissed at him, a coiled asp ready to strike. "You'll be dead, and

THE PRINCESS OF PROPHECY

I will be queen of all of Egypt." She signaled Scylax, and the mercenary tossed his spear aside and unsheathed his sword. "A clean death is too good an end for his treachery. He should suffer first." Her lips twisted into a grin. "Make him watch. Then kill him."

Without further word, the princess spun on her heel and exited the chamber.

"*I don't take orders from you.*" Scylax muttered under his breath, watching the Egyptian wench disappear down the hall. He brandished his sword, taking a few practice swipes in the air.

How had it come to this? Aligning himself with the Egyptian royalty? Bit by bit he was compromising everything he thought defined him as a man.

Make him watch, he sneered at the thought. That was punishment dealt out for one who wronged you, not for some perverted sort of enjoyment. How many of his Brethren had she treated in that fashion?

He pressed those thoughts aside. They did not help. His mission was before him. He had only to suffer through this unpleasantness and be on his way back to Greece, back to Dora. He place the tip of his sword above Paris' neck, the man struggling beneath the hold of the other two guards.

He lifted his sword...

And a searing pain arched across his back. He spun to meet his assailant, surprised to face one of the Trojan guards. He was an older gent with silver-kissed black hair. His bounds had been cut, possibly on the discarded spear Scylax had so carelessly tossed aside. In his hand was a short knife with an ivory handle he'd gotten from the gods-knew-where. It was stained with Scylax' blood.

"Stay away from him," the Trojan warned, his gravelly voice dripping with quiet threat.

"Or you'll do what? Join him in the grave?" Scylax saluted

437

the guard with his sword, whipping it around to test the soldier's agility. The Trojan jumped out of its path, the man surprisingly spry for his age.

And so began the dance, the two men circling one another. For Scylax, it was a welcome reprieve from acting the executioner. It was better to face an armed man, to test his skill against your own. The way of the Egyptians was that of the butcher.

He lunged forward, slicing the Trojan's shoulder, and forcing him back. He stumbled over the prince but regained his balance in a few short steps, his knife brandished before him.

"Why do you bother? You can't win." The Trojan had to know that, and Scylax was curious what drove him to fight regardless. No man was that loyal when the odds were stacked against him.

"I don't care," the guard hissed back. "Better to die in his service than watch a scumbag like you destroy something beautiful."

It happened quickly. Their circling had finally placed the Trojan within reach of the other guards. One of Bay's lapdogs, a thick Egyptian with tattoos circling his arms, stood up and planted a spear through the Trojan's back. The five-pointed tip exploded out the man's ribcage, splattering Scylax with blood.

"IAMUS!" Paris screamed, renewing his efforts to get to his guard, fighting like a possessed animal. The Egyptian guard had to quickly toss the skewered Trojan aside to help his partner subdue the prince.

The craven fool, Scylax cursed at his Egyptian 'helper'. He didn't need the man's aid, least of all in the form of a spear to the back of a nearly defenseless man. "Hold him still!" he shouted to the guards, wiping the blood from his face.

"*Iamus*," Paris cried out again, anguish on his face as he watched his guard bleed out before him.

"I'm sorry," the Trojan gasped, a bloody froth spilling over his lips. "*I'm sorry, My Prince.*" He took his last breath and said no more.

In the commotion, the two guards stationed by the bedchamber had come forward, a Nubian and a mixed breed Egyptian with asiatic features that surely hailed from the Delta — the exact sort of soldiers that made up the core of Pharaoh's army. The exact sort of soldiers Scylax had once declared his eternal enemies. They cast him a disapproving glare, scowling at the bloody mess, as uncomfortable as he in their impromptu alliance.

"Get on with it." The Nubian spat, the drivel leaking down his chin. "If we hurry, Bay might let us have a go." He nodded back to the bedchamber where the princess was screaming as though in the grip of night terrors.

Some part of Scylax heard her cries. A distant part, one he couldn't let take control. He turned back to the prince, placing his sword above his neck again.

"Have you no soul?" Paris shook as he cried out. "Can you not hear her? Do you not care?"

"Shut up!" Scylax clenched his sword, raising it high.

The prince turned his head, his dark accusatory eyes staring straight into him. "You're not a man. You are a dead thing. A dead, soulless beast. All of you are." The Trojan spat at the other guards. "The Gods will curse you for this."

The princess continued to scream, a pitiful, heartbreaking sound. In his mind, her cries blended with those of Heliodora's, and Scylax was forcibly reminded of the night she saved him from this god-accursed land. He was reminded of the price she had paid so he would never again stand where he stood now.

She will forgive me for this... for the girls, she will look past this final act of barbary.

He knew that was a lie. Dora could never forgive this, and he would never forgive himself. His blade came crashing down —

And severed the Trojan's bonds.

Paris looked up at him as one struck, confused by his sudden freedom.

Scylax, however, knew exactly how to act. He reversed his stroke, taking an Egyptian guard across the chest, flaying him open. His blood sang as his metal met flesh, its sweet chorus more heavenly to his ears than all the hymns of Zeus and Amun-Re combined. He wanted more. He'd sacrifice every Egyptian who crossed his path on that altar. Sword raised high, he spun to meet his next offering: the Nubian guard, the first of his brothers to regain his senses.

The sound of metal on metal rang out as he parried the Nubian's thrust. He shoved the man back, daring the few precious seconds to shout over his shoulder to the prince.

"*Go! Save her.*"

Paris needed no further instruction. He leapt to his feet, snatching the discarded blade of his Trojan guardsman. The last Scylax saw of him was the flash of his blood-soaked robes as the prince sprinted to the back chamber.

※

From the moment the guards had lifted her into the air, an all-consuming fear had come over Helen. She was a child again, dragged off by monsters in the dark. She had thought she faced these demons in the temple, but they hovered ever near.

"*No!*" she cried out as loud as her lungs would allow. Over and over again she screamed, kicking and fighting with every ounce of strength she possessed. Her elbow dug into one captor's jaw; her foot into the other's breastbone. She would not be a victim again. She'd make them kill her first.

Her efforts were not enough. Though they were bruised and bleeding, the guards still dragged her into the bedchamber and tossed her down roughly on the bed. One held her arms above her head, the other pinned down her legs. She bucked wildly, trying to throw them off, but they were too strong.

"*No!*" she moaned, the slow realization of her helplessness draining her of strength. "*No...*" The single word became a mantra that she poured all of her resistance in to, as though the word could deny this event from existence. "*No!*"

Bay entered, a vulture waiting to scavenge his meal. She ceased her struggles and watched the man approach her with hate-filled eyes. No other man had filled her with more revulsion. Not even Agamemnon, at his most depraved, had looked at her so.

"Don't look so reticent, Princess," he cooed, removing ropes of gold from his neck and jeweled cuffs from his arms. "You will enjoy this more than you realize."

Enjoy? Was he mad? But Bay seemed to believe it, and he caressed her legs like a lover fulfilling some sick fantasy.

Something inside of Helen snapped. The absurdity of her situation overwhelmed her, and she *laughed*. His hand froze on her thigh, the mocking tone of her laughter cutting right through his slick confidence.

"*You brazen whore.*" His grip tightened, bruising her flesh.

"You pathetic, puny, little man," Helen spat at him, channeling all her Spartan courage. She was not afraid of him. There was nothing he could do to her that she had not already suffered ten-fold. "You think to claim me? If not for your men, you wouldn't be able to lay a finger on me. You are a dog, Bay. A dirty mongrel given treats by his betters."

It was foolish to bait the man, but she could not help herself. She would not whimper before him. She wouldn't give him that power. She couldn't allow it. A lioness raged inside her.

His eyes hardened into lumps of coal, and he ripped at her robes until they fell away in rags. "I was wrong, Princess. You *won't* enjoy this," he hissed. "Let go of her." His guards did as he commanded, and he crawled on top of her.

She was ready for him. Bay pinned her arms down, foolish to believe they were her only weapon. Her knee came up and slammed into his gut, missing his groin by mere inches. He groaned and fell into her chest, just close enough for her other weapon. She bit into his ear. *Hard*. She tasted blood as the flesh tore away, but before she could complete the deed, a fist slammed into her stomach, knocking the air from her lungs.

A string of curses flooded from Bay as he put pressure on his wound. "Hold her down!" She was immobilized again as his guards quickly complied.

Helen wanted to fight back, to scream fury at the puerile man, but everything *hurt*. She could scarcely force air into her lungs. When he came at her again, she knew she couldn't stop him.

Do your worst. Take this body. You will never claim me.

He hovered above her, the foul stench of his breath making her gag. "I will make you scream for this."

"Like hell you will."

Paris stood in the doorway, dagger in hand, his chest heaving. Helen turned to him, and tears came to her eyes. He had come. She didn't have to face this alone. The strength that abandoned her returned with force.

"Get him, you fools!" Bay screeched.

Paris moved lightning quick. He flung his blade, the weapon spinning hilt over tip until it sank into the skull of the man behind her. Without a moment's hesitation he leapt over the bed, spinning in the air like his knife, and landing gracefully beside the guard, retrieving his weapon before the man hit the ground.

The other guard lunged at him with his sword, but he easily shifted out of the blade's path. He slammed his elbow on the guard's exposed sword arm, knocking the man off-balance. While he stumbled, Paris ran his dagger across the man's throat. He fell to the ground, drenching Paris with his crimson tide.

Helen could scarcely move. She watched as her prince, her dark avenger covered in blood, turned to Bay. The chancellor backed away from him, terrified, until he cowered in the corner of the room, unable to retreat any more.

"No, please..."

Paris ignored his pleas, and hauled the man up by his tunic. He placed the edge of his dagger at the man's throat.

"I can't die. Not like this," Bay groveled.

Paris was beyond mercy. He wanted this man to suffer. "You're right." He lowered his weapon, dragging the tip down the man's chest. "Death is too good for you." He mimicked Twosret's words, savoring the fear they evoked in Bay. "I want you to watch as I destroy what you hold most dear." He grabbed the man's scrotum and castrated him like the pig that he was.

Bay screamed and fell to the floor, slipping over the blood drenched tiles. As he fell, the roaring in Paris' ears died down to a dull strum. His vision, once clouded with the haze of violence, cleared, and his stomach twisted as it always did when he was forced to kill. He tossed Bay's mangled organ down on the man and turned away.

"Helen?"

She knelt on the bed, her eyes wide, staring at him as though seeing him for the first time. Her lips parted and a soft moan escaped her lips.

"*Helen?*" He rushed to her side. "Are you hurt?" As he reached for her, he saw his blood-stained hands and pulled back. What sort of terror had he just forced her to witness?

But she was not afraid. Her arms circled around him, and she pulled him to her with a fierce strength. "*Thank you,*" she sobbed into his ear, her hands clinging to his hair. "Oh, thank the Gods for you."

Chapter 38

Brothers of the Sword

PARIS CLEANED UP from the bloodbath as best he could, the red stain of his skin making him feel like a tribute to Ares. He and Helen changed out from their ruined clothes into two of his spare tunics. Once Helen was decently clad, they emerged from the bedchamber, Paris first.

The antechamber was in shambles, the aftermath of a massacre. Jason... *Scylax*, he scolded himself, was with Brygos, the two men helping Ariston sit up.

Paris scouted the room. The Greek had dispatched four fully armed Egyptian guards with clinical efficiency. There was not a scratch on the man, save the blow from Iamus' blade.

"Need I be worried?" Scylax raised a brow. Whether he meant that of Bay's ongoing cries from the back or from Paris himself was left unsaid.

Paris kept a safe distance between them, placing himself between the cutthroat and Helen. "That depends." He held his dagger in a tight grip, ready for use. "Who are you? Why are you here?"

Before he could answer, Helen caught sight of Iamus, and she dropped his hand with a cry. She collapsed beside the fallen soldier, cradling his head onto her lap. *"Iamus, no..."*

Scylax took a step to follow, but Paris barred his path. "Answer me."

The Greek eyed his small blade with a touch of amusement. He was in for a surprise if he judged the threat Paris posed by the size of his weapon. There were more ways to kill a man that just metal.

"I am not your enemy anymore, Trojan." Scylax put his hands in the air. "I don't want to be your enemy."

Were it so simple. Paris had faced his share of assassins in his life, and none had come as close to ending his life as this man here. The second he lowered his guard, Scylax was apt to put a blade in his heart. "And why should I trust that?"

A dark shadow crossed over the man's eyes. "'Have you ever loved someone more than life itself?'"

Paris froze. Those were his words.

"I have," Scylax continued, a bitter pain twisting out of his words. "And she was taken from me. By a queen hellbent on retrieving her lost sister."

"*Clytemnestra* sent you?" Paris blurted out, shaking his head in disbelief.

"In another life, I had a certain set of skills." Scylax' eyes took on a faraway look, as though remembering things he'd rather forget. "I was a mercenary, one of the best of my trade. I tried to leave that life behind, start anew in Mycenae... But some things you can't outrun. Too many other people remembered what I was, and some of them held the queen's ear."

Paris shook his head, puzzling out the pieces. Clytemnestra sent a single man after them? It made sense in an odd way. Why send an army to track down two fugitives? It was a delicate, conniving move. Agamemnon would not show such cunning.

"She took your family?"

Scylax nodded.

THE PRINCESS OF PROPHECY

"Then why didn't you kill me?" Had their roles been reversed he would have let no man bar him from Helen's safety.

"I know what you nobles think about sell-swords like me. You say we have no honor." Scylax spat on the floor. "You're a fool if you believe that. I know the difference between good and evil. I do not blind myself to the atrocities committed by a king simply because I was born on his land."

He was worked up now, stationary but with a simmering rage mounting inside. Paris had no trouble imagining Scylax at the head of army. He would be a fearsome foe.

"Self-indulgent royals bloated on their vanity and pride," he continued on in a rage. "They rule the world, taking whatever they want, *destroying whomever they want*, and all the while the innocent suffer. One day, they will squeeze too hard, and their precious reign will crumble in their fingers. I know that as surely as I know the sun will rise each morning."

He turned to Paris, his ire vanishing. "Just as I know that you are not one of them. There are few good people in this world, Trojan. I could not live with myself if I culled their numbers." He appeared surprised by his own words. "You are... unique."

Paris was speechless. *Meshwesh*, sell-sword, mercenary, cutthroat—he had been raised to hate these men. They were painted as less than human, a tool warlords utilized to swell their numbers.

Scylax, however, was no thoughtless animal. He was a man, no different than Paris. And he spoke true. In all of his diplomatic travels, the number of righteous rulers Paris encountered were few. He was grateful for his outcast status then, and the ill company it spared him. How many nights had he spent in conversation with Glaucus where Scylax' words might as well have been his own?

"I want to believe you," Paris hesitated, the knife still secure in his hand, "but I just don't trust you."

"Then you are learning," Scylax snorted. "I do not ask for

your trust. You are down a man, and another is too wounded to wield a sword. Let me help you out of Egypt." He offered his hand to Paris, placing himself within striking range of Iamus' blade. "Please, don't make my sacrifice count for nothing."

Paris looked to Helen. She still clung to Iamus, but was listening to them intently, absorbing every word. He wanted her input. He had come to trust her insight on reading a man's intent. When she nodded, he finally let the last bit of tension go.

"To the Delta and no farther?"

"And no farther," Scylax agreed.

He clasped the man's arm, and they set about to leave the capital.

The journey through the palace passed in a daze for Helen. They had traveled no more than a hundred feet before pockets of battle broke out before them. Soldier fought soldier, and the halls ran red.

Paris and Scylax were both skilled in keeping them from sight. They ducked into alcoves, flattened against walls, and hid behind pillars until the melee passed.

She saw Setnakhte from a distance once. He pressed back a group of warriors twice the size of his own, calling to his men to rally again. And then he was gone.

They did not leave by the front gates, opting for the royal stables instead. It was there that Helen said her last goodbye to the foreign land, a place rife with conflict and yet beauty as well. As she mounted her horse, she gazed one last time into the palace, a distant figure catching her eye.

Nefertari stood at the far end of the corridor. She watched as their horses filed out of the yard, one hand placed over her heart, the other lifted high in farewell.

Helen mimicked the gesture, hoping the queen understood

how much her kindness meant to her. She prayed the regal monarch would see better days, but some part of Helen knew that was a feeble wish.

Heliopolis itself was completely ignorant of the troubles in the palace. Several shops flew the black flag, mourning their king, but no soldiers marched the streets. The only smoke that filled the air was from the palace.

They reached the harbor with little fuss. A ship awaited them there, as well as Glaucus and Aethra, just like Meryatum promised. They casted off immediately, the Egyptian seamen working the sails to capture as much speed as possible.

Helen sat at the stern watching Heliopolis disappear as they sailed down the Nile. She had come to this city a naive princess in awe of its ageless beauty. Was it prophetic that she left it in flames? If Agamemnon and her sister's fury followed her to Heliopolis, would it not also follow her to Troy? Would there be others, like Twosret, who hid their duplicitous natures behind smiles and well-wishes? Would the next hidden dagger find its mark? She tightened her shawl around her head and steeled her nerves, her fingers twisting Nefertari's gift around her wrist.

Let them come, Helen vowed silently to herself. *This time when they do, I'll be ready for them.*

Chapter 39

Parting Ways

IAMUS' FUNERAL PYRE lit up the delta marshland, its orange flames battling the dark shadows surrounding the smugglers' camp that the Trojans now occupied. Paris had reclaimed his ship at Heracleion with little fuss, only allowing the crew to stop in the security of full night. Tonight, they paid homage to their fallen mate, the crew lifting their voice in song to the memory of the royal guard.

Paris stood beside Glaucus watching the flames crackle against the sky, as though Iamus' spirit danced one last jig. Glaucus was pale about the cheeks, but hale, as though a poisoned arrow were no worse than a bad case of gout. Paris suspected he hid the true extent of his pain, but he had seen his old friend through worse injury, and he was beginning to believe what the oarsmen whispered, that the man was indestructible.

Scylax stepped quietly beside them.

"I'll see you for the announcement," Glaucus grunted and excused himself. The captain and mercenary had spoken little on the voyage from Heliopolis, the confession that the poisoned arrow was his, souring what little camaraderie Glaucus felt for the sell-sword. It didn't help that Scylax was entirely unapologetic about the act, either.

"Are you sure this is what you want?" Paris spied the knapsack on the man's shoulder. Tonight they would part, Scylax off to face the queen and her injustice.

"I will get my wife back, or see those who harmed her pay." There was a finality in his tone that left Paris with no doubts that it would be done. "It is time I remember who my real enemies are."

Paris nodded, knowing better than to wish the man "good speed". He watched the flames climb higher into the night, devouring itself in its urgent appetite. He had a sudden flash of his vision in the temple. Death, and more death. It seemed an inevitable future, yet some part of him wished there was another way.

"Don't fall back to it, Scylax."

The sell-sword arched a brow, studying Paris with a puzzled expression.

"Be better than what they say of you. Don't prove them right."

Scylax fidgeted, shifting uncomfortably. "I am what I am." He sighed with a bit of sadness. "I am not built for a quiet life."

"Then use your skills for something better. It's not too late for you."

"Fight for a cause?" Scylax laughed, he seemed genuinely amused by that idea. "My last one didn't fare so well."

"Well then find another," Paris pressed. "A better one." He did not know why he challenged the man, only that it felt important. Like Meryatum's last words to him professed, the world was truly what its human caretakers made of it, and Paris wanted it to be good.

Scylax studied him with an admiring look, one laced with surprise. He laughed again. "Let me know when *you* find one, Trojan. I might just join you." He held out his arm in farewell, and Paris clasped it. "We'll meet again," he spoke with utter surety. He took two steps into the night and was gone, quiet as the black shadows he favored.

Paris remained outside the gathering for a while, listening to the sounds of the marsh blend with the Trojan dirge. For a moment, everything was peaceful, and he could forget all the things that haunted him. When the song tapered off, he turned to the ship where Helen awaited him.

She was a vision all in white. Aethra insisted the filth from their escape be removed before their announcement, and like any good task-mistress, Paris, too, fell under her scrub brush. It was worth the effort. The matron spent hours with Helen, fixing her charge into a beauty all men would adore.

"Are you ready?" He took Helen's arm.

"Yes." A firm resolve sparkled in her deep blue eyes. He led her before the pyre to where Glaucus stood, finishing his eulogy for the departed.

"Let no man say Iamus did not reclaim his honor. He loved his prince, and in the end, he proved it with his life. His was a good death." Glaucus stepped back as the Trojan guards slammed spear against shield in solid agreement. When the thumping died off, Paris stepped forward.

He stood before the host of one hundred men, the brave soldiers who had followed him through many journeys. Over the past few years they had replaced the family he was born to, caring for him as those esteemed nobles never would. He owed them his life and more. "Iamus died for me, a debt I cannot repay." He lifted his voice, humbled by that loyalty. "Each of you has risked the same, and I believe it is time you know why."

The crew stirred. It was unusual for Paris to share the finer details of his missions. It was their job to obey without question.

"We carry urgent news to Troy." He cleared his throat, making sure they could hear him even in the far back. "War is brewing in the West. Agamemnon craves an empire, and to achieve that, he will try to plunder the riches of Troy." Helen squeezed his arm, giving her gentle encouragement to continue on. "The king must be warned. If any of us should fall, the last among us must carry this news to him."

This caused a ripple of concern amongst his men, but when the muttering died off, they beat their shields. Trojan solidarity. Stronger than iron. He waved them down, grateful for their support.

"But it is not only dire news and warnings we transport to Troy." He pulled Helen before him. "Our hallowed decks carry a great treasure."

She turned to him, her smile more dazzling than a thousand stars. Mighty Aphrodite, how did a lost soul like him win her heart?

"Our stop in Egypt was not without purpose. You are the first of our countrymen to greet her. Bid your new princess welcome. My wife, Princess Helen of Troy."

The camp erupted into cheers, and he lost himself in her eyes. "*My wife.*" He repeated quietly to her, scarcely believing it was real.

"My husband," she whispered back and then kissed him. Whatever came next, they could weather, so long as they had each other.

And so long as there was life in his body, he was never letting her go.

EPILOGUE

The Winds of War

A CHILL wind whipped the sails of the Grecian galley as it set sail from Mycenae's port. Clytemnestra stood at the bow, letting the western zephyrs toss her hair. Every breath felt like the gentle caress of a lover's hand, for every breath brought her closer to Helen.

Menelaus barked a command to his sailors to trim the sails. He seemed in his element in the brewing tempest, his raw power waiting to be unleashed.

Clytemnestra sneered. She was no idiot. Agamemnon thought himself clever, sending his little brother to Troy. Her husband never sent his muzzled dog without purpose. If he meant to provoke a war, so be it. If she was lucky, he'd get himself killed in the effort.

Her husband was a fool, however, if he thought Menelaus commanded this envoy. The court was *her* realm, and she would not be leaving Troy empty-handed. Helen was coming home, whether she wanted to leave the Golden City or not.

Nestra jutted her jaw out, a determined line dominating her visage. She was grateful for the information Astyanassa had elicited from the Trojan guard. A man born under a dark omen would have enemies, possibly many.

And the enemy of my enemy will prove a powerful ally.

She let that factor fill her with confidence. Her weapons were not those of bronze, but something far more powerful. She had plans for that detestable prince, plans he would never be able to counter.

Helen is coming home. It became a mantra, that promise

drilling over and over again into Nestra's brain. *She IS coming home.*

The desperate knot in Clytemnestra's heart would afford no other outcome, and once she was reunited with her twin, everything would go back to the way it was.

Forever.

AUTHOR'S NOTE

In writing this series, my goal was to take a holistic approach in retelling the Trojan War—to incorporate historical data, cutting-edge archaeological research, and classical sources like Homer and Virgil. By blending those elements with an understanding of human nature, I plan to tell the *personal story* of the people who lived so long ago, the people who *inspired the myths*. In Heroes of the Trojan War, the Gods don't walk the earth, but the people who prayed to them do. Hopefully, my readers will experience the ancient world from a grounded, fact-influenced perspective that closely reflects the experience of our Bronze Age ancestors.

Homer's "Illiad" was more than mythology. It was a recanting, albeit fantastical, of an actual historical event. Since no piece of history stands in isolation, to fully depict the significance of the Trojan War, it is crucial to explore the greater, international world of the Late Bronze Age—not just Mycenae and Homer's "Grecified" version of Troy. I had to consider the influence of the other "Super Powers" of that time, among which Egypt was certainly a major player.

Fortunately, for the purposes of this novel, more of Egyptian culture has been preserved than possibly any other ancient society. By studying Egyptian history, I learned that in 1200 BC, the entire world —not just Greece and Troy—was on the brink of war. Rameses II, whom biblical lore often paints as the weak Pharaoh who unwilling set free his Hebrew slaves, was in fact one of the greatest rulers of Egypt. His wars of conquest capped several hundred years of Egyptian domination into the Near East. With his death, came a vacuum of power... where mercenaries, drought, famine, and civil war wrecked havoc in Egypt, ultimately ending the powerful 18th Dynasty—a period of time that coincides with the Grecian invasion at Troy.

It should not be surprising, then, that the people of the Nile left us their own version of the Trojan War, of the impact of the "Egyptian Aphrodite" who visited their shores, and of Egypt's role in that international incident. Herodotus, the first Western historian who lived circa 600 BC (some 200 years after Homer), discovered those tales, and they told a different version of Helen and Paris' fateful journey, one that deeply conflicts the mythology told by the Greeks.

Herodotus' accounts have provided historians with invaluable first-hand information about ancient society, and he is one source of many that confirms how the consequences of the Trojan War were far-reaching. The impact of massive warfare, the transfer of power, and the destabilization of established order had ripple effects across the civilized world—much like it does today. Those factors have greatly inspired this series and The Princess of Prophecy, in particular. Troy and Greece were part of a larger world. This book reflects how the underlying factors that caused their epic clash did not originate nor end with them.

As I continue to write the series, I look forward to highlighting other

THE PRINCESS OF PROPHECY

ancient cultures: of the nomadic Israelite clans across Canaan, of the fearsome warriors of the Hittite Empire, of the rebel coalition members of the Anatolian Assuwa League, and—of course—of the mysterious Sea Peoples, whose war-path unmade the ancient world. The Golden Era of Grecian Heroes has a place amongst a larger story, and I am excited to explore it. Hopefully, with passionate characters and intense drama, this series will shed an intimate light on one of the most pivotal moments in human history.

I am indebted to my many mentors and professors at Berkeley, to my time excavating at Tel Dor—an actual settlement for people displaced by the Trojan War—and the vast network of scholarly work available for public review. In particular, I'd like to highlight the work of Eric H. Cline, whose publications have been tremendously insightful, and to Vangelis Pantazis, who has dared to challenge assumptions held by the academic community. For any budding historians, I highly recommend checking out the publications at academia.edu.

Thank you for your interest, and I hope you enjoy the book!

PHOTO BY: JEFF LORCH

ABOUT ARIA

Inspired at an early age by the adventures of Indiana Jones, Aria Cunningham studied marine archaeology at UC Berkeley. In 2004, she set forth to create her own adventures and helped excavate a Roman palace from 200 AD at Tel Dor, Israel.

Continuing her old world education, she travelled the expansive fjords of Norway, castle hopped from Wales to the Rhineland, and explored the funeral complexes along the Egyptian Nile. She is an avid scuba diver who has navigated shipwrecks on the ocean floor, the immense kelp forests off the Channel Islands, and the legendary Cenote caverns of the Yucatan.

Aria has a Master's degree in the Cinematic Arts from USC and currently lives off the coast of Southern California.

See how the epic began:

BOOK ONE: THE PRINCESS OF SPARTA

Heroes of the Trojan War, Vol. I

"The Princess of Sparta is the perfect blend of history, romance, and action giving this book a broader reach with readers. The characters come alive in this forlorn world of long ago as they share their joy, pain, and struggles. Once you pick this book up, there's no turning back or putting it down!"
—Portland Book Review

Helen of Troy's humble story began as a Princess of Sparta; honorable, loyal, with promise to become a powerful queen. Given in marriage to Menelaus of Mycenae, an abusive husband who neither wants nor needs her, she clings to a prophecy made to her about a great destiny, and even greater love.

That destiny awaits her in Paris, a noble prince of Troy, whose reputation for fairness and fortitude precedes him as an Ambassador. Unjustly cursed at birth by a dark omen claiming he will cause the destruction of Troy, Paris is an object of ridicule amongst the Trojan nobility. He is a man who has never known love.

Until the day the Fates intervene and Paris travels to Mycenae as an Ambassador of Troy. He meets Helen, and the bond of two souls linked by a common destiny is irresistible. He is drawn to the Spartan princess, and she to him. But with relations between their kingdoms under pressure, can the star-crossed lovers risk dishonor and war simply to follow their hearts?

Discover the love story that provoked the greatest war of ancient history and paved the way for the rise of Greece and Rome.

Available at Amazon, iTunes, Kobo, Barnes & Noble, and bookstores everywhere.

Look for

THE
PRINCESS OF TROY

HEROES OF THE TROJAN WAR
VOL. III

Coming Spring, 2016

Visit the author's website for updates, ancient history facts, and insider information on the series at: www.ariacunningham.com

Made in United States
Orlando, FL
05 August 2022